MURDERING LAWYERS

MURDERING LAWYERS
A NOVEL

LARRY FINE

GREY SWAN PRESS

Publisher of Fine Books   Marblehead, Massachusetts

Grey Swan Press

www.greyswanpress.com

This book is a work of fiction. Names, characters, places, and incidents either are products of the author's imagination or are used fictitiously. Any resemblance to actual events, or locals or persons living or dead, is entirely coincidental.

———

100% acid-free paper

Printed in the United States

———

Library of Congress Control Number: 2014935348

ISBN: 978-0-9834900-8-1 (hardcover)
ISBN: 978-0-9834900-9-8 (paperback)
ISBN: 978-0-9834900-6-7 (epub)
ISBN: 978-0-9834900-7-4 (Kindle)

0987654321

To my wonderful wife, Laura Winston,
who for over a quarter of a century has
consistently and thoroughly supported me
no matter what crazy things I try to do; plus,
she's also an all-around sweetie, a person
with whom I never get tired of hanging out,
and (I'd be remiss if I didn't also mention)
she combined genetic material with me and
birthed two other amazing people, Alicia
and Jocelyn.

Law never made men a whit more just.
—Henry David Thoreau

The lawyer's profession is essentially unclean. ...There will always be some lawyer who will jiggle with the facts until the moment comes when he will find extenuating circumstances.
—Adolf Hitler

Do what thou wilt shall be the whole of the Law.
—Aleister Crowley

PROLOGUE

Gerald Thornton, Esq., felt more alive than he had in weeks. His heart beat rapidly and his palm sweated as he signed the Bronx motel register. As always, he signed the name of an old law school classmate who was a partner at a competitive firm. That really amused him.

The young girl hung back a little, as if embarrassed. Thornton doubted that. She was hardly a sacrificial virgin. He had noticed the little strawberry blond when cruising the strip. A couple of times Thornton had just missed his opportunity, watching the kid drive off in another car. Today he had had her in mind when he first set out.

She was barely five feet, with a slight overbite that accentuated her youth. She popped her gum and blew bubbles incessantly. She could be anywhere from twelve to twenty, but Thornton, in his late fifties, didn't care about the truth.

The clerk held up a key. "You'll be in Room 11. You got up to three hours. That's eighty bucks."

Thornton reached into his left pocket and pulled out his pre-counted eighty dollars and shoved it into the clerk's outstretched paw. The man counted the money before handing over the key.

Thornton checked his watch. Three hours. Perfect. His wife expected him home from his business meeting at about ten.

Inside Room 11, the girl proved less shy. After Thornton placed the cash on the dresser, she took off her tank top and un-buttoned her shorts. Thornton sat on the bed and watched, until the little girl had pulled off her bikini briefs and stood in front of him naked, blowing a bubble.

"You want me to do you?" she asked Thornton.

"You know I do." They had already agreed on all services and prices in the car. "What's your name?"

She removed Thornton's tie as she answered. "Suzy." After a moment, without real interest, "What's yours?"

Gerald Thornton didn't hesitate. "David."

Suzy unbuttoned "David's" shirt with one hand while she placed the other in the customer's lap. It was early in the evening and she was already sore all over.

She blew her biggest bubble yet. Then she spit the gum into a Kleenex from the box on the night table next to the bed.

Thornton was relieved to be finally freed of his suit pants. He played with himself for a moment as he lay naked on the bed. Alarmingly, Suzy was already poised to take him in her mouth. Thornton pulled away, grabbed an unlubricated condom from his pants on the floor and presented it to her. Suzy placed it on Thornton and went to work.

As he watched Suzy's head travel up and down his length, Thornton started feeling uncharacteristically potent. Seizing the moment, he pulled out of Suzy's mouth and positioned her in-vitingly.

Once inside, Thornton built to a rapid rhythm. He was undisturbed by the fact that Suzy barely moved. He was getting close.

He stopped abruptly, heart pumping double-time. "What was that?" he asked the girl. "Did you hear something?"

"No. Go ahead, man. Just come."

"I thought I heard someone touching the doorknob."

"No way. Just go ahead."

Thornton resumed his motion, hesitantly at first. Then the fire began to return. He sped up again. He clutched at the little girl as he pumped faster and deeper. He gasped and squeezed his eyes shut as he finished.

Thornton was smiling when the door opened and the four well-groomed young white men came in. He barely had time to pull out and open his eyes wide with surprise. The gun was shoved deep into his mouth and fired.

The four intruders had a lot of cleanup to do. First they chloro-formed Suzy into unconsciousness. Then the men went out to their cars and brought in two empty trunks. Two of the men, one of whom was built like a football tackle, put Suzy into a medium-sized trunk, along with the stained sheets. The big guy sprayed stain remover on the wall and used Kleenex from the night table to wipe away the blood.

Meanwhile, the man with the gun, the one whose right fourth finger ended abruptly at the first knuckle, yanked off Thornton's rubber as the fourth man, a redhead, wiped him from head to toe with a motel towel, soaking up all the bodily fluids. Then both men washed their hands well. "Filthy scum-bag," quipped the gunman, breaking the silence momentarily as they all laughed.

The well-built man and his partner started the difficult task of dressing the lawyer's body. They had to bend parts of his body and gently straighten others. It took almost half an hour. Little was said as they worked. They moved with a speed and efficiency that belied their lack of experience in this particular line of work.

Planning was everything.

After leaving the motel, the two groups split up without a

further word. The football player and his partner brought Suzy to the warehouse on the west side of Manhattan and dumped her out on the cold floor, to be saved for later use. The man with nine fingers and his redheaded associate dropped Thornton off in Central Park, just a few blocks from his penthouse condominium. The gun was placed carefully in his stiff hand, with the suicide note nearby. They inspected their handiwork.

"His will is done."

PART ONE

One

When Marc Wilson arrived at the Manhattan Bar Association hours earlier, he hadn't planned to commit a crime. But now, amazingly, the opportunity was presenting itself and Marc couldn't just walk away. There was no one around to stop him.

I can't believe I'm doing this, he thought as he walked up to the administrative office for all of the Bar Association committees. *After a lifetime of obeying even the most arbitrary rules, I could be barred from the practice of law. And locked up.*

Marc laughed mirthlessly at the thought. It wasn't as if he had a lucrative career and the respect of his peers at stake. Or even any freedom to lose.

I'll just see whether or not the door is locked.

Nine months earlier, Marc had asked the Bar Association librarian if he could just put the card up on the bulletin board or whether he had to clear it with anyone.

The short bald guy shrugged and touched the screen of his iPad. "Just stick it up there. We don't have anything to do with the board."

The bulletin board outside the library of the Manhattan Bar Association was full. Every inch was wallpapered with index cards listing the names and addresses of pathetic losers and the depths to which they would sink. Marc glanced back at the oblivious librarian before stealing a thumbtack and burying another pathetic loser's index card under his own:

MARC WILSON
Available for long and short-term
assignments, per diem, court
appearances, depositions, local counsel.
Top 25% of law school class, Law Review.
Reasonable Rates

The door to the Bar Association administrative office wasn't locked. It swung open noiselessly. *Damn*, thought Marc. *What are you trying to do to me?* He locked the door from the inside.

The lack of security didn't really surprise him. There was no cash around. He wasn't aware of anything in the office that anyone would want to steal. Even the computer was a practically worthless antique.

Still, the computer in the center of the little room was his first stop. He hit a random key and was momentarily stymied. Of course, the computer was locked, and a password was required.

Marc momentarily wrestled with frustration. And relief.

Then he saw the Post-it note between the computer and the phone.

Weeks earlier Marc was in small claims court. He shifted and took a deep breath while his client of several minutes glared at him. Vince had been intrigued to learn that defendants, and only defendants, could have lawyers in small claims court. He had been sold by Marc's pay-me-only-if-you-win guarantee. But he still wasn't sure he was getting his money's worth.

The judge continued as if teaching a first semester law school course, which was perhaps his ambition. Anything was better than small claims. "It seems clear to me that the plaintiff and defendant never had a meeting of the minds over the terms of a contract to provide entertainment for the plaintiff's bachelor party."

"It wasn't *my* bachelor party, your Honor," said the plaintiff. "I was best man."

"Whatever. You paid the defendant to provide strippers, right?"

"Right. And they only danced for twenty minutes and the blond never took off her G-string. They barely let us touch them."

Between the judge's clenched teeth: "So you've said before. You've already painted an adequate picture for the Court."

I went to law school for this? thought Marc. *People's Court would be a step up.*

Marc swallowed hard and jumped in again. "Your honor, my client provided a service. Even if you find that there wasn't a contract, my client earned his payment pursuant to the doctrine of *quantum meruit.*"

Vince the Stripper King looked like he might finally be impressed.

The judge wasn't. "This is small claims court. No Latin here." A bang of the gavel. "Judgment for the plaintiff. Return his full payment. Two-hundred seventy-five bucks."

Vince looked at Marc like *he* should pay the judgment.

⚖️

After successfully entering the password from the Post-it note (*is "Guinevere" this administrator's favorite historical/literary character, daughter, or cat, or perhaps all of the above?)*, Marc located the Ethics Committee directory on the hard drive. He went through the sub-directories, guessing which ones contained proposed revisions to the Code, or memoranda concerning investigations of specific attorneys, or letters of reprimand, cc'd to the State Bar Association. The Manhattan Bar Association didn't have the power to disbar an attorney, but it could and did make damn sure that the State Bar Association took care of things.

The computer files were loaded with the names of the desperate and the greedy. Those who had cut too many corners. Those who had stretched the truth too tightly. Those who showed zeal for false causes ...

Last week: "Tell Marc about your case, Aunt Helen."

This was not the first time that Sylvia Wilson, née Goldberg, had prompted her aunt to tell her son about a lawsuit she was contemplating. Mrs. Wilson often predicted that her son's career would take off as soon as he got the right case. Marc knew his mother was trying to help both of them, and he silently cursed his lowly circumstances.

Two summers earlier, during Marc's second summer of law school, when he had a great job with prestigious Harper, Weiner & Dorn, Marc had barely listened to Great Aunt Helen's lawsuit of the month. He had nodded his head periodically, while thinking how ridiculous it was that this poor old woman expected him to be interested in avenging her latest perceived wrong. He was making over three thousand a week! She couldn't afford him.

Now, a year after his graduation from law school, anyone could afford him. Harper, Weiner & Dorn had decided to optimize profits by downsizing, and so didn't make offers of permanent employment to any summer associates. Meanwhile, other firms seemed to be hiring *only* the associates who worked for them over the summer. Marc had been turned down by firms that paid half of what he'd been willing to accept. He was shut out.

So, a year after his proud graduation day, Marc was living with his mom in Forest Hills, Queens, New York. Upstairs in his old room, surrounded by the wrestling and track trophies of his glory days. The only things added since high school were the once state-of-the-art gaming computer and the fancy synthesizer which were the trophies of his Harper, Weiner summer money.

Marc made his bed most days—not that his mother made him—he knew that it made her happy and it was easy enough. He insisted on buying the groceries with his meager earnings. His mother couldn't pay for everything on a court file clerk's salary, despite her seniority.

Begging for work in person and on bulletin boards hadn't provided a reliable grocery subsidy, so Marc had been forced to secure a steady income as a night shift word processor for the major Manhattan law firm of Samson & Lake. During the last six months, he had become desensitized to the incorrect word usages and glaring misstatements of the law which he typed into the computers each night. At first he had attached Post-its with helpful notes and comments for the attorneys who had scribbled out the briefs, but some of them had complained. Marc now accepted that no one at the firm cared that he could do better.

Marc had vowed that some day he would do much more than pay for groceries. Many times he had promised his mother that he would buy her a place to retire in Miami Beach, near her cousin Gertie, to which she always responded, "You're a sweet boy, but it's not necessary."

But to Marc it *was* necessary. He knew how hard his mother worked, and how much she hated the cold New York winters. In a perfect world she would have retired already, and Marc's time to invest in Florida real estate was fast running out.

The only ship coming in at the moment was Great Aunt Helen. *Please have a good case, Helen.*

"Those good-for-nothings are going to have to pay me! I'll shut them down! We'll see if they find *that* funny!" Aunt Helen was eighty years old and about eighty pounds, running on will-power and spite.

Mrs. Wilson patted Aunt Helen gently on the back. "Don't upset yourself, Helen. Just tell Marc what happened. He'll know what you should do."

Marc braced himself. *Let it be a real case. Mom and I need more than just a new pair of shoes.*

Last year, just out of law school and unemployed, but still hopeful, Marc had endeavored to explain to Aunt Helen why she couldn't sue a local magazine for reneging after guaranteeing her a sweepstakes grand prize. The year before that, Marc had begged off on her proposed suit against the people from Smuckers who had stolen her idea of putting peanut butter and jelly in the same jar.

"I could have died," said Helen. "That applesauce was as slippery as the devil."

Applesauce, Marc considered. *Sounds a little silly at first, but on second thought it has promise. Million dollar lawsuits have been built on more innocuous substances.*

"Would you two like some coffee or tea?"

"Mom, Aunt Helen's in the middle of her story. She doesn't want to be interrupted."

"Maybe a glass of tea," said Aunt Helen, "with a little cream and sugar."

"So, Aunt Helen, did you slip on applesauce?"

"I sure did. Went flying. Almost broke my neck."

Almost.

"When was this?"

"Last month."

"How badly *were* you hurt?" *Let there be some substantial hidden injury.* Helen looked about the same as ever, though. "And how big were your doctor bills?"

"My hip smarted like the devil. For days. I didn't see any quack doctor about it, though. Don't trust any of them."

Stay calm.

Mom chimed in. "Helen was in a *lot* of pain. Isn't that worth something? Is it too late for her to see a doctor now?"

"Well, it won't be as persuasive as if she had gone right away," Marc mused aloud, a hint of cynicism in his voice. "Not that there isn't a doctor out there somewhere who would swear that the applesauce injured every piece of soft tissue in her body."

"Oh, of course we don't want to lie or do anything illegal," his mother said.

"Those can be two different things," Marc pointed out. "People hire these types of doctors to testify every day." He shrugged and added, "But not people like us, I guess."

"Oh well." Sylvia sighed. "I guess we'll never get rich."

Marc felt bad for his mother. She only wanted the best for her aunt and her son. *She watches too much television. She and Aunt Helen have been promised large cash awards by too many lawsuit salesmen.*

For his mom's sake, Marc plugged on mechanically. "Do you have any idea how long the applesauce had been on the store floor?"

Aunt Helen looked confused. "Well, I dropped the jar just ten seconds before. The jar was too heavy. I tried to pick it up and it went flying ..."

Sylvia Wilson shot Marc a look to say that she was as surprised as he was by this latest revelation. "Sorry," she mouthed.

Aunt Helen continued, undaunted. "Wasn't even chunky style ... "

Next?

⚖

Fortunately, Marc was pretty sure that he wasn't mentioned in any of the Ethics Committee sub-directories. Yet. But a stunt like this was a sure way to make one of the Ethics Committee's lists, if not jail. If he got caught.

Marc found the file with the Committee membership list. Unfortunately, he wasn't mentioned there either.

He had been trying to get on the Ethics Committee for almost a year. His former friend Paul was on the Committee, and Paul's career had soared from the contacts, while Marc's had taken a nosedive.

During his year of unemployment, Marc had objectively analyzed all available data and concluded that life was one big conspiracy, with certain members of the New York Bar at the center of it all. All the most successful lawyers were bosom buddies with the most powerful judges, legislators and/or politicians, deciding the fate of the rest of the world at the fourteenth hole. Marc desperately wanted in, but he didn't know a thing about golf.

The first two times that Marc applied to join the Committee, he had received a polite form letter from membership director Gerald Thornton, Esq., informing him that there were currently no vacancies on the Committee.

Just a few days ago, Gerald Thornton had *created* a vacancy on the Committee by committing suicide. Marc read about the death of the prominent attorney and humanitarian in the New York Law Journal just last week.

Marc never understood people like Thornton. The man had had everything. Money, fame, power, prestige ... Everything Marc wanted and didn't have. *If I'd been Thornton, I would have been a damn sight happier.*

Marc had been planning on applying again, as soon as he found out the name of the new membership director. But he'd had the sinking feeling that it didn't matter. His application would be rejected yet again. *What would happen*, Marc had wondered, *if I just showed up at a meeting anyway?*

Then, tonight, they'd closed the Bar Association while he was in the bathroom. Maybe it had been the exciting prospect of the long Labor Day weekend that had made them so careless.

As Marc had wandered the darkened hall toward the front door, he had passed the Bar Association administrative office. He had remembered that the Ethics Committee was short a member *and* a membership director. Marc could take advantage of the temporary confusion that Thornton's sudden death must have caused within the Committee. *I can't do something that ... sleazy,* he had thought to himself. *It's wrong.*

But the door to the office had been unlocked. And he hadn't been able to stop himself.

As Marc added his name to the membership list and printed it, he tried to comfort himself with the thought: *It's a victimless crime.* Then he found the files of letters from Thornton to applicants. As he was writing a form letter welcoming himself to the Committee, he heard someone trying to turn the doorknob.

Just a few days before, Berna Gutierrez, Marc's neighbor in nightshift word processing at Samson & Lake, had returned from a week's absence uncharacteristically quiet. When Marc asked if everything was okay, she said she'd talk to him during a break.

Later, in the deserted cafeteria, over vending machine coffee, Mrs. Gutierrez told him emotionally, "It's my son."

"Paul or David?" Marc asked with concern.

"David. He was almost killed and no one cares!"

"What happened? Is he okay?"

"The bullets missed him, but I don't think he'll ever be okay."

Berna Gutierrez calmed down sufficiently to tell Marc how her fourteen-year-old son, David, had been caught in the crossfire between drug dealers and undercover cops. "He was going to visit a school friend. He didn't know the pushers were using an apartment on the same floor." She shook her head sadly. "For years I've been saving to move to a better neighborhood. I still can't afford it."

"Did the narcs fire in self-defense?" Marc asked. "Did the drug dealers fire first?"

"David says the police fired first. But he didn't even know they were police then."

"Were there other people in that hall at the time?"

"I'm not sure," she said. "I don't think so."

"That's horrible. They should be thrown off the force."

"We filled out a complaint form, but the men in the station treated us like criminals. They kept asking why David was there. And they said 'The boy seems fine. Count your blessings and keep the kid away from crack houses.'"

Marc was too angry to comment. He asked, "Have you considered a civil suit against the police?"

"This afternoon I talked to Mr. Millborne, the partner at Samson & Lake who's in charge of *pro bono* cases. He said the case sounded too hard because the police didn't do anything directly to David. He *also* told me to count my blessings. I *do* thank God that David wasn't shot. I just wish I could take away David's fear. I wish I could give him some reason to respect the law again."

In all of their small talk about the weather, their health and their families, Marc had never mentioned to Mrs. Gutierrez that he was an attorney. He hadn't told any of the word processors.

He decided to break his silence. "I may not have mentioned this before, but *I'm* a lawyer."

"Really? Then what are you doing ...?" Tact pulled her up short.

"Millborne's right. Your son's case will be difficult. You'll have to bring it in federal court, under section 1983 of the Public Welfare Law. You'll have to disprove the officers' stories, prove that they acted recklessly and wantonly. I think the cases say that their actions must 'shock the conscience.'"

"You don't think ..."

"But your story shocks *my* conscience. I think it *is* terrible enough." He ran down his mental checklist. "You'll also have to prove psychological damages, and their foreseeability. Even if you win, the monetary judgment might not be that big."

"I understand that," she said. "Are you saying that you ..."

"I don't have much experience. I don't have an office. I don't even have stationery. But I have a computer, good research and writing skills, and I could use the practice. I'd like to take your son's case." Marc ignored the practical voice in his head that was teasing him: *a difficult case that pays nothing now and not much later ... just what you've been looking for.*

"Thank you so much," Mrs. Gutierrez gushed.

She actually thinks I can do it. She doesn't know I've never set foot in federal court.

"Do you have the time to do this?" she asked.

"Don't worry about that," he assured her. "Time is something I definitely have."

Well, I've finally got a case. I still need some paying jobs, but this is exciting. Can I really do this by myself? If I were at a firm, I'd have support staff to churn out the forms. And partners to review my work and make sure I don't commit malpractice. And I'd have malpractice insurance.

⚖

Again, someone jiggled the doorknob to the Bar Association office. Marc froze and stared at the door. Then he heard footsteps heading away.

Whoever it was might come back in a minute, but he couldn't stop now. He printed two copies of the letter, then exited the directory and switched off the computer's power strip. Quickly, he forged Thornton's signature on the bottom of one copy of the letter, using the bottom of one of his rejection letters as a model. He opened the appropriate file drawer and filed both the letter and the new membership list.

This time he heard the footsteps as they approached. Marc hid under the desk, feeling scared, guilty and humiliated.

What am I doing?

The janitor unlocked the door and flicked on the light, muttering under his breath. He left the garbage pail outside and came in with the vacuum.

As he bent down to plug in the vacuum, his face came within two feet of Marc's. Marc could smell the whiskey the man had been drinking. Marc held his breath as the janitor grunted and stretched for the outlet.

Mission accomplished. The janitor stood up and turned on the vacuum. He began to push the machine about in an unpredictable, unsystematic manner. Marc was trapped because the desk had no opening in the back. He crawled in as far as he could go.

The vacuum began to probe for dirt under the desk. Marc got on all fours just in time to allow the machine to pass under his stomach and bang against the desk back. Then it was gone.

As the janitor circled around to the other side of the desk, Marc peeked out and saw that the janitor was looking the other way. Marc crawled out of the room quickly and quietly. As he fled the building, his pants coated with dust, he tried to convince himself that everything would be okay, that he didn't just do something stupid that would ruin his life.

Two

A week later, Marc received a card "reminding" him about a brief procedural meeting of the Ethics Committee the following Tuesday, September 13. *Could the Committee really have been fooled so easily? Things aren't supposed to work this way.*

He told his mother the shortest version of the story: he was on a committee with lots of powerful, influential people. "That's great," she said. "I'm sure you'll impress them. Maybe they'll give you a job." *Yeah*, Marc thought, *I'm sure I'll stand out as the smartest one there.*

When he told his mother that it was the same committee that Paul Johnston was on, she asked him, "What ever happened to Paul? You two used to spend so much time together."

"We kind of drifted apart. After he started making lots of money and I stopped."

"That's a shame. He seemed like a nice boy."

Paul had been nice, though full of self-pity, back when he couldn't land *any* job during his second summer of law school. Marc had been big about things, paying more than his share of movies and bar tabs. Then, when Paul joined the Ethics Committee right after graduation, Paul's many new contacts had netted him a top job at a prestigious firm. Marc grew to resent Paul, and Paul became uncomfortable around Marc.

"I think your uncle used to be on that Ethics Committee, years ago," said Sylvia Wilson.

"I don't know. He's not on it now. Thank God."

"I don't see why you never got over your grudge against Uncle Charles."

"I don't see how you could have gotten over it. Dad was so angry with Uncle Charles. He really hurt Dad."

"Your father never hated anyone. Especially not his own brother. You don't even know what they fought about, do you?"

"It doesn't matter."

"I'm sure they would have made up eventually, if your father was still around."

Marc remembered that, tough as he could be, his father had always been quick to forgive. But Marc didn't care that his mother was probably right. Hating his uncle made him feel closer to his lost father.

⚖

Marc stopped by Marsha's place without warning. He told her about the Committee, and predicted that this was a turning point in his life.

"Why are you telling me?" she asked, still standing in the doorway. She stood very straight, a posture that accentuated the healthy buoyancy of her beautifully rounded breasts.

"I want to share my good fortune with you."

She blocked his path, while keeping her voice modulated. "I meant what I said the other day. I don't think we have a future together."

Marc had gotten the message a few days earlier. But he wasn't ready to give up yet. He had enjoyed many happy times with Marsha over the last two years. Also, he was afraid to be thrust back out into the dating world. Although he had no physical deformities, Marc knew that his appearance was fundamentally plain. His chief claim to fame and source of pride was having a full, thick head of hair while most of his acquaintances were already missing some on the top or the sides. It would be hard, against-the-odds work to get another woman to acquire a taste for him.

"But things are changing for me," he pointed out. "How can we give up now on all we have?"

"What did we have? We practically never went out. All you ever wanted to do was watch old movies on video."

"That's not all we ever did, and you know it."

"Well, we *did* have great sex," Marsha conceded. "But your mother always ruined it for me. I could hear her rattling pans or washing dishes in the kitchen. I'm too old for that."

"Me too. I'm working on it." He recalled once again that he had been making three thousand dollars a week when he started dating Marsha. Neither of them could have predicted then that they would still be so close with his mother two years later.

"I need to get out," she announced.

"Have you found someone better?"

"You don't really want to know, do you?" She edged him out the door, saying, "Good luck."

The big day arrived. Marc showed up a few minutes early for the "brief meeting to discuss procedural matters." He was scared. Scared of being exposed as a fraud. And scared of success. And what such a success would signify about the universe. *Maybe I've invested too much in this meeting*, he thought. But it was impossible to calm down about it.

The Ethics Committee filed in, in ones and twos. It didn't surprise Marc that almost all the members were white, but he was pleasantly surprised that over a third of them were women, and all age groups were represented. The clearest pattern Marc noticed was that each person was beautifully dressed.

Marc was sitting in the back of the Bar Association meeting room. He had no idea how the Committee members would react to him. *Pay no attention to me*, he thought. *I am not the interloper you're looking for.*

He was excited but nervous at the prospect of seeing his former friend, Paul Johnston. It could be awkward, and Paul might be suspicious. But Marc did miss Paul. They had had some good times together.

A few of the Committee members took seats without noticing Marc, but many nodded or smiled in his direction. A group of four guys approximately his age walked in and sat near the front, turning to look back at him and smile. One of the men was particularly big and muscular, and another had bright red hair. From where he was sitting, Marc couldn't see that the third was missing the fourth finger from his right hand. Marc returned their good-natured stares and smiled nervously. *They seem friendly. There's no reason to assume they won't like me.*

It was 12:30 on a Tuesday afternoon, but surprisingly few of the attorneys gave off the expected air of busy New York lawyers who had barely managed to escape their offices for an hour. *These people really are important.*

On the other end of the spectrum, Marc had strolled down to the meeting room after a routine trip to the Bar Association library upstairs to check on job postings. He'd been more surreptitious than usual this morning, afraid that by some unlucky chance he would be seen by members of the Committee.

A middle-aged woman sat down to Marc's right and greeted him with a smile. She introduced herself as Doris Spender, and Marc thought he recognized the name as one of the only female managing partners at a big New York firm. Marc was alarmed to notice that other Committee members appeared to be watching and listening as he introduced himself.

"Your uncle Charlie's a great man and a brilliant jurist,"

said Doris Spender.

Marc was momentarily thrown. First of all, he so seldom thought about his uncle that he often forgot he existed. Secondly, he almost never talked about his uncle. His brief conversation with his mother a few days ago had been the first time in a year, and he was sure that his uncle never talked about him. Yet, this woman hadn't just guessed, she had *known* that Charles Wilson, the Second Circuit Court of Appeals judge, was his uncle. Had she and/or others on the Committee checked into his background?

"Uh, thanks."

A heavyset middle-aged man in front of Marc turned to face him and said flatly, "Charlie Wilson was the best Committee Chair we ever had. No offense to Bob and the current regime. But Charlie's been doing a lot of good on the Second Circuit, too. By the way, I'm Don O'Neill." Marc shook his pudgy hand.

Just then Robert Baylor strolled in and called the meeting to order. Twenty-four members were present out of a total of thirty-two, including Marc. Everyone faced front. Marc was relieved.

Marc was glad that Baylor didn't make a production by officially introducing him to the Committee. Maybe he knew or guessed that an unofficial introduction had already occurred. More importantly, Baylor didn't denounce Marc or eject him from the meeting.

Did my crazy plan somehow work?

Baylor announced, "In the wake of Bob Thornton's untimely passing, and by the way thank you to all of you who contributed so generously to the scholarship fund established in his name—Bob cared so much about young people—Doris Spender has taken over as membership director. I'm sure she'll do a terrific job, with His help and guidance."

Ms. Spender smiled and nodded at the Committee members, ending by fixing a friendly gaze on Marc. After a couple of seconds, he looked away self-consciously.

At that moment, two men entered the room. Marc instantly recognized the shorter, younger man as Paul Johnston, looking tan, blond and more movie-star-handsome than ever in a Brooks Brothers suit. The other attorney wore an Italian suit that highlighted a lean but muscular form, which denied his sixty-plus years of age. This was a man whose appearance seemed to be the result of total mental and physical discipline.

It struck Marc with a jolt that he had only once before perceived such innate power. Although he had been shorter and stockier than this man when Marc last saw him, Charles Wilson had radiated a similar aura of confidence and influence. *Why does he keep coming up?*

The two men took seats in the middle of the front row, as if the seats had been saved for them. Although Baylor looked vaguely annoyed at their late entrance, neither man had an apologetic word or expression. The older man faced front, while Paul swept the room quickly with a sociable glance. Marc thought Paul saw him, but he wasn't sure.

The meeting proceeded rapidly. As advertised, it was brief, though painstakingly procedural. Several sub-committee chairmen were called upon to report on their sub-committees' progress, self-imposed deadlines, and the times of their next scheduled meetings. No one spoke for more than a minute.

Marc noticed that many of the chairmen followed statements of future intentions or predictions with conditional catch-phrases, such as "if He's willing" or "if all goes according to His plan." *These ethical types are pretty damn religious*, he mused. *Hope I can fit in.*

Marc wondered if he should volunteer to join one of the sub-committees, but he chickened out. He figured he would bide his time a little, insinuating himself gradually.

Baylor asked, "And how are the preparations for the Halloween parties going, Bill?"

Mr. Powerful Italian Suit stood up and addressed the Committee. "Very well. The party for the shelter kids will be held on Saturday afternoon in the basement of my church. Transportation, candy and costumes are all being donated. And *our* party is set for later that night at the Aladdin Club, which we booked for the whole night." He smiled roguishly. "Should be decadent Halloween fun till dawn." He added, "Be it His will."

As he turned to sit, he concluded, "Paul's been helping me, so there should be something for every age and taste." Paul smiled charmingly.

Minutes later, the meeting was over. The next general meeting, scheduled for the second week in October, was being held at Baylor's suburban house. Marc would have to borrow his mother's car and get directions to Dobbs Ferry, a river town in Westchester County, New York.

As Marc and everyone else stood up to leave, Paul and Bill turned and faced Marc. As the two men walked back toward him, Marc couldn't help feeling nervous. First he met their gazes and smiled, and then he glanced artificially to his right for a moment. He couldn't stop himself as he looked away one more time before they reached him.

Paul reached Marc first, grabbing his right hand and pumping it forcefully. "Marc! It's so good to see you!"

Bill waited quietly for Paul's enthusiastic handshake to slow down. Paul turned to him and introduced him. "This is Bill Eckart. Head of the Environmental Litigation department at Ballen, Warren & Dow. Sort of my mentor."

"Good to meet you," Marc managed, shaking the man's hand.

"This is Marc Wilson," Paul continued. "We were friends and study partners in law school. Took turns beating each other on finals."

I had a higher average than you, you Brooks Brothers ass. Marc pumped all the charm he could muster into his handshake and smile.

Bill relinquished the handshake, but immediately placed

his right hand on Marc's shoulder, making Marc feel uncomfortable.

"I could use another one as good as Paul," said Eckart. "The timing couldn't be better."

What's he talking about? Marc didn't dare ask.

"Can I persuade you to join us at Ballen Warren?"

What sort of practical joke?

"But I haven't ..." Marc stopped himself.

"Don't worry if you haven't had environmental defense experience."

How'd he know what I was thinking?

"At least you won't have anything to *unlearn,*" said Eckart. "You'll be a clean slate on which I can write the law of the jungle."

Paul chimed in, "Don't let him intimidate you with his bullshit. He talks tough but he's really a sweetheart. The hours aren't that bad and the pay's great."

"Don't listen to *his* bullshit," Eckart broke in, good-naturedly. "I'm a monster. I eat associates for breakfast. But we'll dine *together* as long as I like you."

During the ensuing silence, it became painfully obvious that Marc had not been contributing much to the conversation. *What the hell can I say?*

"Think about it," Eckart advised, with a final slap on Marc's shoulder. "Call me tomorrow."

Manhattan District Attorney Bob Rosetti shoved most of the hot dog into his mouth as he continued reviewing the file marked "E.C." Practiced as he was at such multiple tasks, he didn't drop a single spicy onion on his shirt. It also helped that he had spent two years in Iraq and had experience eating while contemplating violent death. Few would have considered the text or pictures in the file to be appetizing.

So, the coroner's report had validated Rosetti's hunch that

Bob Thornton was moved to Central Park *after* he died. Thornton had ejaculated shortly before he died, but someone wiped him clean as a whistle. *Why?* Rosetti wondered. *Was sex the motive for the murder, or just part of the method?*

Rosetti thumbed through the rest of his file on the Ethics Committee, trying to make sense of it. First Norm Maxwell, now Bob Thornton. *What's making these bastards kill their own? And how am I going to get to the bottom of it?*

Three

Even in the age of computerized research, the library at the law firm of Ballen, Warren & Dow was almost as big as the one at the Manhattan Bar Association. The stacks of old books and the space to display them were impressive status symbols and reminders of the firm's grand history. The library, with its high ceilings, wood paneling, plush carpet and beautiful East River views, was just as grand, yet comfortable as the rest of the Ballen Warren offices. The library had the extra feature of a huge gold-plated antique telescope that had been a gift from one of the Vanderbilts. Some mornings when he arrived before the crowds, Marc liked to look at boats, Roosevelt Island and Queens through the Vanderbilt telescope.

The library was often empty and Marc liked to spread out and work at its big tables, so that by Friday of his first week at Ballen Warren, Marc was well on the road to intimate acquaintance with Iris, the librarian. He was also getting to know Gina, his secretary, Joe, the guy who stopped by his office to deliver and pick up mail, and Maria, the cashier who rang up his sandwiches in the firm's cafeteria before he wolfed them down at his desk. The firm had all of the services and amenities of a top-flight, mid-sized midtown Manhattan law firm. A firm with one hundred lawyers was considered mid-sized in Manhattan, but huge in many other parts of the world. Marc thought how strange and wonderful it was to be surrounded by helpful support staff. *Hell, it's strange and wonderful to have enough pens and paper clips.*

Marc hadn't seen Maria the cashier on Monday and Thursday, though. On those days he had been forced to find the time for long and expensive lunches on the firm, one with Eckart and Paul, and one to "get acquainted" with Marc's office-mate, Harry, and an executive committee partner.

Marc was doing it and he was loving it.

He didn't mind sharing his twenty-ninth-floor view of the East River and Queens. He knew that such doubling up was paradoxically common at most prestigious firms in the city. The room was big enough, and Harry was good company; friendly yet not too distractingly talkative. As one of the only three black attorneys at Ballen Warren, Harry was candid with Marc, telling him that he wasn't holding his breath to become a partner. Despite having preemptively accepted such a limitation on advancement, Harry put in more than adequate effort, produced good work, and was well liked in the environmental department.

"Except for Eckart." Harry had pointed out. "I don't think he likes me."

"Why not?" Marc asked.

"Why doesn't he like me, or why don't I *think* he likes me?"

"Either."

"I don't know. He sort of ignores me." Harry lowered his voice and ventured, "Must be his Nazi ancestry."

When Marc looked incredulous, Harry laughed. "It's probably just my own racist stereotypes, but the guy *was* born in Germany in the 1940s. Says so in his Martindale-Hubbell listing."

"He doesn't have an accent."

"I guess he got out when he was pretty young." Harry seemed to regret bringing up the subject. "I'm sorry. I'm sure *you* won't have any problem with him."

It was only just over a week since Marc had first met Eckart at the Ethics Committee meeting. He had called Eckart the next day and expressed serious interest. He had visited the firm's offices the following day, to meet one other executive committee partner—a mere formality, Marc was told—and to look over the facilities and meet junior associate attorneys, also a mere formality in Marc's eyes. Although he pretended to be evaluating and deciding, he would have taken the position even if it meant working in a condemned slaughterhouse alongside convicted child rapists. He had started work the following Monday. Under pressure from Eckart, he had stopped playing hard to get. He had considered pretending that he needed to give his "current employer" two weeks notice, but Eckart's calls and his own empty bank account had made a more honest man out of him.

Some of the work Marc had been doing this week was background, becoming familiar with certain key state and federal environmental statutes. This process was rendered more difficult because he found so much in the statutes to be counterintuitive. For example, unless he was missing something major, there seemed to be numerous scenarios in which the most extreme unrepentant polluters would fare better than one-time accidental polluters.

Eckart had advised him to read the statutes and the related treatises immediately, billing his time to a company called Hammond Chemical, for whom he would be doing a lot of work.

"Don't take any of those treatises too seriously, though," Eckart had counseled over a tasty swordfish salad platter at the Manhattan Ocean Club (Marc let Eckart order first, then ordered the same. Paul went for the salmon). "Most of these statutes are still virgin territory for creative manipulation. Anyone who says he's an expert is a liar."

As usual, Marc had nodded with conviction. So far, that

had been enough.

As they were finishing their entrees, Marc decided to broach the subject of his *pro bono* case for Mrs. Gutierrez's son, David. "What's the firm policy on *pro bono*?" Marc asked, a little nervously since he wasn't sure what he'd do if Eckart had said, "We forbid it."

"We think it's important and we encourage it, although finding the time can be difficult. What type of case have you taken on?"

How did he know I already had a case? Marc had been noticing that Eckart was frighteningly good at reading people, or at least Marc. "I took the case just before I met you," Marc told Eckart. "I've drafted the complaint, but I haven't served it."

"Would you like me to look it over?" Eckart volunteered.

"That would be great," said Marc. *What a nice guy!* "It's a section 1983 civil rights case. Fourteen-year-old kid recklessly endangered by gung-ho undercover cops. Actually damages are purely psychological. Probably not big money."

"*Au contraire*, my friend," said Eckart. "Put a case like that in front of a sympathetic jury and you could be looking at a million dollars. The city will appeal, but the verdict will stand. Have you researched the 1983 case law?"

"Not yet," Marc answered apologetically. "I'll start today, now that you've given the go-ahead. And I'll give you a copy of the complaint at the end of the day. But take your time looking at it, of course."

"Be sure to ask for attorney's fees under section 1985 in the complaint," Eckart advised.

Before starting work, Marc had had a brief meeting with David Gutierrez at his mother's Bronx apartment. After the nerve-wracking trip deep into the Bronx, Marc had decided not to visit the actual scene of the incident.

David Gutierrez had told his story without energy or emotion, like he was too tired to experience it again. The young man had been polite, but cynical. "Is there any chance we can make the jury believe me and not the narcs?" Marc hadn't been sure if the young man had a lack of faith in the system, or in his unemployed attorney.

But now an experienced partner was going to review the complaint. And when Marc e-filed the complaint he would be doing it through the Ballen Warren systems, not from his home computer. David Gutierrez had lucked out when Marc lucked out.

⚖

At 11:17 a.m., Friday morning, the blessed event occurred. Joe from the mailroom, making his rounds, stopped in to deliver a pay notification. It was only for one week—after this he would be paid every two weeks—and not as dramatic as an actual check but it was a beautiful and welcome new arrival just the same.

That evening he showed the pay stub to his mother with obvious pride. Mrs. Wilson stared at it for a full minute, mentally calculating his monthly and annual gross and net income. She hugged her beamish boy.

"I'm so happy for you," she said. "You should celebrate."

She was right, so Marc took her out to dinner. *Some might not consider this an exciting celebration,* he thought. *Some might even have friends their own age with whom to party. On the other hand, some might not have grossed over $3000 this week.* He was on the move. Friends would come later, especially after he moved.

He broke the news to Mom over the egg rolls and cold sesame noodles. "Of course, I'm going to get my own place. You'll finally have some privacy."

"Privacy? What do you think I'm going to do with all that privacy?"

Marc shrugged.

His mother continued, "Have you been disturbed by my

many gentleman callers, stopping by at all hours of the night? Have we been making too much noise?"

"Mom! I wish you *did* have gentleman callers! Then you *would* throw me out."

Mom stopped eating her noodles. "I don't want to be a typical Jewish mother, but ..."

"You aren't. You never have been."

Sylvia Wilson smiled happily. "Well, I've got to maintain that image." She dipped the rest of her egg roll in the mustard and duck sauce mixture she had made and stuffed it in her mouth. "I guess I always knew you would move out when you could. I'm happy for you that you can. You haven't found a place already, have you?"

"No, I'm going to start looking this weekend."

"The Sunday Times is best, you know."

"I know." *I'm not sure if that's still true now that all the listings are online,* he thought. "Anyway, you'll be retiring and moving down to Miami Beach before we both know it. I'm still planning to buy that sunny condo."

"You're so sweet, but it's not necessary. I just want *you* to be happy."

The main courses came and the waiter placed them on a Lazy Susan for them to share. But Mrs. Wilson didn't have much use for orange beef and Marc thought chow mein was boring.

Mrs. Wilson broached a new topic gingerly. "So, I'm going to temple on Thursday. I don't suppose you want to come?"

"Why do you ask me every Rosh Hashanah? You know I don't believe in God."

"I wish you wouldn't say that," his mother told him for the hundredth time. "You're just not sure. You're an agnostic."

"Sorry, Mom, but I'm an atheist."

"I don't know how you can say that. How could you possibly be sure? Did God appear to you to say that he doesn't exist? Or did you see His dead body?"

"Come on. I haven't gone with you for four years." Last

time had been the week after Dad died. He had had to try it, one final time. "Stop asking."

"Are you going to go to work on both days?"

"Of course I am. I just started the job."

"They'll respect you more if you *don't* go."

"They don't even know I'm part Jewish, 'cause I don't have a Jewish last name."

"Well, technically you're *all* Jewish, because I'm Jewish. The mother's religion is what counts. That's the way it works in Judaism."

"Technically, I'm nothing because I don't believe in God. That's the way it works in the real world."

As soon as he spoke, Marc started to regret his candor. It was one thing not to go to services, but maybe he didn't have to be so outspoken.

"It's not like you raised me to be orthodox or something," he explained. "I went to temple with you maybe twice a year. We had a Christmas tree, for God's sake. I just never picked up a belief in God. I guess I'm more like Dad."

"Well, I've never pretended to be sure myself. I go largely out of habit, but I don't see how anyone could be sure either way. Including your father."

"But you didn't force him to go to temple, and he didn't stop you. That sort of mutual respect and compromise made a big impression on me when I was a kid."

"It wasn't always that smooth." Sylvia Wilson looked at him wistfully. "I suppose it must have been confusing for you sometimes."

Well, yes, thought Marc. *But not just because of the religious differences.* His father and mother had had such different approaches to raising him and to evaluating his worth.

Marc remembered the time in twelfth grade when his parents had been called to the police station. Marc had agreed to go for the beer after Doug, the class president, and Laurie, the head cheerleader, had suggested it, but he hadn't agreed to the six passengers who loaded into his mother's car with him. They had used Doug's fake ID to buy the beer and a pint of Southern Comfort, and were on their way back to Mike's unchaperoned house, when the police had spotted the overcrowded car and stopped them. Doug didn't say anything when the police came down hardest on Marc. Marc didn't dare implicate anyone so popular.

"It's not like he was driving drunk," his mother had said in an attempt to calm his father. "The other kids were drinking much more than him. And no one was hurt."

"He has to stop making excuses. And to say no to bad ideas."

His father had grounded him for two weeks. The following weekend, his mother had let him go to a movie with friends while she and his father went out.

Sometimes Marc had hated his father for being hard on him. And always being right. *But I never really wanted him gone.*

"We must have done something right, because you turned out so well," Sylvia Wilson concluded. "A smart, successful lawyer, and a nice boy besides. You can be proud when you look in the mirror."

Give me a break. Marc missed his father.

After taking Mom home, Marc was restless. He read from an environmental treatise for an hour. Then he played his synthesizer for a while. He continued to edit a song he'd been composing on the synthesizer and recording as data on the computer.

After Mom went to bed, Marc went out. His first stop was a local Queens dance club.

He built up enough nerve to ask a woman with high blond hair for a dance. "No, I'm with friends," was the response. The second one didn't offer any explanation. Then the group of three beautiful girls dancing with each other ignored him completely.

He returned to the bar and bought a couple of drinks for a couple of women. With the last woman, he worked his prestigious new job into the conversation and finally saw some interest. "So, do you, like, advertise on TV?" she asked.

I have to move to Manhattan.

⚖

Paul told Marc about a hot date he had on Saturday and then asked Marc about his weekend. Their relationship seemed to be picking up where it had left off.

When Marc mentioned his apartment hunt, Paul expressed interest. "I know a couple of people who are looking to sublet. Or they might know some other people. I'll ask around."

"That would be great."

Marc was surprised when Paul offered to join him apartment-hunting one night that week. "I'm always interested in what's out there in the market. Name a night."

"How about Wednesday?"

"Sure." Paul nodded. "If we can escape Eckart before eight." That was a long shot, since neither Marc nor Paul had left the office before ten in the last week.

Marc only received a couple of short-term assignments from other partners. The vast bulk of his work came from Eckart. And the bulk was growing vaster every day. Although hard work had never come naturally to him, he was managing to find the strength to meet this latest challenge.

On Wednesday, half an hour before Marc and Paul hoped to sneak out to look at apartments, Eckart called Marc to his office.

"How's everything going?" Eckart asked.

Marc was quick to respond, "Fine. What's new with you?"

"You keeping up with everything?"

"So far. Oh, I'll get that opinion letter for Hammond Chemical to you tomorrow. Is that okay?"

"Sure. Fine. I have another matter for Hammond that I'd like you to get involved with. Paul just submitted a motion to transfer the case, but discovery is proceeding in the meantime. It's a big commitment, and Paul's got more cases than you do."

"That's true. I'll be glad to help." He was already on the verge of exhaustion from his current workload, but he was resolved to continue doing whatever it took. "What is it?"

"It's an interesting case. Big stakes. Hundreds of people dead in a chemical leak."

Please tell me that our client isn't responsible for it.

"I'll need you to go abroad with me next month," Eckart continued. "Probably a couple of times. Help me with some depositions."

"Sounds ... fine." *Too bland, noncommittal.* "I'd love to watch you handle some depositions." *Too much?*

"We'll be going to Regensburg. In Germany."

Marc knew that the knot that appeared in his gut at the thought of visiting Germany was completely irrational. Even though his Great Uncle Theodor happened to have been killed by a German chemical leak. In the shower. In Auschwitz.

"I'll be glad to go," said Marc. *Does he buy that? He's usually hard to fool.*

If Eckart noticed Marc's trepidations, he didn't comment. "Terrific," he said. "I'll give you more information on what I need in the next few days. And one other thing ..."

"Yes?"

"Do you belong to a church?"

Marc was taken completely by surprise. He yanked his mind back out of the gas chambers.

"Excuse me?"

"A church. Do you belong to a church here in the city?"

"Oh, no. Not here in the city." Marc shifted.

"Well, you know I live just a few blocks uptown. We go to the Immanuel Church on 88th Street. We love it. Do *you* happen to be Lutheran?"

"Uh ..." *Do it,* Marc prompted himself. *Who could it hurt? For all you know, your atheist father could have been born Lutheran.* "Yeah. Sure I am."

But this isn't right. Is he allowed to ask me about this stuff?

"You know, the Committee members are devout. We're all regular churchgoers."

This doesn't seem kosher. Or at least not subtle enough.

Eckart continued with a smile. "Of course, young people these days, they're all either atheists, or else they're much more religious than their parents, more interested in the old rituals."

Marc nodded thoughtfully, agreeing with at least the first half of Eckart's proclamation.

"So I was thinking that you might like to join me and my daughter for services this Sunday."

With only a moment's pause, Marc addressed the challenge. "Sure. I'd love to."

Again, Eckart seemed to buy it.

Am I getting better at lying?

Four

Sunday morning, Marc was tired and in church. He had only been in church a few times before.

He had been forced to lie to his mother about where he was going. She wouldn't have liked to hear that, just days after he refused to join her in temple for Rosh Hashanah services, he was going to a random Sunday service to worship Christ with some Lutherans. So he told Mom that he was going out to brunch with Paul. "Must be a fancy brunch, the way you're dressed," she had said. *I have to find my own apartment*, Marc kept thinking. *And I'm wasting prime looking time this morning.*

Marc hadn't known anything about Lutherans. He had worked up his nerve to ask Harry, who was a Baptist, if he knew anything. "Lutherans are basically Catholics who don't like the Pope," Harry had offered. That was a little comforting to Marc, who had been to two Catholic weddings and seen a few more in the movies. He might be able to bluff his way through.

His comfort level wasn't helped by the proximity of the influential partner who had changed his life by giving him a prestigious, high-paying job. He was the one man who had the most power over his future. Still another unsettling detail was that between Marc and Eckart sat Samantha Eckart, his bewitching daughter. Marc had heard that Eckart's wife had died in an accident a few years before.

The church had room for hundreds, but today it was only three-quarters full. Although some benches were nearly empty, Bill Eckart led them straight into the overcrowded second row. The church was about forty feet tall, with stained glass windows and a balcony that housed the choir and the organ, which was playing softly.

Most of the parishioners were successful-looking couples and families, expensively and conservatively dressed. There did not appear to be many single men and women in the congregation, except for a few older members. Although many of the people seemed to know each other, only a few talked to others in reserved tones, glancing occasionally toward the pulpit to see if the pastor had entered yet. Marc noticed that many of the older parishioners had thick German accents, and he remembered learning in school that Martin Luther himself had been German.

While they waited for the pastor and the late-sleepers to arrive, Eckart and Samantha alternated between greeting incoming church members and making polite conversation with Marc.

Marc wondered at the seating arrangements that placed several parts of his body hard up against Samantha Eckart on the crowded bench. *It can't be that Eckart wants me to rub up against his daughter's shapely butt, can it?*

Sitting next to twenty-three-year-old Samantha Eckart was *too* pleasant. She even smelled wonderful, fresh and clean, yet subtly distinctive. Somehow he was able to differentiate and enjoy her fragrance despite the many offensively strong perfumes nearby.

The forced physical contact made Marc shy. He was embarrassed but grateful when Eckart described him as a clever "rising legal star."

"How does the star like Ballen Warren?" Samantha asked. When he hesitated briefly, she turned to Eckart and said, "Daddy, don't listen."

He had difficulty looking directly into her probing green eyes, framed by well-defined brows that were a shade darker than her long, honey-brown hair. Instead, he became acquainted with the four light freckles on a nose that crinkled when she smiled.

"Well, the lawyers are all extremely bright, and the matters are quite complex and interesting," he began with an air of seriousness, "but I was particularly impressed by the facilities. The marble staircases between the four floors, the two posh reception areas with recreated stones from Pompeii ... even bathrooms are tastefully designed ..." *I'm rambling. Let's wrap this up.* "It's class all the way."

"Thanks. Daddy designed the bathrooms on twenty-nine and thirty-one."

Her smile was so wide and open. It forced her big green eyes into a squint.

A moment later, he managed to wipe the grin off his face. He glanced at Eckart to see if his new boss had observed his total surrender. Fortunately, Eckart was greeting an entering congregation member.

"Thanks again, Bill," said the woman, who looked familiar to Marc. "I never could have gotten past the zoning board if you hadn't hooked me up with Stratton."

"I was glad to help," said Eckart. "I'm looking forward to cocktails on your new deck."

Marc whispered to Sam, "Is that Justice Comstock?"

"Is she a judge?" Sam whispered back. "Mrs. Comstock's a summer neighbor in Saltaire."

"Thanks again," said New York Supreme Court Justice Comstock to Bill Eckart. "I owe you one. At least."

As the judge walked back a few rows, Marc felt validated on his theories of how things work.

Marc looked back at Samantha and tried to think of something to say. Samantha waited patiently, her full lips still curved.

"So, *you're* quite a star yourself," he ventured.

Her face registered surprise and skepticism. "Who told you that?"

"Well, no one told me *anything*, unfortunately. I was bluffing. Trying to draw you out. What do you do, anyway?"

"I'm in my last year at NYU film school. The graduate program. I've made a couple of short films that have been described as 'showing promise.' *No one* has called me a star. Not even Daddy."

"That sounds really interesting." *Shit, that sounded phony, but I meant it!* "Really. I used to see at least five movies a week in college. Had to go to the foreign ones and the silent ones by myself."

"Hmm. Who's your favorite director?"

Marc felt the pressure. "I guess Scorsese's been the most consistently fascinating modern American director."

Samantha pursed her lips and nodded. "Clever. Picking a NYU grad, critically respected, yet well-known, occasionally box office ..."

"Okay," he interrupted, "how about some classic writer-directors of the forties and fifties, like Billy Wilder? Preston Sturges? And, corny or not, I still love vintage Capra. Even *Mr. Smith Goes to Washington* and *It's A Wonderful Life.*"

Marc was on a roll. *Those thousands of hours alone in the dark are paying off.* Countless other directors' names bubbled up to the tip of his tongue.

Marc did not immediately notice that everyone else was standing. He wondered why Samantha had suddenly risen. He noted distractedly that she was almost as tall as he was.

Unlike in court, no one had called out, "All rise!" When Marc finally jumped to his feet, the pastor was already standing behind the wood railing with his back to the congregation, facing the life-sized wooden statue of Jesus on the front wall.

With his eyes closed and his hands spread out together in

front of his face, the pastor led the congregation in a brief opening prayer. Like his acolytes, the pastor wore a white robe, but his had fancy gold embroidery on it in several places.

As the service began, Marc focused on the wooden Jesus on the wall. The figure appeared serene, kind, and wise. On either side of it was a smaller statue of a similar-looking man. Marc wasn't sure if all three figures were intended to be Jesus, or if the other two figures somehow represented the rest of the Holy Trinity, or maybe saints, if Lutherans have saints. The wooden man on the left seemed to have two tablets with Hebrew letters on them under his arm. Maybe he was Moses. Maybe the other statue was Abraham. Marc was in no position to ask.

The service continued. Fortunately, Eckart seemed to concentrate on the service and paid no attention to Marc. Eckart's gaze was fixed on the wooden Christ as he prayed quietly.

Samantha, however, did seem to note and enjoy Marc's confusion as he flipped back and forth between the numbered pages of the service and the numbered hymns in the back of the book—once he had figured out that much.

Because he was working harder than anyone else at following in the book, Marc was often a little behind in perceiving changes in the height of the crowd. He stood and he sat a little late, and he was totally thrown when the congregation went directly from standing to kneeling in one fluid motion. One of the reasons he was so slow in detecting the maneuver was that the couple in front of him seemed to be exactly the same height kneeling as when they were sitting.

Marc was able to relax a little during the sermon. He learned that Lutherans *do* have saints, and this Sunday was dedicated to "St. Michael and all the angels." His mind began to wander as the pastor segued into a sermon about the dangers and evils of greed, starting from Christ and the moneylenders, and focusing on the heydays of avarice in the '80s and '90s and more recently during the credit crisis.

He glanced over at Eckart, who was staring at the pastor

with seeming interest. *Could Eckart have reached his current position without greed? His own and his clients?*

"Money is not the only goal of the greedy," the pastor continued. "We crave fame, power, even love. We are greedy for love. We can't get enough."

Samantha caught Marc looking. She met his gaze frankly. He faced the front again.

The pastor bridged into a discussion of the virtues of charity. *Not too controversial*, Marc thought. *But don't you have to be greedy before you can afford to be charitable?*

He wondered how much money Eckart donated to charities. Probably only a small percentage of his huge annual earnings.

⚖

Dan Lessing and Larry Moore had to miss church that morning. They had more pressing obligations.

As the two athletic twenty-seven-year-olds traveled across the second floor of the Port Authority bus terminal, they noted several groups of teenage boys and girls, some white, some black, some Hispanic. Some were heading for a bus, some from a bus, and some were just hanging out.

Because it was the midtown Manhattan bus terminal, land of the walking dead, no one paid any attention to strangers, except to avoid them. No one noticed Larry's bright red hair or Dan's missing fourth finger.

Dan thought of the work that he had left undone at the firm on Saturday. He might have to go in for a few hours of research tonight after the gathering. He had to be careful not to ignore the conventional aspects of being a lawyer.

"Have you been working every weekend like me?" Dan asked Larry, as the two turned back and continued pacing.

"You mean legal work?"

"Yeah. *This* isn't work."

"I've been working my ass off. And most people at Trell

and Dray have had it slow. *Our* circle of clients keeps getting bigger."

"I'm beat."

"I'll barely be able to stay awake at the gathering."

Dan laughed. "I doubt *that*. You'll be up for *that*."

The two of them walked up to the third floor, while constantly observing their surroundings. "So," said Dan. "Did you hear about that new guy, Marc?"

"Yeah. If it were up to me, I'd take care ..."

Larry slowed his step. Dan noticed too.

The boy looked about sixteen. He was pale white, sitting against a wall. Didn't look like he was going anywhere. Not even for lunch. He hadn't eaten in more than twenty-four hours.

Dan and Larry knew the routine.

Larry held up the crumpled Dunkin' Donuts bag. "Don't you want the last one?" he asked Dan. "You got it coming to you."

"Nah," said Dan. "I had enough already. I feel sick from all the sugar."

The boy didn't try to hide his interest.

"Seems a shame to toss it," Larry mused.

The boy spoke up. "Hey, Mister. Could I have the donut? I ain't eaten since yesterday."

Dan and Larry looked at each other. They shrugged.

"Sure, kid," said Larry, tossing over the bag.

"Thanks a lot." The kid tore the crumpled bag to remove the donut. He took a big bite, creating a powdered sugar beard and moustache.

"Hey, you really are hungry," said Larry.

"You look like you could use more than just a donut ..."

After the pastor led the congregation in the "Apostle's Creed," each member began actively chasing their neighbors' right hands so they could shake them forcefully, smiling benevolently as they intoned: "Peace be with you." After both members of the short gray-haired couple in front of him had pressed his flesh, Marc turned to Samantha.

As he smiled and said his line, she replied and leaned over to plant a quick kiss on his cheek. He must have blushed.

"Peace be with you, Marc," said Bill Eckart, as he grabbed Marc's hand with his two large hands.

Marc breathed deeply with relief. *That didn't go too badly ... Wait! There's more. The Eucharist.*

As the rows began to file out and up to the wooden bar in the front of the church, a sudden discomfort welled up in him. *I don't want to do it. It's sacrilege. To all religions. I don't believe.*

The worshippers from the first rows were already kneeling. The pastor and his acolytes were placing the Host into the open mouths of the believers. *I hope I don't choke on it.*

⚖

The boy had run away from an abusive uncle in Kansas. Dan and Larry didn't ask how. His name was John, but his few friends had called him Gooch. They didn't ask why. He was *very* hungry.

He willingly accompanied them into the taxi for the ride to their "fully stocked refrigerator." Larry and Dan put John in the front of the cab, while they sat in the back. At one point, Larry whispered to Dan, "He's *too* easy. *Too* trusting."

"Not having second thoughts, are you?" Dan sounded scornful.

"Nah. Could take hours to find another."

When they got to the warehouse, John asked if it was what they called a "loft."

"Not exactly," said Dan.

For the first time, Gooch seemed uneasy. "Look, I don't mind if you want to do stuff with me. Just don't hurt me. Can I please eat?"

Dan reached out and placed his four-fingered hand on the boy's cheek and caressed it slowly.

"Take off your shirt."

The boy looked to Larry nervously. Larry's face was without expression.

Gooch reached down and jerked his rock T-shirt up. As the kid had the shirt up over his head, Dan, tired of the game, shoved him over onto the floor. The shirt muffled the sound of the boy's head smacking the wood floor. Gooch lay still.

Marc knelt in place but his mind raced as the pastor approached with the Host.

Marc noticed that most worshippers opened their mouths while the wafer was placed on the tongues, and then drank directly from the same communal wine cup when it was brought to them. *I guess the religious faithful aren't too worried about communicable diseases.* Some people, however, put out their hands for the wafer, and then merely dipped *it* into the wine. *That's a little less disgusting.*

If it weren't for the wine, the wafer would have had *no* taste. It was dry and tasteless as a Passover matzoh.

Marc almost did choke on the wafer. He wasn't sure if he was allowed to chew. Finally, it started to melt in his mouth. It *was* a miracle. He couldn't avoid a momentary image of Jesus, bleeding on the cross, with vultures perched and feeding on him.

Finally, Marc was allowed to follow the Eckarts back to the seats. The service concluded shortly thereafter.

There was no way to leave without talking to the pastor. It was like the receiving line at a wedding. As they approached the exit, Marc saw and heard that the minister was engaging every parishioner in more than a few seconds of conversation. Marc braced himself. *I belong to a church in Queens. What's the name of that church I used to pass on the way to the dance club?*

"Hi, Bill," the pastor beamed as he shook Eckart's hand. "Always a pleasure to see you and your family. And who's this young man with Samantha?"

The pastor grabbed Marc's hand and shook it forcefully.

"That's Marc Wilson. He works at my firm. Nice Christian boy."

For a second Marc feared that he heard irony in Eckart's voice. But Eckart was smiling warmly.

"Fine sermon," said Samantha as she shook the pastor's hand.

"Thank you. But I don't have to tell your family about charity. Thanks again for your latest generosity, Bill."

⚖

"We could at least have given him something to eat," said Larry.

"With all the starving people in this world?" asked Dan.

"Please. Forget ... food. Just ... let ... me ... go."

It took Gooch a little time to get the words out. Dan and Larry didn't know if it was the mental or physical trauma; the hunger or the thirst. In any case, it didn't seem like they'd need the gag.

"You wouldn't want to miss the party, would you?"

"Please." The kid had given up trying to break free, but he still had enough strength to beg. "Loosen the ropes ..."

"Maybe later."

Five

The next week at work was a killer. Fortunately, Eckart had already reviewed Marc's complaint in the Gutierrez case and only made a few changes, so Marc had it filed that Monday morning. Then Marc had to push aside every non-essential project to concentrate on two high priority rush jobs. Unfortunately, he was having trouble concentrating.

To his surprise, Marc couldn't stop thinking about church. Specifically, Samantha. He repeatedly dismissed Sam's image from his mind, along with her voice and her scent. He had to work! Anyway, she was the boss's daughter. Surely that meant trouble. And she was only twenty-three, unsure what she wanted to do with her life. He really didn't know her at all, except that she was a film snob. Maybe it was a typically unconstructive reaction to his urgent need to focus on work, but he had never had such frequent and compelling thoughts about *any* woman before. Not even Gisele Bundchen. Definitely not anyone he'd ever actually met.

Each time his mind wandered, he eventually dragged it back to the two vital projects at hand. One case he had known about for almost a week: the chemical leak at the Hammond

Chemical plant in Germany. He had to help Eckart prepare to take and defend the first depositions in that case. They had plane tickets for the Sunday night redeye to Nuremberg and had to begin the depositions on Tuesday morning. Their return flights had been left open.

The other case landed on Marc's desk Monday morning, with a resounding thud. He had to oppose the emergency motion of the Environmental Protection Agency and the Environment and Natural Resources Division of the Department of Justice, Enforcement Section, to close down Long Island Paper's plant. The Department of Justice's motion for an injunction was returnable before Judge Clemmons of the United States District Court, Southern District of New York, on Thursday afternoon. Marc had to write and file opposition papers before then.

Eckart expressed confidence in Marc as he dropped the full Redweld file folder onto Marc's desk. Marc was amazed and daunted when Eckart informed him that he would be the one arguing the motion in front of the judge on Thursday.

As Marc turned white, Eckart smiled. "Don't worry. I know you're the right man for the job. Besides, Irma Clemmons likes you eager young men better than us crusty old litigators. You'll do great."

Two hours later, Marc had digested the file and was scouring Clean Water Act cases.

Maybe I should call Samantha, he kept thinking. *But what for? What would I say? Even if I had the nerve, I couldn't ask her out this week.*

That night he sat at his desk next to a high stack of cases. After a couple hours of writer's block, he began drafting the memorandum of law and accompanying affidavits. He worked until three a.m., then took the car service home to Queens, thinking he had to get that Manhattan apartment very soon.

When Harry arrived at 9:30 a.m., Marc had already been hunched over his computer for over an hour. "How are you holding up?" Harry asked.

"Okay," Marc muttered. He looked up from the screen. "Why? Do I look freaked out?"

"No more than any of us. What are your deadlines?"

"Well, I have to email these affidavits to the client's plant manager today for him to sign and email back by tomorrow. I want to show a draft of the memorandum of law to Eckart by the end of today. I'm hoping to file the papers tomorrow and get the judge's courtesy copy to her chambers before she leaves."

"First of all, take a *little* pressure off yourself. If the papers don't get brought over and filed until Thursday morning, I'm sure that will be okay. It's not like Judge Clemmons is going to read your papers before the hearing. She's just going to stare you down and say, 'Why shouldn't I grant the government its injunction?' I'll help you prepare your oral argument if you want."

Maybe I should call Sam. Ask her out for Thursday night. I'll be too burned out after the oral argument to work on the Hammond Chemical case that night.

That afternoon, Marc caved in. He figuratively and literally pushed everything on his desk to the side and called her.

Realizing that he had not spoken to anyone in hours, he practiced saying "hello" as he dialed. Then it was ringing.

He resisted the urge to hang up.

"Hello, you've reached Sam ..."

Damn, a machine!

He started to hang up. Then he jerked the phone back to his mouth impulsively. He didn't hear anything.

"Oh. I must have missed the beep. Anyway, this is Marc Wilson. Uh, we met last Sunday. I, uh, work with your father ..."

"Hi." She picked up the phone. "I was screening. I still have an old-fashioned answering machine ..."

"Oh, yeah, me too. Digital, but basically old-fashioned ..."

"Right," she said. "So you made the cut ..."

"That's great. So, how're you doing?"

"Fine. So how did you get my number?"

"From old-fashioned directory assistance. Luckily you still

have a landline and you're the only S. Eckart. Listed, at least."

"Nice investigatory work. So are you at work now?"

"Yeah."

"The way they work people there, I'm flattered that you could make time to call me."

"I doubt you know the half of it. You *should* be flattered." No sense playing not-trying-to-get.

"With your schedule, I guess you'd better cut to the chase. What do you want with me?" she asked coyly.

"I'd like to see you. Hopefully Thursday night, when I'll be recuperating between legal crises."

There was a brief silence. "Aren't you afraid Dad might mind?"

"No. Well, maybe. Would he mind?"

"Probably not."

"Do *you* mind?"

"When do you want to pick me up?"

Marc had thought he would be able to concentrate better after he made the date, but after he hung up, he couldn't stop thinking about *it*.

That evening, Paul agreed to look at the Long Island Paper brief before Marc showed it to Eckart. Marc nervously handed over the twenty-two-page memorandum of law and three affidavits ranging from two to ten pages. Paul's review consisted primarily of flipping pages rapidly, nodding occasionally.

"Looks fine," Paul announced.

"No way. Come on. Be critical."

"Well, I could get into criticizing specific word choices and stuff, but it's really fine. You're going to win. Don't sweat it so much."

"I wish I could be as sure. There is circumstantial evidence that our client is violating the Clean Water Act, and the alleged environmental harm is so serious."

"As you say here, they haven't demonstrated a likelihood of ultimate success on the merits. They haven't sufficiently linked the alleged rise in toxin levels with our client's plant. They're trying to use the claimed emergency nature of the situation as a replacement for cold hard evidence."

Eckart spent even less time looking at the papers. "Good work, Marc. Make a good appearance on Thursday and it's in the bag."

Marc left Eckart's office in a daze. It was only Tuesday night. The papers were only supposed to be in draft form. He should have been thrilled. Instead he was stunned and a little uneasy. Nonetheless, he went home and got a good night's sleep.

On Wednesday, he asked Harry if he would look at the motion papers. "Can I bill it?" Harry asked. "My hours have been a little light."

"Sure. It's Long Island Paper."

Harry read the papers carefully. With Marc's encouragement, he wrote in several corrections. Most were minor, but one change was major, altering the thrust and location of a point in the memorandum of law.

"You're right!" Marc realized. "I think it's much better that way. Why didn't Eckart or Paul catch that?"

"Maybe you'd better leave it the way Eckart liked it before."

"No, this is better. I'll talk to him."

Eckart was on his way out to a meeting. He listened to Marc, and then said, "Either way. It doesn't matter."

Marc stared in disbelief as Eckart departed. *It's so major. How could Eckart think it doesn't matter?*

He made the change and thanked Harry.

When Marc arrived in the courtroom on Thursday, he was petrified. He was sweating, his head was pounding, and he felt like he had to go to the bathroom for the tenth time in an hour. The government had sent three attorneys, one from the EPA and two from the Department of Justice. One of the DOJ attorneys was about Marc's age, but the other two lawyers appeared confident and experienced. Marc still couldn't believe or understand why Eckart had sent him off by himself. Maybe Eckart's confidence was supposed to take the pressure off, but Marc felt like he had been dropped into a pressure cooker.

Eckart miscalculated.

Marc had never even set foot into federal court before, except for the day he'd been sworn in. He had been doing some wishful thinking when he had bothered to get admitted in the Southern District. As a struggling solo practitioner, he had practiced mostly in small claims court, except for the Gutierrez case, with rare appearances in state supreme court—which, despite the inflated-sounding name, was actually only a trial court for cases involving higher amounts of money than those in small claims. This week, Marc had re-learned the Federal Rules of Civil Procedure, which he had optimistically studied for a whole semester in law school. That effort would not be wasted, at least, since Marc had brought David Gutierrez's *pro bono* case in federal court.

The Southern District courthouse, next to the state courthouse on Centre Street downtown in Foley Square, was big, old, and lavishly constructed and maintained. Anyone could see how many more tax dollars were earmarked for furnishing and maintaining the federal courthouses, as opposed to the state ones. One only had to look around in the high entrance hall with working metal detectors and guards, in the high-ceiling well-polished courtrooms, even in the clean paper-and-soap-stocked bathrooms that Marc had visited several times since arriving. This was the big time.

Eight motions were scheduled for 2 o'clock. The attorneys and most of their clients were on the polished wooden benches waiting for the judge's arrival. Marc sat by himself. Even his client wasn't interested in attending.

The bailiff proclaimed, "All rise."

Judge Irma Clemmons looked like one of Marc's mother's

less appealing friends. She was about sixty years old, weighed at least one hundred eighty solidly packed pounds and stood about five-foot-two. Not a speck of makeup or a sign of occasional good humor softened the stark, harsh lines and contours of her big face. The pageboy haircut didn't help either.

"Sit down," she ordered.

Marc had seen from the list posted outside the doors of the courtroom that his case was scheduled to be argued second. Although the suspense was killing him, he was glad to be able to watch another case argued before it was his turn.

"Where are the parties for Aldrich v. General Electric, et al?" the judge asked.

Seventeen people, various attorneys and clients, stood up. A white-haired attorney announced, "Your Honor, the parties are all here except for the second, fourth-party defendant, Joe's Corner Fish Market."

"Then you can all relax until I have heard the other seven matters scheduled for this afternoon."

"Your Honor," the old pro ventured. "I'm sure the other party will be here by the time you've heard the next motion."

"Sid," said Judge Clemmons, "we have known each other for twenty-five years. You know my unbending rules. You'll go last. Now sit down."

Judge Clemmons didn't smile. "United States v. Long Island Paper?"

Marc bolted to his feet a moment before the government attorneys. "Present for the defendant, Your Honor."

"Present for the government, Your Honor."

"Good. Take your places."

The government lawyers moved up from the benches to spread out themselves and their papers at the long wooden counsel table on the right. Marc sat in the middle of the left table, alone with his folder of papers.

Judge Clemmons stared down at all of the attorneys with an unpleasant expression resembling disdain. "I've read your papers already, so I don't want you to bore me by reading them aloud."

Both sides were caught off-guard and rattled. Marc suspected that he was going to have to throw out his carefully prepared oral argument.

"Defense counsel, tell me this," the judge ordered, and then paused. Marc ceased breathing. "Why shouldn't I grant the government's request for a preliminary injunction?"

She's decided against me. It's hopeless. She's decided that my client is an evil environmental rapist.

Then, a moment later, Marc regained control of his mind and body. He took a deep breath. *If she's already decided, I have nothing to lose.*

"The government has totally failed to prove a substantial likelihood of ultimate success on the merits." *That actually came out pretty forcefully. Keep going.* "They have alluded to evidence which they *hope* to be able to produce at some unspecified later date, but such bald assertions alone cannot be allowed to succeed in crippling a vital industry."

The judge was staring at him. She didn't seem to blink.

He continued haltingly. "The government's motion is premature, given the limited extent of their current knowledge and evidence. Shutting down the plant will have such a devastating effect on my client, and on the local economy, as detailed in the affidavits we submitted, that such a step should not be ordered until the government has met the full burden of proving at a trial that the alleged rise in local toxins was due to my client's plant. Unproven allegations alone do not justify the emergency relief which they now seek."

As he was finishing, Marc noticed two of the government attorneys whispering to each other. Then everyone was watching the judge, waiting. Marc fought the urge to continue talking, paraphrasing himself.

Finally: "You are correct. Mark this matter for a full hearing exactly five weeks from today. First Thursday in November.

Until then, no injunction."

"But Your Honor," the senior DOJ attorney sputtered. "The environmental damage being done is catastrophic and irreversible. It cannot be allowed to continue for five more weeks."

"It'll be allowed to continue forever until and unless you prove your case," the judge roared. "And don't waste everyone's time by appealing this order. You know how seldom I get reversed. Just because you work for the government, that doesn't mean anyone should take your word for things. Get off your fat, tax-supported ass and try to assemble some evidence. See you in five weeks."

And that was it. Sudden, overwhelming victory. At least for five more weeks.

The relief was palpable. A couple of moments later it all seemed so obvious. Of course, he *had* to win. Naturally, the government had no case. He stumbled out in victory.

Six

As Marc headed for Samantha's Greenwich Village apartment, he tried not to worry about work and his impending journey to Germany. Tension had already driven from his mind the brief euphoria of the Long Island Paper victory. He wasn't having much success at relaxing until she opened the door and wiped his mind clean.

She had her coat on, but not buttoned, over a scoop-necked peasant blouse, short black skirt, opaque leggings, ankle-high boots with laces and a necklace that looked like a cross but had an open circle at the top. He stared admiringly at all almost-six-feet of her.

"Sorry, you can't come in," she announced. "The movie starts at 10:15 p.m., so we should head out to dinner right away. Where'd you pick?" she asked, as she locked her door and started toward the stairs.

"How does Moroccan sound?"

Without missing a beat, starting down the stairs, she hummed a snake charmer song. "How's that?"

"I think that's how *Baghdad* sounds. Do you know how Morocco tastes?"

They emerged onto the street. "I like couscous."

"Great."

It was less than a ten-minute walk to Lotfi's Couscous. Marc was not thrilled, but also not surprised, to learn that Samantha was a vegetarian. He had gone out with a couple of vegetarians, and both of them had been involved with the arts.

"How much do you mind it if I order meat?" he asked.

"Oh, no, you get what you want."

"Will you be disgusted with me?"

"No. I don't know you well enough."

"When you know me better, you'll be disgusted."

She laughed.

"Is it a health thing, or a spiritual thing?"

"A little of both. That reminds me, have you ever been to church before?"

Marc was taken by surprise. He was about to lie. Then he said, "Not exactly. But I've thought about it. I've always been sort of interested in religion. Took a bunch of classes in college."

"Are you Christian?"

"My dad was Christian, and my mom is Jewish. My dad wasn't religious. I doubt he ever read much of the New Testament, but I've read the whole thing."

"My parents were both religious. But since Mom died, I've only gone about once a month."

"When did your mother die?" *Maybe I shouldn't have asked that.*

"Just a couple of years ago. It was really sudden. A car crash."

"My God! How bizarre! My *father* died in a car accident, five years ago."

"That's a weird thing to have in common," said Sam. "Of course, I mostly feel sorry for *Dad.* He really misses Mom. He's had such a tough life, between losing the family he left behind in Germany, and Mom, and their son, who would have been my younger brother. He died of sudden infant death syndrome in the middle of the night."

At that moment, Marc felt compassion for his rich and powerful boss. And for his boss's beautiful daughter.

"We don't go to our place in Fire Island as often since Mom died," said Sam. "These days Dad mostly brings business associates up there, or loans the house out to them." Sam closed her eyes to free a tear. "Mom was the best swimmer and fisherperson in the family. She and I used to spend most of every summer in Saltaire, while Dad shuttled back and forth to work in the city. The weekends when we were all together were terrific."

Marc's compassion was tinged by a trace of jealousy. At least Sam had some pretty cushy memories. Marc had never been to the posh Fire Island National Seashore. He had always wanted to, but there weren't any hotels there. You had to know people. They didn't even have cars on exclusive Fire Island. Most people took a ferry or a private boat over. Marc's family had taken the subway a couple of times each summer to Brighton Beach, Brooklyn. *Get over it*, he told himself. *For all her wealthy upbringing, she's down to one parent too, just like me.*

They managed to arrive at the Film Forum in time to buy two of the last tickets for the director's cut of Orson Welles' *Touch of Evil*, an assignment in one of Samantha's classes. Fortunately, they agreed on preferring to sit in the extreme front of the theater rather than the extreme back.

Afterward, Samantha invited him up. Since it was after midnight, they both agreed that it would only be for a few minutes. For the first time in several hours, Marc remembered his work pressures.

As she made decaffeinated tea, she seemed to sense his returned tension. "Do you want to talk about your legal crises?"

"Not much." He surveyed her living room, an interesting blend of cinema memorabilia, handmade tapestries, and colorful stones of various sizes, shapes and textures. "Just that I argued and won a motion this afternoon."

"Congratulations."

"And now I have to do lots of work to prepare to go to Germany with your father."

"Oh yeah. He mentioned that you were going with him on that case. Do you like defending corporate polluters?"

Marc felt blindsided. "Well, I wouldn't put it that simply. We represent corporations, and sometimes they're accused of polluting. We also *advise* corporations about the environmental laws and regulations."

"And how to get around them, right?"

"Not necessarily. Sometimes following the law can be the most efficient business course." *Theoretically.*

"I guess you really needed this job, right?"

How should he answer such a question from his boss's daughter? "It's a good job, with a prestigious firm. Also, frankly, it pays well. My mother and I need the money."

"That's it? That's your motivation for destroying the world?" Sam asked.

"I want to help my mother move to Miami Beach," said Marc. "Near her cousin Gertie."

"That's nice, I guess. But do the ends justify the means? Does your mother know what you're blaming her for?"

How much should I take from this spoiled student? "Some people have to work for a living. Not everyone has a parent destroying the environment and making enough money so she doesn't have to." *So much for diplomacy. Or visiting those full lips ...*

She smiled. "Not bad. But save your moral outrage for yourself. And Dad. *I* wouldn't take a penny more of Dad's blood money than I have to. I work part-time as a waitress. Between that, financial aid and loans, I almost pay my way."

She poured them each a cup of tea. Marc welcomed the break in conversation. He took a small sip of the hot tea and widened his eyes in response.

He was glad to change the topic. "This tastes really strong. But good. You're sure there's no caffeine, right?"

"I'm sure," she said as she sat down beside him on the

couch. "It's my own blend of herbs. It's particularly good at reducing tension."

As he blew on it and continued to sip, he became convinced that she was right. "This is just what the doctor ordered."

"I believe that everything we need to be healthy and happy is in the earth, air and water. We just have to know what's what, and we have to protect them from destruction."

"So you're sort of into New Age stuff?" Marc asked. He looked around the apartment. "Crystals and things ..."

"Don't *you* judge *me*," she announced loudly, jumping to her feet and disappearing into the kitchen.

Marc was startled by her outburst. In her absence he thought, *I guess she and I just aren't going to work out.*

She returned seconds later, composed and smiling. Again, Marc was surprised. "Do you want more tea?" she asked.

"No, thank you," said Marc, gathering his nerve. "You knew what I did for a living before you met me," he pointed out quietly. "Why'd you go out with me at all?"

"I don't want to *marry* you," she said. "I just think you're sexy as hell." Her nose crinkled as she smiled self-consciously.

Marc was speechless.

"I hope that wasn't too forward," said Sam. "I can be a bad girl ..."

"I'm looking forward to verifying that."

Sam groaned at his attempt at worldly humor, then kissed him anyway.

The next day, Marc was tired but in good spirits. Even while productively organizing the Hammond Chemical file and simultaneously drafting questions to ask the plaintiff at the deposition, Marc was spurred on by an overall sense that life was good. He couldn't wait to return from Germany.

Later that morning, he received an email from the Manhattan Bar Ethics Committee, reminding him that there would be a meeting a week from Sunday in Dobbs Ferry, New York.

Oh yeah. I'm on the Ethics Committee. Marc had almost forgotten. He had joined the Committee to make contacts and try to get work. When a terrific job offer had come through at the first meeting, he had stopped thinking about the Committee.

He would go, of course. Even if he wanted to, he couldn't just quit so soon. *What would Eckart and Paul think? What would all those other important attorneys on the Committee think?*

Anyway, he *did* want to go. The meeting was another chance to hobnob with the rich and powerful legal elite, this time in their natural habitat. He was sure that the house in a posh river town in Westchester would be worth the trip. Although he was likely to feel out of place, he wouldn't miss the opportunity.

When Harry left at the end of the day, he wished Marc a good trip to the "Fatherland." Then he apologized when he realized that Marc *was* uneasy about the locale.

That night, Marc's mother was less sensitive to his apprehensions. "I'm nervous enough about this trip," he said.

"No, if you were nervous enough, you wouldn't go."

"I have to go. It's my job."

"They wouldn't fire a smart boy like you just because you didn't want to go to dangerous places."

"As usual, you're assuming that others think as highly of me as you do. I like this job too much to take chances."

Sylvia Wilson looked almost beaten. "But Germany ... and on Yom Kippur? It's no place for a boy like you."

Marc ignored the Yom Kippur remark. "I know that Great Uncle Theodor was gassed by the Nazis, but that was a long time ago."

"Forget the '30s and '40s. Look what's going on there right now. Those young thugs, beating up foreigners and minorities. Nothing's changed."

"Hasn't the government cracked down on the skinheads?"

"A few slaps on the wrist," said his mother. "The people running the government now are the kids of Hitler Youth from the '30s and '40s."

Seven

"You'll love Germany," Eckart announced to Marc as they flew through the black night. Somewhere far below was the invisible Atlantic. "Germany's physical beauty is surpassed only by its music, art and literature."

"I'm really looking forward to it," said Marc.

Eckart caught Marc off-guard by saying, "I know that you aren't really."

I can't keep anything from him. Marc began, "It's just that ..."

"That's okay," said Eckart. "Keep an open mind and I think you'll be pleasantly surprised."

"I like German beer," Marc volunteered, instantly regretting the inanity.

"Who doesn't? Of course, we won't get to see or drink much on this trip. Maybe next time we'll spend a whole weekend."

"When are the next depositions?" Marc was anxious to steer the conversation in a legal direction.

"Two weeks from Thursday."

"And what if Paul's motion to transfer the case to Germany is successful? Will these depositions be admissible in

German court?"

"Yes, to the same extent as they would be in the U.S. When we get back to the office, we should have received plaintiffs' opposition papers. We'll make our reply papers concise."

Marc nodded. *Great, more work.*

After a lull, Eckart asked, "Are you in touch with your Uncle Charles?"

Marc didn't expect that question. "Not really."

Eckart looked a little disappointed. "When was the last time you saw him?"

"A few years ago."

"That's a shame. You should contact him. Catch up on things. I'm sure that a lot has happened to each of you in the last few years."

What's it to you? Marc wondered. Rather than get into a heated discussion of his family life, Marc asked Eckart, "Do you still have family in Germany?"

Eckart answered in a matter-of-fact tone. "They all died in the war."

"Sorry." Marc wondered which side had killed them, but he didn't ask.

"It's wonderful to visit Germany now. The reunited country is alive with such hope and promise. It's been so long."

Marc nodded thoughtfully. He chickened out of mentioning the recent incidents of racial intolerance, xenophobia and hate crimes.

Marc and Eckart didn't have a chance to see Nuremberg during this trip. They were just passing through. As they took a taxi to the train station, all Marc could tell was that Nuremberg had a lot of dangerously aggressive drivers, including their own.

As he paid, Eckart spoke rapid German to the cab driver. At the harsh guttural sound, Marc fought to drive from his mind a memory of a documentary about Hitler's rallies, held in this very city. He realized that he was prejudiced against the German language. *Better get used to it.*

They took the express train to Regensburg. The train pulled out on time and pulled in on time, exactly an hour later. In the interim, they passed through lovely green countryside, interrupted by gingerbread houses and the occasional fairytale castle.

They took another taxi to their hotel, the Roter Hahn, at Rote-Hahnen-Gasse 10, where they separated for an hour. Having enviously watched Eckart sleep like a blissful child for most of the night, Marc decided that forty minutes of concentrated sleep would be better than nothing.

Forty minutes and only one remembered World War II dream later, Marc bolted up at the sound of the alarm and dressed quickly. He met Eckart in the lobby, and the two of them set out for the Bavarian Hammond Chemical plant.

The taxi driver took them through the medieval-looking city of Regensburg, past churches, museums and towers. Then they crossed the Stone Bridge, *Steinerne Brucke*, built speedily as a result of a pact with the Devil, according to Marc's guidebook, over the Danube and out of the city. They drove ten more kilometers northeast to the outskirts of the Bavarian Forest, or *Bayerischer Wald*. The plant was set in a clearing, but behind it were trees as far as one could see, growing denser in the distance. As a matter of fact, the Forest extended across the Czech border into Bohemia, to form Central Europe's largest forest region.

The building was three stories high. From the top floor where they sat waiting, Marc looked down at the tops of a series of eight storage tanks almost half as tall as the building itself. To the west, Marc thought that he could see the meager remains of the gypsy encampment that had been less than a quarter mile away.

Marc turned back to his legal pad and wrote in the date at the top of a page. He fully understood his role in this client meeting to be that of a mute secretary.

Ludwig Helfferich, plant manager, was short, round, and friendly. His roly-poly shape, combined with the rosy hue of his cheeks, the good humor in his eyes and his wild uncombed hair, made Herr Doctor Helfferich look like a playful little boy or even a doll. This was despite that he was over 70 years old.

"Wilhelm!" he cried out in a high-pitched voice, embracing Eckart. "How was your trip?" he asked, in German.

"Gutt," Eckart responded. "This is my associate, Marc Wilson. Marc, this is Doctor Helfferich."

The plant manager grabbed Marc's hand with his own meaty mitt and shook it enthusiastically.

"Pleased to meet you," the man gushed. He spoke English well, but with a kooky accent that, to Marc, sounded like a fake mad scientist cliché.

"Good to meet *you*."

"Are you two hungry?" Doctor Helfferich asked in English. "Your stomachs must be confused from the time change. Would you like to eat breakfast or lunch while we talk?"

"Whatever," said Eckart.

They followed the plant manager to the plant cafeteria. The food fulfilled most of Marc's preconceived notions: various sausages, sauerkraut, and boiled potatoes. The only disappointment was that, instead of stout German beer, the beverage of choice for this business lunch seemed to be sparkling water.

After they started eating, Eckart began by saying, in English, "You've already told me much about what happened. Now, before your deposition, I want to go over some details."

"Of course. Ask me questions."

Marc put down his knife and fork and picked up his pen and pad.

"What type of chemicals do you manufacture here?"

"Umm, pest ... icides," Herr Helfferich answered slowly and carefully.

"Where are the chemicals stored prior to being transported away?"

"In eight big tanks behind the building." Helfferich stabbed a sausage, sawed it in half, and shoved it into his mouth.

"How far away are the nearest houses?"

"Over five miles away." Marc couldn't help seeing large chunks of partially chewed bratwurst. Thankfully, no pieces escaped.

"Why is the plant located so far from the city?" Eckart asked. He wasn't eating.

"In case of an unlikely chemical leak." Finally, Helfferich swallowed. He filled up again. "No one would have been hurt if not for those damn gypsies!"

"How long has the plant been here?"

"Twenty years."

"And how long were the gypsies there before the incident?"

"Three or four months."

"When was the incident?"

"Last December 27. A strange young man released the MIC gas from its tank. We informed the proper authorities immediately."

"Who was this stranger?"

"We do not know. He had no connection to the plant. His name was Struger."

"Where is this stranger now?"

"He was killed by the gas he released. We found him next to the tank. He was holding the axe which he used to break through the tank wall."

"Do you know why he did it?"

"I have no idea. He must have been crazy."

"Don't speculate about anything you don't know," Eckart advised. "Although you might want to volunteer that his head was shaved."

"I will."

Eckart looked over at Marc to make sure he was taking notes. Satisfied, he continued. "What about the employees? How were they protected?"

"This plant is air-tight and self-sufficient. The workers do not go out during the day."

"But one employee *did* die, correct?"

"Yes. Herr Walther. He went out to his car and was exposed."

"Did any of the gypsies survive?"

"Almost all of the one hundred or so gypsies died within hours. A few individuals lasted several days longer."

"Just say 'no' then. Is the pesticide in question *so* deadly?"

"That many deaths were against the odds." The plant manager swallowed and considered carefully. "But the MIC gas was concentrated. The wind must have blown it straight to them. Also, maybe gypsies do not have any immunity to the toxins of civilization."

"Okay, Ludwig. Don't let them get you speculating like that, though."

Eckart relaxed and took a piece of bratwurst and sauerkraut. "You know, as a practical matter, you're lucky they were only gypsies. The plaintiffs' attorneys have been having a hell of a time finding claimants. The dead gypsies didn't leave estates, and their living relatives are virtually untraceable. That should severely limit what they can hope to recover. Although American juries are notoriously generous in their estimation of the value of life. *Any* life."

"That is why they sue in America, correct? And that is why you are having the case moved to Germany?" Herr Helfferich asked.

Eckart smiled. "Sure you're not a lawyer, Ludwig?" After talking to Ludwig for several more hours, Marc and Eckart spent a couple of hours going over and adding to their list of questions to ask the plaintiff whom they were going to depose. Then they called a taxi and returned to their hotel. They separated at 5:15 p.m., agreeing to meet in the lobby at 8:00 o'clock to go out for a fine dinner.

Although he knew he should be tired, Marc was still running on adrenalin. He decided that he might as well see a little of the city. He may not have wanted to come, but he wasn't going to miss the sights. According to the guidebook he had brought along, everything was in walking distance.

Marc started with the Reichstag Museum, with its beautiful Renaissance paneling and fittings, and its preserved torture chamber. From there, he sped east to a dense cluster of ecclesiastical buildings known as the *Domstadt*. He headed to the church, the *Dom* itself, anxious to verify the bizarre details described in his guidebook.

Normally, Marc wasn't particularly interested in churches or religious art. In previous trips to Europe, he had realized how different travel must be for religious Christians. Europe was one huge church-visiting opportunity. For people who cared about churches, there must be little time to do anything else. Marc managed to locate all five of the church's quirks. A relief on the left main pillar of the facade, just as described in the guidebook, depicted greedy little Jews dancing around a golden calf. More creatively, a relief on the left-hand pillar of the southern entrance showed allegedly Jewish figures suckling on a great sow.

In the church itself, Marc stared in wonder at the sixteenth-century wooden crucifix on the south transept wall. As promised, the contorted Jesus had real human hair. Apparently, Judgment Day had not yet arrived, because the hair had not grown to knee-length, as predicted.

On the way out of the *Dom*, Marc spotted the pair of fourteenth-century figures in the niches on either side of the western nave entrance. He might have guessed that the thin figure on the right with the knowing smile was the Devil, but he needed the guidebook to tell him that the hag on the left was the Devil's grandmother. The book said that the figures were there to remind the congregation that, as soon as they left the safety of the church, evil and temptation awaited. Marc was skeptical that "good Christians" put the Devil and his kin in their churches.

As a companion stop on his whirlwind tour, Marc headed south a couple of blocks to the *Neupfarrkirche*. This church occupied the site of a razed synagogue, and had been planned as a vast pilgrimage church dedicated to the Virgin as thanksgiving for deliverance from the Jewish peril. A couple doors down, in the entrance of *Neupfarrplatz 7*, Marc found the pilfered Jewish tombstone, "the ultimate status symbol for medieval Christians" according to the guidebook, set into the wall.

Maybe Mom was right, thought Marc. *Maybe nothing's changed here in six hundred years. Maybe the sooner I'm back in New York the better.*

After a simple dinner and a few beers, and an early night's sleep, Marc found himself sitting on one side of Eckart while Ludwig Helfferich sat on the other. Also sitting at the long table was an American attorney for plaintiffs, as well as local German counsel, an impartial translator and a stenographer.

Plaintiffs' American counsel had agreed to hold the depositions in Regensburg, although their local counsel's office was in Munich. In exchange, Eckart had agreed not to dispute the right of plaintiffs' counsel to question the defendant first.

It was slow going. The plaintiffs' American attorney, Joseph Paddington of Geller & Hamlin, asked questions in English, which the translator repeated in German. Ludwig answered each question in German, which was followed by a translation.

Eckart had anticipated virtually every question asked by plaintiffs' counsel. Ludwig was a well-prepared witness, wisely asking for repetition or elaboration of every conceivably ambiguous question. Paddington was understandably dogged and skeptical on the issue of the inexplicable saboteur, but Ludwig refused to speculate as to the man's motivations. After Paddington had attempted to ask similar unanswerable questions three or four times, Eckart stated that he had allowed plaintiffs' counsel considerable latitude, but now he "had better move on to questions within Doctor Helfferich's direct knowledge."

They broke for an hour lunch, which the plaintiffs' attorneys had brought with them. At six p.m., Paddington asked whether they wanted to break for the day.

"Aren't you almost done?" Eckart asked.

"Not too far. But we could finish tomorrow morning, before you depose my client."

"You're not tired, are you, Ludwig?"

"No," the plant manager answered, back to his smiling self.

"Why don't you just finish your questioning today?" Eckart was well aware of the litigator's trick of adjourning a deposition at the end of the day, although it was basically finished, in order to buy time to think of follow-up, questions and to discuss the deposition with colleagues. "Then we could even come out to Munich tomorrow and save you and your client a trip out here." He knew that the plaintiff to be deposed was an unemployed gypsy with no other pressing engagements, but he assumed that Paddington and his German associate wouldn't mind saving a trip back to Regensburg.

Paddington whispered briefly with the German attorney. As a result of the calling of his bluff, plus his pleasure at the thought of sleeping later in Munich, Paddington asked four more token questions and then adjourned.

Marc and Eckart exchanged friendly farewells with Ludwig Helfferich. "That wasn't so bad," Ludwig said, chuckling. "Thanks to you, Wilhelm." The little fat man hugged Eckart. "And you too, Mr. Wilson." He pumped Marc's hand hard. "I may call you Marc?"

"Sure," said Marc, forcing a smile. *Why shouldn't we be buddies?*

⚖

The next morning, Marc and Eckart boarded an early train for Munich. The trip took just under two hours. They checked into a new hotel, a modern, comfortable establishment named Adria on the edge of Munich's museum quarter, then headed to the German lawyer's office.

"This should work out well. Today's deponent is just one

of dozens of named plaintiffs. He won't know much. I'll polish him off, and then we'll be able to catch the end of Oktoberfest. We'll fly back to New York from Munich tomorrow morning."

The lawyer's office was strictly second-rate. The paint was old and cracking. The walls were devoid of art. Marc guessed that gypsies couldn't get first-class attorneys in Germany.

The plaintiff, a fellow named Litvak, was the brother of a man who had died in the gypsy camp near the Bavarian Hammond Chemical plant. He didn't dress the way Marc had expected a gypsy to dress. He wore faded Levis, a green polo shirt, and Reebok sneakers. Marc wondered if these clothes were his "Sunday best." Litvak looked completely out of place, uncomfortable and intimidated.

Eckart conducted the deposition in German, barking questions at the deponent in a tone that seemed skeptical and scornful. The man responded reluctantly at first. Later, he snapped his responses angrily with barely a moment for reflection.

Marc watched Eckart and Litvak, while listening to the translations of their exchanges. He took copious notes on the proceedings.

Naturally, Litvak had no information about anything that had happened at the Hammond Chemical plant. He had only limited information about his brother's illness and death, as Eckart and Marc had expected. The only witnesses with first-hand knowledge of the deaths were all dead themselves. Marc mused that, if Hammond Chemical had repaired the broken tank and disposed of the saboteur and the one dead employee, there would have been no hard evidence linking it to the gypsy deaths. Of course, people might have suspected. All those sudden deaths and nothing around for miles except a factory manufacturing deadly pesticides.

The witness had lived with his older brother, who was a recent widower. In response to Eckart's series of questions, Litvak delicately related the fact that he had been carrying on an affair with a married woman in Regensburg at the time of the incident. Consequently, he traveled to and from town whenever her husband was away. That December, he had spent Christmas with the woman. When he returned to the camp around noon on December 28, almost everyone was already dead.

As Litvak described the scene of horror he'd found, Marc was uneasy anew. It was so horrible, all those dead gypsies. *Too bad that skinhead, Struger, was dead already. But I hope we can find out if anyone else was in on it with him.*

At one point, Eckart asked about the dead brother's general health. The deponent answered forcefully. "My brother was never sick a day in his life," the interpreter translated. Litvak remembered something. "Except on that December 26, when he came into town to meet us. He was having trouble breathing, and chest pains, and he was so tired he left early."

Marc was surprised, but Eckart moved on. "Were you the first one to go to the camp on December 28th?"

"I may have been. It was horrible. All of them, lying scattered about ..."

"Thank you, Mr. Litvak."

"They'd been murdered!"

Eckart's face betrayed only a moment of irritation. "Are you a forensics expert, Mr. Litvak?"

"Uh, no."

"Are you an attorney?"

"No."

"Then please do not volunteer medical or legal opinions."

As Litvak listened, he was looking down and it was impossible to predict how he was going to react. Then his head shot up and he spat out several phrases in some Slavic tongue. Marc was pretty sure he had heard the word "Nazi."

Eckart pretended he hadn't heard the tirade. The others seemed to take their cue from him, and the deposition proceeded smoothly to its conclusion.

They were finished in time for a late lunch.

"What did you think?" Eckart asked.

Marc was surprised by the question. "Um, very good. For one thing, we can dispute causation or argue mere exacerbation of a preexisting condition. That was a surprise when he said that his brother was sick the day *before* the chemical leak."

Eckart shook his head regretfully. "That would be nice, but it won't work. So what if the man had a little hangover the day before? Our best defense, applicable to every plaintiff, remains the unforeseeability of the unaffiliated saboteur."

At first Marc felt embarrassed to have suggested the pre-existing condition defense. Then he thought that Eckart had been too quick to dismiss it. Eckart was so opinionated and so sure of himself.

Which was not to de-emphasize the importance of the saboteur. Marc drew considerable comfort from the saboteur. He was relieved to believe that their client wasn't really responsible for the deaths.

Several sausages and beers later, Eckart cut Marc loose.

"I apologize, but I have some personal matters to attend to. You'll have to enjoy Munich and Oktoberfest alone. Not that that should be difficult for a young man."

Marc was caught by surprise, but he quickly realized that this was a positive development. Eckart added, "Although I'm sure that my daughter will be interested in hearing all about your trip."

Even though Eckart was smiling, Marc got nervous. He had wondered if Eckart knew about his date with Samantha, and if so, what he thought about it. *Oh well, at least he was smiling. For the moment.*

What sort of personal matters does Eckart have to attend to? Does he have a woman in Munich?

After changing out of his suit, Marc wandered around Munich, guidebook in hand. He had resolved to see some of the historical highbrow sights, like museums and even churches, before getting lost in the vast tents and steins of Oktoberfest.

After viewing the palace open to the public as the Residenz

Museum, and the *Schatzkammer* with its fabulous collection of treasures including the Bavarian crown jewels, he walked a few blocks southwest and came to the *Frauenkirche,* or Dom. Like the Stone Bridge in Regensburg, legend had it that this church was built with the help of the Devil, who was subsequently outsmarted. *Evidently, the Devil was a prominent, though much-maligned, patron of architecture in Germany during the Middle Ages.* Marc pondered the black footprint made by the Devil when he stamped his foot in rage, three hundred years earlier.

To save time, Marc hailed a taxi. His nervousness wasn't aided by the fact that the driver spoke to him quickly in German, and clearly spoke no English. Nonetheless, he climbed in and announced, in his best but still awful German accent, "Oktoberfest." He doubted that the driver was fooled.

At the outskirts of the converted *Theresienwiese* meadow, he left the cab and walked toward the cavernous tents of Oktoberfest. Each major brewery had its own tent. Each tent was full of loud, happy people, Germans and tourists. Tonight, here, it was impossible to tell that any Germans were having trouble getting along with foreigners.

At first, Marc was overwhelmed. He was repulsed by drunkenness on such a colossal scale. He stared at the most Aryan-looking males with uneasy suspicion.

Many hours, many pretzels, two half chickens and countless beers later, Marc lost any reservations, as well as most of his sense of balance. He generously sampled dark beers, amber beers, malty beers, full-bodied beers ...

At 10:30 p.m., he was in the tent run by Hofbrauhaus, the state brewery whose permanent home was probably the most famous building in Munich. He had made friends with a bubbly blond Aryan with decent, though slurred, English. Her name was Ilsa. He allowed her to lock her arm in his as she sang some ridiculous drinking song.

By eleven, both of Marc's arms were locked with his neighbors', and they were swaying in unison. Marc had learned a couple of lines of the song and, at Ilsa's prompting, he sang out: *"In München Steht Ein Hofbräuhaus, so trinken eins, zwei!"* It meant something like, "We've got a great brewery here in Munich, so drink up, one two!" As he looked around him at the smiling, laughing faces, he felt a sense of wellbeing. He was just one of the crowd. He was one with the crowd.

A few minutes later, the tent was closing and fights were breaking out among the reluctant departers. Somehow, even these conflicts seemed almost friendly. Nevertheless, partially snapped back to reality, Marc managed to duck a punch, but not to remain standing. After a couple of moments rest, he scooped himself up and headed fairly straight for the exit. He was successful in escaping.

But he had lost Ilsa.

Eight

It was Friday morning when Marc finally returned to his office at Ballen Warren. He had slept more than twelve hours, managing to recover from jet lag and the lingering effects of Oktoberfest.

He had lots of work to do on his other cases. He wouldn't be having much of a weekend. Still, there were a few activities for which he would have to make time. The most certain given was that he would be traveling to Dobbs Ferry for the Ethics Committee meeting. He'd have to borrow his mother's car. He hoped to combine two other things on Saturday: seeing a new apartment prospect and Samantha.

During the flight home, as Marc had striven to hide the telltale signs of his hangover, Eckart had been particularly friendly. At one point, Eckart had announced that he knew the perfect place for Marc to move into.

How did he know I'm looking? As usual when Eckart surprised him like that, Marc had wondered whether someone had told him, or he was guessing, or whether he was a mind reader.

"A friend of mine is looking to sublet a big, bright, and beautiful one-bedroom apartment immediately," Eckart had told him. "Confidentially, he's been looking for a while and he's negotiable."

Marc called Eckart's friend and set up an appointment to see the apartment. Then he called Sam and asked if she'd like to come along, and then grab a bite to eat. She agreed, saying that she was "anxious to hear all about Germany."

When he got home after ten that night, his mother greeted him enthusiastically. "I can't help it. I missed you, and I worried about you," she said in his ear as she hugged him. "I guess it's good practice for when you move out."

"Is everything okay?" he asked.

"Of course, honey."

He returned the conversation to the previous topic. "Actually, I might be moving out soon. Mr. Eckart gave me what sounds like a great lead. I'm looking at it tomorrow."

Although he had had Chinese food delivered to the office earlier, he peered into his mother's refrigerator, checking for snacks.

"There's some leftover meatloaf ..."

"No thanks. I was looking for something a little lighter ..." *Like an anvil.* He took a Dannon yogurt and started to open it.

"By the way, can I borrow the car Sunday afternoon? It's for a Committee meeting." He knew his segue was artificial but it worked.

"Of course. Are you going to have to work this weekend?"

"Yes. Tomorrow."

"Are you going to see Mr. Eckart's daughter this weekend?"

"Yes, nosy."

"I'm not trying to pry. But I'd love to meet her."

"Maybe soon."

Marc met Samantha in the lobby of the building. There was an awkward moment as their lips seemed to head for each other, then detoured at the last moment for platonic cheek kisses. Perhaps the watchful eye of the silent doorman added to their slight unease.

"I got the keys from the doorman. The owners, your dad's friends, moved out already. Let's go up."

Marc looked to the doorman, who expressionlessly waived them onward and upward. They crossed the ornate yet tasteful burgundy lobby to the elevator bank. They silently rode the spotless chrome and brass elevator to the fourteenth floor. Marc considered grabbing Samantha and kissing her properly, but felt inhibited by the camera in the ceiling of the elevator.

The apartment was perfect. The owner had left most of the impeccable furnishings. Despite many obviously appealing details—the large living room and bedroom, and an eat-in kitchen with a Sub-Zero refrigerator—Marc and Samantha were each inexorably drawn to the sliding-glass door leading from the living room to the terrace.

"Your father didn't even mention a terrace!" Marc sputtered, as the two stared out in wonder across East Seventy-Ninth Street, over a church and far downtown.

"It's great," Samantha stated simply.

Marc turned and stared at Samantha. She gave him the kiss he'd been wanting to give her.

"You've made me lightheaded," he said. "We'd better go inside where it's a little safer."

That night, he called the owner of the apartment and got him to agree to a twenty-one-hundred-dollar-a-month rent and a two-year lease, which the owner would email to Marc immediately. Marc could move in as soon as the owner received Marc's check for first and last month's rent. For Manhattan, twenty-one-hundred dollars was a steal. Marc knew that the guy must be paying more than that in monthly maintenance fees alone, let alone his mortgage.

Best of all, Marc could afford it now, because he had a great job. He might be working hard, but it was well worth it.

Marc lay awake in his small childhood bed, too excited to sleep. Soon he would be sleeping in a queen-sized bed on the fourteenth floor of a doorman building on the upper east side of Manhattan. Marc thought again about how he had turned his life around. By breaking into the Bar Association, getting on the Ethics Committee and meeting Eckart. *Crime's not supposed to pay*, he thought to himself for the thousandth time.

And tomorrow was another meeting of the Committee. Who knew what new advances his career might make?

The house was on a steep, narrow, winding street named Villard. Like its neighbors, Baylor's home was over one hundred years old and four stories high. With some embarrassment, Marc parked his mother's Oldsmobile behind a BMW and an Infiniti, blocking half of the thin street.

The meeting was called for two p.m. Marc assumed that such timing was designed to give the many religious Committee members the opportunity to go home between church services and the Committee meeting. Marc had intended to arrive about fifteen minutes early, counting the number of cars in order to determine whether to go in yet. However, a couple of wrong turns delayed his arrival until one fifty-nine.

He walked quickly up the long driveway to what he guessed was the main entrance. The minute he entered the living room he felt out of place. He was the only one who was wearing a suit. He had meant to ask Paul about the dress at suburban meetings, but he hadn't seen him on Friday.

He felt a lot better when Bob Baylor recognized him and greeted him in an extremely friendly manner. "Marc!" he proclaimed, like they were old friends or relatives. Baylor shook his right hand, while clapping him on the back with his left.

Everyone seemed much more friendly and relaxed than at the previous meeting. Several of the casually dressed men and women introduced themselves to him and pointed him toward snacks and refreshments. It was hard to believe that these were the same powerful, influential people who had been at the last meeting at the Bar Association.

Doris Spender was particularly effusive in her greeting, actually hugging him and giving him a peck on the cheek. Marc must have blushed in surprise.

Marc saw Paul and Eckart chatting together in a corner. As he started in that direction, he encountered the four young men he had noticed at the first meeting. The most solidly built of them—he'd definitely been on a college football team—yanked his hand and shook it energetically. "Hi. You're Marc, right? I'm Joe Garrett. This is Scott Seldano, Larry Moore, and Dan Lessing."

As he shook Dan's hand, Marc noticed that the man was missing his fourth finger. Marc forced himself to look at Dan's face, driving thoughts of the nine-fingered villain from Hitchcock's *The Thirty-Nine Steps* from his mind.

"You're at Ballen Warren, right?" asked Dan.

"Right."

"Eckart bust your ass over there?"

"Well, he keeps me busy."

"We're all *way* too busy," Larry chimed in.

"Welcome aboard!" Scott announced.

"I'm sure we'll see lots of each other," said Joe.

Marc agreed and said how good it was to meet them all. Then he made his way over to Eckart and Paul, who also greeted him enthusiastically.

Paul asked, "How did you like the apartment Bill steered you to?"

"It was incredible. Perfect. I've already negotiated a price and taken it. Thanks so much."

Eckart made a "don't mention it" face. "So when are you moving?" he asked.

"As soon as you allow me enough free time to pack and unpack," Marc joked, then worried that Eckart would be offended by the grain of truth in the quip.

"So you're giving your mother back her privacy, eh?"

Paul teased.

"Yep."

"You're a good son," Eckart said. "Hey, I just had an idea. Your mother works in the clerk's office in Queens County, doesn't she?"

"Yes," Marc answered, shocked at Eckart's knowledge of his life.

"I just remembered. Justice Green over there needs a new secretary. Would your mother be interested? I'm sure it would pay more, she would keep her seniority, and Sam Green is a real sweetheart."

"That sounds great. I'll ask her." *She'll go for it in a minute,* he thought. *She's really been getting sick of that clerk's office lately. Could Eckart know that?*

"Please do," said Eckart.

"Thanks again." Marc was spooked by this level of thoughtfulness.

"So," said Paul, "how wasted did you get at Oktoberfest?"

Marc smiled guiltily and changed the subject. "Is that Justice Williams over there?" Paul and Eckart each nodded. "Is he on the Committee?"

"There aren't any judges or clerks officially on the Committee," said Eckart. "But the Committee has many *friends.*"

Just then Baylor announced that the gathering was about to convene. Everyone began filing out of the living room, through a door and downstairs to Baylor's basement. Marc took his cue from Eckart and Paul, however, who seemed to be waiting for the rush to end before they moved.

When the three of them finally did enter Baylor's basement, the Committee was packed in pretty tightly. Standing in the back of the room, it was hard for Marc to see over the rows of people in front of him. Baylor must have been standing on some type of platform, because Marc could see his head and shoulders as he faced the front of the crowd.

Marc was surprised and confused to note that Baylor was

wearing some sort of black robe that made him look like a judge. Marc glanced over at Paul and Eckart, but they had disappeared. Marc presumed that they had moved further up, but he decided to remain in the back of the room.

"Brothers and sisters," Baylor greeted them in a friendly but formal tone. "I'm glad you could attend. First, let us briefly discuss business."

Are we here for something other than business? Marc wondered. *Are we going to see a movie?* he joked to himself.

"In the last several weeks, we have made considerable progress against those who do not share our ethics. We now have evidence against Manning, Farnsworth, Hill and Cobb."

Many in the crowd applauded or shouted "Here, here."

"We are expecting any day now to get evidence on Kraft and Young, who have caused more than one Committee member discomfort. Young is obviously unaware of our newest rules extending corporate affiliation restrictions to spouses, but we're trying for something more serious."

More applause. *They take the job pretty seriously and personally,* Marc thought. *Hate to be on their bad side.*

"Does anyone here have progress to report, or individuals who require the attention of a subcommittee?"

The crowd was silent. A middle-aged man named Upjohn spoke up. "There's a snotty-faced kid named Winston at the Public Defender's office. Got no respect."

"See me later with the details," Baylor instructed. "Anyone else? No? Okay. Enough business."

Marc was confused and a little spooked by the nasty tone of the last exchange. *I guess this kid Winston must have done something pretty damn unethical. Just because Upjohn doesn't like him, it doesn't mean he prejudged him.*

"Today's service will be on the short side." *Service?* "Some of us have pressing commitments. But, don't forget, the Halloween party is coming soon." Baylor was grinning uncharacteristically.

Marc wondered what sort of service was about to take

place. *Surely not everyone on the Committee is Lutheran. Is this going to be some sort of non-denominational prayer session?*

What about the separation of church and state? Bar Association committees are arguably quasi-governmental bodies. Like influential religious people really care, Marc thought. *The President of the United States still asks for God's help as part of his oath of office.*

Maybe that's why the Committee has some of its meetings at members' houses. More freedom, less like official promotion of religion than if they were meeting in the Bar Association building. Once again Marc found himself thinking, *What am I doing here with these ultra-religious types?*

Someone carried a large wooden cross onto the platform, struggling awkwardly with its weight. The man attached the cross to nails already in the wall behind the platform, evidently for this purpose. Marc chuckled silently with combined amusement and vicarious embarrassment. The man had hung the cross upside down.

At this point, Baylor reached back, grabbed a black hood attached to his robe, and pulled it up and over his head. Then Baylor pulled some sort of necklace over his head and smoothed out a silver star that hung from it.

Two other people in black robes with raised cowls joined Baylor on the platform. Baylor and one of the new hooded figures took two steps back, away from the spectators, while the other mysterious individual stepped forward. Marc could only make out a small fraction of the newcomers' facial features, not enough to recognize them now or identify them later. Also, he still couldn't see lower than their shoulders, due to the rows of Committee members in front of him.

As Marc wondered about the purpose and origin of the black cowled robes, the man next to him handed him one of his own. Evidently, the robes were being passed out, down each line of Ethics Committee members. Most people in the room had already received and donned theirs.

It took Marc several moments to figure out how to wear the garment. At least now he wouldn't stand out in his suit. The cowl severely limited his field of vision. He strained to watch the activities on the platform in the front of the room.

Marc was so stunned by the events unfolding in front of him that he had ceased trying to figure out what was going on. His last wild guess was that this was some sort of religious ceremony combined with a fraternal-style initiation ritual. Now he was just watching and listening, waiting anxiously for further clues.

The ceremony began with several minutes of Latin. In general, the man in front spoke first, sometimes at length, and Baylor and the other person on the platform responded briefly. *Like Eckart said the other day, some young people in particular seem to be returning to the older religious rituals.* At various points, Marc could tell that the front man, the celebrant, was raising up objects and waiving them about, but he couldn't always tell what the objects were. He managed to make out some type of incense boat, and an ornate golden cup. He also couldn't see the low table from which the man was evidently retrieving these items.

Eventually, a gong was struck three times. Marc didn't know where the gong was. The leader of the service cleared his throat and finally addressed the crowd in English. His style was formal and dramatic. It seemed likely that he was following a prepared text, but he had evidently committed it to memory. Marc focused on the man's mouth, which was the only facial part completely revealed to him.

"Therefore, Oh mighty One, we entreat You that You receive and accept this sacrifice, which we offer to You on behalf of this assembly, upon whom You have set Your mark, that You may make us prosper in fullness and length of life, under Thy protection, and may cause to go forth at our bidding Thy minions, for the fulfillment of our desires and the destruction of our enemies."

Despite Marc's relative lack of familiarity with Christian

services, this prayer struck him as odd. For one thing, the prayer was surprisingly forthright in its request for destruction of enemies, as forthright as Upjohn had been earlier. In that way, the prayer sounded like something that the Old Testament Israelites might have chanted before confronting a Canaanite army.

The celebrant continued, his thick lips opening and closing like rubbery curtains. *I know this person*, Marc realized with a shock. *But who? Did I meet him somewhere outside the Committee?*

"Therefore, in the unity of unholy fellowship ..." *What?* "We praise and honor first Thee, Satan, Lucifer, Morning Star, and Beelzebub, Lord of Regeneration ..."

As he stared at the speaker's moving mouth, Marc's line of vision, already restricted by the cowl, seemed to shrink further. The man was screaming in his face. Marc felt lightheaded.

"And your servants, Belial, Prince of the Earth and Angel of Destruction. Then Leviathan, Beast of Revelation. Abaddon, Angel of the Bottomless Pit. And Asmodeus, Demon of Lust."

Marc couldn't see anything but the mouth, and he couldn't turn away.

"We also praise and honor the mighty names of Astaroth, Nergal and Behemoth, Belphegor, Adramelech, Baalberith, and all the nameless and formless ones, the mighty and innumerable hosts of Hell, by whose assistance may we be strengthened in mind, body and will."

In the silence that followed, Marc broke out of his fixation and looked around anxiously. For a split-second, he half-expected to see some or all of the demons who had just been named.

There was only a room filled with people. Fellow Committee members. *Or were they?* He couldn't be sure what lurked within the sea of faceless hoods.

I have to get out!

He was right near the back door. He could just run.

But why should he run, he thought. He wasn't really in

danger. He would wait until the ceremony was over.

He couldn't leave anyway. *What would they think? What would they do?*

A woman in a nun's habit ascended the platform. *What can she be doing here?* He looked away.

He looked around. *No one's paying attention to me. Maybe I should leave.*

Marc heard a new sound. The trickle of water in a metal receptacle. Involuntarily, he searched for the source of this strange new counterpoint to the rapturous words of the "deacons." When the flow had ended, the "nun" presented the chamber pot to a "deacon."

I should go.

The man received the pot of liquid with reverence, saying, "I am the Alpha and Omega, the beginning and the end. I will give freely unto him that is athirst of the fountain of the water of life."

Baylor produced a large rubber phallus. He dipped it into the fluid in the pot. Marc couldn't see what Baylor did next, as he cried out: "In the name of Satan, we bless thee with this, the rod of life."

I've got to get out of here!

As the celebrant raised a holy wafer, then returned it to the unseen altar table, Marc at last summoned the will to move his bones. No one seemed to notice as he headed for the door.

His hand on the knob, nearly free, Marc had to look back once more. For the first time, the positioning of the crowd enabled him to see the "altar" upon which the ritual objects rested: it was a beautiful naked woman, smiling with serene pride. The celebrant stood between her legs, the golden cup sat below her flat belly, and the holy wafer had been placed between her full breasts. As the priest reached for the wafer and pushed it inside her, the woman moaned softly.

Marc cursed as the door slammed behind him.

Nine

At Samantha's beckoning, Marc climbed onto the bed, kissing her deeply as he slowly entered her for the first time. He kissed his way down her neck and shoulder while he matched her rhythm. He licked the birthplaces of her perfect breasts as she moaned. He felt his own tension mounting.

As he reached down to suck one of her tall pink nipples, he noticed something disturbing. Instinctively, he pulled out and away. The damp holy wafer was nestled between her heaving breasts.

"Hail Satan!" a deep voice cried out. Marc spun around to face the newcomer.

The man pulled back his black hood. "Isn't my daughter good enough for you?" Eckart screamed. "No man pulls out of the high priestess!"

Marc scrambled to his feet. A crowd of faceless hooded figures stood silently in the background.

"You have been chosen!" Eckart announced, pulling open his black robe to reveal a huge erection.

Marc feared that Eckart intended to force his swollen manhood on him.

"Come in to me, Father Satan!" Samantha's eyes were blazing with lust. Her legs were spread wide and pulled up to her head, as if she were a contortionist.

As Eckart approached his daughter, the hooded crowd began to chant. "Go, Satan! Go, Satan! Go!"

Marc tried to scream. No sound would come. He tried to run, but he couldn't move.

Eckart paused at the foot of the bed, turning to face Marc with a grin. "I'll do you next."

⚖

Marc bolted awake, drenched. He didn't know what to do.

He was nervous about going to work. How many people at the firm were involved? And what were they involved in?

Yesterday at the meeting, he had learned two things about the Ethics Committee. First, it seemed that the Committee tended to investigate people it didn't like. He couldn't be sure to what extent the investigations and their results were or weren't legitimate.

Second, he had learned that the Committee worshipped Satan.

It's really too crazy. Just thinking it made Marc think that *he* must be crazy.

Had he hallucinated? He'd never done so before.

Had he misunderstood? Only if "Satan" and "Lucifer" were new ways of pronouncing "ethics." And only if the naked woman being used as a table really *was* a flesh-colored table with coincidental bumps and curves.

Had a joke been played on him? This last choice was possible, although incredibly unlikely. These high-powered millionaire law firm partners had many better things to do than playing jokes on the newest and least successful member on their Committee.

Maybe it was more than a joke. What if it was part of a

complex, vicious plan to punish him for tampering with the
Ethics Committee membership files? Again, Marc doubted that
these people had the time or interest. They could probably get
him disbarred with five minutes' effort.

*So, say the Committee members worship Satan. What does
that mean, exactly?*

Were they evil? Most of them seemed so nice.

Did it mean that they were dangerous? Well, these were
successful, influential attorneys. He had known that they were
potentially dangerous long before yesterday. But were they
dangerous to people who didn't deserve to be hurt? Were they
harming innocent people? he wondered. Not that he knew of.

*Are they dangerous? Would I be safer if I convinced them
I was on their side, or if I disentangled myself from them completely?*

How could Marc disentangle himself? Would he have to
leave the city, the state, the country? Or would he have to tell
the police or the Bar Association about the Committee and
seek protection? What if the Bar Association was in on it too?
And the police? Paul had said that the Committee had many
"friends." Even if they weren't in on it, what would/could the
authorities do? *Would they believe me?*

I'm going crazy, inventing evil plots. All Marc knew for sure
was that he had to go to work. He wasn't prepared to make a
snap decision to stop practicing law and live with his mother for
the rest of his life.

Marc spent a paranoid morning at the office, although he knew
there was no reason to think that the whole firm was in on it,
whatever *it* was. Paul and Eckart were the only firm members
whom Marc had seen at Ethics Committee meetings.

He stayed at his desk, working on the reply brief on the
Hammond Chemical transfer motion. After reviewing the oth-

er side's papers in opposition to the motion to transfer the case to Germany, Marc began performing electronic legal research from his computer terminal. He didn't say more than three words to Harry, even though observation and logic told him that Harry was not well connected enough in the firm and the legal world in general to be part of any evil conspiracy.

When Marc had to go to the library for a treatise which wasn't on-line, he was careful not to make eye contact with anybody. This was pretty easy, since the attorneys at Ballen Warren were usually busy and preoccupied.

As he was poised to enter the spiral staircase that connected Ballen Warren's three contiguous floors, Marc noticed that Paul was a couple floors below, heading up. Marc wheeled about smoothly and started for the elevator banks.

He slipped out to a nearby typical Manhattan salad bar for lunch. As he picked at the ill-advised assortment of incompatible hot foods he had piled into the plastic carton—foods whose origins were variously and vaguely Chinese, Italian and American—his thoughts wandered back to yesterday's events.

In the light of early afternoon Manhattan, the situation appeared even more unreal. Everything seemed completely normal at the office. *The world couldn't go on so normally if the city's most powerful lawyers worshipped Satan. Could it?*

On the way back to his office after lunch, Marc couldn't resist the temptation to look at the attorneys whom he passed. They all walked quickly, with determined looks on their faces. What were they intent on? They all seemed to be rushing about on secret evil missions.

A couple of senior associates looked at him oddly as they passed. Maybe he had been staring. *Are they in on things?* He turned to watch them whispering as they walked on. *Do they know that I was at the Committee meeting yesterday? Do they know that I ran out on the meeting?*

He tried to regain his composure in a stall in the twenty-ninth floor men's room. As he sat in the empty bathroom, calming down, he heard the front door pushed in loudly and abruptly. He peered out through the crack in the stall. The intruder came into his line of vision. It was Eckart!

Eckart's office was on the thirtieth floor. *What's he doing in this bathroom?* Marc wondered. *Could he actually be looking for me?* Eckart was heading toward Marc's stall. Marc resisted the urge to lift and hide his feet. It was too late anyway.

Maybe Eckart just looked for me in my office. He might have guessed that I'd be here. Or maybe he just has to piss.

Marc saw Eckart pull out his large penis, then turn to a urinal. Eckart stood a couple of steps back from the urinal, aiming up. Marc couldn't help remembering his nightmare from the previous night.

Marc hadn't breathed since Eckart walked in. He was terrified without rational cause. He felt trapped and helpless in the stall.

Eckart cleared his throat. *He's about to speak!*

A junior associate walked in. Marc saw the subtle look of discomfort on the associate's face as he considered the etiquette of pissing near a powerful partner. Should the young man pull up right alongside Eckart, showing that he was secure? Or would that be too presumptuous, or too gay? No matter what, he would scrupulously avoid looking even in the general direction of the partner's penis.

The associate surrendered the game entirely, heading for a stall despite his initial obvious interest in a urinal. He tried the door to Marc's stall.

Marc managed to stop himself from yelling, "Occupied!" Once the young man discovered this fact himself, he slithered over to the next stall and locked himself in. Marc could tell by the placement of his neighbor's feet that he had decided to make it look good by sitting down.

As Marc and the other associate waited out Eckart's urination, the humor of the situation caught up with him and relieved his tension considerably. Nonetheless, he waited as first

Eckart and then the other man exited the room before he did so himself.

Marc made it through the day without any face-to-face encounters with Paul or Eckart. He had bought himself more time to figure out what to do. He was happy to arrive home at a relatively early hour, 9 o'clock, prepared to sidestep conversation with his mother.

He was stunned to find that his arrival home had been preceded a few minutes earlier by a visit from Paul. Marc found Paul having a friendly talk with Mrs. Wilson in her living room.

"Hi, honey." She greeted Marc with a kiss. "I was just having a little chat with Paul. I haven't seen him in so long."

"Hey, Marc," said Paul. "Did you forget that I was stopping by?"

"You didn't tell *me*," Mrs. Wilson stated, with a trace of irritation at her son's lapse in etiquette.

"It wasn't exactly a firm plan," Marc responded, happy to try redirecting his anxiety into annoyance.

"Harry and Joe are meeting us at the restaurant," Paul informed Marc. "How soon can you be ready?"

"I'm glad I didn't make anything special for dinner," Mrs. Wilson muttered.

Paul and Harry didn't get along, and Paul knew that Marc knew that. I guess he just wants to get me by myself so we can talk. But what is there to say?

Marc looked at Paul's smiling face, detecting a sense of urgency below the surface. *It's Paul*, he thought. *I should give him a chance to explain.*

"Okay. I'll be ready in two minutes."

As Marc ran up the stairs to his room, he heard his mother asking Paul, "So, what's new at work? Marc is so happy about working with you at that big firm, and on that Committee ..."

"It's not like you think it is," Paul began to explain.

"What do you mean?" Marc could never have had this conversation with Eckart, but he couldn't manage to be scared of Paul. They'd spent too many late nights together, sometimes studying, sometimes getting thrown out of closing bars, sometimes both activities in a night. Tonight, however, Marc planned on sticking with the one beer in his hand.

"We know you ran out on the ceremony."

Shit! Who's we?

Paul continued. "But no damage has been done. That can't be reversed, anyway. You just overreacted."

Marc picked his words carefully. Paul was evidently speaking to him in a semi-official capacity. "I was surprised by some ... unusual events, at the meeting. I mean, the ceremony."

"Well, you knew that some of the Committee members are pretty religious."

"Religious?"

Paul lowered his voice, although no one was close to their table. "Satanism is a religion. Just like any other religion. Despite the teachings of Hollywood and Stephen King. And heavy metal music."

Marc digested this. "I once saw a woman on some R-rated HBO reality show make the exact same statement. I was skeptical."

"*Most* of us aren't really religious at all. I like some of the philosophy, though. The emphasis on assertive individualism, kind of like Ayn Rand or Dianetics. That and the hedonism of the old Hellfire Clubs and Aleister Crowley's circle. But I don't think of myself as religious."

"So you're just humoring the old guys?"

"Sort of. Most of us were raised as Satanists, and we're hesitant to break away."

Marc was stunned. "Were your parents Satanists?"

"Yeah. Just kind of reformed Satanists. We didn't go to services that often. Still, it paid off when Dad heard about the Committee. He's just an accountant from a small suburban coven, but he managed to get me in."

Marc didn't say anything.

"You look really stunned," Paul continued. "What's so surprising? The problem is all the misinformation about Satan-worshipping. I mean, it's not like we sacrifice babies or anything."

"Well, that is a relief," Marc laughed, relieving much of the tension. "Still, I did see some pretty unusual stuff going on yesterday."

"Weirder than a Catholic mass? Or an orthodox Jewish service? Religion is just weird, period. But we all get jaded to how strange even the most familiar religions are."

"I don't know of any religious ceremonies involving naked women," Marc stated simply.

"And you're proud of that? Religious services are dull enough. Why not have a naked woman or two? The human body is a wonderful gift. It was given to us by the godhead to enjoy."

"Well, lots of religions don't emphasize enjoyment."

"I know," Paul said with disdain. "Stick with the Committee, Marc, and you'll have fun. That's why I'm in, for the fun and the contacts."

"You make it sound like a fraternity. Or a country club."

"Exactly. That's all it is."

"Even if I bought that, I've never been in a fraternity. Or a country club."

"What are you, too good for us?" The question was posed as a joke, but Marc caught its serious implications. Who was he to reject these powerful people if they actually wanted him?

"It's hard to adjust. I wasn't raised with Satan, you know." On the other hand, I wasn't raised to fear Satan either, except in movies.

"We know."

That's when it hit Marc. *They know! They know I don't belong on the Committee! So how ...*

"We admired your persistence and your initiative. Breaking into the Bar Association computer was a clever idea. You had no way of knowing that it couldn't work."

"That's it? You've just been toying with me?"

"No. We want you."

"Why? What do I have to offer?"

"Unlike Lou Grant, we *like* spunk. As well as a willingness to bend and break rules to accomplish worthwhile ends."

"Those qualities are all too common. Especially among lawyers."

"Ah yes, that's certainly what the public thinks. But I assure you that the Committee is *very* selective."

"I'm flattered, I guess."

"So keep taking advantage of this opportunity. Don't throw away your career just as it's blossoming. Move into that beautiful new apartment. Get your mother that promotion. Continue doing good work for Bill. Keep attending Committee meetings. The Halloween party is coming up ..."

"What's *that* going to be like?"

"It's just a wild party. No one gets sacrificed. Nothing bad happens. Only good stuff. And great stuff. Halloween's America's national holiday celebrated by everyone. On Halloween, *everyone* loves the Devil. It's our Saint Patrick's Day."

"Let me see if I have things straight. All I have to do is keep showing up for meetings, right?"

"That's it," said Paul. "You don't have to become a deacon or anything. You just have to sit through, or stand through, the occasional meeting and/or ceremony. It's nothing. Just a bunch of nice, friendly, powerful people getting together once in a while and helping each other out. They'll take care of you and everyone you care about. You can count on them."

Paul ordered them a couple more beers. "Stick around, kid. You and me are going places."

Marc surprised himself by downing the beer as soon as it arrived.

⚖

His mother was still awake at eleven-thirty when he returned home. She expressed surprise that he had been drinking on a work night.

"Just a few beers. Nothing to worry about. In fact, nothing to worry about at all."

"Were you celebrating something?" Sylvia Wilson asked.

"You bet. We were celebrating your promotion."

"What?"

"Are you willing to advance in the world?"

"What are you talking about, honey?"

"Bill Eckart said he could get you promoted. To a judge's secretary. It would pay more, get you more prestige, keep your seniority. Interested?"

"Well, sure. That would be wonderful. Isn't Mr. Eckart a nice man! I'm sure he thinks highly of you."

"He knows how to take care of friends. You gotta say that for him."

"It's so nice of both of you to think of me," she said as she planted a kiss on his forehead. "You're a good boy."

"Least I could do. From now on, Ma, you and me are going places. We're gonna grab the ... what do you call it? Brass ring. No more hesitating. I'm not afraid to get ahead. It's not going to kill anybody if we get a few breaks."

"Well, you certainly seem to be getting what you want. I'm very proud of you. I just hope you're happy."

"Thanks, Mom. That means a lot."

⚖

"I can't believe he doesn't want us to kill O'Neill after all," Dan complained. "I already cancelled a date for Friday. And I was looking forward to seeing that fat fuck's eyes bulge out of his big pumpkin head."

"There's nothing to say about it. The Master has spoken," said Scott. "He's going to kill O'Neill with his own magic. Knight too."

"I guess the sacrifices have been working pretty well," Larry speculated.

"Yes," said Joe. "You can see it in his eyes. He is growing very powerful. And we have bound him closer to our Dark Lord with each life we've offered up. He can kill with a word."

"Satan bless him and protect him!"

"For his is the power, and he will lead us to glory!"

"So," said Dan. "What's with that new guy, Marc Wilson?"

Ten

The next day, Marc took out a little time to work on his *pro bono* case for David Gutierrez. An attorney representing the City of New York had left a message requesting an extension of time to answer the complaint.

Even though attorneys routinely give each other a minimum of one or two extensions to answer complaints, Marc was reluctant to extend too much courtesy to the other side in this particular matter. As he explained to the city attorney, Joe Dinaro, "every day justice is delayed, a young man continues to suffer pain and disillusionment."

"Whatever," said Dinaro. "Are you going to give me a month? Or do I have to talk to the judge?"

"Two weeks. The judge wouldn't give you more than that. They just scheduled us for a conference on November 6. I'll send you a copy of the notice."

Marc hung up. *End of Round One. Nothing for me to do until the conference. Except I should have discovery demands ready to send out when I receive their answer.*

Gina, his secretary, brought in a couple of messages she'd taken while he was on the phone. Samantha had called.

He didn't know what to think, what to do. He was dying to see Samantha, but he wasn't sure he should. She was Eckart's daughter. She had probably grown up worshipping Satan.

So what? Like Paul said, she probably doesn't sacrifice babies or anything. What does religion matter? After all, my parents had a mixed marriage.

Now that he was thinking about it, Marc was becoming curious to find out what Samantha knew about her father, Satan and the Committee. But he would have to be careful.

He made a date for Friday evening.

Then he had to speak to her father. Although he could not help looking at Eckart a little differently, he was proud of how naturally he managed to act. After discussing the motion to transfer the Hammond Chemical case to Germany for five minutes, Eckart literally patted Marc on the back, saying, "Right. Keep on hammering at the location of all the evidence and most of the witnesses in Germany, and the interest of the German people in adjudicating the matter in their own country. You got it. Just get it down on paper by Monday."

Bolstered by the compliment, Marc gathered up the nerve to say, "I told my mother about your offer to help, and she was very excited."

"Terrific. Consider it done. Justice Green trusts me, I trust you, and you trust her. I'm sure she'll be perfect."

Marc took a few hours Thursday morning to move into his dream apartment. Since his new building was a co-op with a doorman and elevators, he had to abide by the house rules, which included moving only on weekdays.

He didn't have to hire any of the dozens of inexplicably Israeli moving companies in the city. It was a happy coincidence that he didn't own much and the well-furnished apartment didn't need much. His synthesizer, his computer, some clothes, and thousands of CDs and DVDs fit into two trips with his mom's car. He left thousands of books behind at his Mom's apartment (*I'm going to start buying e-books!* he thought). Each drive from Queens to Manhattan took just over half an hour.

After carrying his last things up to the apartment, he only had to wait another hour before the most important piece of furniture, the bed from Dial-A-Mattress, arrived.

In penance, he worked until after midnight. After a great Burmese dinner—how he loved Manhattan!—Marc and Samantha arrived at his new address. After Marc said hi to Eric the friendly doorman and responded to his assessment of the weather, they crossed the plush burgundy lobby into an elevator of polished chrome and brass.

"I haven't fully unpacked yet," Marc apologized as he groped his way into the dark apartment, banging his foot into a box of records on the way to the standing, three-bulb living room lamp. In the moment before he turned the switch, he noticed anew the beauty of nighttime Manhattan as viewed from his living room.

Marc hadn't found the nerve or wit to probe her religious beliefs at dinner. However, basking in the smiling warmth of her presence and admiring her sweet natural beauty—he couldn't detect any makeup—he felt convinced that she could not possibly have any dark secrets.

But how could she have been raised by Eckart and not know he was a Satanist? And not worship Satan herself?

"I have a confession to make," she said as she sat down on the couch.

Marc was stopped in his tracks, which had been leading to a chilled bottle of champagne. "What?"

"I brought along one of my films. So I could make you watch and see your reaction."

"That's not such a bad confession," he yelled from the kitchen as he pulled the champagne out of the refrigerator. "Here *I* am, trying to get you drunk and take advantage of you."

He popped the cork with impressive speed.

"I have the same plan, but I'm not even paying for the champagne."

Marc hoped that she wasn't kidding. For weeks, he had been dreaming of seeing her magnificent body. While awake.

They clinked glasses and drank, while Sam pulled a DVD out of her shoulder bag and popped it into Marc's new blu-ray player. Marc was nervous. What if he didn't like it? How should he react? Was it a drama or a comedy?

It was under five minutes of video. The camera work and direction were generally simple and unobtrusive. It was a devastating nightmare.

A little girl, maybe twelve, and her mother stood side by side in a yard, talking and hanging clothes on a line. They spoke about household chores, then homework, and then boys. The two talked openly and good-naturedly about sexual experiences and the relative merits of different positions.

Then the little girl asked, "Do I have to go to church Sunday?"

Her mother turned on the girl and struck her to the ground. The girl struggled to her feet, bleeding from her hands and her cheek. She pummeled her mother without effect.

As her mother began to walk toward the other end of the wide yard, the little girl clasped her hands together, closed her eyes and mouthed silent words of entreaty. She opened her eyes to see a white Cadillac approaching from far off beyond her mother.

The girl called out, "Mother!" The woman turned to face her. Neither said a word as the Cadillac slowly approached.

At this point, the camera work got tricky. Quick cuts from the girl's point of view to the mother's. To the driver's. The "camera" ran over the woman and headed toward the girl.

A two-shot revealed the Cadillac pulling up next to the girl. The driver's tinted window opened mechanically. A smiling white-haired man leaned out to say, "Hey, little girl. Want a cookie?"

The girl approached the car with curiousity. She opened her mouth and he reached out and placed the chocolate-covered wafer on her tongue. He caressed her cheek.

"There's plenty more where that came from. Wanna have a good time?"

She touched her own cheek as she went around to the passenger side of the Cadillac. Once she got in, she couldn't be seen through the tinted glass.

The car sped away, dragging the dead mother behind it.

"Wow!" was all he could say at first.

"Why, thank you," she said, laughing self-consciously. She had watched him nervously throughout the short video. "Not what you expected?"

He blurted out, "Who could expect that?"

Sam laughed again.

"I'm speechless. That was really heavy. What does it mean?"

"Whatever you want. You don't have to give an immediate intellectual critique. It's supposed to be appreciated on a gut level, at least at first."

"I can see that. I have to digest it. I need time." *And a whole roll of Rolaids.* "Can I borrow the disc?"

"Sure. I'd like that."

"So, how come you're still going to church with your dad?"

She was surprised. "What does that have to do with the film?"

"Isn't it a statement against organized religion?" *The work of a Satanist?*

"No. And it isn't autobiographical either. Not particularly."

"Your mother was very religious, though, right?"

"Well, yes. She was incredibly religious. Sometimes even Dad couldn't keep up with her. But really he's devout too. They taught me to believe in God. I do, and I try to act like it. Although I don't go to church *every* week any more. And I often feel unworthy."

Sam was convincing. It seemed that Eckart, somehow, had hidden his true beliefs from his wife and daughter, while paying extensive lip service to Christianity. *I guess Satanists are used to masking their true religion. Like the Jews of fifteenth-century Spain who pretended to convert to Catholicism in order to avoid torture or expulsion.*

"But your mother *was* killed by a car ..."

"Don't over-analyze the film," she ordered. "You're not my shrink."

"Sorry." He poured himself more champagne. "It looked very professional."

"Thanks. I got an A-."

"I'm glad you brought the disc. I wanted to see what you do. I knew it wouldn't be boring." He added, "Unlike what I do."

"What about your hobbies? I've been wanting to hear you play your synthesizer."

He briefly feigned modesty and reluctance, but he was thrilled. This put things way ahead of schedule. Soon he'd be showing off in his bedroom.

"I haven't had much time to play lately."

He turned on the Korg synthesizer and the computer to which it was attached. "I'm supposed to have the capability to match music to video with split-second accuracy, so I ought to be able to score your next movie. But I only understand maybe a tenth of the software."

He played back some tracks of a song that he had written and spent the last six months, on and off, recording. It was melodic stuff, on the edge of sappy. He started to play a piano sound along with the pre-recorded tracks of strings, horns and guitars. He grew bolder in his improvisations as he perceived that Sam was impressed. It had been a long time since he had played for a woman.

She stood behind him as he played, watching his hands and the computer screen that indicated the notes he was hitting. He continued playing as she began to give him a needed and appreciated back rub. Then her hands encircled his waist and worked their way up. She leaned in and kissed his neck.

The song file ended and he stopped playing. "Don't stop," she whispered.

"Any requests?" he asked.

"Anything," she whispered provocatively.

As he began to play an old mellow composition, she unbuttoned his shirt. His lifted his elbows up to allow her to come around to his front. He struggled to maintain rhythm as she kissed and licked her way across his partially revealed chest.

Then she stood in front of him, unbuttoning her shirt. She unhooked her black bra and held her breasts up toward him. He fixated a moment on a brown star-shaped birthmark, previously hidden at the bottom of her left breast. Then she placed in his waiting mouth a subtly sweet nipple that became his new focus. He sucked and licked the swollen pink button hungrily, while his hands remained imprisoned by the keyboard.

"Please," he mumbled, his mouth still pressed against her breast. "I have to hold you."

"Not yet. I want more mood music."

She unzipped him, reaching in to grasp him for the first time. He lifted himself slightly off the stool as she slid his pants and underwear down to his ankles.

Her mouth felt too good.

Moments later, he hit rewind and play on the computer. As his own notes played back like a player piano, he grabbed her firmly and carried her to his new bed.

"Let me go," she said softly.

As he laid her down gently and kissed her stomach, he noticed that she was quiet and still. Staring at the ceiling.

"Sam, is everything okay?" he asked.

She turned to him, looking disoriented. Then she smiled and kissed him roughly.

He forgot his questions as she massaged him back to life. She fished a condom out of her bag. First she mounted and rode him aggressively, her breasts rising and falling with her motion. Then she collapsed herself upon him until every inch of her luscious front was pressed against him. His hands squeezed their way down her back, coming to rest in a tight grip on her gently moving buttocks. He couldn't hold her tight enough as the pressure built within him.

Just then a car alarm went off. And kept wailing. Somehow it sounded as if it was in his apartment.

It didn't hinder them. It couldn't. Nothing could.

As her cries became more frequent and staccato, he increased his rhythm until he had caught up with her.

Samantha pulled off slowly. She grabbed a handful of tissues from his night table and removed his condom for him. She tossed the wad of tissues into the trash.

"Two points," he said. "Thanks."

The car alarm continued to blare.

As Marc propped himself up to gently kiss one breast, then the other, he noticed with happy surprise the thousands of lights outside his window. The car alarm died in mid-wail, allowing him to hear a car screech to a halt while still another driver threw all of his weight against his horn.

I'm in the Big Apple!

Eleven

They began to wake at the same time. Samantha snuggled up against Marc and he casually threw an arm over her.

He was struck by how beautiful she looked in the morning. Even the bed creases in her face appealed to him. Her bright eyes were squinting and her adorable nose was crinkling as she stared fondly at him in the incoming sunshine. Her disheveled hair, falling in shiny tangles over one side of her face, was sexy as hell. He couldn't imagine her looking bad.

I could really get used to this, he thought. *And I think I'm growing on her. She hasn't mentioned my job lately. Does it still bother her?*

Neither of them wanted to get out of bed, so they didn't. Sam answered the question that Marc wanted to but would never ask, murmuring, "Last night's sex was great."

She's not exactly the flowery, romantic type.

"Does it bother you to talk about sex?" Sam asked.

"Not at all."

"I've been around, you know. I don't pretend to have been a nun."

"Does your Daddy know about your wild life?" Marc

asked jokingly.

"Definitely not," she said.

"Does he think you're still a virgin?"

"No. He knows exactly when I lost my virginity."

"What?" Marc was caught off-guard.

"When I was five, I had this serious bike crash, skidding down a big hill. I was bleeding all over. According to the pediatrician, I lost my virginity to that bike."

"Sounds pretty rough."

"It was horrible at the time. But later I appreciated it. No one could tell when I started having sex for real, not even the family doctor. I would have hated the idea of the doctor telling Daddy."

"Doctors don't do things like that. They're sworn to secrecy."

"But Dad paid the bills. And he's so nosy and overprotective."

"So why do you still tell him your business?"

"What do you mean?" Sam asked.

"Why did you tell him you and I were going out?"

"*I* didn't tell him that."

"What? He knows. He mentioned it to me."

"Didn't *you* tell him?" Sam asked.

"No way."

"Oh well," Sam said. "See? Dad's nosy. And he has a way of just knowing things."

"I've noticed that. I often feel like he knows what I'm thinking."

"He probably does. He's always been uncanny that way. Makes him a great litigator. But a difficult dad."

Sam felt Marc's tension. "But let's not talk about Dad," she suggested.

"He's not exactly a turn-on," said Marc. "At least not for me," he joked.

Marc didn't go in to the office until Sunday morning. He worked efficiently, with only an occasional flashback to Sam's body, until midnight.

The next morning he showed the Hammond Chemical reply papers to Eckart. Eckart made minimal changes and then signed the brief and the affidavit that Marc had drafted for him. He emailed an affidavit to Helfferich in Regensburg for the man to sign and send back as soon as possible.

Eckart reminded Marc to attend to any deadlines in his other matters, and then prepare for the depositions of two more plaintiffs in Munich on Thursday. They would fly out Wednesday at noon.

On the plane to Munich, Marc reviewed plaintiffs' responses to his firm's first set of interrogatories. As requested, plaintiffs' counsel had provided information concerning the two expert witnesses whom they had retained to date: who they were, and what they would testify about. This information, by pinpointing plaintiffs' contentions, could be helpful to Marc in preparing for tomorrow's depositions.

One of plaintiffs' experts was a coroner from Munich, a medical doctor who had examined several of the dead and found high levels of cyanide in the blood of each of the decedents. According to the coroner, the cyanide had the effect of depriving the body of oxygen and causing severe heart palpitations. As a result, most of the "victims" suffered almost immediate death from respiratory and/or circulatory failure. The three individuals who survived for several days each had lower levels of cyanide in their blood and died from cardiac arrest that the doctor attributed to the cyanide.

The other expert was a doctor of pharmacology, who would testify generally about the properties and lethal nature of cyanide in the form of methyl isocyanate gas (MIC), and the fact that Hammond used this gas in the production of several of their pesticide products.

Eckart was reading *Forbes* magazine in the aisle seat next to Marc. When Marc looked up from his papers and glanced in his direction, Eckart closed the magazine and asked, "What is it?"

"I have to answer their interrogatories next week. Who are our experts?"

"We don't have any."

"We don't?" *Don't big complex cases always have lots of experts?* "How are we going to dispute their experts? It's probably already too late to examine the bodies."

"We're not going to dispute their experts. We can't. We know that methyl isocyanate *was* released and did kill at least most of those people. Helfferich said so. Remember, he called the authorities himself on the twenty-eighth."

Eckart continued over Marc's surprise. "We're going to stipulate that plaintiffs died of cyanide poisoning, then try to exclude all the inflammatory material plaintiffs will seek to admit about the symptoms of cyanide poisoning, etc. Our defense is that the saboteur's act was a superseding cause. It was unforeseeable and couldn't have been prevented by any reasonable precautions. That's our best and only hope. It also happens to be a winner."

Marc was trying to follow. He decided to embarrass himself now in order to avoid disappointing Eckart later. "How do we prove that?"

"First of all, I contend that the plaintiffs have the burden of proof on that issue. But," he began ticking off fingers, "we put on witnesses from the plant about its good safety record, witnesses from the company which manufactured the holding tanks about how strong the tanks are, witnesses from the town about how crazy this skinhead Struger was. Maybe we get one expert, someone to testify that Hammond's plant met and exceeded the industry standards for German chemical factories."

Marc managed to write it all down on his yellow lined pad. Eckart reopened *Forbes*, commenting to Marc, "This case will keep you plenty busy."

⚖️

As Eckart grilled his second gypsy of the day, Marc started to lose concentration. This deposition was going very much like the previous two. He hadn't written any notes on his pad for over ten minutes.

He thought about gypsies. The word evoked memories of bygone ages. He pictured the character actress Maria Ouspenskaya playing the gypsy woman who explained lycanthropy to Lon Chaney, Jr. in *The Wolf Man*. It was her longhaired jewelry-laden son who bit Lon Chaney in the first place.

Then he pictured Maria and her son being herded through the gates of Dachau concentration camp and separated. The son's long hair is shaved off entirely before he is sent to build roads. Maria, too old to work, is delivered without delay to the open doors of the busy ovens ...

Am I helping the Nazis to kill the gypsies all over again? Marc wondered.

"Most died so quickly," the interpreter translated for the benefit of Marc and Paddington. "I was lucky to survive. A couple of the others who returned to camp with me on December 28 died shortly afterward."

Marc looked up. *How could that be?*

Eckart didn't seem to have heard the witness's last statement. "What else did you do on December 28?" he asked.

"The men from the chemical company arrived just a few hours later, with doctors and nurses from the hospital. There wasn't much they could do."

"What did *you* do?" Eckart repeated.

"The chemical people drained our well, then gave us lots of bottles of water. They said that some of the gas could have gotten into the well ..."

It had been a long day of not very responsive witnesses. Eckart snapped, "Did *you* yourself make any further observations concerning the deceaseds on December 28?"

"Not really."

"Thank you."

⚖️

"These depositions have been useless," said Eckart. "These people don't know anything that can help us or hurt us. They're ignorant."

Eckart wasn't angry. He just looked and sounded tired.

"Let's have a great dinner, then get some rest," Eckart decided. Marc thought that there was no such thing as a fine German restaurant, but he was wrong. Located in a converted sixteenth-century cellar, the Preysing Keller was as fine as any French restaurant. During his meal there, Marc managed to clear his mind of dead gypsies. The only drawback was that they had to keep their suits on.

This was the sort of International Lifestyles of the Rich and Famous scene Marc had dreamt about during his long, lean period. It would have been a lot more fun with a date, especially Samantha. But her dad wasn't so bad.

Eckart had insisted that they both order the famous three hundred deutschemark price-fixed seven-course meal. *Eckart obviously likes me*, thought Marc. *And knows what I like. He treats me well. He's a pretty good guy.*

Oh yeah, he worships Satan, Marc couldn't help remembering. *So, who am I to judge?* He sipped liberally from the subtly powerful red wine whose cork Eckart had smelled.

The food was light and sophisticated, like French, but there were local meats and vegetables in abundance. Marc was feeling stuffed after the second-course lentil soup.

He and Eckart were each drinking their third glass of wine, when Eckart said that Marc had been doing a fine job at work. "You're a bright young man. I'm glad I picked you."

"Thanks. I'm glad too."

"You could do some good work on the Committee, too. The Committee needs bright young men. With lots of energy."

"I'm sorry about the last ..."

"Say no more," Eckart cut him off. "I'm sure you'll prove yourself. You'll love the Halloween party, if I do say so myself."

"I'm sure you and Paul did a great job organizing. I'm looking forward to it." *What the hell is going to happen on Halloween? Can I handle it?*

After some strudel and fresh fruit, Marc and Eckart went back to the hotel. Eckart repeated his claim of fatigue. Although Marc was a little tired from the wine and the strain of conversation with Eckart, he was hoping for a second wind. He planned to change clothes and head out again.

He had read about dozens of nightspots in his guidebook, but his current low energy level led him to set out for the nearby and tried-and-true Hofbrauhaus. He was curious to try the landmark Hofbrauhaus itself on an ordinary weekday night, having previously only experienced the Hofbrauhaus Oktoberfest tent.

Marc walked south on Widenmayerstrasse, along the banks of the River Isar, then headed right on Maximilianstrasse, soon passing the chic Madison Avenue-style shops and prestigious private art galleries. At the intersection with Marstallstrasse, by the historic and exorbitant Hotel Vier Jahreszeiten, he turned left and found the beloved Hofbrauhaus, founded by Duke Wilhelm V in 1589. The current building itself was "only" as old as 1896.

He was surprised by how seedy the immediate neighborhood was: a handful of establishments had neon signs promising "frauleins" and depicting women in G-strings and pasties. Marc wondered if the strippers had also been there for hundreds of years. He pictured a frightening line-up of aging Marlene Dietrich look-alikes.

Even though it was a Thursday, there were a lot of people drinking a lot of beer at the Hofbrauhaus. The mood, while relaxed and festive, was not quite the ecstatic abandon of Oktoberfest. Marc did not feel as comfortable and welcome as he had on that night.

There didn't seem to be anyone in charge of seating. Marc chickened out of joining a crowd at one of the long tables, opting instead for one of the few smaller tables, which happened to be unoccupied. He surveyed the historic interior.

It was a huge hall, with a roof ornately decorated with geometric patterns and flowers, curving downward to meet pillars that combined to form arches. Bright lamps hung from the highest point of each roof arch. Patrons swayed from side to side on the hardwood benches to the rhythm of the loud oompah-pah band, each member of which had a red nose to prove that he liked to take breaks.

After fifteen minutes, Marc thought, *I might as well be in the Sahara.* The few times that a waitress, her hands full of precariously balanced huge beer steins, seemed to notice him at all, she looked vaguely annoyed.

Marc began to get more than a little annoyed. His mood was further soured by the steady stream of laughter that seemed to be coming from all the other customers. The music was getting pretty damn grating. *Who do these people think they are? Is beer reserved for the Master Race?*

Marc summoned his nerve and stopped the vaguely annoyed waitress when she passed near unencumbered. "Why can't I get service?" he demanded.

She pointed to his table and said, "*Stammtisch.*" Had he been insulted? "Reserved," she added, with surprisingly little accent. "For only regulars."

"But ... But they're not here tonight."

The waitress shrugged. "Same at all beer gardens. Move."

"Why didn't you tell me before?"

"Same at all beer gardens." She moved on toward the bar.

He could sheepishly move over to another table, asking if the locals minded if he joined.

"Screw this," he muttered as he sped toward the door. He thought he felt more than one pair of baleful eyes staring at his departing back.

He had planned on beer hall hopping, but he was discouraged. Maybe he'd be better off trying out a slightly less German hangout. He decided to find a taxi and head north to one of the "bohemian" areas, Schwabing or Haidhausen, Munich's answers to Greenwich Village. He'd try the Wunderbar, then maybe the Nachtcafe.

As he walked along, he couldn't resist the temptation to look across the street at the strip joints. He wondered how authentically German a place called "Hollywood Strip" could be. He was a little curious ...

Then he thought of Samantha. He remembered Eckart's words to him during their last trip to Munich, undoubtedly intended to inspire guilt as he "enjoyed Munich alone": "I'm sure that my daughter will be interested in hearing all about your trip."

Marc and Sam had never talked about an exclusive relationship. In fact, they had never talked about having a relationship except that time when Sam had said that she *didn't* want to marry him. But Marc had felt himself getting closer and closer to her, and he thought and hoped that she felt the same way. He couldn't wait to see Sam and tell her about his trip. He realized for the hundredth time how dangerous it could be, going out with Eckart's daughter. Of course Eckart would be watching him, judging him in every way.

As he was thinking about Eckart, he thought for a moment that he saw him across the street. *I really am obsessed.*

To humor himself, he stopped and squinted in the inadequate street light. *It is Eckart!* Marc was almost sure.

"Eckart" walked quickly into "Hollywood Strip."

Must have been mistaken, Marc thought, at first. Then: *No, I couldn't have been wrong.*

Marc couldn't believe that it had been Eckart, and he couldn't believe that it hadn't been. He had to go in and find out.

But what if, by some strange chance, it *was* Eckart? He had to proceed with caution, to avoid embarrassment for all concerned.

He paid the admission charge and headed in cautiously. It was dark in the audience. Those already inside would be able to see him, but he couldn't see them.

He didn't linger in the doorway. He cut immediately to the right, feeling ahead of him as he proceeded as far right as he could go.

He found a seat in the back right, near a small table, and then began visually searching among the patrons in front of him, as his eyes grew accustomed to the dark. A leggy blond was just starting to strip out of her shorts, T-shirt and Rollerblades, to the haunting strains of the Beach Boys singing "California Girls." A moment's study revealed that her face was older than her body.

It *was* Eckart, sitting alone across the room from Marc. Eckart was staring fixedly at the blond stripper, nursing a drink.

It wasn't like going to a strip joint was the most shocking thing in the world, especially for a single man. But Marc just didn't think it was in keeping with Eckart's character.

Eckart turned and looked to his right. Marc instinctively, dropped his head onto the table. Maybe Eckart wouldn't see him. Or maybe he would pay no attention to such an anonymous drunken mass.

Keeping his head on the table, Marc watched Eckart through narrowly opened eyelids. Eckart wasn't looking at him. He was watching the approach of a tall, wiry youth, probably twenty-two, twenty-three years old. The new arrival's thinness was accentuated by his dark attire.

The young man sat down gracefully next to Eckart without asking permission. The youth smoothed down his wild hair with his left hand. For many moments, neither he nor Eckart said a word as the two stared at the nearly naked blond.

After a while, Marc realized that Eckart's lips were moving. The two *were* speaking to each other, without facing each other.

The other man's gaunt face was sharp and frighteningly

skull-like, in stark contrast to Eckart's full handsome features. There was something else unnerving about his appearance that Marc couldn't quite place.

As the young man once again adjusted his hair, Marc noticed the subtle shift in the entire scalp line. It was a hairpiece. The whole thing. The youth must be completely bald.

Pretty unusual for a kid to be that bald. Marc stared at the young man through his slightly open eyelids. The face was hard, unbelievably hard. A face with no pity, no compassion. The face of a Nazi. This kid was a skinhead. No doubt about it.

Why was Eckart watching strippers with a skinhead?

Maybe the kid knew Struger, the saboteur. Maybe Eckart's doing his own legwork, finding witnesses to testify about Struger and his sabotage plans.

Why wouldn't Eckart have told Marc about it? Wasn't meeting Nazis in porn theaters too dangerous for one lone man?

Something very strange is going on. But it was none of Marc's business. He didn't have to know what it was. He wouldn't confront Eckart about it. In fact, it was important to him right now to get out of this place *without* being seen by Eckart. He didn't *want* Eckart to try to explain to him.

Should he try to slip out? Too risky. Might attract attention.

Marc thought that his best bet was probably to stay right where he was, continuing to act passed out. Hopefully Eckart would leave soon.

Someone grabbed Marc from behind and shook him. He smelled strong cheap perfume.

"Get up, honey," the barmaid ordered loudly. Through his squinted eyes, Marc could see Eckart and his companion look over in his direction. "Buy a drink or move on."

Marc kept his head down, thrusting his right hand into his pocket and pulling out some bills. He reached back and felt the woman's leg.

"Hey!" she yelled. She quieted when he found her pocket and shoved the bills in. He had no idea of the denominations of the bills.

He held his breath as she examined the money. She grunted something in German, but her tone was clearly extremely appreciative. *How much did I tip the woman?* he wondered.

"Auf Wiedersehen," he growled lowly to the woman.

"Danke." She moved on.

Eckart was standing and heading toward Marc! *Has he recognized me? Should I confess? Or run?*

Marc remained perfectly still as Eckart approached. He forced himself to breathe regularly.

Eckart went past him. Was he going to sneak up from behind?

Marc heard a door open and close. He recalled now that the bathroom was behind him.

This was his chance. He'd make his break now. The skinhead didn't know him. And he'd never see him again.

Moaning slightly, Marc revived himself slowly. The kid didn't seem to be paying attention.

The youth bolted up and walked out.

Marc was surprised. *I guess they finished their discussion.* He was afraid that Eckart might come out of the bathroom at any moment. Standing up quickly and without stopping to look around, he sped out the door.

He stopped just outside the theater, looking both ways for a sign of young "Adolf." It seemed that the youth had already vanished.

Wrong. Just then "Adolf" rushed out of the theater, literally bumping into Marc.

"*Achtung! Vorsicht!*" the youth shouted at him, flashing a small but sharp knife.

Marc held up two open hands and backed away silently.

"*Schwein! Dumkopf!*" The young man branded him, taking a step forward. But the youth's intensity was dying down. He seemed to be losing interest.

Marc turned and started walking, fast. *It probably isn't per-*

sonal. He doesn't know me. He fought the urge to run. He fought the urge to stop and turn. He thought he heard footsteps behind him.

He looked back as he turned the corner. The street was deserted.

Twelve

"Please thank Mr. Eckart for me. Actually, I'd like to thank him myself. I'd like to meet him."

"That's not necessary, Mom. I'll thank him for you."

"Judge Green is so nice. Poor man's a widower. Wants me to start on Monday."

"That's terrific, Ma. I'm sure he'll love you." It was strange talking to his mother on the phone. Marc had seen her practically every day for the last couple of years, and consequently had had few occasions to talk to her on the phone.

"So when do I meet the other Eckart? Your girlfriend."

"Soon, Mom."

"Are you seeing her tonight?"

"Yeah."

"That's nice. Why don't you two come over for dinner next Saturday."

"That's Halloween." He had a quick flash of childhood memory: there were few holidays better than a Saturday Halloween. "I have two Committee parties that day. One in the afternoon for some children from a shelter. And one at night for the Committee itself. No dates allowed."

"That's too bad. How about Friday? I'll make brisket."

"Maybe. Except Samantha's a vegetarian."

"A what?"

"Don't worry. She may not eat poor defenseless animals, but she's still a nice girl."

⚖⚖

"Let me go," said Sam, pulling away from him in her bed.

"Are you kidding? What's wrong?" When she didn't respond, Marc said, "I'm sorry it slipped out so undramatically, but I meant it."

"You shouldn't have said it," Sam whispered, staring away from him.

"I thought you might be starting to love me, too."

"No," Sam said simply.

Marc felt stupid. But he couldn't give up easily. *I couldn't be so wrong, could I?*

Slowly, Sam turned around to face him again. "Don't claim I ever misled you," she said. "I told you up front that I didn't want to get involved. I just thought you were cute."

"But then we got to know each other better ..."

"Why do people think sex has to involve love?"

"Are you really that cold?" Marc asked.

"I guess so," she said, pulling on pants. "I told you long ago that I didn't respect what you do for a living. I don't know how anyone can defend companies like Hammond Chemical."

She doesn't even know about Hammond Chemical's Nazi ties ... "That's my job ..."

"It's what you *do*. It's what you're willing to stand for." She yanked yesterday's shirt over her head. "How can I respect you?"

"You know I don't like it. But I have to ..."

"You don't *have* to do anything," she announced. "Some people refuse to be corrupted. They stand up for what they believe in."

"Why aren't you going out with one of those saints? Is anyone really as holy as you?"

"I never said I was perfect. Or even *good*. But I can still get pissed off when I see wasted potential. You're not even addressing your issues."

"Well, what if I changed? What if I quit?" *Am I bluffing? Testing her?*

"Don't be flippant with me."

"You won't even give me a chance? Did you go out with me *because* you knew there was something wrong with me?"

"What are you talking about?"

"You don't want to be in love," Marc accused. "Isn't that right?"

"Don't you fucking cross-examine me!" she yelled, throwing his clothes at him. "It's pathetic, the way you shift blame from yourself. Take a good look in the mirror."

⚖

Marc told his mother that he had to work all day Friday, so he and Sam would have to take a rain check on dinner at her place. Then he did work until after midnight on Friday, and four hours on Saturday.

He had been so busy with Hammond Chemical and other emergent matters that he hadn't done much work on the opposition to the Long Island Paper injunction. Now that the permanent injunction hearing was coming up on Thursday, he had a lot to do in a short time. Hopefully, Eckart would take a little more interest in this determinative hearing than he had in the preliminary one. Even though Irma Clemmons had ruled in his favor once, he was still frightened by the prospect of presenting his full case to that vicious man-eating judge.

At 1:20 p.m. on Saturday, he had to leave the office and meet his Committee obligations. He went straight to Eckart's church, Immanuel, to help set up before the kids from the shelter arrived for the Halloween party at three.

Eckart had already been there for hours, supervising the decorating and the unloading of donated gifts and refreshments, when Marc arrived in his rubber Frankenstein mask (he planned to rent a fancier costume for the party that night). Samantha was there too, blowing up balloons and setting out candy with help from Paul. She greeted Marc politely, but didn't have anything to say to him. Marc tried to sublimate Frankenstein's pain by hanging plastic cobwebs.

Eckart had elaborate makeup surrounding the fake axe seemingly embedded in his skull. During the course of the party, he occasionally bit into packets of fake blood, which came trickling out of his mouth to great effect. Most of the kids loved it, and only one kid screamed.

Paul, who was wearing an outfit from an Orvis catalog with a wide-brimmed hat and a whip, informed Marc that he was Indiana Jones. Samantha was dressed as a white witch. She looked like the singer Stevie Nicks in her white lace and white satin cape, with several rings, necklaces, bracelets and charms.

The kids had a terrific time. They loved the costume contest, the grab bags, the candy and the ghost stories. They even listened politely, shoving whole candy bars in their mouths, during the brief ceremony in which the chief administrator of the shelter handed Eckart a plaque made out to the Ethics Committee for its many good works.

It was sad at 6:00 p.m. when the kids had to be herded reluctantly onto the bus that would deliver them back to their shelter.

"Spit blood again," one six-year-old Hispanic child begged Eckart, as the latter waved at the departing children.

Eckart imitated Boris Karloff's voice as he yelled, "Happy Halloween." As he smiled widely, blood gushed out from between his perfect white teeth.

"Cool!"

⚖⚖

Larry tousled little Superboy's hair as he handed him a Snickers.

"It's a good thing Superboy here's off-duty," he said. "Otherwise a couple of bad guys like Freddy Kruger and Jason could be in big trouble."

"Not Superboy. I'm Superman!" screamed the insulted child as he headed across the lawn toward the next house.

"Ungrateful shit," Dan observed, slamming the door.

"Shouldn't have given him that Snickers. We're running low. Gonna have to make our move soon."

"Have to anyway, or we'll miss *tonight's* party."

"Got to stop being so picky." Larry stared out the peephole at the latest batch of approaching trick-or-treaters.

"The boss wants the mother to be young and stacked. Sounds good to me too." Dan's leer was hidden by his hockey mask.

⚖️

Larry was anxious to get back to New York. They had left the firm at eleven and arrived at this randomly selected Philadelphia suburb just after one, scoping out the neighborhood for hours before they broke into this house on a corner. Dan had remarked that it was "dangerous to leave your house unattended on Halloween. Well, we'll do them a favor and man the fort. Put on the outside light so nobody throws any eggs."

Larry opened the door for two kids and their frumpy mothers. He couldn't tell what the kids were supposed to be, and he was too tired to ask. He gave them each a lone Starburst and sent them on their way before they could complain.

He kept the door open a crack to watch the two approaching figures. "Whoo baby," Dan muttered. "That's the one." He stepped back and left Larry alone at the door.

The previous two kids and their mothers had already turned onto the next block. For the moment, no one was in sight except one Teenage Mutant Ninja Turtle and his voluptuous young mom.

"Hello there, little Turtle." *Talk to the kid and the mom will follow.* "You look pretty darn tough. Are you?"

"Cowabunga, dude," the little blond boy gargled.

"I bet you wouldn't be too scared to come into my haunted house for a Snickers bar, would you? Even though it's being guarded by a monster?"

The boy looked at his delicious mother. Larry detected a slight hesitation.

"Your mom's probably too scared, but you're not, are you?"

"No way!"

"We'll both face your monster, thank you," she said, sizing "Freddy" up. "If you've got a Snickers in there for me."

"You bet. Moms get two!"

Larry opened the door wider, proudly showing off the cobwebs and skeletons hung all around. "There's the treasure chest of Snickers!" he proclaimed, pointing a few feet into the living room. "Only a few feet away, but the path is dangerous!"

As they walked in and toward the chest, the woman asked, "Are you the boy who's in college?"

"What?" Larry asked as he closed the door.

"I mean when you're not Freddy Kruger. Are you the Clarks' oldest boy?"

"No, *I* am." Dan appeared in their path, smiling under his mask, two hands behind his back.

The woman recovered from her surprise and laughed nervously.

"Hey, little toad," said Dan. "Guess which hand."

"Turtle," the kid muttered, reaching out to touch Dan's right hand.

"Good one, kid." Dan put out his right hand and gave the boy a Snickers bar.

"Now Mom."

"Is mine in the other hand?"

"Well, maybe. But maybe it's not a Snickers ..."

"Bobby, let's go."

As she turned, Dan grabbed her from behind with his right arm while thrusting the chloroform-soaked handkerchief in her face with his left. As her struggles died down, his right hand began to wander over her fine figure. Soon, however, the dead weight was too heavy and he let her drop.

"Hey, Bobby Toad. You're next, little bugger."

The boy ran straight for the front door, right into Larry's grasp. Larry removed his hand from Bobby's mouth just long enough for Dan to replace it with the chloroformed handkerchief.

Larry turned off the outside light.

Thirteen

arc wasn't shocked to find that the Ethics Committee took Halloween seriously. The Aladdin Club was a hot, state-of-the-art Manhattan dance club, and the Committee had bought it for the evening.

Everyone who normally worked at the Aladdin had been paid for the night and sent home. Eckart and Paul had brought in their own "skeleton" crew to run the place, including a female deejay and a couple of lighting men. Marc wondered if they worshipped Satan, too. *I suppose that's a requirement to get in the door. What am I doing here?*

Marc was a little intimidated and disoriented when he opened the door and entered the club, after being passed through by two large bouncers with massive facial scarring that he hoped was makeup. At first he didn't recognize any of the guests in their costumes.

He'd never been to the Aladdin Club, so he could only imagine what it looked like on a normal night. The pentagrams and upside down crosses hung everywhere glowed pale green and blood red in the overall low lighting. There were pockets of illumination in the darkness. Strobe lights repeatedly crisscrossed a huge banner depicting the head of a generously horned goat. A flickering yellow spotlight shone on what seemed to be a medical school skeleton. A steady red spotlight highlighted the round platform located in the center of the room.

There were already dozens of people, milling about and making trips to and from the open bar. Organ music in a minor key was playing softly in the background.

Paul, still Indiana Jones, easily recognized Marc, despite his General's uniform. Paul gave him a warm greeting as he ran by to talk to the lighting people. "Catch up with you later!" Paul yelled back at him. "Enjoy!"

More guests were coming in, and Marc was starting to recognize some of them. Judging from the number of people already there, the guest list must have included many "friends" of the Committee as well as members.

It seemed like these Committee people were friendlier every time Marc saw them. No doubt it was partly due to the quantity and quality of the free alcohol flowing around this place, but it was really strange the extent to which everyone was laughing and showing affection for their fellow Committee members.

Joe and Scott came over to him and, to his amazement, hugged him. Marc didn't know what to say to them. "How's it going, guys?" he asked, striving to match the general enthusiasm level of the room.

"Great!" they both responded. "It's Halloween!" Joe continued. "It's finally here!"

Marc looked at Scott's wedding ring and asked, "Too bad no dates, huh?"

Both of them stared at him like he had announced his own castration. "You kidding? I'll see her tomorrow, but tonight's Halloween!" Scott and Joe searched his face for some intelligence.

"'Course I'm kidding," Marc recovered. "It's Halloween!"

Soon thereafter Marc proclaimed a thirst and set out for the bar. On the way he encountered a tipsy Doris Spender in, of all things, a ballerina's costume.

"Marc!" she yelled. She grabbed his face in both hands and gave him a loud kiss on the lips. "I hope you'll be my partner later."

"Sure, later," he said, patting her on her thick exposed shoulder as he passed. *What are we going to dance to, Swan Lake?* In line for his drink, a pair of attractive young women, whom he had noticed at the last meeting, introduced themselves. *This night is really playing out like a dream.* The bartender handed him his gin and tonic.

As much as he appreciated it, Marc thought to himself that it probably wasn't a wise career move for these two young female associates to have come dressed as a cheerleader and the Catwoman. Cindy, the Catwoman, looked particularly wonderful in her form-fitting black leather.

"You're new, right?" Cindy asked.

"Only to the Committee."

The cheerleader smiled, but Catwoman smiled wider. "Good. I'm tired of the same old people. Need new blood."

How suggestive is she trying to be?

She grasped his arm firmly. "I love men in uniform. Can I count on you later?"

Very suggestive.

He thought of Samantha. *Was there any chance of a future with her?* He had no reason to think so, but he couldn't stop hoping.

"Maybe a quick dance," he said matter-of-factly, striving to keep double entendre out of his tone. *That was tough.*

"She only likes *long, slow* dances," the cheerleader informed him.

"I'll take whatever you've got," were the Catwoman's departing words. "Later."

He made his way back toward the door. Dan and Larry were just coming in, dressed as Jason and Freddy Kruger, shaking hands all around and laughing. Marc headed over to say hi.

Then the mood lighting switched off. Pitch black.

There was no panic. Only tittering and buzzing and quick intake of breath.

A low-pitched rumbling began, building in volume until it was near deafening. Then the rumbling stretched out into the mirthless laughter of a giant.

"Greetings, my children. You are all welcome, my beloved. Let us bring Hell to earth!"

Two large lit candelabras appeared and traveled slowly across the room. The crowd separated to clear a path for the candles as they proceeded toward the center platform, which could only then be seen. The candelabras were handed to the beautiful naked woman who lay on the platform. It was the same woman who had served as an "altar" for the last service.

A black-robed man stepped onto the platform and stood motionless, holding a squirming, squawking chicken. The two black-robed deacons appeared on either side, each holding an ornate chalice. The whole scene was surprisingly well revealed by the flickering candlelight.

With a quick wrenching movement the priest tore the head from the creature and held the two parts high. The blood spurting from the head and the body painted the cloaks of all three men dark red, as the deacons held their cups so as to catch the blood.

Then they placed the chalices on the "altar's" stomach and began to speak in Latin. The red spotlight came back on, pointing at the platform with a decreased intensity. The platform began to revolve slowly, allowing the crowd on every side an equal view.

The service began and proceeded much as the previous one had, including that Marc remained as far from the proceedings as possible. Once again, black robes were passed around and donned by the crowd. Despite his discomfort, the idea of cheerleaders, ballerinas and vampires alike wearing black hooded robes tickled Marc a little.

One good thing was that the service did not seem designed to involve participation from the congregation. Furthermore, between the low light and the hoods, Marc felt fairly secure in his anonymity.

The celebrant held up a chalice of chicken blood, but replaced it on the altar without drinking. He continued, "Renouncing the spiritual paradise of the weak and lowly, we place our trust in Thee, the God of Flesh, looking for the satisfaction and fulfillment of all our desires in the land of the living."

Then he chanted a corruption of the Lord's Prayer:

"Our Father who art in Hell, hallowed be Thy name. Thy kingdom is come, Thy will is done, on earth as it is in Hell! We take this night our rightful due, and trespass not on paths of pain. Lead us into temptation, and deliver us from false piety, for Thine is the kingdom and the power and the glory forever!"

"Let reason rule the earth," the deacons intoned.

Later, the priest threw the holy wafer to the floor and trampled it. Then he lifted the chalice high once more, spoke some Latin, and drank deeply.

Marc was disgusted. He couldn't help thinking *I hope that was a free-range chicken.*

Marc was nervous to notice that several chalices were now making their way through the crowd, with each person taking a sip. *Could there have been enough blood? Or enough chickens?*

He knew what to do. When a cup came to him, he put it to his lips and tilted his head back. He kept his lips closed tight. He was nonetheless relieved to smell wine, not blood.
Guess Paul was right. The average person on this Committee isn't that weird.

The celebrant led the group in their first and only responsive chanting. "Great One, hear us now as we invoke Thy blessing: In the pleasures of the flesh and the tranquility of the mind ..."

The crowd responded, "Sustain us, Dark Lord!"

The responsive chanting continued for several minutes. Marc grunted along. He was a little surprised to learn that, al-

though he had not been raised religiously, even he had difficulty saying "Dark Lord" and "Satan" out loud. It really was a
strong taboo. Fortunately, grunting and muttering responsively
seemed sufficient to get him through the moment.

Marc looked around in wonder at the sea of cowled figures,
free from such taboos. These mavericks were free from most
man-made limitations. They claimed to worship reason. For a
moment he envied them their freedom. Then he remembered
that some of them drank chicken blood. Well, every group had
its fanatics.

"We are kindred spirits, demon brothers, children of
earthly joy. With one voice we proclaim ..."

"*Ave, Satanas!*"

"Arise, invoke the blasphemous Name. The Lord of So-
dom, the God of Cain, joy to the Flesh forever!"

"*Ave, Satanas!*"

The celebrant bowed before the altar, then turned and
raised his left hand with its fingers in two groups, like the Vul-
can greeting from *Star Trek*. "*Ego vos benedicto in nomine magni
dei nostri Satanas.*"

Every person in the crowd held up his or her left hand
with the same Sign of the Horns. Marc held up his hand, but he
couldn't make the fingers separate properly.

"*Ave Satanas*," said the celebrant.

"*Ave Satanas*," the congregation chanted once more. "It is
done."

The tableau held for another minute. Then the spotlight
flicked off and the candles were blown out. Recorded music began to play, gaining rapidly in volume. Marc released much tension as he chuckled. It was the Rolling Stones classic, "Sympathy
for the Devil."

The deejay's voice was mixed in over the vamping rhythm
track. "Alright, boys and girls, ladies and gentlemen, witches
and warlocks, sluts and studs, let's party!"

The former low lighting with pockets of brightness was restored. Almost in unison, people were shedding their robes and tossing them into piles against the walls. Young and old alike began to dance.

The song seemed more authentically pagan and carnal than Marc had ever noticed. At first it seemed like everyone was dancing with everyone. They danced wildly, primitively, like the natives in *King Kong* or other movies of the 1930s.

Marc danced, but he couldn't match their abandon. He felt out of place, like a prude at a nudist colony.

A new trend emerged. Men and women began to pair up and dance closer. Some started to kiss. Some started to grope.

Paul stopped on his way by. "Having a good time?"

Marc nodded with feigned enthusiasm.

"You've got to start going with the flow, man. This is called 'fun.' You better look into it." Paul leaned over and embraced Marc, while whispering urgently in his ear: "They're watching. Get involved. Show that you belong."

Paul pulled back and grinned. "Better choose soon, son," he advised. "The judges usually grab the best babes."

Paul danced away, aimed straight for a voluptuous brunette who was already surrounded by guys.

Marc searched the room from a corner. Who was watching him? He couldn't tell, but he believed Paul. He overcame his nerves, put a smile on his face, and danced into the fray.

The music had shifted to a less well-known but also primitively rhythmic piece. Marc was only a little surprised at this point to see a pair of large breasts go dancing by him. He was more surprised to see the erect penis of the man pursuing her.

All around him, men and women were shedding their clothing. Costumes were strewn all over the dance floor.

He was starting to feel more and more conspicuous. He wished he still had the hooded cowl on to shield his identity. He wished he had worn the Frankenstein mask. To stall for time, he started to take off his costume.

He bravely stripped to his underwear, but it wasn't nearly

good enough. He was now in the minority merely because he was still standing. Over a dozen couples had sunk to the floor already, creating the impression that the ground was alive and undulating. One couple rested their heads on the buttocks of another, while a third pair occasionally rolled into both. Some couples linked together into long daisy chains of lust.

What could he do? He had to do something.

She was only wearing the Catwoman mask now. She danced up to him and smiled. Her breasts didn't move much when she danced. *Probably fake. Nonetheless, hugely appealing.* His eyes were captured by the neatly shaved cleft below.

"Came for my dance," she murmured. She grasped his nipples between her fingers as she kissed him. Then she felt for the stiffness she knew she'd find.

I've got to do it. I'm being watched. And it's not like Cindy thinks I love her.

As she reached into his jockey shorts, he thought, *Samantha was the one who broke us up. Still ...*

None of his inner conflict reduced his erection at all. He was poised to surrender, when he remembered ...

"Condoms. I think I have one in my wallet. In my uniform."

As he located the General's pants in the nearby pile of clothes, Cindy spoke in a slightly irritated tone. "Come on. We don't need that. I'm on the pill."

"What about ...?"

"*We* don't get *that*," she responded incredulously. "What are you so worried about?"

Marc palmed the condom and dropped the pants back into the pile. *Is Cindy a fanatic?*

People were watching. He had to get back on track.

He knelt in front of her and pulled her toward him. Her irritation died down as she started to moan.

He put the condom down next to him. He put off the issue for now. He would convince her when the time came. He would satisfy her. And the Committee.

Soon he lay on the hard floor with her on top of him, each tasting the other. His misgivings were melting away as was all resistance. He closed his eyes tight and thought only of sex.

Then she shifted position. She climbed off him then replaced him in her mouth. Now their only point of contact was his penis. All sensation was focused at that one spot. The woman seemed inspired anew, showing increased skill and motivation. He was awash with lust.

His eyes still shut he pictured the tongue that flicked so delicately along his length and against his base, the full lips which pursed so tightly about him as they traveled up and down with increasing speed. The woman was a virtuoso.

He opened his eyes and lifted his head to see for real. But Cindy was gone. The woman in whose mouth he was deeply buried was completely unfamiliar. Or was she?

Her graying hair looked like it had been cut in a bowl. The Phantom of the Opera mask attached to her middle-aged face only added to the surreal nature of the scene. He couldn't see her body.

She paused and looked up at him. She smiled and asked, "Are you ready for me now?"

When he didn't respond, she added, "I hope you don't mind that I got rid of your little friend. She didn't know how to give real head."

As she spoke she stroked him with an expert touch that felt magnificent even now. *Who the hell are you?*

The woman rose to her knees, her breasts dropping down low to rest on a roll of fat. So much for lust. So much for recognition. Surely he had never seen a woman who looked like this. ...

"I'm sorry ..." he began.

She paid no attention, leaning forward to reach under and grab his buttocks. "I was looking all over for this tight butt," she announced. "I noticed it last month. And I'll enjoy it again when you're in my courtroom next week."

What? No! For God's sake, no!

"I knew you'd have a big young dick!" United States District Court Judge Irma Clemmons informed him. "I'm dying to ride it!"

He was stunned. He was horrified. He was paralyzed. But he was still erect.

He couldn't say no. His mind stepped out for a while.

PART TWO

Fourteen

Marc tried to lose himself in his work. Unfortunately, it was hard to convince himself that old-fashioned legal research and writing were still relevant to successful litigation. Was he involved in any cases that weren't fixed?

Many things from the last few months—*hell, years*—were much clearer now. No wonder Eckart hadn't been the least bit worried about the previous Long Island Paper hearing in front of Judge Irma Clemmons. Hadn't Eckart even said something to the effect that she liked "eager young men?"

Part of Marc thought that he shouldn't bother spending another minute preparing for the full hearing Thursday, but he couldn't suddenly stop acting the way he'd been taught to act as a lawyer. Anyway, surely he had to make it look good. Otherwise, wouldn't the lawyers on the other side figure things out?

He wasn't looking forward to the hearing, but he wasn't dreading it either. He had felt numb for days. He would do whatever he had to do. There was nothing to worry about, nothing to think about. No choices to make.

When Harry had asked him how his Halloween had been, Marc had answered, "Same old thing. What'd you do?"

"The usual for me too. Helping my folks at the front door for a couple hours, then went out drinking with a few buddies." Harry chuckled. "Frankly, I could use a woman."

Marc had stopped trying to call Samantha. He didn't know what to say to her anymore.

Paul asked Marc if he was available for a double date with two sisters on Saturday. Marc begged off. "You're going to miss something special," Paul warned Marc, shaking his head at the thought.

Marc thought of Cindy, the Catwoman. He wondered if she had given him a moment's thought since Halloween. Somehow, he doubted it. He was curious as to how she would respond to a call, but not curious enough to do it. He had a feeling it would be considered gauche. Why couldn't he just wait until the next orgy, like everyone else?

On the flip side, he drew some comfort from his theory that Judge Clemmons was unlikely to call him for a date. He was more concerned about what she would do at the next orgy, whenever that was. He only knew that the next *meeting* was in three weeks. How personal was the judge's interest? Was she done with him or not? She hadn't given any clear indications, merely muttering "see you in court" as she climbed off him and walked away, to rest or to find another young stud, Marc surmised.

He was sure that she would be completely professional at the hearing Thursday. She would never let on in front of the other side that she had engaged in unethical *ex parte* "communications" with him. He would have to be just as professional. He doubted that he could look her in the eye. *What part of her should he look at?*

Irma Clemmons stared at Marc. She had been staring at him for several minutes in the same inscrutable, unblinking manner that he had noted the last time he was in this courtroom. Last time, Marc had feared that she was pulling apart his arguments in her head. This time he suspected that she was pulling off his pants and giving him head. For just a moment, he flashed back to how great her mouth and tongue had felt. *Christ, get a grip!*

He remembered, with a smile, the old public speaking trick of imagining your audience naked. *You probably aren't supposed to picture your audience raping you.*

"But counselor, how can a man be raped?" Judge Clemmons demanded of him. "Isn't it true that you in fact loved it?"

"Excuse me," Marc spoke up. "What did Your Honor ask me?"

Irma Clemmons frowned and repeated, "I asked what you thought of the government's statistics concerning the increased incidence of cancer in the area of the plant?" *Why was she pursing her lips? Was it some sort of secret signal, or just a facial tic?*

"Well, even if fully documented, it would be wholly inconclusive," Marc recovered. "Plaintiffs still have not established any evidence of causal link. They haven't provided sufficient foundation concerning their base numbers, nor have they proved that my client's plant was the only new variable introduced during the period ..."

She turned her attention to the opposing attorneys, finally. "What does the government have to add to its papers?"

The civil servants never had a chance. For one thing, the senior DOJ attorney was doing all the talking, while his tall, muscular young sidekick merely handed the older man documents as he referred to them. *A little research might have told the plaintiffs that the old guy isn't the Judge's type.*

After Irma announced her finding for the defendant, she immediately called the next case. Both Marc and the DOJ senior attorney muttered, "Thank you, Your Honor," as they gathered up their papers.

It's over! I survived! As he headed toward the back doors, Marc thought he could feel two unblinking eyes staring at his butt.

Later, Marc realized that he might have been wrong about whose eyes were watching him. Or there might have been more than one pair.

As he crossed the first floor lobby, thinking *another successfully fixed hearing*, he heard footsteps behind him. When he turned around, a burly man turned away suddenly and conspicuously. Marc faced front again and said goodbye to the armed security guards as he hurried out of the building.

At the bottom of the court steps, Marc looked over his shoulder to see the big man at the top of the stairs. Marc made a fast right and headed toward Chinatown. He looked behind him periodically, but didn't see any sign of pursuit.

Strange. The man had been looking at him both times that Marc had turned. There was something intimidating about the guy. He had a long scar on his right cheek, and the heavy build and hard expression of Mob muscle. If Marc owed money to a loan shark or a bookie, he would have been petrified.

Marc figured that he would catch the 6 train at the Canal Street stop in Chinatown. The Muscle must have read his mind, because he intercepted Marc a few steps before the subway entrance. *How'd this guy move that fast?*

The man planted a heavy arm around Marc's shoulder. "Hey!" Marc exclaimed in surprise. Moving quickly, he managed to remove the arm and wheel about to face the stranger.

The man's face was transformed by a wide grin. "Nice move, Marc. May I call you Marc?"

"What the hell should I call you?"

"How about Bob?"

Marc couldn't help be a little amused by this surreal scene. "Do you have a last name?"

"Yeah. Rosetti."

Bob Rosetti? Robert Rosetti? Where have I heard that name?

"Are you the Manhattan D.A.?" Marc asked incredulously.

"Bingo. You like dim sum?"

"Well, yeah." *What the hell could the Manhattan D.A. himself want with me? How does he know my name? And what does dim sum have to do with anything?* "But I already ate lunch. It's 3:15."

"There's always room for Mandarin Court dim sum. Follow me."

"I've got to get back to the office ..."

"I think you'd better give me a few minutes." Rosetti stopped smiling.

Marc didn't have the nerve to defy the D.A., but he could mess with him a little. "You paying?"

"Me? With taxpayers' money? On a civil servant's salary? Get out of here. You young kids make more than me."

Rosetti was serious about his dim sum. Watching the man grab plates off the cart as it went by, Marc thought that this meeting might be just a pretext for dim sum, rather than vice versa. Marc found something amusing about the sight of this big bruiser in a well-worn suit delicately manipulating tiny Chinese dumplings with chopsticks. Marc picked on his vegetable dumplings, nervously anticipating Rosetti's questions.

Marc's wildest fears were realized when Rosetti stated simply, "I think there's something fishy about the Ethics Committee." Marc struggled to keep a poker face, allowing himself only a mildly inquisitive look. "I've been looking into it since the Thornton murder."

Thornton murdered? I thought he committed suicide. It was in all the papers.

At first Marc tried to maintain his composure. Then he realized that shock *was* the appropriate response to this statement about Thornton. He was glad that Rosetti had brought up something he knew nothing about. He went with the shock.

"So, you act surprised," Rosetti observed. "I know that you've only joined the Committee recently. I admit I can't be sure how much you know. I don't know if everyone on the Committee knows what's going on."

"What *do* you know?" Marc asked with genuine interest.

"I know that Thornton was moved after he died. The coroner confirmed my hunch that he'd just had sex, but someone had cleaned him off afterward. Someone concerned with his reputation."

"But wasn't the suicide note in his handwriting?"

"It looked like it. Impressive work."

"Why wasn't this in the papers?" Marc asked.

"Oddly enough, no one asked me. The papers just accepted the suicide story and let the whole thing die. I've been supervising the investigation myself."

"What made you suspicious to begin with?"

"It was too much like that other death, two years ago. Norm Maxwell, Secretary to the Ethics Committee at the time. Also committed suicide. Also found in a deserted public place. I was suspicious at the time ..."

"What's the connection to the Committee?"

"I'm working on that. I figure either they both found out something, or they threatened to go public with something. What was it?"

"Don't ask me."

"I'm asking for your help, at least."

What else did this guy know? What did he want from Marc? Could Marc get away with turning him down? Marc wasn't prepared to give up everything on the spot. *What would it accomplish?*

"What can I do?" Marc asked. "I'm the new guy. I don't know anything." *That's practically true. All I know is that they worship Satan, which isn't a crime. It's protected by the First Amendment. And they invite judges to their parties. I don't even know for sure that the judges are influenced by the Committee.*

Rosetti stared him down. "You folks on the Committee really are successful, aren't you?"

"There are a lot of high-powered types on the Committee," Marc agreed. "I'm just a junior associate."

"At a prestigious firm. By the way, congratulations on your recent good fortune. I understand that you were unemployed until a couple of months ago."

"I was a solo practitioner," Marc corrected stiffly. "It wasn't going so well ..."

"How did you get on the Committee?"

Marc hesitated. "I wrote a letter to Mr. Thornton asking to join."

"Really?" Rosetti asked skeptically. "I've been trying to get someone accepted onto that Committee for months. How'd you do it?"

"Timing, I guess. Thornton had just died." Marc mentally patted himself on the back for his skillful blending of fact and fiction.

"Did your luck have anything to do with your uncle's former association with the Committee?"

Good question! I've wondered that myself. You've done your homework.

"Not that I know of."

"Funny thing," Rosetti seemed to be musing aloud. "Seems like *lots* of Committee members have become judges ..."

Was Marc supposed to comment? He got up the nerve to ask what was on his mind: "Why are you talking to *me*? How'd you pick me?"

"Like you say, you're just a junior associate. Just starting out in life. Wouldn't want to take the wrong fork in the road, go astray ..."

"So you only have my welfare in mind? Even though I can't help you?"

"Maybe I already have more senior Committee people working for me ..."

"Then why bother with me?"

"I told you ..."

"Why bother trying to get someone into the Committee?"

"That was a test of their procedures." Marc didn't buy this.

Rosetti was bluffing. *Right?*

"Why are you handling this personally?" Marc asked.

"Why not? It's a big case, involving far-reaching corruption in high places. It's sensitive and important. I'm interested." Rosetti moved on. "So tell me, how do they decide who to let in? What do they all have in common?"

He doesn't know? Then he doesn't know anything. And no born-and-raised Satanist is going to tell him. I'm probably his only hope. Does he know that?

Marc offered a guess. "They're all dedicated to the promotion of legal ethics?"

Rosetti didn't smile. "I hope this doesn't mean that you've decided to play it cute. *Cute* isn't *smart.*"

"Look, I don't know anything about Thornton's death. I never met him."

"Okay. What do you know about?"

Marc shrugged. "I'm new."

"Don't you even know how you got on the Committee? What do you have in common with them?"

"Nothing," he answered, attempting conviction.

Fifteen

Marc had to be in the Southern District again the next afternoon, Friday, on David Gutierrez's civil rights case. In his comfortable chambers, Judge Kelly asked Marc if he had sent out discovery demands yet.

"Yes," Marc responded. "As soon as I received defendant's answer I served interrogatories, document requests and deposition notices."

Judge Kelly turned to the government's attorney, Joe Dinaro. "Have you sent out your discovery demands?"

"Not yet, your Honor. I'm working on them."

"When are the depositions of defendants scheduled for?" the judge asked.

"The subject police officers are to be deposed beginning on December 10, after I've received and reviewed their discovery responses," Marc answered.

"Okay," said the judge. "Let's keep this case moving. I don't want to see any government delays."

"I assure you, Judge, that we will move this case ..."

Judge Kelly cut the man off impatiently. "Don't tell it to the judge," he instructed. "I'm overdue in my courtroom. I'll leave you in the capable hands of my law clerk, Jim. He'll help you set up a full discovery schedule." Jim had just walked in, holding a legal pad. "I want to see you back here five weeks from yesterday at 2:00 p.m. sharp. If you haven't conducted at least one deposition on each side by then, I'll hold you both in contempt. Officially."

The judge fled the room, leaving them to work out the logistics of discovery. Jim, playing the good cop, apologized for Judge Kelly's temper and expressed the hope that this case could be resolved quickly and amicably. Jim suggested that the defendant should depose the plaintiff on December 11.

Marc was relieved that D.A. Rosetti didn't show up at the meeting, or outside Judge Kelly's chambers. The man had made it clear that the discussion was not over and that he would contact Marc again. Marc needed time to come up with a plan. He had to figure it out by himself, having decided not to discuss Rosetti with anyone on the Committee.

He couldn't stop himself from turning and looking back periodically, just to make sure no one was following. *How had Rosetti known where I'd be yesterday? How much does he know about me?*

Marc was giving the U.S. Marshals by the front door his usual friendly wave when they surprised him by stopping him. "You Marc Wilson?" the bigger one asked.

Amazed, Marc nodded.

"Then you're not leaving," the man informed him.

"I thought you were the guy," said the other one. "You fit the description."

"What's going on?" Marc asked, momentarily holding his anxiety in check. He glanced apprehensively at the guards' guns. *At least they haven't drawn them yet,* he thought. *Is this it? Am I under arrest? Funny, somehow I wouldn't have thought the city D.A. would arrest someone in federal court ...*

"We don't know," the other guy said. "Just got orders to send you up to seventeen."

"What?"

"Seventeen. Take the elevator up and someone will meet you there."

Very strange. "You guys do this often?"

"We do what we're told," was all he could get from them.

Well, there was no way out. He headed for the elevators. What if he didn't go to the seventeenth floor? Would they come after him?

On the way, he looked at the building directory. *Of course, the Second Circuit Court of Appeals is up there.* The place to appeal adverse decisions from the federal trial courts of New York, Connecticut and maybe other states that Marc couldn't think of right now. He'd never been up there. Why was he going now?

He stepped into the elevator.

He didn't know anyone connected with the Court. A classmate used to clerk for one of the Second Circuit judges, but by now he had moved on to a high-paying private practice job. Marc couldn't name practically any of the appellate judges. Except for his uncle, whom he hadn't spoken to in over five years. That had been just a few months before his uncle was appointed to the federal trial bench. Three years before he had been promoted to the Second Circuit Court of Appeals.

Could this have something to do with the Committee? How could it? But what else could it involve? Before joining the Committee, Marc *never* had anything to do with powerful people.

The elevator doors opened and Marc stepped out. He didn't recognize the robed man who moved quickly to trap and squeeze him in a vise-like grip. Marc struggled helplessly in the man's thick arms.

"Marc! It's been so long!"

His attacker let go and stepped back. "Let me look at you."

It was Charles Wilson. It *had* been a long time. And Marc had never seen him in judicial robes. He had aged twenty years in the last five, growing more round, more bald, more haggard overall.

Still, the man exuded the same aura of strength and influence as ever. His eyes, now surrounded by dark rings, still
pierced whatever they fastened on.

"Uncle Charles," Marc stated, unsure how else to minimize the awkwardness of the moment.

"Come, join me in my chambers." Charles Wilson led the
way down the hall. "In here."

Marc paused at the threshold. *I've got to go in. How could I
justify refusing? Other than mentioning that he broke my father's
heart.*

Uncle Charles noticed Marc's hesitation. "I suppose this is
rather sudden. I hope you don't still hate me."

Marc couldn't hold it in. "You really hurt my father." He
added, "I admit I don't know what the fight was about. But my
father was a fair man ..."

Charles Wilson was silent. Marc watched him carefully.

"I'm so sorry," his uncle said, his voice cracking. "I miss
him so much ... It must have been so hard for you."

"It still is."

"Of course."

Marc followed his uncle into his chambers, then further
into his office. His uncle sat down on a couch, and he sat on a
loveseat facing him. Marc grew uncomfortable under the other
man's stare and looked around the office.

There were plaques and certificates that Marc couldn't
read from where he sat. There were pictures of Charles Wilson
at various dinners and ceremonies with various state and city
officials, only a few of whom Marc recognized. There were older
pictures of Charles Wilson and his late wife, Charles Wilson and
his baby son shortly before he died, and Charles Wilson and his
brother, Mitch. Marc's father.

Marc couldn't help being nervous. He noticed how quiet
it was and realized, with surprise, that he and his uncle were
alone. No law clerks or secretaries around. And it was only
3:10 p.m. But it *was* Friday.

"Don't be nervous," Judge Wilson instructed. "I just want to talk a little. I've missed you."

That was a strange thing to say. It wasn't like he used to take Marc to ball games or anything. They used to see each other at Thanksgiving dinners. Once in a while they talked.

Then Marc remembered what he had forgotten, that Uncle Charlie *had* always shown interest in him. Always asking him what he was doing in school, what he wanted to be when he grew up. Always performing hokey magic tricks like pulling coins from Marc's ears. Always slipping him a few bucks, telling him to "spend them wisely."

"How's your mother?"

"Okay. Still getting by."

"How is her new job going?"

"How'd you know about that?"

"I've always kept up with you two. I wanted you to do well."

Very touching. How come you never helped us out? "Well, things have been looking up a little," said Marc.

"Is your mother seeing anyone?"

The question caught Marc by surprise. "No. She hasn't. Guess she misses Dad too much."

"That's unfortunate. You know, I tried to help your mother back then, get her on her feet. She was too proud."

Proud, eh? For all her preaching to me about forgiving and forgetting, my mother's been holding a grudge too, hasn't she?

Charles Wilson continued. "Now I'm so glad to finally have been able to help you. I'm happy that you seem to be fitting in. I was a little worried when you ran out on your first mass, but you seemed to enjoy your second one."

My God! How much does he know?

"I know *Irma* enjoyed it."

Marc almost died. He managed to sputter, "Was it you all along?"

"When Doris Spender told me about the stunt you pulled

with that computer, I was delighted. It was beautiful. It would have worked if we were a normal committee. She asked me what to do, and I said, 'Welcome the boy aboard. He's a real Wilson!'"

"But no one said anything ... Did they all know?"

"Many did. But they knew to treat you well and give you some time. That Johnston boy did a fine job, helping you adjust ..."

"Paul? Paul was working for you?" Marc was dizzy.

"Sure. And for you. We just wanted to make sure that you got along, appreciated the opportunities, and didn't do anything rash. It's worked out great. I figured now you were ready for this little talk."

Bob Rosetti was locking his desk and his office for the day. He promised Marge that he'd be home early today, with the groceries on his list. As he rang for the elevator, he thought about Marc Wilson. In addition to wanting to break the secret of the Ethics Committee, Rosetti really was concerned about the kid. He hadn't been bullshitting him. He hated to see these fresh-faced kids getting involved in shady deals.

Can't take it too personally, he reminded himself. *These white-collar punks are no better than the street kids.*

In the old days, Rosetti had handled mostly street crime. Eventually he had realized that these kids had been hard long before he ever saw them. Nothing for him to do but put them away. For the second, third, fourth time. Best for everybody if they killed each other in jail. Seemed like none of these kids ever got rehabilitated.

But a boy like Wilson; he's poised on the edge. He's sweating out his choices, all confused. He still has a chance to stay clean.

As he left the courthouse and headed down the nearest subway entrance, Rosetti's thoughts turned to his own boy. Soon Bob Junior would be going off to kindergarten. Rosetti wished again that he could afford thirteen years of private school, four years of college and endless graduate school for both Bobby and his little sister, Margaret. He hated the thought of his kids having to face the cruel world. Especially Manhattan. He wished they never had to leave the apartment.

Rosetti knew the circuitous underground path to the Lexington line trains without looking at the signs or thinking about it consciously at all. That left his mind free to continue his litany of family worries. *Maybe I can afford a few years for each kid at St. Matthew's.*

Rosetti didn't notice the two men following him. He didn't understand what was happening when they caught up to him and walked on both sides of him, matching his pace perfectly. As he turned to see who was on his right, each man pressed an object against Rosetti's side. "Keep going," said the young man on the right side. "Don't try anything."

Rosetti kept walking at the same pace. *Stay cool. Bide your time. You're tougher than they are, but they've got guns.* He looked at the young man on his left, taller and almost as solidly built as Rosetti. "Just like the other guy said. Head for that exit ahead," the man ordered.

The three men left the subway station in lock step. When Rosetti saw that they were heading for the Lexus with the open door, he weighed his chances of making a break. They weren't good. He would die. Along with other innocent people.

"What do you want with me?" he asked.

"Just get in. We'll talk in the car."

I can't run. I've got to stay alive. For Marge. And the kids. Maybe they do only want to talk. What could they gain by killing me? I'm just a civil servant. I'm replaceable.

Once in the back seat of the car, surrounded by the two men, he asked again, "What do you want?"

"We're taking you to a party," said the driver with the missing finger. "But you better take a nap first ..."

Rosetti fought back instinctively when the chloroform-covered handkerchief was thrust into his mouth. He flailed powerfully, bruising both men before he fell away into unconsciousness.

Charlie Wilson walked over to the loveseat and spontaneously embraced Marc. He sat down next to him. "I'm so happy. You know, Marc, I've had a wonderful career, but I've had a lot of tragedy in my family life. I lost my darling son when he was less than a year old, and my lovely Martha just a few years ago." His voice was sad and tired. "And my little brother. I always tried to look out for Mitch. Especially after our parents died. I helped him through college, helped him get set up in business."

Although he hadn't wanted to, Marc felt bad for his uncle. But he had to know. "What was the big argument between you and my father?"

The power balance in the room shifted in an instant. Now Marc was staring at his uncle, while Charles Wilson looked away awkwardly. Marc waited anxiously. He had wondered for five years. He thought he would never find out.

His uncle buried his bullet-shaped head in his arthritic hands. "I was such a fool!" Marc waited impatiently for more. Charlie Wilson looked up at him with five years of regret. "It wasn't really an argument," he stated. "We both knew I was wrong. We only disagreed as to whether it was his business."

The man jumped up and began to pace. "He didn't want me to ruin my life. And Martha's. I couldn't stand being scolded by my little brother." Charles Wilson stopped at the other end of the room. "Of course he was right. I shouldn't have had the affair. And I should have broken it off immediately. But Mitch couldn't even understand. It was so foreign to him."

Marc had never guessed this. Now, years after Martha's death, it didn't seem so shocking.

"Your father guessed. He was justly harsh with me. He gave me an ultimatum: break off the affair and confess to Martha, or he couldn't stand the sight of me." He finally looked at Marc. "I was proud. With no cause to be. I told him that no one gave Charlie Wilson ultimatums. We said many things that night ... If only I could take them all back. You always think there'll be time ..."

Judge Wilson was crying. Marc felt embarrassed to be seeing this. Should he leave? Should he hug the guy? Or should he slug him?

Then Marc stopped thinking about his uncle. He remembered Mitch Wilson. He could be hard on you when you'd done something wrong, make you feel like the smallest, meanest boy in the world. It only made things worse that Mitch Wilson had seemed so consistently, unthinkingly moral himself. But it made it all the more glorious when he praised you. Which he might do later the same day, because he was always quick to forgive. His smiling approval had been the most wonderful prize Marc had ever won.

Charlie Wilson stopped talking when he saw the tear on Marc's cheek. He sat back down next to Marc, put an arm around his shoulder and pulled Marc toward him. Marc didn't resist. "I screwed up," his uncle said. "But give me a chance. I want to be family to you. And to Sylvia."

Marc didn't know what to say. He changed the topic. "So, how important are you on the Committee?"

"I'm not on the Committee anymore."

"Right. I guess you're one of those powerful 'friends of the Committee' that Eckart talks about."

"How's he been treating you?" Wilson changed the topic.

"Eckart? He treats me fine. Do you know him well?"

"Fairly well. He's dedicated. Very ambitious. Like me in some ways."

"I guess so. I didn't see *you* at either of the services," Marc stated. "Were you there?"

"Oh yes. I never miss a service. They wouldn't let me."

"What do you mean?" Marc stared at his uncle in confusion.

"They need me." Marc focused on the man's familiar mouth. "I may have stepped down as Committee Chair, but I still ..."

"It was you!" Marc couldn't contain his astonishment. "You led the services! You're the priest!"

Charlie smiled. "I thought you might have figured that out before now. Well, now you know."

"But how can that be? You grew up with my father ..."

"Of course I did. We were raised as Satanists."

Marc couldn't speak. Charlie Wilson continued. "But your father was never very religious. We always had trouble making him go to services. Then, first winter solstice back from college, he announced to the family that he was an atheist. He never went to mass again. Eventually, your grandparents accepted it."

His uncle looked at Marc's limp form. "You look pretty surprised. I know he didn't raise you in the religion, but I thought he might have told you something about your heritage ..."

So ... It was Marc's heritage. It was in his blood. *No wonder I can't seem to fight it.*

⚖⚖

Bob Rosetti woke with a start. He would have jumped up, but he was tied to a bed. He would have yelled, but he was gagged. He was completely naked, his arms and legs each tied to a different bedpost. *Where the hell am I? What am I doing here?*

He recalled the smell of the chloroform. He remembered the young men who had grabbed him in the subway. He had seen the faces of all three men. He was going to die. His struggle against the ropes that bound him resulted in pain, but no progress.

How would his family get by? Thank God he had insurance. Would they know how much he had loved them?

Outside, Dan was pulling up to the cheap Bronx motel

with the prostitute. He had carefully chosen the stoned black teenager. When Dan had handed the boy the hundred-dollar bill, his dull eyes had shown their first spark. When the kid put a hand on Dan's crotch, Dan had immediately grabbed that hand and removed it, squeezing hard. "Not me," said Dan. "I've got a *friend* who's dying to meet you."

"Oh. Don't hurt me, man."

Dan parked right in front of the unit. "My friend's a little freaky," Dan told the boy.

"Hey, man. I don't do no freaks."

"Not *that* freaky. It's just that he likes being tied up."

The young man shrugged. "Oh. That ain't nothing."

"I've already done that part. He's in there, waiting for you. Keep him tied and gagged, but make him feel good. Okay? I'll give you another fifty later."

"You gonna watch?" the kid asked Dan with only mild curiosity. "That would be another fifty anyway."

"Nah. I'll just hang around out here. But I'll go in a moment now, just to introduce you. What's your name?"

"Derek."

Dan unlocked the door. Good. All the ropes were still intact, and Rosetti was awake.

Dan introduced the two men. "Bob Rosetti, this is Derek. Derek, this is Bob. Bob has a little problem getting it up, so you'll have to be a little patient with him. You can tell it'll be big when he's ready, though."

Rosetti's eyes were bulging. He was writhing madly, his massive muscles bunching as he strained against his bonds. The growling noise was muffled by the gag. "Oh, and don't mind if he struggles a little. That helps get him hot. Nice muscles, don't you think?"

Derek kept nodding as he took his shirt off to reveal a scrawny body. "I ain't gonna spend more than half an hour, you know."

"That's fine," said Dan. "I have confidence in your abilities.

Oh, and don't forget to use a condom."

The boy was insulted. "'Course I will," he spat, producing a condom from his pocket. "Don't know where you motherfuckers been."

Dan ignored the insult and played out his part as gracious host. "Well, have a good time, you two. I'll be outside."

After Dan left, Derek took off his pants and knelt next to the bed. Rosetti was still squirming around, pulling against the ropes. And he was still completely limp.

Derek couldn't even put the condom on until he got the customer a little hard, so he reached over and started to massage him with both hands. When it wasn't working so well, he got some K-Y jelly from his discarded pants and put a little on his hands. He worked patiently and silently.

What the fuck is going on here? Rosetti wondered. *Is this going to be a blackmail scheme or what? Get off of me, you fucking queer!*

In the unnatural quiet, Rosetti could hear the faint sounds of the boy's hands as they slipped up and down, spreading the jelly. To Rosetti's disgust, he was starting to harden.

Get the fuck away from me. I got a wife and kids.

Now the boy had rolled the condom onto Rosetti's hard length and buried him deep in his warm mouth. Rosetti's writhing couldn't shake the boy, who was moving steadily and with determination, ignoring Rosetti's muted screeching and grunting as well.

Rosetti ceased all sound and motion. Derek stopped and looked up to see what was going on. Rosetti managed to make choking sounds that the kid heard.

"Don't die on me, man," he said. "I don't care what you like, I'm taking that thing out your mouth."

Yes! Rosetti braced himself. *Be cool.*

The boy untied the handkerchief holding it in place, and pulled the other handkerchief out of Rosetti's mouth. "You okay?"

Rosetti sucked in air in big gulps. "Listen, kid," he said as calmly as he could. "This is a set-up. For both of us. Untie me before they come back."

"You don't want no blow job?" Derek asked in dull confusion.

"Let me go!" Rosetti yelled. "They'll kill us!"

The front door burst open. Dan grabbed Derek and held the chloroformed handkerchief over his face until he slumped over.

"Help!" Rosetti screamed. "Help me!"

Dan thrust the gag back into Rosetti's open mouth. Then he closed the front door and locked it.

"We were just trying to show you a good time," Dan explained, as he put his rubber-gloved hand in the pocket of the boy's pants. "What a spoilsport!" He grinned widely when he found the hoped-for small switchblade.

After killing Rosetti with several swipes of the knife, Dan washed the blade well. He put it and the DA's wallet in the kid's pants. *The boy will run for sure. And just as surely get caught,* he thought. Dan congratulated himself on choosing Derek. *The police will never believe him.*

Dan was disappointed that Rosetti hadn't come. He had felt strongly that a sperm-filled condom would go a long way toward selling this scenario.

Oh well, he thought, pulling out his own condom. *They'll never test the sperm.*

Sixteen

On Saturday night, Marc had a dinner date with his mother. He couldn't think of anything better to do, having hung up before Sam picked up the phone.

Mrs. Wilson was thrilled to have "company," and made her driest brisket. Watery spinach and baked potatoes rounded off an acquired taste of a meal for which Marc had been homesick.

Sylvia Wilson was happy and talkative. She spoke of family and family friends. She spoke of politics and world affairs. But she spoke most effusively about Justice Green.

"He's so smart, but so nice. And he's such a gentleman. He's always complimenting me on my outfits."

"Is the judge hitting on you, Mom?"

"Oh, no!" Mrs. Wilson wasn't the type to blush, but her sheepish facial expression was obviously her equivalent response. "I'm sure he has many lady friends. He wouldn't be interested in me."

"But you like him, don't you? Is he good-looking?"

"No, I don't really think so. It's just been too long since I've spent much time with *any* man."

Marc and his mother both chewed.

"What's the story with Samantha?" Mrs. Wilson asked.

"Well, it didn't really work out."

"Whose fault was that?"

"It's not always somebody's fault," he responded automatically. "I don't want to talk about it. Please."

"As you wish. How's work then?"

"Okay."

"Did you have to work today?"

"Of course."

"I'm proud of you and all," she began, "but you really should slow down."

"I can't."

Sylvia Wilson shook her head in concern. "Oh, that reminds me. Well, not directly, thank God, but speaking of hard-working lawyers, what do you think about what happened to that poor man?"

"What are you talking about?"

"That D.A. The one that got murdered yesterday evening."

"What?" Marc snapped straight up in his seat. "Not Bob Rosetti?"

"Yes. Did you know him?"

"Uh, I, uh, just met him. Uh, once. What happened? How did he die?"

"Calm down, son. I'm sorry to break it to you like this. It's been on the news all day." She looked over at the clock. "It's probably on right now ..."

Marc ran into the living room and switched on the TV. The anchorperson was finishing a story about a city teacher who'd been stabbed. "Are you done with dinner?" Sylvia asked.

"Sorry, Mom," Marc muttered. He added, "It was great. I'm stuffed."

The anchor picked up some papers. "For the latest on the death of Manhattan District Attorney Robert Rosetti, let's go live to Carol Anello. Carol?"

"Thanks, Bill," said Carol. "I'm here live in the Bronx, in

front of the Happy Hour Motel. It was here, at this day-rate motel, known to cater to male and female prostitutes and their clients, that the naked body of Manhattan D.A. Robert Rosetti was discovered late last night by a motel employee. Mr. Rosetti was nude, tied to a bed and dead, having been stabbed several times with a small blade. Now we have word that the police have picked up a suspect. The suspect, seventeen-year-old Derek Jones, was in possession of Mr. Rosetti's wallet and a switchblade that they believe to be the murder weapon. Mr. Jones has a record of arrests for solicitation, but the motive for the murder is believed to have been robbery."

"Well, you never know ..." said Mrs. Wilson.

"Robert Rosetti first made a name for himself during the first Gulf War, where he was the most decorated man in his unit. Attending law school upon his return to the U.S., Rosetti became well known and respected as a tough, determined District Attorney, always particularly hard on juvenile crime and vice. The Manhattan District Attorney's office is in turmoil following the revelation of its chief's shocking death, although Acting District Attorney Jill Montana is already working with the police on the case. Questions and mysteries now surround the man and the circumstances of his death. One can't help but wonder: what sort of double life was Robert Rosetti leading? And was his work affected?"

"Maybe all that work affected *him*!" Mrs. Wilson suggested.

Marc continued staring in silent shock.

"Naturally, this terrible tragedy has come as quite a shock to Mr. Rosetti's wife, Margaret, who survives him with their two children. Joe Milton is live at the Rosettis' apartment on the Upper East Side."

As the show cut to a reporter badgering a crying woman, Marc considered the news. His first, automatic response had been *Jesus, the Committee killed Rosetti!* Now, just a few moments later, calmer reasoning had returned. *That's crazy. The Committee's made up of powerful, greedy networkers, not cold-*

blooded killers. They don't go around murdering people.

He grew calmer still. Anyway, it wouldn't even make sense. What could have been the motive for killing him? His death isn't likely to halt the investigation of the Committee. Rosetti must have been working with assistants on the case. What would the killer have to gain?

So, it was just a coincidence. And a bizarre, tragic news story. Marc was relieved when the show cut back from the hysterical wife to the cool blond anchor.

For a second he selfishly wondered if Rosetti's death meant that *he* was off the hook with the D.A.'s office.

"Did he seem gay to you?" Mrs. Wilson asked.

⚖⚖

On Thursday, Marc accompanied Eckart to federal court on the Hammond Chemical case. Eckart explained to the judge, paraphrasing and excerpting Marc's brief, why the case belonged in Germany, not New York. Eckart had invited Marc along, evidently just for the show.

Eckart argued with the calm, persuasive authority of a brilliant and seasoned attorney with a fix in, Marc surmised. Possibly to make it look good, Judge Pierson reserved her decision. Her clerk would post the opinion online when it was ready. Marc wondered if the clerk had already written the decision.

That night, as usual, Marc watched the news for updates on the Rosetti murder. He had seen friends and family interviewed. Most had expressed shock that Rosetti might have been gay, but a few claimed to have suspected. A manager of the Happy Hour motel said that he thought Rosetti had been a regular motel client. The police examined the motel register from last Friday and found a signature in the name of Vito Corleone that looked like Rosetti's handwriting.

The big story tonight was that Derek Jones, the young, black, drug-addicted, male prostitute murder suspect, had pled guilty to involuntary manslaughter at his arraignment. Carol Anello added, "Acting District Attorney Jill Montana has recommended the acceptance of this reduced plea on the condition that Jones receive the maximum sentence for the lesser crime and undergo drug rehabilitation. This plea marks a drastic change in the defense strategy. Just yesterday the defense was continuing to claim that D.A. Rosetti had been killed by a young *white* man who had originally hired Mr. Jones to provide sexual favors to the Manhattan D.A. at the Happy Hour Motel. Police were unconvinced by the suspect's story, having found both the murder weapon and Mr. Rosetti's wallet in Mr. Jones's pocket at the time of his arrest. Mr. Jones's sentencing has yet to be scheduled."

The next morning in the office, Marc received a phone call from a stranger. The woman identified herself as Sarah, and said that they used to have a mutual acquaintance. "Could you meet my new boss for dim sum?"

Shit! Marc had been expecting something like this. *Might as well get it over with.*

Acting District Attorney Jill Montana was already waiting by the crowded bar when Marc arrived at Primola. Marc had chosen the time and location, partly because he had been busy at work all day Friday, partly to test how important he was to the D.A., and to attempt to take some control over circumstances. Other minor motivations had been his uncluttered social calendar, as well as the extremely pleasant appearance of the new D.A., as seen on the TV news.

Ms. Montana was about forty and Marc thought she bore a striking resemblance to Jennifer Connelly, an actress whose body of work Marc had always enjoyed. Although her blue suit was tasteful and professional, Marc was most appreciative of how well tailored the suit was. Marc had worn *his* best-fitting suit and shirt for the hell of it.

Out of curiosity, Marc pretended not to notice or recognize Ms. Montana, and walked toward a different end of the bar.

A few moments later, she walked over to him. "Marc Wilson?" she asked him.

"Yes," Marc admitted. "But how did you know?"

The D.A. smiled self-consciously. "You want to see if we can get a table?"

Marc shrugged, but she was already talking to the hostess. The woman showed them to a small centrally located table.

"Do you have anything a little quieter? More in the corner?" the D.A. asked.

"Sorry. You want to wait?"

"How long?"

"Fifteen, twenty minutes?" the hostess asked them.

Montana looked around in disappointment. "I guess this is okay," she said.

"Good!" the hostess beamed, disappearing instantly.

"A little noisy," the D.A. commented to Marc. "And cramped." The tables on each side of them were less than two feet away.

"So, what's this about?" Marc pressed, ignoring her discomfort.

Jill Montana looked nervously at each of the two couples surrounding them. "I think you know. You spoke to ..." She lowered her voice further, bringing her head closer. "Rosetti."

"You mean *he* spoke to me."

Acting D.A. Montana maintained low, even tones. "Cut the semantic bullshit. Who killed Rosetti?"

"You mean it wasn't that black kid on the news?"

"You tell me."

"All I know is what I saw on T.V."

"You're that uninformed?"

"Isn't the kid going to jail?"

"It looks like it."

"Would you care for cocktails?" the waitress asked them.

"No thank you," Montana answered.

"No thanks."

"Are you ready to order dinner?"

"Sure," said Marc. "I'll have the calamari fra diavolo with linguine."

"Oh, let me see," Montana stalled. "Uh, I'll have the angel hair in light crème sauce."

"Very good," the server commented and walked off.

Marc asked the troubling question. "If you don't think he did it, how can you let Derek Jones go to jail?"

"The kid confessed!" she pointed out angrily. "What can I do? Refuse to let them lock him up? I don't have anything concrete enough. I'm not going to jump the gun." She eyed Marc across the table. "Unless you can tell me right now that you'll give me evidence of who did it ..." After a moment: "Too bad. I'm going to build a strong case before I show my hand."

"Why do you think the Ethics Committee had anything to do with his death? Wasn't Rosetti working on several investigations?" Marc was sincerely curious, and sufficiently ignorant to act innocent.

"Why should *I* share anything with *you*?" Montana's tone was turning antagonistic. The couple to their right turned and looked at them for just a moment.

The pastas arrived and a busboy came by with a pepper mill. "Fresh pepper?" he asked. They both refused politely.

"Look," said Montana, "I could use help. And, on the other hand, I don't particularly want to send you up the river. If you really don't know much about the Committee yet, I'd like you to make an effort to find out more and pass it on to me."

"I don't know if there's much to find out," said Marc.

Acting D.A. Montana twirled a forkful of angel hair, then pursed her full lips in thought. "A lot of people would consider Satan-worshipping a big story."

How could she know that? Rosetti didn't seem to. They must already have an agent on the Committee, as Rosetti implied.

No! Have to hang tough. Can't let her bluff me into giving up my career for the sake of her religious prejudices.

"What are you talking about?" Marc asked convincingly, committing himself to ignorance.

"You really are full of shit. I was hoping you wouldn't be." She took a big mouthful of angel hair, speeding up the meal.

"What do you mean? Did you say '*Satan*'?"

"I suppose you'd take an oath that you've never been to a black mass ..." Now the couple on the left glanced over discreetly.

Marc gave her a look like she was kidding. "Not lately anyway." Marc forced a laugh and held up his right hand. "I swear."

"Yes, but who do you swear *to*? I can't trust you."

"I can't *understand* you." Marc thrust several tentacles of spicy calamari in his mouth.

"Look, I'm just going to say a few more things and then the show will be over: you're free to pretend you don't understand. I know that most people on the Committee don't take the religious part seriously. I know that mostly it's just a corrupt favor-swapping network. But I think that one or two individuals on the Committee have started to take *Him* a little more seriously. And I think that those individuals are responsible for killing Rosetti and Thornton, and several innocent young children."

Children? Is she insane? Where is she coming up with this wild shit?

"You *are* crazy, aren't you," Marc stated matter-of-factly. Despite his certainty, he felt a little queasy.

Montana was similarly straightforward and unemotional. "If you don't know now, someday you will. When you realize I'm right, if you haven't been indicted yet, see me."

Seventeen

The next Ethics Committee meeting was the Tuesday afternoon before Thanksgiving, in the Bar Association building.
The meeting was short and business-like. The only religious ele-
ment, other than the occasional muttered "be it His will," was a
brief generic prayer said in honor of not just one, but *two* Committee members who had died since Halloween. Both men had
died of massive heart attacks within a week of each other. Each
man had been over sixty, with a hearty appetite for beef and
pork. Marc only remembered Don O'Neill vaguely as the man
who had praised Charlie Wilson so highly at the first Committee meeting Marc attended.

Baylor was genuinely upset. "Don O'Neill and Sam Knight
were two of our oldest and most valued members. They were
the backbone of our Committee. We will all miss them terribly. I
know that many of you were at their funerals." He made it sound
like each man had more than one funeral. *Probably did,* Marc
thought. *A public ceremony with a priest or minister. Followed by
what? A midnight visit to the gravesite? And a few blasphemies ...*

Baylor lowered his gaze slightly as he intoned, "O Great
and Powerful One, we commend to You Your servants, Donald

and Samuel. We know that You have called them to You as part
of Your mysterious plan." Many in the room joined Baylor as
he continued: "May You find them worthy, O Mighty One, to
continue to serve You, sitting at Your left hand among Your vast
and awesome legions."

Marc glanced around the room to judge the reactions of
individuals. In general, the older members appeared to be more
affected by the deaths. Paul, sitting next to Marc, looked like he
had other things on his mind. Joe, Scott, Dan and Larry, sitting
right in front of Marc and Paul, didn't seem to be paying much
attention either. Joe was whispering something to Scott.

Eckart, sitting three rows ahead of Marc and Paul, had
taken Doris Spender's hand to comfort her. He looked almost as
sad as she did.

"When we lose beloved colleagues like these, it's difficult
not to stop and think about our own mortality." Baylor paused,
mastering his emotions.

Joe whispered to Scott again. Marc only caught one word:
"devout." Scott nodded. Dan softly shushed them both.

Just then Baylor remembered to add, "Anyone who has
not yet done so is invited to make a donation to the American
Heart Society in their names."

Committee members are dying fast, Marc thought. *At least
these last two died of natural causes.*

Marc spent Thanksgiving with Mom and Great Aunt Helen,
who was "feeling a little better, thank you sweetheart." Helen
had supposedly found some crackpot lawyer to take her applesauce case. *I suppose someone should check if the guy's passed
the New York bar*, Marc thought. *On the other hand, Helen's so
happy, why mess with it?*

Sitting next to Great Aunt Helen, Marc was glad that he
had a job. *It's worth it*, he thought. Helen was impressed with the

big fresh turkey and assorted side dishes that Marc had picked up from a caterer this year, as well as the breathtaking bouquet of flowers that he had sent to his mother yesterday. The large arrangement sat smack in the center of the dinner table, squeezed into his mother's only vase, a tall, thick glass tower. Sylvia Wilson couldn't take her eyes off of it. *She's so easily pleased. I can't wait till Chanukah, when I'll replace that gold necklace she lost in August.*

Marc's thoughts turned once again to Samantha. *We just weren't each other's type*, he thought. *But I don't care. I really miss her.*

"It's been cold lately, don't you think?" said Helen.

Marc's mother joined in enthusiastically. "It sure has been. And it's supposed to get even colder this weekend!"

"That's what I heard on Channel 4," said Helen.

"I just can't take the winters like I used to," Sylvia Wilson announced.

"I'm still working on that place in Miami Beach, you know," said Marc. "I want you to retire and move down there, just like Cousin Gertie. What about you, Aunt Helen? Do you want to go too?"

"Oh no, thank you. I wouldn't know what to do in Florida."

"What a sweet boy," his mother said. "But really, you've got to stop worrying about *us*."

"Who should I worry about?" Marc asked. "Who's more important than my family?"

"I'm just glad that *you're* happy," his mother said. "You seem to be doing so well at your new job. All you needed was a chance to prove yourself."

Marc squirmed in his seat.

"You should be proud. I certainly am," Sylvia Wilson said with a big smile. After a moment's thought, she added, "Wherever he is, I'm sure your father's proud of you too."

"Do you even know what I do?" Marc blurted out.

"You write briefs and go to court, right?" said Aunt Helen.

"Do you know who I work for?"

"What's wrong, honey?" Sylvia asked.

Marc continued. "I defend companies that destroy the environment. Usually they only kill animals, but sometimes they kill people too."

"I'm sorry," said Sylvia. "I had no idea ... Really ..."

Marc was silent as his mother put her hand on his and patted him gently.

⚖

When he showed up without warning, Marc was sure that the first expressions on Sam's face were surprise, happiness, and possibly affection. He held onto that image as Sam regained her composure and asked, "What are you doing here?"

"I want to make some big changes in my life."

Again, Sam's face betrayed her briefly before she smoothed it. "Good. But what does that have to do with me?"

"I have to talk to someone. And there are several reasons why it has to be you. Can I come in?"

After a moment, Sam stepped aside and beckoned Marc into her apartment. Marc sat down on her couch.

"I'm sick of defending polluters," he said.

Sam looked skeptical. "So, are you going to quit your job?"

"I wish it were that simple."

"There you go again, with the excuses ..."

"That's not it. There's more than just pollution going on. And I'm in deeper than you know."

"What are you talking about?"

"I can't just walk away. I have to do something positive. Something to stop all the corruption."

"So now you're going to be a crusader?" She was still skeptical, but interested.

"Your father's involved in at least some of it. That's one of the reasons I wanted to talk to you."

"My father? He's done something worse than just defending polluters?"

I have to tell her before I go ahead with this. I think I can trust her. I have to. Where to start?

"First of all, there's something fishy about that chemical leak in Germany. It's possible that your father knows what really happened and is helping to hide it."

"What makes you think so?"

"It's all circumstantial. Some discrepancies on dates that your father dismissed too readily, and some Nazi connections."

"What?"

"It's a long story. But I want to investigate further, get to the bottom of it. How do you feel about that?"

Sam looked him in the eyes. "I can't believe Dad's involved. But I'm certainly not going to tell you to forget it. You *should* want to find out what really happened."

"I've also seen circumstantial evidence that certain judges are corrupt."

"*That* doesn't surprise me," said Sam.

"These judges, and the Ethics Committee, and your father, they're all bound together by a common interest." Marc watched Sam intently. "Do you know what they have in common?"

Sam shrugged. "How could I know? I'm not even in the game."

"They all ... Every one of them ... They worship Satan."

Sam laughed. "I always knew lawyers were evil. I should have guessed that they'd worship Satan."

"What makes you think I'm kidding?"

Sam stopped laughing. "My dad goes to church every week. He does charity work. You're crazy."

This was a big mistake. "You were right before. I *am* just making excuses. I've been working too hard."

"Has this all been some sort of joke, or what? Are you going to quit or not?"

"No. I enjoy working with your father too much. It's just

that I've been missing you ..."

"I think you should leave now."

On his way to the door, Marc said, "You won't tell your father about this meeting, will you?"

"I'm going to try to forget it myself."

Eighteen

Marc needed more information. His rash conversation with Sam drove that point home. He didn't understand what a Satanist was, let alone what the Satanists on the Committee were doing.

He was resolved to change his life. But he couldn't quit his job and the Committee blindly. He had to know more about the Committee in order to understand what he was involved in and how to get out. Staying at his job and on the Committee a little longer would give him a chance to gather more information.

If Jill Montana was right and some of the Committee members were responsible for murders, then he wanted to know who they were. So he could watch his back more effectively. And so he could work with Montana to get them locked up.

But I can't talk to the D.A. until I know more. No sense running the risk of someone on the Committee finding out that I've collaborated with law enforcement until I have sufficiently useful information. Also, I'll be in a better position to bargain my way out of conspiracy charges once I've determined whether or not there is a conspiracy, and who is involved.

Marc decided that he'd begin shadowing members of the

Committee the upcoming weekend. First, he wanted an answer to the general question: what's a Satanist? He began his investigation in the same way that he, as a junior associate attorney, would start any project. That meant research.

The Internet yielded hundreds of crackpot sites with snippets of inherently unreliable-looking information. This project was going to require fieldwork.

It was more like researching for a term paper than a brief, so the Manhattan Bar Association library would be of no use. Marc started by visiting an occult bookstore in the East Village called the Magick Circle. The shop was much more eclectic than he required, boasting sections on New Age, Wicca, Shamanism, Tibet, Gnosticism and more. The portion of the store devoted to Satan was disappointingly small and tame, focusing more on antiseptic-looking history books than topics like how to vivisect a sacrifice. Nonetheless, Marc felt nervous and awkward, especially when fending off an offer of help from the tall salesperson with a serpent tattoo on his bald head. *Would a devout Committee member shop here, or would these books be kid stuff?* After a short while, the combination of burning incenses and exotic-herbs-by-the-ounce made him dizzy and forced him to leave empty-handed.

The Forty-First Street branch of the New York Public Library provided a much more comfortable, familiar environment in which Marc could get to know Satan. Marc sat at a table in a far corner of the second floor, surrounded by books on the occult, witchcraft, and Satanism. He imagined some friend of his mother's wandering by and noting the ominous collection of titles on his table. "I'm working on a screenplay," he would explain.

Marc had known a little about the occult and Satanism, mainly from movies and television. And from things he had guessed at Committee ceremonies. But now he wanted a more comprehensive understanding of the history and belief systems of Satanism. He wanted to figure out the origins of what he had seen so far, and to speculate intelligently as to what an individual with more extreme beliefs might do.

It was confusing. The books agreed on some things and disagreed on others, focusing on different individuals and themes. But, after many hours, Marc began to see some of the common links between many of the forms of mysticism. As he skimmed through book after book, he took a few notes on each of many topics, supplementing his file by copying whole pages full of additional details that might or might not turn out to be relevant.

One book traced the development of the concept of Satan, from an occasional incidental reference in the latter half of the Old Testament to the popular star of stage and screen of today. To the early Jews, the word "Satan" meant "accuser" or "adversary," and many scholars think that Satan was originally intended to be purely figurative, with no distinct spiritual being at all. Satan's role first expanded after the ancient Jews of Babylonia were exposed to the Zoroastrian religion, and its teachings of the eternal struggle between the forces of light and darkness, by their Persian liberators, circa 535 b.c. During that time, Judaic demonology thrived, and Satan became the serpent that tempted Eve, the originator of all evil and the author of death. Satan made his first appearance as a major character in the contemporaneously written book of Job, discussed extensively by Carl Jung as a vital bridge between the Old and New Testaments.

For over a thousand years, as Christianity was spread around the world by soldiers and missionaries, local pagan traditions became blended with the newer Christian customs. The Celts of Wales and Scotland maintained some of their Druidic beliefs, the Egyptians held on to elements of their cult of Osiris, the Greeks retained a love for their wild fertility gods, Dionysus and Pan. In Scandinavia and what was to become Germany, the Teutonic peoples continued to worship their warlike deities, including the treacherous horned god Loge, or Loki, even after adopting Christianity.

In the Middle Ages, the Church turned first outward to the

Middle East, launching the bloody Crusades against the fast-growing Moslem masses. After many years of bloodshed and defeat, the Church finally called the troops home and turned its sights inward. The Holy Inquisition was established to battle the perceived growing tide of blasphemy within the Church itself.

Besides the unfortunate individual Christians and thousands of Jews who were tortured and/or killed by the Inquisition, many whole sects were banned and destroyed entirely. First hit were the Manichaean sects, such as the Cathari, the Albigenses and the Waldenses. Ironically, the Cathari had condemned the *Catholics* for not renouncing all Jewish influences and sources, because the Cathari believed that the Old Testament God was cruel and capricious, the equivalent of Satan.

According to one source on Marc's table, some philosophers and theologians have written that the Cathari were partly right. The Old Testament God, Yahweh, *was* part "devil," in that he could be angry, vengeful, destructive. Christianity split God into Jesus and Satan, attributing all violence and destruction to Satan. Over the years, some Satanists and a few Christian philosophers, such as Clement of Rome, have considered Satan as part of a trinity: God the Father, Jesus and Satan.

The author of one of the books Marc was reading made the point that, although many religions have postulated a symbol of evil, only under Christianity has a separate movement developed to worship the anti-God. The author speculated that Satanism was the result of Christian repression. By defining all self-indulgence as evil, Christianity created an unprecedented gap between its followers' conscious and unconscious minds, and an irrepressible obsession with forbidden carnal pleasures. The Christian Church created Satan and gave him awesome power and appeal.

Almost all of the volumes Marc perused mentioned the medieval Knights Templar as an important influence on most modern occult societies, although the Church banned the group way back in the 14th Century. Allegedly, this elite society of war heroes from the Crusades had picked up blasphemous practices from the Moslems and Gnostics with whom they had had contact.

Rumors continue, however, to this very day that the secretive and powerful Templars survive and carry on their mysterious rituals. It is undisputed that their influence is still felt in the secret Masonic orders, whose structures and beliefs they inspired. First, came the Freemasons themselves, then the Bavarian Illuminati, founded by a law professor who believed that the whole world should be ruled by the few as Enlightened as himself. In the late 1800s, the British Golden Dawn Society thrived, boasting illustrious members such as William Butler Yeats, Algernon Blackwood, Sax Rohmer and Bram Stoker. Aleister Crowley first belonged to the order of the Golden Dawn, then became most closely associated with the German *Ordo Templi Orientalis* (the "O.T.O.").

Didn't Paul mention Crowley that night he started to explain the Committee to me?

At that moment, Marc's phone rang four times and his answering machine kicked into action. "I can't come to the phone right now," it said. "Please leave a message when you hear the beep."

"Hi, Marc. This is your Uncle Charlie calling. Sorry I missed you. I'd like to get together with you sometime soon. When it's convenient." The voice was smooth and friendly. "Why don't you come over for dinner next Saturday? You can bring your mom. Or your girl. Or both. Give me a call when you have a chance. But you'll have a hard time convincing me to take no for an answer."

Meanwhile, Marc was finding that historians varied drastically

in their assessments of Aleister Crowley. Was he a writer, a phi-
losopher, a prophet, a demon, a performance artist, all or none
of the above? Did he have any talent at any of these roles? Most
agreed that he was a heroin addict, a bisexual and a pedophile.
Some speculated that satisfying his varied and voracious hedonistic urges was the primary motivation for his life and writings.

Although Crowley called himself the "Great Beast 666,"
and the English press dubbed him "the wickedest man in the
world," most historians considered the term "Satanist" to have
been inappropriate in relation to him. Crowley attempted to em-
ploy the scientific process to create a system he called "Magick,"
a sophisticated mixture of Hebrew Kabbalistic and Egyptian
magic, combined with elements of Tantric yoga.

Crowley's system placed vital importance on sex as a
means to power. By bastardizing previous theories of sexual
control into practices of sexual indulgence, Crowley created an
appealing system and drew followers to his abbey in Cefalu, Sicily.
In the frontispiece to his 1904 *Book of the Law*, allegedly dictat-
ed by the guardian angel, Aiwass, Crowley introduced his variation on the words of the French philosopher-satirist Rabelais:
"Do what thou wilt shall be the whole of the law."

Crowley's followers revived barbaric rites dating back to
the Dionysian cults of ancient Greece, similar to but more intense than the purely hedonistic couplings of the socially elite
eighteenth-century London Hellfire Club. *Paul mentioned
them too.* Mussolini expelled Crowley and his people from
Sicily after a male follower died from drinking the blood of a
distempered cat.

In a book entitled *The Nazis and the Occult*, Marc learned
that one of those influenced by Crowley's writings was Dr.
Karl Haushofer, a German geopolitician and occultist. Having
traveled to Japan and Tibet and become an expert on Eastern
religions, Dr. Haushofer's theories on metaphysics were as influential on his disciple, Adolf Hitler, as was his theory that Germany's conquest of the world was justified and necessitated by

the German people's need for "living space." Before World War I, Haushofer was in close contact with the British Golden Dawn Society at the time it was headed by Aleister Crowley. In 1910, Crowley had published a tract concerning the origins and powers of a magical Indian symbol employed by the Golden Dawn, the swastika. Crowley later claimed that the Nazis had stolen the sacred swastika from him.

The Nazis only sometimes paid lip service to Christianity. Jews were reviled because, in addition to being genetically inferior and "unclean," they allegedly engaged in Satanic practices and blasphemed against Christianity. The Nazis openly criticized contemporary Freemasons for similar reasons. Yet it is clear that Hitler and the Nazis were in fact Satanists, who claimed to carry on the traditions of the oldest Masonic orders such as the Templars.

The Nazis' occasional efforts to link themselves with Christianity were themselves blasphemous. For example, art shops in Berlin prominently displayed portraits of Jesus Christ, surrounded by similar paintings of Hitler. Yet a Nazi tract bearing the title "What the Christian Does Not Know About Christianity" made this blunt statement:

"If Jehovah has lost all meaning for us Germans, the same must be said of Jesus Christ, his son. He does not possess those moral qualities which the Church claims for him. He certainly lacks those characteristics which he would require to be a true German. Indeed, he is as disappointing, if we read the record carefully, as is his father."

The coming of a German Messiah had been predicted for years by a small inner core of the mystical, anti-Semitic Thule Society, led by a man named Dietrich Eckart. It was the well-connected Eckart who first introduced Hitler into Munich high society and promoted him as "the long-promised savior."

Marc couldn't find any more details about Dietrich Eckart, like where and when he was born, where and when he had died, what family he had left behind. *I'm sure it's a common name*, he thought.

At that moment, Marc's phone rang two times and his answering machine greeted the caller.

"Shit!" Jill Montana hung up before the beep.

Marc's research continued chronologically and returned him to the United States. Marc read that during the last few years before Crowley died of his heroin addiction in 1947, the U.S. branch of the O.T.O. was conducting massive orgies on huge estates in Pasadena, California. Led by Jack Parsons, one of the inventors of rocket-propulsion, and L. Ron Hubbard, science fiction writer and future author of *Dianetics* and founder of the Church of Scientology, the U.S. O.T.O. devoted itself primarily to the self-assigned task of incarnating the Biblical Whore of Babylon through sex and incantations. Parsons proved to be infertile, and he blew himself up during strange chemical experiments in his basement.

As Marc's reading took him into the sixties, he finally started recognizing some names and incidents, although he hadn't been born yet then. Marc learned that San Francisco had been the center of both the flower people and the Satan people. Charles Manson, who was known to refer to himself as Christ *and* Satan, was associated with The Process, a religious organization founded by Robert and Mary Anne DeGrimston after they met at the London Scientology Institute.

Robert DeGrimston became convinced that he was Jesus Christ, but The Process taught that Jehovah and Satan were coming together for the last days, and that anyone who committed himself or herself to either path would achieve salvation. DeGrimston preached that Armageddon should be hastened by confusion, murder and death. Like Manson, DeGrimston actively recruited from violent biker groups, such as the Hell's

Angels, Gypsy Jokers, Satan's Slaves and the Straight Satans. Although the Process has been officially disbanded since 1974, DeGrimston's writings have been credited with inspiring numerous serial killers, including New York's own Son of Sam killer, David Berkowitz.

According to several sources, the most influential Satanist to come out of San Francisco, or anywhere, in the last fifty years, was Anton LaVey, the founder of the Church of Satan. At the height of his fame and influence, the ex-circus performer attracted celebrities like Sammy Davis, Jr., Keenan Wynn and Jayne Mansfield. Marc thought it odd that he had never heard of the man, but the books said that LaVey had been keeping a lower profile since the late '70s. Once a media darling, LaVey more recently avoided the spotlight without explanation. Membership in the Church of Satan dropped from its high-point in the sixties, but millions of people and numerous covens and Church of Satan splinter groups continued to read and use his seminal bestsellers, *The Satanic Bible* and *The Satanic Rituals*, as starting points in Satan worship.

Having traced the history of Satanism from ancient times to the present, Marc found himself with two crucial questions: how many people worship Satan in the United States today, and what sort of things do these people do in the name of their Dark Lord?

"What did the boss say he wanted Sunday?" Dan asked.

"Just the basic this time," said Larry. "Nothing special."

"Good. You know *my* preferences."

"Can't she be a *little* older?"

In a way, the question of what sort of things Satanists might do was easier, because Marc was convinced by his research and the media that there was little that *some* sick and dangerous individual wouldn't do. Marc had often seen stories in the tabloids and on TV about the ritual abuse and/or murder of children. Not just on Dr.Phil either, but on *60 Minutes, Dateline* and other prime time "news magazines."

Marc had listened skeptically while seemingly reputable psychologists and psychiatrists told of troubled adult patients who have regressed through hypnosis to recall previously-repressed traumatic childhood experiences in which they were forced to participate in brutal Satanic rituals, sometimes by their own parents. Ten, twenty, thirty years after the fact, patients supposedly first "remembered" being serially raped by cult members, or being forced to slay others their own age with sacrificial daggers. Of course, equally well-trained psychologists have expressed skepticism concerning these stories, speculating that some of their colleagues are, possibly inadvertently, planting suggestions that inspire these Satanic "memories."

How could people be so evil? Marc skimmed a popular book from the '90s called *People of the Lie*, by psychiatrist M. Scott Peck, author of the bestselling self-help volume, *The Road Less Traveled*. Marc was surprised to find that Peck believed in the existence of the spirit of Satan, and the need for exorcisms. Peck also believed in the existence of truly evil men, whose narcissism is so total that they lack all capacity for empathy. These sociopaths are greedy in every way and totally unconcerned about the effects of their actions on others.

The question of how *many* Satan-worshippers there were currently, and to what extent they were organized, was harder to answer. Although a purportedly comprehensive FBI study from the '70s found no evidence of organized Satanic violence in the U.S., many remain unconvinced. An officer in the Beaumont, California police department was quoted as estimating that ninety-five percent of all missing children are the victims of occult-related abductions. An intelligence officer with the San Francisco

Police Department wrote a nationally circulated memorandum listing "Satanic" items of evidence for investigators to look for at a crime scene. A Boise, Idaho-based newsletter known as *File 18* purports to monitor criminal cult activity and assumes the existence of an international Satanist conspiracy.

"Time's almost up." The librarian came by to announce that closing time was only ten minutes away. A few of the books in Marc's pile caught her eye. "I'm a writer," he mumbled.

Enough of this book learning. I've got to find out what's really going on here and now.

⚖⚖

It was dark. And hot. And smelly. There was lots of sweat and stuff, and the baby needed changing. The little five-year-old girl could barely move without hitting the crying baby that had been squeezed into the cage with her. She wished the baby would shut up.

The girl could barely see the shapes of the dancing grown-ups in the flicker of the candles. She couldn't see faces or recognize anyone. She could only tell that there were men and women and they didn't have clothes on anymore either.

The girl had still been dizzy when they had taken off her clothes and pushed her into the cage. She wondered how cherry Kool-Aid could have made her so tired. She still felt like she might be dreaming.

What was she doing here? What were they going to do to her? Where was her daddy?

Big hands opened the cage and reached in. First the baby was pulled out and taken away. *Good. It was smelly and noisy anyway.*

"You're next," said the deep voice. "Come on out." Her muscles were too cramped, and the cage was too high up. He had to reach in and drag the little pretzel-girl out.

She was so happy to be out. She felt comfortable in his big strong arms. She couldn't make out his face but his voice was familiar and soothing. "You're so pretty," he said. *I am?*

When he started to kiss her all over, she felt funny. "Let me go," she said, her voice coming out like a whisper instead of the scream she wanted to make.

When he put her down and the others started to kiss and touch her, she got really scared. She lay still on the table, staring straight up. There was nothing she could do.

"Not yet," he ordered.

Samantha Eckart sprang up in bed, clutching the covers tightly against her drenched body.

Nineteen

Thursday morning, Marc stared angrily at the government's discovery responses in the Gutierrez case. The attorney for the city had left many questions unanswered, asserting that they were irrelevant and burdensome. *Judge Kelly isn't going to let them get away with that.*

The phone on Marc's desk rang. Marc could see on the display line that the call was from Eckart. Usually Marc liked that display feature, but sometimes he hated the choices it offered. He didn't feel like talking to Eckart, but was there anything to be gained in the long run from ducking him?

Marc always felt awkward with Eckart, but now he was particularly uncomfortable as a result of the combination of owing Eckart a memo on some new water pollution regulations and planning to investigate the secrets of the Ethics Committee and discuss them with Acting D.A. Montana. Plus, he hoped that Sam hadn't said anything to him about their last conversation. *Oh, what the hell ...*

"Hi, Bill," Marc answered. *No point in pretending he didn't know who was calling.*

"Hi, Marc. How's it going?"

"Fine. What's up?" Marc fought the urge to bring up the water pollution memo preemptively.

"Not too much. Mainly I was wondering what you were doing for lunch."

That was a surprise. Marc hadn't eaten with Eckart since the last German trip. Still, it wasn't so unusual, given the fact that Eckart always made some effort to treat Paul and him as friends and near peers. *Well, might as well go all the way with it. He's my boss. Can't put him off like my uncle.*

"Bringing in from a salad bar," Marc answered, "unless you have any better ideas."

"How about Smith and Wollensky's Grill? I'm afraid you haven't been eating enough red meat. You're not losing that killer instinct, are you?" Eckart joked.

"Au contraire," Marc joked right back. "I'm working my way up the food chain."

Although there were other worthy choices on the menu, Marc and Eckart both ordered steaks. To Marc's intense relief, Eckart did not bring up either the memo or the Acting District Attorney. To his excruciating discomfort and surprise, however, Eckart asked Marc, "What happened with you and Samantha?"

How much does he know? And how does he know it? "Well, Samantha's terrific," Marc began nervously. "But we just weren't right for each other."

"That's too bad. What happened?"

Marc looked down at his plate and cleared his throat. *Could Sam have told him anything about our last conversation? Or could he have guessed what I'm planning?*

"Never mind," said Eckart good-naturedly. "I'm just being nosy and overprotective. So, have you now been in touch with your uncle?" Eckart asked.

Still reeling from the last subject, Marc shrugged absent-mindedly. "A little."

"Have you been to his house?"

"Not for many years."

"Hasn't he invited you lately?"

"How do you know that?"

"Many on the Committee know of your uncle's interest in you. As I told you before, you should get to know him better."

Marc decided to take one step out onto a limb in order to learn something. "My uncle didn't get along with my father. I don't really like my uncle."

"I know," said Eckart, sending chills down Marc's spine. "But it doesn't mean you shouldn't get to know him better." Eckart was leaning in close to Marc now, speaking in low, almost fatherly tones. "Charlie Wilson's a very important, powerful man. And *he* likes *you*. You could learn a lot from him. We all could. Take this advice seriously."

What could Marc say? Something diplomatic. Something other than the fact that he had already left a message turning down dinner with Uncle Charlie this Saturday. "I take everything you tell me seriously," he assured Eckart sincerely. "I appreciate your concern for me and my career."

Something alarming happened on the way back to the office. As he and Eckart approached their building, Marc noticed her from half a block away. He instinctively turned to Eckart, who didn't seem to have noticed anyone unusual. To her credit, Jill Montana must have spotted them too. When Marc looked ahead again, the Acting D.A. had vanished into the crowd.

A few minutes later, Marc came back down to the lobby alone. He took a walk, tracing a three-block circle of the building. Despite his intention of being vigilant, she snuck up on him at a street corner and subtly brushed against him. Hiding both his surprise and his irritation, he pretended to ignore her. She did likewise as she crossed the street and picked up her pace. He followed at a distance as she walked five more blocks, then descended into a subway station. They each swiped a Metrocard, then proceeded to the deserted northernmost end of the platform.

"Damn it," he whispered forcefully. "Stop hanging around

my place of business!"

"Why do you care? Who on your squeaky clean Committee would care if you talked to the D.A.?"

"I honestly don't know. But if there's *anything* to your suspicions, I don't want to be seen with you."

"*Is* there anything to my suspicions?"

"I don't know. But maybe I might find out."

Montana calmed down and looked interested. Marc tried to ignore her physical charms, reminding himself that her interest was purely in justice. Whether or not that involved putting him behind bars.

"I'm not making any promises," Marc explained. "It's just that *I* want to know what's going on myself."

"What do you know so far? What makes you think something's going on?"

"Really nothing," he replied. "I don't have anything to tell you now."

"How long am I supposed to wait?" she asked as the train started to pull in.

"Don't call me," he advised. "I'll call you."

"I'll give you two weeks, unharassed," she announced. She turned and took a few steps south, putting distance between them before the train stopped. "Then you won't be able to get rid of me."

The next stage of the investigation was finding out what a specific Satanist does with his Sundays. According to Marc's research, many Satanists celebrated Sundays as an anti-Sabbath. Since Joe Garrett had made some sort of religious comment about the two Committee members who died, Marc decided to start by following him. *Maybe he's a fanatic?*

It turned out that following someone is surprisingly easy. Especially in New York. Lots of crowds to blend into, even when it isn't Christmas shopping season, plus the average New Yorker's in his own world anyway. Joe Garrett was an average New Yorker, in that respect at least. He *never* looked behind him.

Joe didn't leave his west side apartment building until 11 a.m. *You're missing church, aren't you?* Marc thought.

Joe picked up a bagel of some sort a block away, then headed over to what turned out to be his friend Scott's apartment. Fifteen minutes later they both came down and picked up a car from a nearby parking garage. Scott was driving. *Scott owns and garages a car in Manhattan?! A Lexus yet! Is he rich or insane?*

Fortunately, Marc had no trouble getting a cab. There was no avoiding the cliché, so he milked it: "Follow that car. Keep an average of two car lengths behind and there's an extra twenty in it for you."

Joe and Scott found a metered spot on Forty-First Street and Ninth Avenue next to the Port Authority Bus Terminal just before noon. They sat in the car. And sat. Marc had the cab driver circle the block, then park a short block above Joe and Scott. The taxi's meter kept running. The cab driver remained silent and uninquisitive.

Marc watched Scott's car with an old pair of small but powerful binoculars. He could see the car well, but he couldn't see the passengers from his angle. Periodically, Marc scanned around the car, attempting to ascertain if they were looking at something in particular or waiting for someone. The only person nearby was a Salvation Army Santa.

At approximately 12:20 p.m., three people came out of the Bus Terminal and headed toward the car. Marc recognized Dan and Larry from the Committee, but he didn't recognize the little blond girl with them. He supposed she could be a ten-or eleven-year-old niece of one of them, but somehow he doubted it. First of all, these four didn't strike him as the type who got together on a weekend to hang out with young relatives. Also, there was something strange about the girl. She looked tired, kind of weak and sort of sad, despite the fact that her face was smudged with chocolate ice cream. And the brand-new Barbie doll in her arms clashed with her worn and dirty clothes.

Marc absorbed all this in the minute between when the three walked out of the Port Authority, located the waiting car, and climbed into it. Then he told the cab driver, "Follow that car again. Please."

They went down and further west, parking on Eleventh Avenue in the high 20s. Marc asked the driver to double-park, then follow the five slowly at a distance after they got out of the car. It was a calculated choice between risks. There were few cabs or people in this neighborhood.

The five stopped and went into an entranceway. Marc could see through his binoculars that Dan pressed an intercom button. Marc was pretty sure that it was the top button on the right side. A moment later, all five disappeared through the inner door.

Marc handed the taxi driver fifty bucks and thanked him. "Need a receipt?" the driver grunted. "No thanks," Marc answered as he disembarked. He almost laughed at the thought of submitting this receipt to the firm for reimbursement.

Marc found an entranceway across the street, not too close or too far, with a view of the other entrance, and he waited. *What the hell could be going on between those five in this deserted area?* His curiosity grew as more and more time passed. He sat down and continued his vigil.

A few minutes before 2 p.m., four more people arrived. Marc recognized each one as a Committee member between the ages of thirty and forty. They buzzed and went up. *Did the Committee call a meeting without telling me?* he wondered.

After that, they came in ones and twos. Although Marc couldn't always see their faces, he recognized all but a few of them from the Ethics Committee. One or two seemed familiar from elsewhere, while a few seemed totally unfamiliar.

A chubby graying woman with a pageboy haircut arrived alone in a cab. Marc realized with a chilling certainty that this was Judge Irma Clemmons. *Must be sex involved,* he surmised. *But they all can and will do that at the next Committee party.*

Why this unofficial meeting?

Marc didn't see the woman until it was too late. She yanked open the door to the entranceway he was in, startling them both. For a moment Marc was afraid that it was someone from the Committee who had spotted him, but his fears proved as groundless as hers. "Who are you?" the stranger demanded nervously. "Why are you lurking around here?"

"I am not lurking," he insisted. "I'm just waiting for a friend."

"Who?" she immediately demanded.

He tried to look at the list of occupants but she was blocking it. He cursed himself for not having checked the list earlier so he would be prepared.

"Are you going to leave, or do I have to get you thrown out?" She pressed a buzzer. In response to the deep male voice from upstairs, the women said, "Manny, there's some guy down here and he's ..."

Marc cut his losses and exited. He could see out of the corner of his eye that more people were arriving across the street, but he didn't allow himself to look as he walked with a steady pace to the next corner. At that corner he turned and walked toward Tenth Avenue. He circled the block, then turned cautiously back onto Eleventh.

It was 2:15 p.m. No one else arrived for the next hour. His curiosity got the best of him and he carefully approached the building. After looking slowly in all directions, he entered. He looked at the top right intercom button, which read: "ZZZ Warehousing, eighth floor." The building only had eight floors.

After another survey of his deserted surroundings, he broke out some pins and old credit cards. For the last several days, Marc had been practicing and refining the lock-picking techniques he had learned in college when he or his friends had forgotten their keys.

Marc was glad that the area was so deserted, because it took him a full two minutes to open the door. Still, he was excited and proud when it clicked open. *Shit, I guess I have to go in now.*

Once inside, he passed up the elevator for the stairs. *They might hear the elevator. And it might open right onto ZZZ Warehousing and a crowd of hardcore Satan-worshippers.* The stairwell was unlocked. He took the eight flights slowly, pausing in the middle to make sure he didn't get too winded.

Marc opened the door to the eighth floor slowly, peering out cautiously. There was no one around. Although ZZZ Warehousing was the only occupant of the floor, there was an inner door past the elevator, marked "ZZZ Warehousing." Marc quietly and carefully tried to turn the knob, but it was locked.

Sounds were muffled by the door, but Marc could tell that things were pretty loud in there. Music was playing, of which Marc could only really hear the drums. He thought he heard some high-pitched yells. He couldn't tell if they reflected pleasure or pain. The sounds seemed to be coming from a distance, rather than the immediate other side of the door, but he couldn't be positive.

Did he have the nerve to pick this lock, with all of them in there? He judged the distance from the entrance door to the stairwell door, in case he had to run for it. Only a few feet, and he was fast. How could he walk away without knowing what was going on in there?

The door was locked, but not bolted. He paused every several seconds, listening for new sounds from inside, imagining a group of people lying in wait for him on the other side of the door. The lock released and the door swung out a fraction of an inch before Marc steadied it. He held the door and his breath for a full sixty seconds. Nothing happened.

He widened the infinitesimal crack almost imperceptibly and began to peek in. *Thank God the door doesn't creak.* Marc could see part of a normal-sized room, which led into a huge open space, the door to which was half-open. He didn't see anyone in the immediate room, and he could tell that the people and the noise were in the big adjoining room. He continued opening the front door slowly until he was in.

I've gone crazy, he thought. *What will I say if they catch me?* Sweat rolled down his face. It didn't help that he had been struck upon entering by a furnace-like blast of heat. *What are they doing in there?*

After closing the front door quietly, he hugged the far walls as he crept toward the half-open door to the next room. He flattened himself against a wall and peered in through the crack between the door and its hinges.

The inner room was vast, appropriate to a warehouse, or to a very expensive SoHo loft. The people were on the far side of the room, literally surrounding the round raised stage, which was empty except for a thick metal rod sticking straight up from the center. The almost two-dozen naked bodies were strewn fairly evenly around all 360 degrees of the stage's arc. It took Marc's eyes a few moments to adjust to the flickering candlelight and distinguish the human forms and what they were doing.

At first it looked like the Committee orgy, right down to Irma Clemmons bucking on top of one of the younger men. Everyone was moving, some feverishly, some slowly but insistently. They joined in twos and threes and fours. To his surprise, Marc noticed that some of the groupings included women on women and men on men, something he hadn't seen at the Committee meeting.

The accompaniment was merely the sound of drums, without melody. The rhythm droned on and on, altering slowly over time. There were no high-pitched yells now, only low moans.

Again Marc wondered why these people had kept this meeting a secret from the general Committee. What was so different about this gathering?

First Marc noticed the blood on the empty stage, next to the metal pole. What had he missed? Then he saw a man rise up from the writhing mass and stand on the platform. The man was wearing a goat mask with horns, and an enormous golden extension attached to his erect penis. A blond woman disengaged from a brunette and knelt before the goat-man on the stage. Marc recognized Cindy, the Catwoman from Halloween.

"Take me next, Dark Lord," Cindy begged, caressing the gold extension.

"Do you withhold anything from your Dark Lord?" the man demanded. His voice was familiar.

"I withhold nothing!" she shouted. "My body and soul are only for Satan."

Even so, Cindy couldn't help but wince and grit her teeth in pain as the man first drove the large rod of gold into her. But then she seemed to love it, thanking him with every stroke and begging him not to stop.

Marc had to look away. That's when he saw it. Her. Discarded in a far corner of the room.

Marc had never seen a dead body before. He stared at her through his binoculars. There was no sign of breathing. She lay on her back, naked except for the frayed ropes around her red wrists. Her eyes were closed, but her limbs were frozen in unnatural positions that suggested anything but peace. Her legs were spread wide, with the area between dark red, as was the floor beneath her. It wasn't clear whether she had died before or after. Marc couldn't help but wonder what had happened to the Barbie doll.

He felt his throat and stomach going into spasms. He closed his eyes as he tried to steady his breathing. His knees started to buckle and he leaned against the wall.

He opened his eyes again. *Thank God, no one's seen me. He would creep right out of here now, and they'd never know ... Shit! Someone just stood up and he's heading this way!*

Marc turned and walked faster than he had originally planned. He didn't look back as he went through the outer door. But, as Marc's hand grabbed the stairwell doorknob, he saw the other man open the front door. And the other man saw him.

Marc yanked the door and ran. Although he didn't hear

any pursuit, he didn't stop running until he hit the street. Then he walked fast until he reached his apartment.

What the hell can I do? The man who had seen him had been Paul. And, Marc now realized, the goat-man had been Eckart.

Twenty

What the fuck do I do now?

Marc paced his living room several times, then dropped like a dead weight onto his bed. *I've got to try to think this over logically. No matter how inapplicable logic seems.*

Should I run to the police? Try and get them to go back to that Eleventh Avenue warehouse with me? Somehow he couldn't picture any positive results from such a course of action. If he found a cop open-minded or loony enough to believe him, he had the feeling that all traces of the vile ceremony would have vanished, as in a second-rate horror movie. Anyway, the police might not even be able to obtain a search warrant based on his crazed ramblings.

What were his other choices? Montana. I've got to get to Montana. Maybe together we can stop them.

Marc looked around the apartment. *I've got to get out of here. What do I definitely need besides what's in my wallet?*

The buzzer sounded. It was his doorman. He hadn't ordered food and he wasn't expecting a visitor. Who could be visiting him now? He didn't want to know. He stood up and paced. The buzzer again.

Damn! I shouldn't have come back here. Marc didn't pick up the intercom to respond. His building was small enough that the doorman probably knew that he was in, or thought to himself that he hadn't seen Marc leave. Hopefully, the doorman hadn't volunteered that information.

Who's on duty now? Marc wondered. Was it Eric the friendly gossip, or Hector the strong and silent? *Let it be Hector.*

The buzzer again. The sound was like nails on a black-board. *Why doesn't whomever it is just leave?* Marc's sense of foreboding continued to grow. No casual visitor would be this persistent and this obnoxious.

Marc cursed himself for not leaving sooner. He felt trapped. Now he'd have to wait a while, to make sure that the visitor left. As far as he knew, there was only one way in or out of his building. *Too bad these fancy, modern high-rises didn't have old-fashioned fire escapes.* He considered the distance between balconies and then recovered his senses.

The buzzer hadn't sounded for two whole minutes now. He'd give it another ten minutes, then take the stairs to avoid the elevator security cameras. He tried to relax.

The phone rang. Had he left the ring on the loudest setting? *Stay calm. Screen it through your answering machine.*

The machine picked up on the fourth ring, informing the caller that Marc wasn't available. When the beep sounded, Marc heard: "Hi Marc. This is Paul." Paul sounded pretty nervous. "I think you're really home, but I don't blame you for not wanting to talk to me." *Good. I wouldn't want you to blame me for anything.*

"Come on. Please pick up. Just for a minute. I have to explain. There really is an explanation. I'm not really with them." *Sure.* Marc remembered the last time that Paul had come to him and claimed, "It's not what you think." That time Paul had managed to convince him that the Committee was purely a social and professional organization composed of nice, fun-loving people. What story was he selling now? Or did he really want to do *more* than just talk to Marc?

Paul continued. The machine was set on unlimited message length. Marc wondered if it was too late to switch it now ... "Look, there's a limit to how much I can discuss over the phone. Especially while you're recording. In fact, I would appreciate it if you erased this message."

After a few moments, Paul begged again, "Please, Marc. Please pick up. We've *got* to talk. I can help you. I've learned a lot. Things you should know. Look, you're safe up there. Your doorman won't let me up, and he's bigger than me. But I'll wait down here all night if I have to. You can't avoid me. You have to talk to me. So just pick up already."

He's right. And I could learn a lot from him, and maybe make a deal. That is, pretend to believe that I've made a deal. I'd still rather talk with Paul than the others. Especially Eckart.

"Spit it out," Marc commanded. "What do you want?"

"I've got to talk to you in person."

"The phone's close enough. Tell me what's going on."

"I can't talk about these things on the phone. And, by the way, turn that fucking answering machine off *now*."

Marc hit rewind on the machine. "Done. Now talk."

Exasperated, Paul suggested a plan. "Why don't you come down for a few minutes. We'll talk in plain sight of Bluto, your giant doorman." *Must be Hector.* "I swear on my life that you'll be safe."

"Well, okay. Your life will be the collateral. I think the doorman did time in his country. Wait outside the building, right in front of the glass door. I'll come down, talk to Hector, then join you. You'll have two minutes, then Hector will enforce the vagrancy laws."

"Done. Get the hell down here."

Marc slammed the phone, then threw on his sneakers and a jacket. He pocketed his Swiss army knife, for the hell of it. He paced the narrow width of the elevator on the way down.

Marc suspected that Hector was really a nice guy under his

gruff, taciturn six-foot-two inch muscular exterior. For all Marc knew, Hector had hours of jokes and stories to share with the few Spanish-speaking residents. But all he ever did when he saw Marc was nod slightly and grimace, which might have been his way of smiling. Marc had never tried to talk to Hector, beyond saying "Send him up" whenever Hector buzzed that he had a visitor. Hector said "visitor" pretty well, but he seldom repeated names accurately. Actually, his most common announcement was "Chinee," which meant that a Chinese guy had arrived with food, even if the guy was Japanese, or the food was Italian.

"Hi, Hector," Marc said with a smile. He was glad now that he had taken the trouble to learn the names of the few doormen.

A half-nod and a grimace. Then: "Visitor from before, outside door." Marc was impressed by the rhyme.

"That's what I wanted to talk to you about," said Marc. "This visitor, he's no good. He's ..." *Why did I take French in high school? Not that I remember any French either.* "He's just got out of jail. Penitentiary."

"*Oh, la penitenciaria, si.*"

"Right." Marc nodded. Marc was watching Paul who was watching him through the glass door. "So, keep an eye on us, okay? Make sure he doesn't kill me. You know, *muerte.*" Marc put both his hands around his neck and pantomimed choking. Marc saw Paul smile. *Was that a good-natured smile?*

Hector nodded. "I watch," he stated in his deep voice. Marc felt reassured. Hector seemed to understand, at least a little. Hopefully, if the pantomimed scene were to be reenacted in earnest Hector would do more than just watch.

Marc shook Hector's hand, leaving a twenty-dollar bill behind as he took two steps forward and grasped the handle of the front door. *I hope that's a sufficient tip for this service.*

"Step back two steps," Marc said, as he opened the door. Paul walked back two steps. "Open your hands and hold them out." Paul did. "Keep them that way."

"That's going to get tiring," said Paul. Marc turned for a

split second, verifying that Hector was indeed watching.

"Okay then," Marc responded. "Clasp your hands together on top of your head."

Paul shrugged. "Stupid, but easier." He complied.

"What do you have to say to me?" Marc asked.

"A lot. But I'll start with the fact that I'm not really a part of that group you saw. That was the first meeting I've been to, and I was there for a specific reason. And I had no idea ..."

A young couple from the second floor almost hit Marc with the front door. "Sorry," she muttered. The two were dressed for a nice dinner.

After the couple was gone, Paul said, "This isn't the best place ..."

"Don't worry about that. Just go on."

"I had no idea how far gone those guys actually are. It was horrible, but I couldn't stop them ..."

"Did you try?"

"No, I couldn't. Not today. It would have ruined my chance to stop them for good." Paul really did look shaken. "I don't think I could have stopped myself from screaming, if it hadn't been for the drugs. I still feel a little strange."

"What do you mean?" Marc remembered that Paul had had a strange, confused look on his face at the warehouse.

"There was something in the wine," Paul said. "Or more than one thing. I had a few hallucinations at first, some mystical, some psychedelic. I also felt detached, outside my body. Made me feel like nothing was real." Paul stared carefully at Marc. "I wasn't completely sure that I saw you there. Thought that could have been an illusion. But you're acting like you were there."

Marc didn't say anything.

"Come on, help me out. You *were* there, right?"

"Where?" Marc asked innocently.

"Fuck you if you're fucking with me."

Paul closed his eyes and held his forehead. "My head feels like it wants to float away. Look, it doesn't matter if you were there or not. I need your help. I was going to come to you after this meeting anyway. I swear. On my life."

"Okay, assume I know nothing. Now tell me everything. But start with why I should believe anything you say."

"First of all, let me reassure you. I didn't tell anyone that I saw you there. As far as anyone knows, I just got up to piss. Which I did have to do. But if I was part of them, I could have told them about you and they could have sent someone to take care of you by now."

"How do I know you're not that someone?"

"Marc!" Paul looked shocked and hurt. He didn't budge as the old woman approached the building with her dog.

"Here we are, Bijou," she announced to her companion. "No, Bijou, go *around* the men."

Paul and Marc stood silently while the spry little dog licked Paul, then Marc. Marc had to loosen up and give Bijou a quick rub behind the ears.

"Come on, Bijou," the woman said. "Say goodbye to the nice young men." As she finally reached Hector and the door he was holding open for her, Bijou caught up and ran ahead of her. The door closed behind them.

Paul earnestly proclaimed, "I've always been your friend. How can you think that I ..."

"A lot of friendly people are doing really unfriendly things. You're the one who painted a rosy picture of the Committee and its members ..."

"I'm also the one who warned you that you were being watched at the Halloween party," Paul pointed out.

"You lied when you made me think the Committee was harmless."

"No. The old core of the Committee was the way I described it. They were loyal to their friends, good-natured, and into harmless fun." Paul lowered his voice as he continued. "Sure, they might have lied and cheated a little, stolen useful information and hidden damaging facts, discredited competitors, even fixed some trials, but it was all to further the important interests of clients and friends."

"You didn't mention those things ..."

"I didn't realize you were *that* naive. The important thing is that no one got hurt in the old days. Physically, I mean. But now the old Committee is going fast. First Bob Thornton, then Sam Knight and Don O'Neill." Paul lowered his voice to a whisper. "And Doris Spender and Bob Baylor are due to go any day now."

"What? What do you mean, 'due'?"

Paul looked around. "Could we please go somewhere, instead of standing out here on the street? How can I talk about this stuff here? Won't your doorman testify that I was the last person to see you, if you disappear?"

Marc tried to size up his old friend. "Do you have any weapons?"

"No. I swear." Paul pulled his coat pocket and his pants pockets inside out, revealing only a wallet, keys and gum.

"Shit. I was hoping you did, so you could give them to me."

Paul pondered the situation. "How about this: I give my wallet with all my identification to your doorman, then we go to your apartment to talk. If you don't come back down with me, he can call the police, identify me, and give them my wallet."

"Do you speak Spanish?"

"Yeah."

"Okay. You explain it to him. Slowly. And don't try anything. I took a few years of Spanish myself."

The two of them went inside. Paul handed Hector his wallet, making a point of showing him his driver's license and saying his name. Marc heard key words such as "telefono," "policia" and "asesinar," which he assumed meant "murder" or "assassinate." Hector just nodded gravely and put the wallet in a drawer, like it was all in a typical day's work for a New York City doorman. *Does he really understand?*

"Tell him we'll be down in fifteen minutes," Marc instructed, "or he should call the police."

Paul told Hector.

"Okay then," Marc said. "After you."

Paul went ahead and rang for the elevator. Paul stepped onto the elevator first. A middle-aged man appeared as the doors were closing, and Marc graciously pulled them open for him. The man nodded gratefully, but then got off on the second floor.

Marc and Paul eyed each other anxiously for the next eleven floors, each turning occasionally to stare at the security camera in the ceiling. Then the doors opened on the "fourteenth" floor.

Marc handed Paul his keys. "Use these two, then give them back before you go in," Marc ordered.

Paul held the door open for Marc, who walked in briskly and turned on lights on his way to the kitchen. "Are you going to get some knives?" Paul asked jokingly, a second before Marc returned with the biggest knife in the apartment. "Is that a Ginsu?"

"Shut up," said Marc, killing the faint smile that had come involuntarily to his lips. "You're not going to make me relax." Nonetheless, Marc settled down onto the couch, resting the knife on his lap. He remembered what he had seen today, and his resolve returned. "Now tell me, why were you in a room with a dead naked little girl?"

Paul got serious too. He sat across from Marc on the loveseat. "I didn't want to be. I never want to be again. I want to shut them down. With your help."

Marc was going to do this in an orderly, dogged fashion. "Why were you there?"

"I've been infiltrating. I had gained their confidence, and this was the first mass that I was invited to."

"Who are *they*?"

"The neo-orthodox. The born-again Satanists."

Born-again Satanists! Marc digested that concept for a

moment. Eckart had once spoken of some young people being more devout. *To think I was skeptical of that* New York Times Magazine *article about America returning to religion!* "But what do they want?"

"To gain spiritual and secular power through the adoration of Satan in the old-fashioned ways. They also hope to eventually bring Satan to life on Earth. But in the meantime, most of them seem to really enjoy the old-fashioned ways. Like rape, torture and death."

These folks aren't into doing things halfway. It was hard to take such wild words seriously. Then he remembered the little girl.

"How did you know that they existed?"

"Eckart had dropped hints for a little while. He'd say that 'some people' were dissatisfied with the leadership of the Committee. He'd say that some wanted to return to the older, more spiritual ways. For a while he wouldn't say who he was talking about. He'd act like he wasn't a part of the dissention, let alone its leader."

"What would you say back to Eckart?"

"The first few times I just sort of grunted and nodded. Then your uncle talked to me about Eckart ..."

"My *uncle*? Charlie? What does he have to do with this?"

"Well, your uncle had been friendly and helpful to me, ever since you joined the Committee. He had approached me then, said he knew that you and I had been friends once, and asked if I could help ease your assimilation into the Committee. Naturally, I wanted to do that anyway."

Oh, yeah. Uncle Charlie did say something about Paul helping him out with my adjustment to the Committee.

Paul sounded sincere when he said, "I really had missed you. I was sorry that we had drifted apart after graduation. I guess I was so wrapped up in the Committee that I didn't have time for anything else. Plus, I was overly uptight at the time about keeping the secrets of the Committee. I became insulated."

Marc had missed Paul too, but he was determined to keep this conversation moving constructively and unemotionally. "Do you know that I don't really like my uncle? That he hurt my father years ago?"

"No, I'm sorry to hear that. Your uncle seemed pretty nice to me."

"He definitely can act nice, but I still don't trust him. What did Uncle Charlie want from you?"

"He had guessed that there were more orthodox elements developing in the Committee. And he had guessed that Eckart was involved. Your uncle wanted me to get into the splinter group, find out what they were about, and report back to him. Despite the risks, it seemed like the best course to follow. I had the feeling that Eckart was going to force me into the splinter group eventually, and I would have had no way out. This way, I would help Charlie Wilson bring down Eckart, then your uncle would get me an even better job."

"I thought you liked Eckart. I thought you and he were as tight as can be."

"It's just business. Eckart thinks he can fool people into thinking it's personal, into giving him undying love and loyalty. But I know that's bullshit. And now I know that he's a murderer. And worse. And powerful, in secular terms and allegedly spiritually. He's got to be stopped."

"Did Eckart have anything to do with the recent deaths on the Committee?" Marc asked, suspecting the answer.

"Anything to do with them? Eckart murdered those people. He brags about it to those in the splinter group. He says that he killed Knight and O'Neill, and that he did it with magic. Eckart claims to be the most powerful magician on the Committee. Even more powerful than your uncle, who's the keeper of the spellbook. Not that your uncle uses the book much. Which is one of the reasons why Eckart says we should all follow *him*."

"You've heard Eckart say these things?"

"Eckart says Satan came to him in a dream and told him to

lead his people back to the old ways."

"Why would he kill Knight and O'Neill?"

"For the same reason that he killed Thornton, although he had that one done the secular way. For the same reason that he's announced he's going to kill Doris Spender and that impotent figurehead, Bob Baylor. He's getting rid of the old guard, the secularists who support Charlie Wilson. Your uncle's the real power behind the Committee, but most of his solid support is gone or going fast. Eckart's taking over."

"Do you believe that Eckart really has magical powers?" Marc asked.

"The guy's definitely got *something*. I never really believed in magic, although my parents did. But I don't see any other explanation for these 'coincidental' deaths."

No. Marc wouldn't believe it. There had to be a scientific explanation.

"Knight and O'Neill died of heart attacks, right? Were either of them autopsied?" Marc asked.

"I think O'Neill was. But they didn't find anything suspicious. They were just middle-aged guys with high cholesterol who worked too hard. Eckart brags that his magical murders leave no clues. Just a few chest pains, a little shortness of breath, then bang ..."

Where had Marc heard about such symptoms? Germany. Many of those gypsies had those types of symptoms days before they died from the poison gas. But it couldn't be connected ...

Marc realized he had loosened his grip on the knife. But he wasn't ready to tell Paul about Jill Montana. "You said you wanted my help," Marc said. "What did you mean? What are you planning to do?"

"Well, I have to report back to your uncle and see what he wants to do. But I think we might try to blackmail Eckart and the neo-orthodox types to cut it out. The next big ceremony is scheduled for the morning before Christmas Eve. A few hours before the full Committee 'Christmas' party. I don't know where these people get their stamina," Paul muttered. "Maybe I can sneak you in to take pictures or something, then we can use them against these people. Something like that."

"Something like that," Marc echoed. "We'll have to keep thinking about this." He'd tell Montana about Paul, see if she wanted to trust him.

"If only we could go to the D.A.'s office," said Paul.

Does he mean it, or is he testing me?

"But that's out," said Paul. "If it was anyone other than Eckart's whore ..."

"What? Are you talking about Jill Montana?"

"Of course. Didn't you see her writhing, shrieking in pleasure until she passed out? There's something special between her and Eckart. He fucked her first."

Marc remembered Eckart the goat-man rising out of the mass of moving bodies, seeking new flesh. Had he just pulled out of D.A. Jill Montana? "Jesus! I didn't see her in that sea of bodies. I can't believe it!"

"I think the splinter group had something to do with the murder of her predecessor, Rosetti. That Montana's ambitious, and I'm sure her connection to Eckart didn't hurt."

"Can you prove this?"

"Well, she has a spider tattoo on her ass. Left cheek."

"Something I can verify easily."

"Lots of people know about that tattoo. Joe Garrett told me she did him, Scott, Dan, and Larry at one time, a few months ago. At a ceremony on Fire Island, at Eckart's summer place."

Marc was distracted by the image. "I'm not about to ask those bastards."

"Of course not. You'll just have to come to the ceremony on December 24th. See for yourself."

Should I believe him? I can't afford not to. I can't tell Jill Montana anything unless and until I find out that Paul lied about her.

If she is a Satanist, why would she have pushed me to tell her things she already knows? Maybe she's been testing me, trying to find out if I told anything to Rosetti. If I'm a security risk.

The intercom buzzer went off, alarming them both. "Should I answer it?" Marc asked Paul.

"Of course. We have to keep acting like nothing's different. For now."

For now, I'll go along with you, not trusting you too much. I want to know what you and my uncle come up with.

Marc went to the intercom and pressed the button to speak. "Yes? What is it?"

"You okay, Mr. Wilson?" Good old Hector had noted the passage of exactly fifteen minutes.

"I think so."

Twenty-One

Marc was happy that he had to take the depositions in the Gutierrez case the next morning. There wouldn't be any time to worry about anything else. Unfortunately, Joe Dinaro called at 9 a.m. to say that his clients, the police officers, wouldn't be able to attend the depositions today.

"Neither one of them?" Marc asked.

"Things came up. Is your client ready for tomorrow?"

"Get out of here. I'm deposing your clients first."

"There's no priority in federal court."

"We'll discuss that, and your incomplete answers to interrogatories, with Judge Kelly on Thursday."

Marc tried to do other work. In some ways, the day felt like *déjà vu* with the morning after he first learned that the Committee worshipped Satan. Now, in retrospect, he realized that his highly emotional response to that revelation had been an overreaction, leaving little room for him to escalate his anxiety now.

The stakes were much higher now. Some of these people were much more than mere eccentrics. Back then, Marc had wondered what these people were capable of if he crossed them. Now he knew what Eckart himself would do, without a second thought, if he caught Marc betraying him.

Marc let Gina answer his phone calls, internal and external, and he only emerged from his office hourly to check his messages. Eckart called Marc at 11:05 a.m. Terrified by the man as he was, Marc still had to call him back, and promptly. Marc couldn't act suspiciously.

When Marc called Eckart at noon, he was only slightly relieved that he wasn't there. It only delayed the inevitable.

At 12:33 p.m., there was a knock on Marc's closed office door. The door opened as Marc called out, "Come in." Marc was stunned as Eckart walked in. Eckart almost never went to an associate's office. *Guess this is an honor.*

"Hey, Marc. How're you doing?" Eckart asked.

"Pretty good. How about you?"

"The usual madness," Eckart replied.

You got that right, Marc thought. "So, you called? What's the story?"

"Just wanted to give you a *few* days' notice that the day you've been dreading is coming up."

"What do you mean?" Marc asked.

"We're heading back to Germany. Thursday morning till Sunday night. So put out your other fires quickly and efficiently. Or get volunteer firemen to help."

Marc sensed that it was no use telling Eckart he had a conference in his *pro bono* case on Thursday. "Are we doing more depositions?"

"No, those were mostly useless. We're going to meet with an investigator we hired over there, and some of the witnesses he's scared up. If we like any of them, then we'll give their names to plaintiffs, who'll want to depose them."

"What do you want me to do to prepare?" Marc asked. *Assuming I'm crazy enough to go back there with you.*

"Don't worry about it now. We'll discuss it on the way over." *That seems strange.* "Concentrate on freeing yourself up. Oh, but don't give any of your work to Paul. He's been acting too stressed lately."

⚖️

Paul *was* looking stressed when he met Marc in the salad bar.
And hearing that Eckart perceived him as acting stressed didn't
help. "It's hard acting like nothing's changed," Paul said.

"No shit. You don't have to draw me a diagram of what
that's like."

The two of them were sitting in one corner of the crowded
salad bar, at one of the few tables small enough for two. Both of
them had displayed an uncharacteristic lack of appetite. Each
of their hot and cold salad combos had weighed well under a
pound. Both men were picking at the vegetables, Chinese chick-
en dishes, and pasta that had merged in their plastic containers.
Each took note of the other's nervousness.

"So I just can't imagine traveling back to the Fatherland
with our boss," Marc told Paul. "Spending all that time with
him, so far from home, so close to the ovens."

"You've got to go, you know. Otherwise the game will be
over. They'll know you suspect, and they might guess I told you.
We'll lose our chance to gather ammunition against them from
within, and we'll be at their mercy. We might as well change our
names and leave the country."

"So you're saying that I have to leave the country either way."

"Very funny. You're going to be on that plane Thursday.
And don't worry about your *pro bono* case. I'll charm Judge Kelly to death."

"Why don't *you* go to Germany and I'll charm Judge Kelly?"

"Eckart wants *you*, Marc Wilson. You're really moving up.
Maybe he'll invite you to join his circle ..."

"Maybe he'll invite me to a Nazi rally. I told you about that
skinhead in the strip club, right?"

"Yeah. I wonder what the boss-man was doing with him."

Neither of them having taken a bite in several minutes,

they took their trays toward the trash and recycling bins. Marc stopped on the way past the vegetables, half-consciously noticing that something was odd.

Even from the back, there was something familiar about the man with the brown leather jacket. The man was the only one standing over the salad bar without a plastic container of food in his hands. As the man turned away from the bean sprouts, Marc saw that he held only a half-empty Evian bottle. Marc almost dropped his tray when he recognized the skinhead from the Hollywood Strip.

Before the youth could see him, Marc hurried away to dump his trash. His mind was reeling. What could this mean? Should he tell Paul?

I'll test him. "Have you ever seen that guy before?" Marc asked Paul.

"Which guy?"

"The one in the leather jacket. Heading for the door."

"No. Who is he?"

"It's the skinhead from Germany. Eckart's friend."

"Maybe we should follow him," said Paul.

"Yeah, that's probably a good idea."

Marc wondered what he'd do if the skinhead was waiting for him outside. *Maybe I should start carrying a knife or something,* Marc thought. *Yeah, like I'd really use a knife. Even on a Nazi.*

Marc was mostly relieved not to find the guy. By the time they hit the street, he had already vanished.

Marc went back into the salad bar, wandering over to the bean sprouts. Paul followed him, even more confused than Marc as to what they were doing.

"Marc! Paul!" Doris Spender spotted them before they saw her. "How are you two doing?"

"Fine."

"Okay, how are you?" Marc asked, genuinely happy to see this completely unintimidating woman who had always been so friendly to him. Then he remembered that Eckart had sworn to kill her.

"I'm great, thanks," said Doris.

Marc noticed that Doris Spender's salad really was a salad, consisting solely of assorted raw vegetables.

"Yes, I like my vegetables," she said, observing his gaze. "People make fun of me. Especially the bean sprouts. I love my bean sprouts," she said. She reached under the plastic guard for the bean sprout serving tongs, but they were missing.

"Do you have a cholesterol problem?" Paul asked.

"Nope. And I never will," she answered definitively, taking tongs from the neighboring pea pod dish and digging deeply into the bean sprout mountain.

Marc's brain struggled to make connections in the limited time available. The skinhead and his bottle. Eckart and his plan to kill Doris. Dead gypsies.

Marc grabbed a tissue out of his pocket and sneezed. Hard. So hard that the tissue flew out of his hands, under the plastic guard and onto the bean sprouts. The bean sprouts which Doris Spender had gathered between the tongs for her lunch.

Dozens of nearby patrons stopped what they were doing, staring at the Kleenex as if transfixed. Some, including the heavy twenty-five-year-old blond who was next in line, expressed their disgust both visibly and audibly. One man muttered something about needing "even bigger sneeze guards." Another man pointed out "nothing would stop a guy like that."

"Sorry," Marc mumbled. *What a shot. I could go professional.*

"Uh, that's okay," said Doris graciously, relinquishing her grip on the bean sprout tongs. "I've been eating too much anyway."

Marc walked briskly to the door, an instant celebrity. He didn't slow down until he was a couple blocks away.

Paul caught up and said, "Good work. No one will be eating *anything* from that salad bar for weeks."

Afterward, Marc had time to sit down and construct a

theory as to how everything connected. Evidently Eckart had brought the skinhead over to kill people for him with a German poison stored in an Evian bottle. A mysterious, traceless poison that caused people to die over the course of a week or two, seemingly of heart disease. The same poison that was fed to the Regensburg gypsies.

That was why Litvak's brother had exhibited heart disease symptoms days *before* the well-known gas leak. And why others who hadn't been present during the gas leak had died days later. The poison must have been in the camp well, which Hammond emptied out to cover the evidence. Marc guessed that a worker who couldn't contain his hatred for gypsies had put the poison there. Probably Herr Walther, the one plant employee who *did* die, supposedly by accident.

Helfferich and the others who ran the plant must have been horrified when they learned that their top-secret poison had been used. Not that they minded the loss of a few hundred annoying gypsies. But not in their own backyard. There would be no way to hide the chemical plant's involvement in the sudden deaths. So they had hired or convinced Struger, the skinhead, to release the cyanide gas. Then all they had on their hands was a run-of-the-mill leak of an ordinary pesticide ingredient.

Then all they needed was a clever, sympathetic lawyer. Marc was amazed at how neatly it all fit together. And maybe that lawyer was interested in testing out the secret poison for his own uses. And in impressing people with his ability to make his enemies die mysteriously, as if by magic.

"I always wake up soon after he pulls me out of the cage. I don't know exactly what they're going to do to me, but I'm really scared. Why do you think I keep having this dream?"

Dr. Emma Kierst looked up from her notes into Samantha

Eckart's anxious face. "Recurring dreams are common. There's nothing to worry about."

"But why would I dream about some sort of Satan-worshipping cult?" Sam hadn't told Dr. Kierst of Marc's rantings about a Satanic conspiracy. She wanted to know if there were other factors that could have planted such thoughts into her unconscious.

"I doubt that the cult has any direct significance for you. The scene is evidently symbolic of a situation in which you feel helpless, trapped, suffocated. Tell me, how is school?"

"Okay, I guess."

"Not too enthusiastic," Dr. Kierst commented. "In the dream you are being used or sacrificed, forced to serve a cause in which you don't believe. Are you still sure about your chosen profession?"

"I think so. Although the grading is so arbitrary and unpredictable."

Twenty minutes later, Samantha thanked the psychiatrist and left her office, feeling a little more relaxed. Dr. Kierst kept Samantha Eckart's file out on her desk.

⚖

That night Samantha Eckart didn't wake up from the nightmare at the expected moment. Her consciousness was split between her adult persona and that of the little girl in the dream. Part of her realized that she was dreaming, and that she was due to wake up. Part of her was frightened to death.

After the man yelled, "Not yet," the others stopped touching her. She lay very still on the table, squeezing her eyes shut.

I've got to wake up, thought grown-up Samantha, watching from inside the little girl. *I don't want to see anymore.*

The girl heard the baby crying next to her and opened her eyes. "Stand up," the man ordered, propping her next to the low table on which the writhing baby lay. "Before the real fun begins, there's something that you have to do."

Fun? thought the little girl. *I don't believe that. I want to go away. I will go away. I'll just leave my body and go to sleep.*

No! thought big Samantha. *Don't sleep, wake up!*

The man opened her hand and placed a little knife in it. She looked at him, being careful to look only at his face.

"Stop the baby from crying," he said. "Give it peace."

The girl kept looking at him like he wasn't speaking English.

"Go ahead," he said, taking her hand in his and moving it toward the screaming infant. His voice was so familiar ... "I love you."

WAKE UP!!!

⚖⚖

Tuesday morning, Marc got a call from Doris Spender. The image of the Kleenex in the bean sprouts returned to embarrass him, but it was far from her mind. "I hate to be making these calls," she said, "but Bob Baylor died last night."

Paul had just one minute earlier walked into Marc's office with the library copy of today's *New York Law Journal*, which had a front-page blurb about Baylor's fatal heart attack.

"That's terrible, Doris," said Marc, gesturing to Paul that the call was related to the news about Baylor. "Had he been sick?"

"Not that anyone knew. But he loved a good steak. I used to beg him to eat more vegetables."

It's just as well he enjoyed those steaks, thought Marc. *Since Eckart and his skinhead friend were just going to poison him anyway.*

"Anyway, the funeral is Thursday."

"Oh, I'm sorry I won't be able to go." At last, one good thing about this Germany trip. "I'll be out of the country with Bill Eckart. Have you called him yet?"

"Oh yes. He was so supportive. The man's so wise and philosophical ..."

⚖

"Marc, *please* call me. I have to talk to you," was the needy message on his answering machine that evening. Sam had also called him at his office and left less emotional messages with his secretary. Marc checked and found that he had also missed calls to his cell phone. *I never even felt it vibrate.*

Marc was concerned by the tone of Sam's voice. On the other hand, he couldn't help but be excited that *she* had to talk to *him.*

She answered his call after the first ring. "How quick can you get over here?" he asked. She arrived twenty-five minutes later.

She held him close. Marc couldn't help becoming aroused by her proximity, but he kept his embrace platonic. They sat on the couch, still touching.

"What's wrong?" Marc asked.

"I've been having nightmares," she blurted, then began to sob. "I'm sorry. I don't have any right to do this to you. Not after the way I've pushed you away."

"What is it?" he asked.

"But there's no one else I can turn to." She managed to catch her breath. "I dreamed about a secret ceremony. Everyone was wearing robes. At first."

"I'm sorry," said Marc. "Did I give you nightmares, with my talk about Satanism and the Committee?"

"No, that's not it. I keep having the dream, almost every night now. But it's not about the Committee. It's another group. And I'm a little girl in the dream."

"Don't worry," said Marc, his hand massaging her neck. "It's just a dream."

"It always ended at the same point, when he was taking me

out of the cage. Until last night. Last night I couldn't wake up. He gave me the knife and I couldn't wake up."

"Shhh," Marc soothed. "Everything's okay."

"He gave me the knife and he said he loved me. He loved me when I stabbed it. I took the knife and I used it. At first I just touched the baby gently, but it cried and screamed anyway. They were chanting and he was touching me and saying he loved me and then I stabbed and stabbed and the baby still screamed and blood came out and all over and ... and ... *then* I woke up."

Marc held her very still.

"But it doesn't feel like a dream," she continued, her voice flat. She sucked in a deep breath, then let it out. "It feels like a *memory.*"

Oh, God.

Marc remembered the articles he had read about alleged Satanic ritual child abuse. He recalled that these memories could be hidden for decades. But the people on television had displayed countless other symptoms. Most of them had been dangerous sociopaths. *Sam's normal!*

"But how can that possibly be?" she asked. She looked him in the eyes and grabbed his arm tightly. Then she spoke slowly and deliberately. "Tell me, what have you learned about my father?"

Marc didn't answer right away. Sam pressed. "Is my father a murderer?" she asked simply. Slowly, Marc nodded. "So he made *me* follow in his footsteps," she said.

"You were a child."

"Tell me everything."

Marc couldn't deny her. He spoke slowly and watched her each moment to see how she was handling the information. Sometimes, she stopped him to ask questions. Always, she remained calm.

Afterward, she asked, "So when is Paul going to talk to your uncle?"

"I think today or tomorrow."

"I want to help you."

Marc caressed her cheek gently. "How old were you?" he asked quietly. "In the dream?"

"Five. Somehow I know I'm five."

"That's when you had that terrible bike accident, right?"

"That's what he told me to say. It's been coming back to me. I only tried to tell Mom once. She hit me. We never talked about it again."

He held her silently for many moments. His lips touched her creased forehead, then her nose and eyebrows. She reached up to meet his lips with hers. He whispered, "I missed you." She kissed his neck and ran her hands down his back. He responded by pushing against her gently until he was on top of her, his head buried in her thick honey hair.

At first she responded hungrily. Then suddenly she tried to push him off of her. But he was too big.

At first she froze, then went limp. Marc noticed and stopped moving. "What is it, honey?" he asked.

Sam sprang back to life, flailing against him with all her strength. "Get off me, you big fat pig!" she shrieked in a desperate high-pitched tone. "You're killing me!"

Marc jumped up like he'd been burned. He took several steps back, and watched Samantha with concern. It was excruciating, being afraid to touch her, to try to comfort her.

Samantha was already back in the present, looking shaken and embarrassed.

"I'm so sorry," said Marc, at a loss for more.

"Don't go too far away," Sam said softly. "Play something for me," she asked. "Please."

Marc turned on his synthesizer and played a song for Sam. In time, she approached him slowly and put her hands on him lovingly.

Twenty-Two

Marc was too busy at work to talk to Paul the next day, as he had planned. Marc spent every minute until 10 p.m. researching, writing and running around. He had so many pressing matters that he was actually able to force himself to concentrate. He put the finishing touches on reply papers in one case, asked opposing counsel for and received an extension on interrogatory responses in a different case, then tried to finish two research memos for Eckart. It was annoying and unfair that Eckart, who knew Marc's work load better than anyone, was insisting on having the two memoranda on unrelated cases to take with him on the flight to Germany.

Marc figured that he would call Paul when he reached his apartment, then maybe they'd meet somewhere. Marc was anxious to speak with Paul to find out if he or Uncle Charlie had formulated a plan to shut down the Satanic splinter group. He also wanted to discuss with Paul whether there wasn't some way Marc could still beg off the Germany trip. Failing that, he wanted to solicit Paul's opinions on Marc's best course of action in response to various frightening German scenarios that Marc's overheated imagination had been creating.

When Marc opened his apartment door at 10:35 p.m., he was surprised to find that he had left the living room light on. He headed straight for the refrigerator and a Heineken. He popped the top and took a swig before he heard a drawer closing in his bedroom.

Marc put down the beer and grabbed a long serrated knife. Who could it be? He headed for the bedroom, knife held ready.

The door opened and she stepped out calmly. She looked great in a surprisingly small red leather dress and high heels. She smiled at his menacing pose. "What are you going to do with me?" D.A. Montana asked in a provocatively husky tone.

Marc was surprised and relieved. And turned on. Then he remembered that Jill Montana was probably a Satan worshipper and a murderer. And Eckart might have done it to her with a long gold rod. He shivered at the mental image.

"Well?" she asked, losing patience. "Are you going to kill me or not?"

"Maybe. What are you doing here, and how did you get in?"

"I told you I'd come to you if you didn't come through with some information fast."

"How'd you get past the doorman?"

"Simple. I waited till he was helping someone with packages, then I helped myself to your spare keys and ducked into the stairwell. He never saw me."

Eric's getting way too sloppy, Marc thought. *Hector never would have let her by.* "Is sneaking past doormen and breaking into apartments standard D.A. procedure?"

"No, but I didn't want to be seen. Or turned away. Or avoided." She walked past him boldly, coming to rest on the couch. "Won't you join me? Preferably without the knife."

"I've been meaning to contact you," Marc said, lowering the knife but not approaching closer. *To verify Paul's stories.* "I don't have anything to tell you, though. As far as I can tell, the Committee is on the up-and-up. These people are respectable, they go to church regularly and give generously to charity. What could they be doing wrong?"

"I know all that," the D.A. snapped. "Don't give me a press release. Tell me what's really going on."

"Nothing. Really."

Her voice softened. "Don't you trust me?" she asked.

No, thought Marc. He was becoming increasingly certain that he could not trust her. She really didn't seem professional.

"You should trust me," she said. "I'm on your side. I want to help you out of this mess."

"I know," Marc lied. "Of course I trust you. You're the D.A."

"I'm not just the D.A. I'm a person. I care about you, and what happens to you." She stood up and walked toward him. He tightened his grip on the knife, but stopped himself from lifting it. He couldn't let her know that he knew her secrets.

Jill Montana only stopped when she was three inches away from him. He could feel her cool breath on his face as she said, "I want to help you every way I can." Marc couldn't help thinking of her spider tattoo.

Before he could respond, her lips were on his and her entire body pressed up against him. He felt her firm breasts against his chest and her tongue entering his mouth, even as he dropped the knife to the floor. A moment later he recovered from his surprise and pushed her away. He headed for the front door and opened it.

Montana's eyes were bulging with anger. Marc glanced at the knife at her feet and regretted leaving it there.

"Sorry," he said, attempting to smooth the situation. "I have a girlfriend."

The D.A. had returned to a professional manner. "No, I'm sorry," she said, heading for the door. "I'm sorry you don't have anything for me."

Why are you so sorry? he wondered. *Are you sorry that there may not be a need to kill me?*

⚖⚖

Paul had returned home at 8:35 p.m. and left messages on Marc's answering machine and on his cell phone, asking Marc to call him. He was anxious to discuss strategy with Marc. He wished Marc would call already. Paul was dead tired.

Just before 9:30 p.m., Paul lay down in his bedroom with a legal thriller he'd been reading for some time. It was so unrealistic and boring that Paul was snoozing fitfully by 9:45, with the book draped across his chest and the lights still on.

Minutes later, Paul didn't hear the soft sounds of his front door's locks being picked by a pro. Even if he had, he would not have had much time to react. The Medeco bolt lock took a little over a minute, after which the bottom lock surrendered in seconds.

Outside the bedroom, the intruder heard Paul stretch and turn over. The youth paused motionlessly for a full sixty seconds before proceeding soundlessly into the bedroom.

A light dose of chloroform deepened Paul's sleep while the intruder used nylon stockings to tie Paul's arms and legs together in tight, complex knots. Minutes later, Paul woke up as a gag was being taped in his mouth.

Paul struggled against his bonds, which gave just enough to avoid injuring him but not enough for him to escape. His eyes widened, then blinked in amazement and terror as he stared up at his captor.

"You know me, eh?" the youth asked in surprisingly good English, tinged with a German accent. "My name is Otto."

Paul stared up at the young skinhead's phony hairline and skull-like face. Paul tried to speak, to make some intelligible sound, but it was hopeless. How was he going to beg for his life?

Paul wondered how the young man had gotten past the doorman. Otto didn't volunteer the information that he had climbed over from another building of roughly the same height. Otto had enjoyed the exercise. It reminded him of hunting wild boar with his father in the Hartz mountains, but this was much easier. The roof of Paul's building hadn't even been locked. And there was no danger of this weak American turning and charging him.

Paul strained against the nylons again. The skinhead leaned down and brought the heel of his right hand to within a couple inches of Paul's nose, while pounding the bed with his left. As Paul squirmed to the side, the fear on his face even more intense, Otto laughed.

Regretting his orders not to leave any visible wounds, the young man produced a needle, intravenous tubing and a bag of clear fluid. Otto had planned to put the drug in Paul's lunch the following day, but Paul had been making too much trouble. Otto connected the tubing to the needle.

I'm going to die, thought Paul. *Isn't there anything I can do to save myself? Who can help me?*

The phone rang. Otto turned and stared at it for a moment, then connected the tubing to the full I.V. bag.

Eventually the ringing stopped.

Marc didn't know whether to be annoyed or worried when Paul didn't answer his phone. Where could Paul be? Could something bad have happened to him? Or was he busy getting laid? Could even Paul think about sex tonight?

Marc had stepped out into a stairwell and used his cell phone to call Paul. As soon as Jill Montana had left his apartment, Marc had looked around for signs of bugs or cameras, but he quickly realized he had no idea how to look. The invasion of his privacy and space, by a hardened Satanist, had been unnerving to say the least.

Marc decided to head over to Paul's place. It was only a few blocks away, and Marc wasn't going to be able to fall asleep until he looked into this anyway. Maybe Paul would be home, or done screwing, by the time Marc arrived there.

Paul's doorman was almost as big as Hector, and no friendlier. When Marc asked the man to buzz "Paul Johnston in 11G," he did so without a word. Five seconds later, the doorman said, "No answer."

"Give him a moment, please," said Marc. Still no response. "Could you buzz him again, please?"

Before complying, the doorman gave Marc a look that could fry eggs. There was still no answer.

"Do you know if he's up there?" Marc asked.

The doorman stared at Marc, then said, "No."

At great personal risk, Marc asked, "No, he's not up there, or no, you don't know if he's up there."

The man surprised Marc by answering, "The latter."

"Thanks. Do you remember if you saw him go up tonight?"

"Yeah."

"But you don't remember if you saw him come back down?"

"Exactly. There's a chair over there."

Marc nodded, then sat down in the chair and left the man alone. Time passed.

Where could Paul be? Or why would he be ignoring the buzzer? Marc couldn't help but feel tense. He had a feeling that Paul was in danger. Hell, he had a feeling that he was in danger himself.

But if Paul was in danger, wasn't he likely to be elsewhere? This doorman looked like he could protect the tenants in his care. But where could Paul be? Anywhere.

More time passed. *Wouldn't the doorman have seen Paul if he went out again?* And why would he have gone out again after calling Marc?

Marc walked over to the doorman and asked, "Could you buzz Paul Johnston again?"

The man nodded tiredly, then pushed the buzzer for 11G. Nothing.

Then someone buzzed the doorman. It turned out to be 8J. "I'll get it ready for you," the doorman said. He walked back toward the mailboxes, ducking into a big closet where packages and dry cleaning were stored.

Marc's mind raced with the sudden possibilities and he acted swiftly. Remembering Jill Montana's successful caper earlier this evening, Marc stepped behind the doorman's desk and opened the cabinet full of keys. *Where's 11G? Shit! They're coded somehow. Why aren't our keys coded?* he wondered.

There was a chart taped to the front desk that broke the code. *58!* Marc grabbed the keys on the hook marked "58" and ran toward the nearest stairwell. He wasn't quite fast enough.

"Hey!" the doorman yelled. "Come back! I'll call the police, then come after you myself!"

Marc was in the stairwell and still running. *I guess I'm no Jill Montana,* he thought as he huffed and puffed. *Not too smooth. Paul better be there to call off the manhunt.*

The buzzer from downstairs sounded yet again. Otto looked down at his "patient" and said, "You have annoying friend. *Ist Marc Wilson, ya?*"

Shit! How much do they know about Marc?

Weiß er mehr als er sollte, auch? Otto thought, troubled that Marc also might know more than he should.

Otto held the drip-bag a little higher, hoping to accelerate the flow of poison into his victim. Paul stared up at the half-full, half-empty bag. He had ceased his useless, undirected struggle. He needed some sort of opening, some opportunity, or he would die soon. His mind was working hard, trying to devise a plan, but he had nothing to work with. He had little movement in his hands and feet, and his feet were asleep. He could move his body as a whole, which wasn't attached to anything other than itself, but Otto was standing right over him. Was there anything that could distract Otto? If only Paul had been a ventriloquist, then he could throw his voice without moving his taped lips. *Or if only I had telekinetic powers ...* Paul thought.

The phone rang. An unfamiliar voice said, "Hello. This is the doorman. I don't know if you're home or not, but some crazy man just grabbed your keys and started running up the stairs."

"*Was ist es ...*" Otto dropped the I.V. bag on the bed and looked toward the front door.

"I'm calling the police, but I can't leave my post without relief." Pause. "Just thought you should know." Click.

Otto bolted from the bedroom, heading for the front door. He had to keep them out. Should he chain the door? No, that would give it away that someone was home. *Ich muss schnell denken*, Otto knew he had to think fast. For the first time in an active day, he was sweating.

Otto felt around in his back pocket, pulling out some coins and a used toothpick. He dropped the coins and yanked the front door open. *Gut. Keiner hier noch. Töten Sie nicht Wilson hier wollen. Zu unordentlich,* he thought, not wanting to kill him here because it would be too messy.

At the same time as Otto was opening the door, Paul rolled off his bed onto the carpeted floor. The impact was painful but bracing. The needle pulled out of his arm in mid-air, falling nearby with the rest of the apparatus still attached.

Otto was concentrating completely on the task at hand. He shoved the toothpick into the Medeco lock, then snapped it off, leaving the tip behind.

Paul worked his way over to grab the deadly needle.

Otto used a key to push the piece of wood deeper into the lock, out of plain sight. That should work. It would have to.

Paul used the needle to make a hole in the stocking tied around his hands. He pulled on it, starting a run.

Otto slammed and locked the door.

Paul stopped pulling and covered the run in the stocking with his hands.

Marc was wheezing as he passed the tenth floor. He had considered switching to the elevator part of the way up, but he couldn't stop and wait for it.

Marc wondered if the doorman would come after him, or was already there. Could the man leave his station? Hopefully not, but he could call the police, as he threatened.

Marc burst out onto the eleventh floor and ran to Paul's door. No point in knocking now. He examined Paul's key ring, then pushed a key into the top lock.

Otto dumped Paul's squirming weight back onto the bed. *"Ich sollte ihre Kehle,"* Otto whispered feeling that he should just cut Paul's throat. *"Schau mal, Sie machten das kleine Loch größer. Es verblutet,"* Otto said, upset that Paul had made the little hole bigger and that it was now bleeding. He wiped Paul's arm with a dirty tissue, but not before a drop of blood hit the blanket.

They both heard the sounds of Marc struggling with the lock.

After Manny the doorman called the police, he paced back and forth impotently. What was going on upstairs? He had to go stop this guy.

When Mr. Silverberg from 9C walked in, Manny blurted, "There's an emergency on 11. Can you stand here for a couple minutes?"

Silverberg shrugged and said, "Sure."

Manny was ringing for the elevator seconds later.

Otto became concerned by the continued sounds of lock and door jiggling. He crept over to the front door in order to hear and see better, to gauge the intruder's chances of success. Otto pulled his switchblade and held it ready.

Thattaboy, Marc, thought Paul. *But watch out for that Kraut waiting for you.*

Paul worked on spreading the run in his bonds.

Marc was stymied by Paul's locks. One key seemed to fit the top, or almost did. But it wouldn't turn. The other keys didn't fit at all. He tried several keys on the bottom lock and one worked, but the door wouldn't open because the top was still locked. He tried the other keys on the top lock again. He forced a key in, then had difficulty removing it. He tried just twisting the doorknob in frustration. *That would be funny if it opened right up.*

Could Paul have changed his locks and neglected to replace the keys downstairs? Maybe. Should Marc try to break down the door? He'd come this far already. *No, that would be crazy.* Anyway, he probably couldn't really break down a door. He'd never tried.

Marc looked back at the elevator and the stairs. He had to decide on a course of action. Soon the doorman and/or the cops would arrive. He was already in some shit, but it would be much worse if he managed to break down the door.

He should probably just give it up and go. He banged on the door for the hell of it. "Paul, are you in there or not?"

The sudden banging on the door startled Otto for a moment. Then he tensed and held the blade higher. A few moments after that, he started to relax.

Paul's hands were free. *I probably only have a few more*

seconds to plan, he thought. *Should I stay here and pretend to still be helpless, then grab him when he gets close enough? No. Realistically, I don't think I have the cool nerve for that one. Should I hide, under the bed, in a closet, or something? Or should I try to sneak up on him?*

Marc heard the bell before the elevator doors opened. On an impulse, he ducked around the corner. Manny the doorman charged toward Paul's front door and began pounding on it. "Come out or let me in, you crazy man!" Manny yelled.

Guess this is my cue, Marc thought. *Maybe I can still give up this wild goose chase and stay a free man a little longer.*

Otto had been about to return to the bedroom when this new threat arrived and started pounding and screaming. This really was serious. It sounded like the doorman who had called before, and he sounded big. The man evidently thought that Wilson had used his keys and was already in the apartment. This guy wasn't going to rest until he got in.

Otto couldn't think of a smooth way out. He'd have to just stab Paul and the doorman. At least he was planning to head back to Germany tomorrow anyway.

Paul was unbound and crawling slowly and quietly into the living room. *Great. Otto seems really distracted.* Paul wondered if he should just yell out to the doorman, let him know the story? *No,* he thought. *It would be better to conceal his situation until he could deliver the telling blow.*

While Manny pounded on the door and yanked on the doorknob, Marc was pressed up against the wall, making his way carefully toward the stairwell. Then Manny looked over and saw him.

"Hey, is that you?" Manny cried out. "What are you doing there?"

Marc pulled open the stairwell door and hit the stairs at full-speed, taking three at a time. Manny started after him, then switched to the elevator. It came right away, but stopped on two different floors. When Manny reached the lobby, Marc was gone and Mr. Silverberg was confused.

Otto was relieved that all the fools had gone. He turned and saw Paul, almost upon him.

Twenty-Three

The flight to Germany was scheduled for 10:20 a.m. Eckart had called yesterday and said that he would pick Marc up at 7 a.m. on his way to Kennedy Airport. Marc wasn't offered a say in the matter.

Marc called Paul's home phone and his cell phone at 6:00, 6:30 and 6:55 a.m. Each time voicemail answered. *He's not home, and he hasn't checked messages,* Marc thought. *Did he get lucky and go home with some beautiful stranger last night? How could he do something like that at a time like this?*

Paul better be okay. If something happened to him, I could be next. How can I be going to Germany with Eckart today? Guess there's no way to avoid it. Not without admitting that the whole jig is up. That would end my investigation of Eckart and the Committee. And maybe my life, too.

Marc tied his tie and sealed his suitcase. *Might as well go downstairs and wait for the hangman.* He consoled himself with the plan that he would call the firm from the airport and speak with Paul then.

On the dot of 7 a.m., a black sedan from the ABC Car Service pulled up in front of Marc's building. As the driver put

Marc's suitcase in the trunk, Marc climbed into the back of the car. Eckart smiled and wished Marc, "Good morning."

Marc smiled back and echoed Eckart's sentiment. Then neither man spoke for two minutes. Marc was glad not to have to make conversation, but uncomfortable about the silence nonetheless. Casually, he pulled the *Times* out of his briefcase and stared sightlessly at the front page. After a suitable period of time, he turned the page.

Marc looked at Eckart out of the corner of his eye. Eckart's eyes were closed and he seemed to be dozing. *Great*, Marc thought. *Just relax, get your beauty sleep. Don't feel like you have to entertain me.*

Now Marc was able to concentrate enough to read a few pages of the newspaper. It was a slow news day.

"How's your uncle?"

Marc almost jumped. He turned to meet Eckart's stare. "Okay, I guess."

"Haven't you been to his house yet?"

"No, not yet," Marc answered apologetically, falsely implying a plan to visit his uncle.

"What did I tell you?" Eckart asked.

"I know ..."

"I asked you to do something for me. And for you. And what have you done?"

On this last line, Eckart's voice rose to a near-thunderous volume. This was by far the most confrontational Eckart had ever been with Marc. And the closest physical proximity in which Marc had ever been trapped with Eckart. What could Marc say?

"I'm having dinner with him next Saturday," Marc blurted. Somehow, the lie relaxed him. For good measure, he added, "I was going to have dinner there *this* Saturday, before this German trip came up."

Eckart looked pleasantly surprised. He nodded slowly. "Good boy," Eckart said seriously, without obvious humor or irony in his voice or face. Then the partner snapped instantly into his cordial small talk personality. "Do you have any plans for Saturday night? Is there anything left in Munich which you haven't done?"

Marc answered on autopilot, while wondering *why does he care about my relationship with Uncle Charlie? Does he think I can spy on Charlie for him? And is that what Uncle Charlie wants from me: to spy on Eckart? But Charlie's already got Paul for that* ... Which reminded him: *Paul better be okay!*

The car seemed awfully small. Marc opened his window a crack, hoping that a little fresh air would alleviate his claustrophobia. Thank God, they were approaching LaGuardia. Kennedy was only a few miles farther. That meant that it could be anything from ten minutes to an hour from here, depending on traffic.

Plenty of time for Eckart to bring up another really uncomfortable topic. "And how's my daughter?" he asked.

Could he know that we just got back together? And does he know about his share in the responsibility for our reunion? "Uh, she's good."

"I haven't seen her for some time. She's always so busy. I guess she makes time for you, though."

Marc reeled at the subtle animosity in Eckart's comment. Aimed at him *and* Sam, it seemed. "Oh, I've only seen her once in the last month. She *has* been incredibly busy." He made a mental note: *got to make Sam visit her dad some time soon. Or at least call. And try to act natural. Can't afford to let him get suspicious. Not until we have at least some type of plan.*

"She's a tough kid," said Eckart. "Always been her own boss."

Marc doubted that was true. But he hoped it was coming true, with a *little* help from him.

"I miss those old days," Eckart mused aloud. "She was cute as a button."

Marc was caught off-guard by Eckart's sentimentalizing.

He felt kindly toward the man for a fraction of a second. Then he remembered the things Eckart had done to his little daughter and he wanted to throw up. And to kill the man.

There was uncomfortable silence until the car pulled into the labyrinth of Kennedy Airport. As the driver threaded his way toward Lufthansa Departures, Eckart said, "By the way, did I tell you that we won the motion to transfer?"

At last, business. Marc thought back ruefully on the days when he had been nervous about discussing the *law* with his boss. "No," Marc answered. "When did that happen?"

"We got the decision in the mail yesterday. It was short and to the point. The judge paraphrased your brief in several spots. Good work."

Just a week ago this news and praise would have made Marc feel much better. "How does this affect us?"

"Not much right now. We still have to do the same investigatory legwork. Our defense is the same: unforeseeable external sabotage. I think the German courts will be receptive to our arguments."

I'll bet, thought Marc. *Even if the new judge isn't in Eckart's pocket, he probably won't be a friend to gypsies.*

The driver helped Eckart and Marc remove their bags from the trunk. Marc and Eckart had each brought one bag and a briefcase to carry on.

All during the time that they were checking in, then going through security, Marc was having difficulty hiding his anxiety.

After they finally got to the gate, Marc excused himself to go to the bathroom. "Might as well leave your stuff with me," Eckart suggested, walking over to a seat and placing his case next to it. "No sense carrying it to the john."

"Oh, of course." Marc placed his suitcase and briefcase next to Eckart's. "Thanks."

Marc looked around for bathrooms, hoping they'd be far away. *Damn, what were the odds?* There was a men's room just a few yards from where they were sitting. Marc headed for the bathroom, turning back only momentarily at the entrance. Eckart didn't seem to be watching, so Marc quickly changed course and continued past.

Marc walked at a rapid pace away from Eckart, following signs toward the next bathroom area. It was almost an hour until their flight was scheduled to take off, but Marc wanted to return before Eckart had a chance to miss him.

It was 9:25 a.m. Paul usually arrived at his office at about 9:15. Marc pulled out his cell phone and punched in the numbers. "May I speak to Mr. Johnston?" Marc asked Paul's secretary without identifying himself.

"He's not in yet. Can I take a message?" she asked.

"Uh, no thanks. I'll call back." *Stay calm. He's only a few minutes late. So far. I'll call back, just before boarding.*

Without much hope, Marc tried calling Paul's cell phone again. The voicemail picked up yet again.

Marc went to the bathroom, then hurried back to Eckart. Fortunately, Eckart didn't look up as Marc approached. Marc muttered, "Hi," pulled a book out of his briefcase, then sat next to Eckart.

At 10 o'clock the airline announced that the flight would begin boarding in just a few minutes, "Thank you for your patience. We are endeavoring to stay on or close to schedule."

I have to call again. But what will I do if Paul isn't there? Will I still go to Germany?

Of course I'll still go to Germany. How could I not go? Plus I'll probably be safer in Germany than in New York. While I'm there with Eckart on official business, I'm his responsibility, right?

"At this time we'd like to board all those with small children ..." the airline worker announced.

Shit!

"I'll be right back," Marc told Eckart.

"Where are you going? We're boarding."

"Phone's dying. Need to buy one of those emergency boosters ..."

"Forget it," Eckart said forcefully. "It's too late."

"Uh, I just have to make a quick call ... to my mother."

Before Eckart could protest again, Marc ran off twenty feet and used his cell phone to call the office. Eckart was watching him with interest, but he was just out of earshot.

"Hello, is Paul Johnston there?" Marc's voice almost cracked from the tension.

"No, I'm sorry, he's not in right now."

Marc wasn't surprised, yet he was stunned. And terrified. "Wait," he said. *Maybe I'm jumping to conclusions.* "He's not in *right now*? Has he come in today at all?"

"No, he isn't in yet. Who's this, please?"

Marc felt like he was falling. Eckart was waving to him impatiently. He seemed miles away.

Marc tried one more time. "Did Paul call in? Did he say where he was? When he's coming in ..."

"No, I'm sorry. Who is this?"

Marc hung up and started walking toward Eckart. "What was so important?" Eckart asked. "You could have called from the plane."

Marc didn't answer. He picked up his bags and got on the boarding line. Eckart picked up his one bag and stood behind Marc. "What's going on, Marc? Is something wrong?"

"Nothing," Marc muttered. He couldn't manage more.

Paul's dead! The conclusion seemed inescapable.

Marc couldn't mourn Paul now. What was he going to do?

The line moved up and Marc shuffled along with it.

The logical thing was still to go to Germany. Surely Eckart wouldn't kill him there.

The airline worker took Marc's boarding pass from him, scanned it, and handed a piece back to him. Eckart stepped up behind him.

This was it. Marc felt trapped as he started down the tube to the plane. The open door and the smiling flight attendant beckoned him on, but he couldn't make himself go. Marc stopped just short of the plane. Eckart bumped him, then stopped.

Logic didn't matter anymore. Marc couldn't get on the plane with this killer. He couldn't go to Germany.

At least I know New York.

"I've got to do something," Marc mumbled as he turned around and started past Eckart.

"What? Where are you going?" Eckart followed right behind.

The gate agent tried to stop Marc. "What are you doing?"

"Forgot something ..."

"The plane's about to leave," the man said. "There's just one late arrival left to board ..."

As he pushed past the worker, Marc collided with the late arrival. He and Otto the skinhead recognized each other instantly and simultaneously.

Before either one could act, Marc was grabbed from behind. With one strong arm around Marc and the other squeezing his shoulder, Eckart spoke firmly and loudly. "Come on, Marc. Flying is perfectly safe. Did you take your pill?"

"Ohhh," said the airline worker, nodding his understanding. "There's no reason to worry, sir. Flying's safer than driving."

"Poor fellow," said Otto, shaking his head sympathetically and putting a hand on Marc's other shoulder.

Marc was surrounded. Everything was out of control. Nothing was safe anymore.

"Come on," said Eckart in a patronizing tone, while tightening his iron grip on Marc's shoulder. "Turn back around and let's get on that big bad plane."

Marc spun around, twisting free of Eckart's grasp and taking one step back. Eckart looked surprised. He reached out to Marc but never connected. Without further thought, Marc smashed his right fist into Bill Eckart's iron jaw. Eckart looked shocked, but the blow only sent him staggering back two steps.

Marc turned again to face the airline worker and the skinhead, each of whom looked surprised themselves. Marc dropped his briefcase, elbowed past the worker, then threw his heavy carry-on bag at Otto. In the split second before impact, the skinhead unsuccessfully tried to duck, leaving himself off-balance enough that the impact of the luggage sent him sprawling.

Marc ran. Out past the metal detectors, slowing down as he got onto the "down" escalator to Arrivals. Once outside in the standstill traffic of the Arrival pick-up area, he stopped for a few moments while looking around for pursuit. He didn't see anyone yet, but he couldn't wait on the long line for taxis. If any one was coming after him, he'd be a sitting duck there.

Marc chased a Budget Rent-a-car van that was crawling in the traffic. He persuaded the driver to open the door although he wasn't near the curb. Then he slouched down low in his seat, far from the one other passenger.

"Not much luggage," the driver commented. *Not anymore, anyway.* Marc pictured his medium-sized suitcase, soon to be sitting on a deserted German baggage conveyor belt.

"Where you from?" the driver asked him with idle curiosity.

"Intercourse, Pennsylvania."

PART THREE

Twenty-Four

When the van dropped him off at Budget, Marc had no idea what he was going to do next. *I guess I should try to find out exactly what happened to Paul.*

Then Marc remembered David Gutierrez. Paul had promised to cover the conference in Marc's *pro bono* case. Judge Kelly was going to go through the roof when he heard that neither deposition had been conducted. Although it was the government's fault, if Marc didn't show up Dinaro might be able to blame the delays on Marc and his client.

I can't let David and Berna Gutierrez down, whatever my problems are. Theirs is the only worthwhile case I have.

Marc had the cab drop him off a block from Paul's apartment. Although Marc regretted the loss of his luggage, it was nice not to have anything to carry.

It was shortly after noon, but a television newsperson was already reporting from outside. Marc joined the gathering crowd and heard the reporter saying that Paul Johnston had been a young rising star at the prestigious mid-town law firm of Ballen Warren & Dow.

Fuck. I was right.

"According to detectives on the scene," said the reporter, "the handsome young attorney was stabbed and brutally beaten almost beyond recognition with the base of a track and field trophy. Police are unsure as to the motive."

As Marc pushed in closer to the reporter, he heard her introduce Manny the doorman. "We understand that you were on duty last night, when this brutal murder evidently occurred."

"It wasn't my fault," the man protested. "This crazy man held me at gun point, took the keys and went up to Mr. Johnston's apartment."

What is he saying? Marc wondered.

"I went up and chased him away. I didn't know he had already gone in and beaten the poor guy to death."

As Marc turned to leave, he heard Manny describing the killer as "average height, average weight, with brown hair and brown eyes."

Thank God, I'm average.

Marc was walking up the big steps to the Southern District federal courthouse by 1:40 p.m. Dozens of attorneys and a handful of clients were trying to get through the metal detector for their 2:00 p.m. hearings. Marc had to wait almost five minutes for his turn. It felt strange not to be carrying a briefcase to place flat on the X-ray conveyor.

Marc set off the metal detector. One of the three armed U.S. Marshals stopped him and ordered him to empty his pockets. Marc threw his change, wallet and big chain of keys (work, home and Mom's house) into the plastic tray and walked back through. Success. He grabbed his possessions and headed across the high-ceiling entrance hall toward the elevator bank.

Marc rode to the sixth floor in an elevator crowded with lawyers. He looked around him with thinly veiled uneasiness. Marc was relieved not to see anyone he knew, considering that most of the attorneys he knew were Satan-worshippers and/or killers. Even so, he eyed the men and women beside him suspiciously.

On the sixth floor, Marc walked past the doorway marked "Private" into the hallway where the judge's chambers were. Judge Kelly was one of the few federal judges who allowed attorneys into his chambers—outer chambers, to be sure, not his office itself. Most judges had conferences in their courtrooms.

The attorneys from three other cases were there, but not Joe Dinaro, the government attorney in Marc's case. Marc hung his overcoat on the coat rack and waited with the rest of the attorneys in the front area by the judge's secretary/receptionist. One by one, each case was called and the lawyers involved proceeded into the judge's chambers.

Dinaro arrived at 2:20 p.m., during the second conference, apologizing to the receptionist. "Sorry. I had another conference and I couldn't get anyone to cover."

Dinaro sat across from Marc and took a brief out of his briefcase. Marc stared at him balefully, while the man at least pretended to be studying the document in front of him. Dinaro flipped the pages with a little too much show.

It wasn't until the fourth time that Jim the law clerk came out into the waiting area that he greeted Marc and Joe and said, "Come on in and let's get started."

As Marc had guessed, Judge Kelly was angry when he heard that no depositions had taken place. Unfortunately his anger didn't seem to be aimed at Dinaro.

"Why didn't you produce your client to be deposed?" the judge asked Marc, while Jim watched and took notes.

"Me?" Marc was caught by surprise. "I was supposed to depose them first ..."

"There's no priority in federal court," the judge reminded him.

"I know, but defendants didn't even answer our interrogatories properly ..."

"Mr. Wilson, do you remember what I said 5 weeks ago?" Judge Kelly questioned.

"Yes, you said you'd hold us in contempt ..."

"Correct. How come you remember now, yet didn't act accordingly?"

What sort of persecution is this? "But defense counsel called me the morning of their deposition and wouldn't even explain ..."

"That's no answer, Mr. Wilson. Face up to your own responsibilities."

This is totally unreasonable. But don't forget, the judge is always right. At least until the appeal. And you can't appeal a tongue-lashing anyway.

"I'm sorry," said Marc. "If you give me another chance, I'll put off everything else to move this case forward."

"You're damn right, you will." The judge kept pushing, unsatisfied by Marc's pledge. "You'll produce your client within the week, for defense counsel to question from day to day until he's satisfied."

"But what about *my* discovery?"

"If you don't like their answers to interrogatories, make a motion. But see if you can come up with deposition dates which are convenient for the officers."

"But Your Honor ..."

"I'll see you back here in exactly another 5 weeks." Judge Kelly looked straight at Marc and added, "You'd better get your act together. And show more respect." Without another word, Judge Kelly vanished into his inner office.

Jim the clerk repeated, "Five weeks. January 22nd. We'll see you back here then."

"Right. Thank you," said Dinaro as he darted toward the door.

"Thanks," Marc muttered as he stood up to leave. He was moving slowly, still dazed from the unexpectedly personal battering.

Dinaro was long gone by the time Marc reached the outer

door. "Wait a minute," Jim called after him. "Marc? Can I talk to you for a second?"

Marc stopped, looking disoriented. What could Judge Kelly's clerk want to discuss with him? Without Dinaro around, such a conversation would be an improper *ex parte* communication. *Am I supposed to explain the rules of ethics to a federal judge's law clerk?*

"Oh, Peg," the law clerk said to the receptionist. "Could you go get those books I asked for? Now, please?"

"Sure, Jim. Will you cover the phones?"

"You know I will. Thanks, Peg." To Marc, he said, "Could you come back in for a moment?"

Marc shrugged and followed the man. "I guess. What is it?"

"Sit down." Marc complied. "Sorry the judge was so hard on you just now."

Marc said, "I was just surprised that he let the government attorney off so easy."

"We're sorry you were so upset. Especially in light of your current problems."

"What? What do you mean?"

"We know you've been confused and upset lately."

Marc couldn't believe his ears. "What? Who told you that?"

Jim looked at Marc with feigned concern. "Bill Eckart's been worried about you." *Eckart?* "Says you've been awfully moody."

Uh oh. Marc jumped to his feet.

"Sit back down." Jim's voice had taken on harsh tones, but not as harsh as the gun in his right hand.

It was too far to the door. Marc sat on the couch. Jim stood over him, four or five paces away.

"I always feel so safe in this courthouse," Jim began. "Some people put them down, but the U.S. Marshals really do a good job. With their metal detectors, they make sure that no one brings guns in. Except the marshals themselves. And the judges.

Did you know that judges are allowed to carry guns into the courthouse? We've got gun control here."

"Does Judge Kelly know what you're doing?"

"You leave him out of this!" Jim snapped. "He's busy. But of course, as his senior law clerk, *I'm* really the one who makes the decisions around here anyway."

Stay calm. Keep him talking while you think of a way out.

"What have you decided to do?" Marc asked.

"I hate that!" Jim exclaimed, taking two steps closer to Marc and waiving the gun wildly. "Lawyers are always bothering me to find out if there's a decision yet. I'll tell you when I feel like it!"

He's really enjoying this. I wonder if this is his first time terrorizing an attorney. With a gun ...

Marc was quiet, waiting for Jim to feel like talking to him. Marc continued to face Jim, while searching out of the corners of his eyes for something, anything he could use.

But Jim wasn't saying anything. He was just breathing heavily, acting like he was trying to psyche himself up for something.

Finally, Marc asked, "Did Eckart get off the plane? Are you taking me to him?"

Jim laughed mirthlessly. "Maybe in the long run." Jim took one more step closer to Marc, so that they were only separated by three or four feet. "You stayed behind after the conference," he recited as if by rote. "You were angry about how the judge treated you. You argued, you wouldn't leave, then you grew violent ..."

"What are you talking about?" Marc asked, as he peripherally noticed a formidable dagger-like letter opener ten feet away on a desk. That was all he'd found so far, except for a heavy ceramic vase on the windowsill.

"You grabbed the sharp letter opener from the desk and came at me with it. Luckily I knew where Judge Kelly keeps his gun ..." Jim was sweating and trembling, like he might pull the trigger at any moment. Yet he didn't.

Marc couldn't believe the audacity of it. Could they expect to get away with this, in the middle of the federal courthouse? Then again, did they *care* whether or not Jim's story was believed?

Marc voiced his suspicions. "You won't get away with it."

"Yeah, right. You *would* say that."

"No, I mean the *Committee* will get away with it, but *you* won't. Judge Kelly will probably say that *you'd* been acting moody lately. He'll turn you over to the cops in a minute. Unless he kills you first, and says that I did it."

Jim massaged his scalp with his left hand, while trying to hold the gun steady with his right. "No! You don't know!"

Marc reached into his pocket as he observed, "I guess they didn't teach you this stuff at Yale, or Harvard, or wherever you went to law school. They covered how to steal, but not how to kill." Marc pulled his hand out of his pocket. "Or how to avoid being a fall guy." Marc felt like Humphrey Bogart with this "fall guy" stuff.

Jim was holding the gun with both hands now. The sweat was rolling down his face and landing at his feet. Marc's face was almost as wet.

"Save your own life," Marc counseled. "Let me go. Fire one shot after me if you want."

"They'd kill me."

"For one little fuck-up? Wouldn't they let you try–?" In mid-sentence, in one quick fluid movement, Marc hurled his heavy keychain at Jim's face and threw himself to the floor in front of the couch. Jim fired a fraction of a second too late, the bullet traveling through the back of the couch. The keys caught him in the right side of the face just a moment before Marc rolled into his legs and pulled them out from under him.

Jim managed to hold onto the gun, but not to fall well. Blinding pain shot up Jim's spine from the impact. He fought his way through it and tried to sit up, but Marc jumped on him and drove him back down.

Marc grabbed at the gun with two hands. The phone rang, but they both ignored it. Marc managed to pry the gun loose and toss it to the left, just as Jim brought his left arm around to bash into Marc's unprotected back. Jim rolled Marc over and got on top of him, but Marc slipped out before Jim could secure his grasp.

Jim was closer to the gun. Marc knew he couldn't catch him in time, so he headed the same way but with a different goal. As Jim snatched up the gun and lifted it to aim, Marc spun around with the ceramic vase in both hands. Marc used his body's momentum like a discus thrower and sent the vase hurtling the four feet between them. Jim's mouth was open when the projectile struck his forehead and sent him flying backward. This time the gun went flying also.

Marc scooped up the gun and aimed it at Jim. The clerk was dazed, but still conscious. He laughed. "What are you going to do now? Shoot *me*? You *know* you can't do that. You'd never make it out of this building alive." He coughed a couple of times. "And if you did, I'd pity you then."

Shit. He's right. Marc leaned down and smashed the gun against the top of Jim's head. There was no visible blood, but this time Jim was unconscious. Marc put the gun in the inner pocket of his suit jacket.

Marc looked back at the door to Judge Kelly's inner office. Could the judge still be in there? Surely he'd heard their struggle. He must be in on it. Was he cowering in a corner? Should Marc go in there? *No, just get the hell out of here while you still can.*

Marc grabbed his overcoat from the rack and placed the gun in an inner pocket. He played with it, trying to minimize the bulge of the gun, then went out the door into the hall. He passed several other judge's chambers on the way back to the elevators. He also passed Judge Kelly's secretary, who was carrying two books and heading back to chambers. To Marc's chagrin, she saw him, recognized him, smiled, and said, "Hi." At least she probably didn't know his name, not that it would be hard to figure out from the judge's calendar.

Marc smiled back, nodded, and turned the corner to the elevator bank. He pressed the "down" button several times. He looked around nervously, but no one else was in sight. He noticed and stared at the three-dimensional flower-in-a-square pattern on this and every other ceiling in the building. He pressed the elevator button again. Then he pressed the "up" button too. He had to at least get off the floor. He looked for the stairway entrances.

An elevator opened and he jumped in. The elevator went up to the tenth floor, then down to five and three. Finally, Marc reached the first floor and walked briskly toward the front entrance/exit.

Marc slowed down as he saw the activity ahead of him. There was a line of people waiting to leave the building, and there were twice the usual three marshals on duty. As Marc shuffled toward the end of the line, Marc saw that the marshals were making people go through the metal detector on the way out, in addition to on the way in. The last person on line turned to Marc and said, "How do you like that? I'm going to be late getting to the Eastern District. Just 'cause some psycho picks today to attack a judge."

"What?" Marc asked with genuine surprise. *A judge, not a law clerk? I guess that was the only way to mobilize the U.S. Marshals this fast.* Marc was still surprised and impressed by the marshals' quick response.

"Some guy tried to kill Judge Kelly. Didn't like a ruling or something."

"Jesus! Is the judge alright?"

"I think so. Someone said his law clerk saved him. Said the guy's name was Winston, Wilson, something like that ..."

Marc tried to think of options. There was no other exit. What could he do?

Marc wondered if the marshals knew what he looked like.

They probably had a description. *Who called them? The receptionist or Judge Kelly?* Marc remembered how the marshals had stopped him on his way out the last time he had been here on the Gutierrez case. That time it had been to talk to his Uncle Charlie on the seventeenth floor. But he had been the only one passing through at that particular time. Maybe this time they wouldn't recognize him from the description. Maybe someone else in line would look more like him than he did.

Just then Marc felt the weight of the gun and looked down at the bulge in his coat. He wouldn't pass visual inspection, let alone the metal detector. He had to inconspicuously step off the line and leave the gun in a bathroom or something.

Marc had turned and taken two steps when a man at the front of the line pointed at him and yelled his name. *Damn! Dinaro! What's he still doing here?*

Dinaro broke out of the line and started toward Marc. "That's the guy! Marc Wilson!" he yelled. A couple of U.S. Marshals pulled their guns and followed. Marc reacted instinctively, breaking to the right and turning the corner.

He was in the jury selection area. Without thinking, Marc stopped short at the door to the main juror's waiting room, then strolled in calmly. Without hesitation, he headed straight back a few rows in the large double room and sat down next to a young man in slacks and a tie, as if he were returning to a seat he had been occupying all day. Marc looked around him.

In contrast to Marc's last few moments of headlong flight, practically no one in the jury room was moving at all. Most people seemed frozen, staring sightlessly into space. An industrious handful read newspapers and magazines in slow motion.

The assemblage was a tribute to the democratic system. There were men, women, youngsters, oldsters, white, black, Hispanic, Asian, rich and poor, to name just a few categories. Of course the rich white men were most likely to be excused before serving their full two weeks, and so were under-represented, but at least they had to show up.

It seemed that Marc's quick and decisive move had paid off. Dinaro and the marshals must have run past the jury room in their search for him. *I wonder if Dinaro is enjoying this?*

Surely they'd be back eventually. Marc took a deep breath and considered his next move. He felt a sudden sharp pain in his gut and massaged it gently, while surveying his surroundings.

Marc had never picked a jury himself, but he had watched jury selections. He knew that one way of dividing these people into two distinct categories was that some of them were dying to get out of jury duty and some of them were actually dying to get picked for a jury, preferably a long murder trial. Marc had never been on jury duty and a law school professor had told him that neither he nor any of his classmates would ever be picked for a jury. But he had always thought it would be fun watching other attorneys sweating, trying to convince him of the merits of their pathetic little cases.

A woman walked in and handed a piece of paper to the man standing at a podium. The man announced, "I'm going to read a list of names. If you hear your name called, stand up and wait over here near me."

The man began to read the list. At first he paused after calling each name, waiting for the person to stand and approach. After the first half dozen names, however, he picked up the pace and the potential jurors stood up and sauntered over with more regularity. Marc followed the young man in the next chair when he got up. It was the safest way out of this room.

Soon the caller proclaimed, "That's it. All of you whose names I just called, follow Sarah here to Judge Carter's courtroom. The attorneys there will have some questions for you."

Marc and the potential jurors all followed the woman as she headed toward the elevators. Marc looked casually to the right as they passed the entrance area on the way. The line to leave the building was longer than ever. Marc kept moving with the crowd and got on one of the two elevators they were piling into.

As Marc had feared, Judge Carter's courtroom happened

to be on the sixth floor. Well, maybe Marc could make use of this stop. It had occurred to him that the only way he was going to make it out past the marshals was with a powerful escort. Marc could draft such a companion with the bulge in his coat, but he was reluctant to involve more people and hold an innocent judge hostage. So, the daring alternative was to revisit Judge Kelly and draft his aid.

No. That's impossible. By now, the judge must be surrounded by Jim, his secretary, and maybe a U.S. Marshal or two.

The elevator stopped at six and they pushed their way out, then waited for the other elevator to arrive. Marc was alarmed to notice Jim the clerk waiting for a "down" elevator. Marc turned away and burrowed deeper into the crowd. The next time he looked, Jim was gone. *I guess he's going to join the search.*

The other elevator of jurors arrived and they all started across the hall to Judge Carter's courtroom. Marc lagged behind the group. He would sneak off to a bathroom for further planning.

Marc couldn't believe his eyes. Now Judge Kelly was standing at the elevator bank, pressing the "down" button repeatedly. He looked distracted and hurried. There were still many people milling about in the hall, but Marc couldn't wait. He walked rapidly until he stood right behind the judge.

At that moment, the elevator right in front of Judge Kelly opened. There was no time for Marc to make himself known and stop the judge from boarding. Marc jumped on the elevator behind the judge, pushing past him. The judge turned to face the front without noticing Marc.

There were three other people in the car. The elevator stopped at the fifth floor and picked up two more people. As they pushed in, Judge Kelly happened to look around him. His eyes popped when he saw Marc, but Marc made sure that Judge Kelly felt the gun through his suit jacket before he could say anything.

Marc took the initiative, speaking in a casual tone, not too soft or too loud. "Judge Kelly. I've been *desperate* to see you," he said. Two people looked over at them briefly, then looked away. "I'd do *anything* to talk to you." Marc punctuated the word "anything" with increased pressure against the judge's back, in an attempt to prove that his desperation could drive him to risk a gunshot in a crowded elevator. It worked well enough to keep the judge quiet until the second floor.

When the doors opened on the second floor, Marc nudged Judge Kelly out. "Come on," he said. "This is our stop." Marc wasn't about to get off on the first floor, near the exit and the marshals. Not until he'd had a long talk with Judge Kelly.

The judge did not immediately comply with Marc's request. He too must have been thinking about those marshals on the first floor. The elevator doors started to close.

A man in the front caught the doors and pulled them open. "Here you go, Judge," said the man. "These doors don't give you a chance."

The judge had a vaguely sick look on his face as Marc followed him closely out. The doors closed all the way this time and left Marc and Judge Kelly alone in the second floor elevator bank hall.

Fortunately, the U.S. Marshals didn't have enough personnel to cover the whole building, but police were no doubt on the way. Marc had to bring the judge in line and execute his plan quickly.

"Let's go to that bathroom over there," Marc instructed. "I have to powder my nose."

Once again, Judge Kelly hesitated for a moment. Marc felt another sharp pain in his side and his gut, and he grimaced. Kelly stared at him, sizing him up.

Marc flashed the gun momentarily, speaking softly but forcefully. "I'm just a poor schmuck whose career is over. I'd like to get out of here alive, but my second choice is to blow your fucking head off."

Twenty-Five

While Marc was threatening Judge Kelly's life, Samantha Eckart was talking to Dr. Emma Kierst. Sam lied and said that not much was happening in her life.

Dr. Kierst was surprised. "Well, what about the dream? Have you still been having that dream with the girl in the cage?"

Sam shrugged. "No. It's weird, but I seem to be over it."

All the way to Dr. Kierst's office this morning, Sam had thought about what she should say to the psychiatrist. *I can't tell her what I've been finding out,* Sam had decided. *She's met my dad. He pays her bills. I can't tell her his secrets.*

Dr. Kierst jotted down some notes, then looked up and changed the subject. "Anything going on in your love life?"

"Surprisingly, yes. I got back together with Marc. But now he's in Germany with my father." *The murdering Satanist.* The thought rose up with a sudden intensity that made her want to scream, to smash something, to tell her psychiatrist everything.

But Sam resisted the impulses, turning her thoughts back to Marc. "I think Marc is actually good for me," she said.

⚖

Once in the bathroom with Marc, Judge Kelly caught him off-guard with his innocent-sounding question. "Why are you doing all this? Why did you attack Jim? What do you have against me?"

Marc blinked in amazement. Then he recovered, steadying the gun as he snarled, "Get off it. You're in on it with all of them. You can't get away with this act."

"What do you mean? You need help. You're completely paranoid. All I know is that you attacked Jim, then wrestled my gun away from him. Why'd you do it?"

It was possible. Marc didn't want to take a chance on killing an innocent man. And the judge could really help him if the man really was clean, and if Marc could convince him of things.

"Who called security?" Marc asked. "You or your secretary?"

"She did. Then she woke me up. I'd been taking a nap."

Could the judge really have slept through the sounds of the fight in the next room? Including the gunshot?

As if in response to Marc's mental questions, the judge explained, "The walls in this old building are extremely thick. And I sleep with headphones and loud classical music."

That seems weird enough to be true.

"How did your clerk get possession of your gun?"

"Jim knows I keep it in a desk drawer in the outer chamber. So he appropriately utilized it when you started threatening him with the dagger ..."

"I did *not* threaten him!" Marc exclaimed, a little louder than was prudent. "Don't you know that he's corrupt?"

"I don't believe you. But why do you care what I believe? *You* have the gun."

At last! The judge was thinking now. Maybe he was innocent. And maybe he could be convinced. Marc made the attempt. "I care what you believe because I'm *not* a crazy fiend who attacks clerks and judges. Some powerful people are trying to kill me."

Or maybe the judge was just stalling for time. Marc looked around the bathroom quickly. He was lucky that no one else had come in. *Yet.*

"Look," said Marc. "I don't know if you're in on it or not, but I know one thing. You're going to get me out of here. You and I are going to go down there and walk past those U.S. marshals. Or else we'll die together." He added, "And I'm sorry if you were innocent after all."

Judge Kelly didn't move or say anything. "Do you understand me, Judge? I've got nothing to lose." Marc held up the gun under his jacket and aimed it at the judge.

The judge looked cool, but he couldn't hide the sweat stains radiating out from under his arms. Marc could smell both of them. They smelled like hunted animals.

"Okay," said the judge, nodding slowly. "I think you at least believe that you're telling the truth. About this conspiracy. And about killing me. I'll help you out. Don't shoot me." The judge paused at the door. "You know I have a wife and two kids, right?" Oddly enough, Marc couldn't tell if this comment was serious or tongue-in-cheek.

"All the more reason to do what I say," was Marc's quick, convincingly hard-boiled response. "We'll take the stairs to the first floor. There'll be a line of people waiting to get searched by the marshals, as a result of your panic call. You'll cut that line and take me with you. At all times, I will stay no more or less than two paces behind you. I won't miss. Now go!"

The two stepped out into the second floor hall. Only one other person was there, waiting for an elevator. Marc followed Judge Kelly past the middle-aged attorney to the stairwell.

So far, so good. But how was Marc ever going to get past the crowds downstairs? And could he keep Judge Kelly scared of him when they were both surrounded by armed marshals?

"Wait," Marc ordered, as the judge was poised to open the door to the first floor.

Judge Kelly turned back to face Marc and the judge's own gun. "Don't worry. I told you I would help you. I give you my word that I won't give you away." The judge turned back toward the door.

"No, wait," said Marc, brandishing the gun. "Maybe we should try the Pearl Street exit, downstairs."

"I'm sure there are just as many marshals there by now," the judge answered with growing impatience.

"Well, step away and let me peek out." The judge took a step to the left. "Go back two steps," Marc instructed. The judge complied.

Through a tiny crack he made in the doorway, Marc couldn't see much, except that there were a lot of people all around. And he could hear the sounds of many excited people. After just a moment, he wheeled around to make sure of his prisoner, pointing the gun where the judge had been.

"Drop your hands down against your sides," Judge Kelly ordered Marc. The judge was one step lower and to the left of his previous position, with a pistol trained dead on Marc's heart. Marc had only a second to acknowledge that he could not re-adjust his aim before the man could shoot and kill him. Marc dropped his hands.

"Put the gun back in your jacket. Slowly." Marc did. "What made you think I only had one gun?"

"But why didn't you ..."

"I figured that your plan was the most likely way for you to get killed. Either by me or by one of our excellent marshals. With lots of witnesses to confirm your dangerous state. So don't chicken out now. Go!"

Judge Kelly fired his gun. Marc's heart stopped. Had he been shot? He didn't feel anything.

Then, despite the fact that he knew it was what Judge Kelly wanted him to do, Marc ran. He flung the stairwell door wide and ran.

After Samantha Eckart finished her session and left, Dr. Kierst continued taking notes for two more minutes. Then she made a phone call.

"It's Dr. Kierst again," she began. "Sorry to bother you. But I thought you should know that Samantha seems to be in a new phase."

"What do you mean?" the man on the other end of the line asked.

"She's no longer willing to talk about the dreams. She says that they've stopped. But I fear that her recent memory flashes are moving from her unconscious to her conscious mind." Dr. Kierst paused, wondering if further explanation was necessary. "I think she knows. But she may be going through denial."

"Could she be just pretending?" he asked.

"That's a good question. I don't know. I'll have to observe further."

"I'll observe as well. It's been too long since I've seen my daughter."

"Very good," said Dr. Kierst. "Let's both keep an eye on her."

"Thanks for keeping me so well informed. Naturally there'll be a nice bonus for you this month."

⚖

Despite Judge Kelly at his back, Marc didn't run far. Not to the waiting marshals, two of whom were looking in his direction. He took four steps, then twisted sideways and jumped through the doors of a crowded elevator before they could close. Unfortunately, having connected with Marc's shoulders, the doors opened again, resulting in annoyed sighs from a couple of the passengers.

Marc saw Judge Kelly approaching from one side and two marshals from the other as the doors met and the car started upward. Marc attempted to catch his breath, assuming an innocent expression as he looked around the elevator. Most of the passengers were minding their own business, but a few were giving him suspicious glances. For the hell of it, Marc looked at his watch: 3:10.

The elevator stopped at two, four, five, seven, eight, and ten before Marc decided what button to push.

It was business as usual on the seventeenth floor of the federal courthouse. The atmosphere at the Second Circuit Court of Appeals was as still and rarefied as ever. No marshals running around here. Yet.

The clerk's office was immediately opposite the middle elevator. The door to the courtroom was at one end of the hall, marked 1705, and the Court of Appeals judges' chambers were in the adjoining hall past the door marked "Private."

Marc figured that court was probably still in session and he should look in. Because Court of Appeals judges take turns hearing arguments in rotating panels, Marc had no idea whether Charles Wilson was on the panel today. The odds were probably only about 25 to 33 percent. *Please be there. And, please, help me.*

The entrance to room 1705 was a nondescript single door, as opposed to the polished wood double doors that opened into most courtrooms. Upon opening the door, Marc discovered that it opened into an anteroom that in turn led to the courtroom. The waiting room was comfortable, with plush carpeting and couches, and a walk-in coat closet.

Marc pushed gently against one of the double doors, then walked quietly into the courtroom. Despite his stealth, a few of the attorneys seated about the large, well-maintained room turned to stare. Who was he, entering so late in the session?

Three old Second Circuit judges were seated high above the sweating lawyers they faced, shielded by thick dark wood. Marc, never having been here before, didn't recognize any of them. As Marc walked out, the same few attorneys watched him in annoyed confusion.

The seventeenth floor was still quiet. Marc walked past the door marked "Private" toward Charlie Wilson's chambers. He knew that Second Circuit judges didn't routinely show up on days when they weren't on the panel, but it was possible. Although Marc still disliked and feared his uncle, he found himself hoping desperately that Charlie Wilson would be there. Only he had the power to help Marc now. But would he? Wilson had said that he wanted to help Marc and his family.

Marc tried to soothe his own fears and misgivings about the man. Wilson couldn't be in on the current plot to kill Marc. Jim the clerk had mentioned Eckart. Marc knew from Paul that Uncle Charlie saw Eckart as an ambitious rival, not an ally. Unless Jim had dropped Eckart's name just to throw Marc off ... No, surely Marc was thinking *too* deviously now, even for these people.

The secretary offered Marc a friendly smile, which expanded to a goofy grin when he said that he was Judge Wilson's nephew. "Is he in?" *Please.*

"He's in his office with Moira, his clerk." *Thank God.* "Is he expecting you?"

"I don't think so. I think it's a surprise. Will he be long?"

"I don't think so. They've been in there a while. Why don't you just take a seat and relax. You want to hang your coat?"

"No thank you."

Marc took a seat, but he couldn't relax. A couple of minutes passed. Marc couldn't wait much longer, especially since he was starting to hear loud voices from the hall. Coming closer.

"I'm in sort of a rush," Marc told the secretary, as he rose to his feet. "I'll just be a minute."

He headed back toward his uncle's office before the woman could stop him. He stopped at the inner door and took a moment to knock. When his uncle called out, "Who is it?" Marc answered at the same time as he opened the door.

"Marc, my boy!" Charlie Wilson jumped up from the couch to embrace him. Marc was relieved to receive such a warm welcome, but he still couldn't convince his body to respond to the hug.

Moira the clerk smoothed her skirt as she stood and approached the two Wilsons. As the curvaceous redhead smiled at him, Marc forgot all his troubles for a few seconds.

"Moira, this is my handsome and brilliant nephew, Marc. Have you met?"

Moira nodded hello. "Not formally."

She *did* look sort of familiar. But where could he ... *The Halloween party!* Of course Marc had noticed her then, but she had been occupied. By *two* guys.

"Do you two want to be alone?" she asked.

"Thanks, Moira. You and I are basically done anyway. I probably won't be in again until Friday, but you know where to reach me."

Just then they all heard the loud voices in the outer office. Moira went out to investigate, while Charles Wilson hung back a moment. He had seen Marc's tense reaction to the disruption.

"What is it?" Wilson asked.

I've got to trust him a little. "They're after me," Marc answered in a low voice. "Judge Kelly tried to kill me, then told the marshals that *I* tried to kill *him*."

"Come with me," Uncle Charlie instructed.

"I'll stay ..."

"It's too late to hide," Wilson said into Marc's ear, then grabbed his arm and started him on his way out.

"... only the judge's nephew. I don't know his first name," the secretary was saying as they approached.

The marshal's deep voice betrayed impatience. "But is this nephew average height, brown hair, brown eyes, about 30 ..."

Charlie Wilson began speaking just before he turned the corner to the reception area. "What's all the racket?" Marc hung back, just around the bend.

"Sorry, Judge Wilson. It's just that there's some wacko on the loose, tried to take a shot at Judge Kelly. Coincidentally, his name is Marc *Wilson*."

"My God!" Wilson exclaimed. "I hope you find the man. How could such a thing happen in a federal courthouse?"

"I know how you feel. We have marshals going from floor to floor, and the police should be here by now."

"Well, I was just going out for an early dinner with my nephew, Joe here." Judge Wilson looked behind him and Marc materialized, a smile plastered on his face. Fortunately, the marshal wasn't one of those who had chased Marc downstairs, but the big man stared at him nonetheless. "Do you think it's safe?" Wilson asked.

The man turned his gaze back to Judge Wilson. "Oh, I'm sure it is. He's just one guy, and this place is crawling with law enforcement agents."

"All the same, would you accompany us?" Charlie Wilson asked, as he put on his coat. Marc's stomach dropped out, and he looked down to help mask his anxiety. "I'd feel much safer."

"Yeah, okay, Judge," the gruff man replied, sizing up Marc again, deciding that he must be okay. "I was going back down soon anyway."

Moira looked at them with mild curiosity, as if she knew something was going on but didn't care too much if she ever found out what. The secretary said, "Have a nice day, Judge" as the three of them walked out.

Marc was starting to feel strangely calm. He felt secure in his uncle's company. Charlie Wilson had the power to open any door. But could even Judge Charles Wilson help him if Dinaro or someone else who knew Marc was waiting downstairs?

Dinaro wasn't downstairs. *Thank God. Maybe he's going from floor to floor with bloodhounds.* It looked like every other attorney in Manhattan was. The line to get out was longer than ever, with other people milling around and rubbernecking. Two city policemen were manning the exit along with the three U.S. Marshals. Marc assumed that there were more cops searching for him upstairs.

Their escort led them almost to the front of the line, saying to the other marshals, "Let Judge Wilson and his nephew out. They're in a rush."

The ordinary path to the exit doors had been blocked off with rope, forcing everyone to exit through the metal detector, which was normally only used for screening those on their way in. Marc had hoped that his uncle might be allowed passage through the roped-off area, but cutting the line like this was the next best thing. In a minute they'd be through the metal detector and out! Maybe his luck was starting to change.

God, I'm a fool! Marc remembered the weight of the gun in his coat's inner pocket. *I forgot to dump the gun!*

The group of attorneys in front of them had passed through the detector and were retrieving their briefcases from the x-ray conveyor belt. Charlie Wilson was poised to walk through when Marc stepped up behind him and smoothly thrust the gun into his uncle's right pocket. Charlie Wilson didn't hesitate or acknowledge the delivery in any way. The metal detector sounded as he walked through.

The judge immediately calmed the law enforcers who surrounded him instinctively. "I'm so sorry. I forgot I had this." He placed the gun in a tray with his keys and went back through the machine without event. He retrieved the gun and keys as Marc dropped his metal objects in the tray and went through the detector.

"Good luck, boys," said Second Circuit Court of Appeals Judge Charles Wilson. "I hope you catch whoever you're after, so we can all relax."

Twenty-Six

Charlie Wilson owned the largest, most lavishly decorated brownstone home in Manhattan. Or so it seemed to Marc, who didn't have much to compare it with. It was over seventy years old, the gray stone exterior dotted with gargoyles, each one distinct from the rest. Seeing Marc's interest, Charlie gave him a tour of the seven bedrooms, library, study, living room, large dining room, small dining room, music room, party room, kitchen and four bathrooms, laid out in four stories connected by stairs and an elevator. It was obscenely large for just one person.

Actually, five people lived there. Marc was introduced to the cook, the maid and the butler, having already met Tony, the chauffeur, when he drove them uptown from the federal courthouse. Marc noted that all of the men working for his uncle were large and tough looking, especially Tony. Marc guessed accurately that these men served the extra function of providing protection for his uncle. Coincidentally or not, Donna the maid was attractive.

Donna brought them each a beer and took their coats as Marc and his uncle settled down in the living room to talk. To Marc's surprise, the beer was domestic: Budweiser. The living room was a distinct space that led at one corner into the large dining room, which had a dumbwaiter connecting it to the kitchen on the ground floor. Both the living and dining rooms had high ceilings and many windows that looked out from the second floor onto quiet Seventy-Fourth Street, between Madison and Fifth Avenue. As Marc sat back in a plush old chair, sipping the beer in this comfortable fortress, he couldn't help but feel safe. He should have come here days ago.

"What would you like Antoine to make for dinner?" Donna asked them.

Charlie looked to Marc. "What do you feel like?"

"Can he really make anything?" Marc asked in wonder.

"The man's a genius. He possesses an overstocked pantry, a library full of cookbooks, a photographic memory, a golden palate, and the reverse engineering skills of an industrial spy."

Marc rubbed his aching gut. "Too bad my stomach's been killing me all day. Like someone's been driving in spikes. Must be all the excitement."

"That's a coincidence," said Charlie Wilson. "I've had pains like that for a couple of days now. Sharp pains in my side and my stomach. And a little shortness of breath. I must have eaten some MSG. I'm allergic."

That *was* a coincidence. There was something alarming about this coincidence that Marc couldn't quite pinpoint.

"I suppose we'd both better have some mild vegetable soup," Judge Wilson told Donna.

"You got it," she declared with a pleasing smile, then disappeared.

Poison! Could we both have been poisoned by Eckart and his henchman? Marc felt dizzy and nauseous.

"Eckart must be trying to kill us," Marc said to his uncle. Marc told his uncle of Eckart's boast that he was killing senior members of the Committee. Then Marc told him that many of the dead people on the Committee had had the same symptoms of chest pains and shortness of breath before having sudden magically induced heart attacks. Marc decided to hold back explaining to his uncle that Eckart's secret weapon wasn't magic, but a slow-working, traceless German poison administered by a young Nazi assassin.

Judge Wilson didn't seem surprised by what Marc had told him. Maybe he'd already heard it all from Paul. "So you think we're going to go the way of poor Bob Baylor and Doris Spender?"

"When did Doris Spender die?"

"Just last night. Also a heart attack. I suppose she had chest pains beforehand, but I hadn't talked to her for a couple of weeks."

So. The skinhead got to her after all. Marc wondered how many days ago Doris had been poisoned. *How much longer do we have? Marc longed to know. When were we poisoned?*

Marc felt numb. He couldn't understand a word his uncle was saying. Marc was under a death sentence. Which had already been carried out. *Could there be an antidote?* he speculated wildly. *Or is that stuff just in the movies?*

Then his mind snapped around one hundred eighty degrees. *This is crazy. I'm not going to die. Where and when could I have been poisoned?* Eckart wouldn't have bothered trying to get Marc on that plane to Germany if he'd already been poisoned. *And why would they still be trying to kill me at the courthouse if I'd already been poisoned? Maybe the pains were just ordinary pains, like an ulcer, or heartburn, or just nerves. Maybe it's all in my head.*

What about Uncle Charlie? Were his symptoms mere heartburn too? Marc wondered. *Too big a coincidence.*

"Tell me more about that bastard Eckart." Wilson didn't look scared. He looked invigorated.

"I don't know that much," Marc muttered. He told his uncle about the aftermath of the orthodox ceremony, about the phallus of gold and the terrible fate of the little girl.

"Has Eckart tried to get you to give him information

about me?"

"Yes, but I know less about you than I know about Eckart. He kept telling me I should get to know you better."

"He probably hired you to get to me. No offense to your legal abilities."

"Then he didn't get his money's worth," Marc commented.

"But you're here now," his uncle pointed out.

"What do you mean?"

"How do I know that you haven't sought me out now to gather information for Eckart? Well, your incredulous expression right now goes a long way toward convincing me. But surely Eckart said negative things about me, trying to poison you against me."

"Not really." He knew he didn't have to bother.

"I take it from your predicament today that you're on the outs with Eckart. That's too bad. Your relationship with Eckart could have been useful."

"It's too late for that now. Just as it's too late to save the life of Paul Johnston, your last spy." The memory roused Marc to anger and remorse.

Charlie Wilson became quiet. "I'm sorry. I know you two were close. I didn't think they'd act so quickly and ruthlessly. Eckart must be close to making his final move for control of the Committee. None of us is safe now."

"That reminds me," said Marc. "Would you mind giving me back that gun?"

Uncle Charlie smiled. "Of course. Good idea. You *should* have a weapon." His uncle presented Marc with Judge Kelly's gun.

"Thanks." Marc looked at the gun in his hands, felt its smooth weight, turned it over. He fought a momentary irrational urge to shoot Charlie Wilson between the eyes. *He gave me the gun*, Marc reminded himself. *And rescued me from an impossibly dangerous situation. He's on my side.*

"What about your mother?" Charlie asked.

"What do you mean?"

"Where is she? Is she safe?"

Jesus Christ! "You think they might go after my mother?"

"I wouldn't put it past them. She could be a weapon against either of us. Let me send Tony over to her place, to stand watch outside. I'll get her a guard of her own tomorrow, or we'll send her out of town." He hit an intercom button on the wall and asked for Tony.

"Thanks," said Marc, hoping that his uncle was overreacting, but wishing that he'd thought of his mother sooner. *I'm selfish and thoughtless. And too inexperienced at this sort of thing.*

Tony appeared, listened to his instructions, and then vanished. "He's a good man," said Charlie Wilson. "Been with me sixteen years. Would give his life for me and mine."

Marc was relieved to have the big bruiser on the job, protecting his mother. In general, his uncle seemed to know what he was doing and Marc was glad that he had come to Charlie Wilson.

Marc realized that this could be a chance to get some information on what the warfare on the Committee was all about. "What does Eckart want?" he asked.

"Power. As much as a man can have," Wilson answered. "And he knows the best way to get power is through the Committee. So he wants to rule the Committee."

"To replace Baylor?" Marc asked.

"To replace *me*. I thought you knew." At this point, Marc was barely surprised. "I've ruled the Committee for six years. Baylor stepped in as official figurehead after I was appointed a federal judge. No judges on the Committee's official roster, as you know."

"So Eckart wants to use his splinter group of fanatical Satanists to oust you?"

"That's right. He's evidently convinced them that I'm not devout enough, that I don't love Satan, that I don't want to bring about the reign of Satan on earth. He's right. I like Satan right where he is: in the hearts of all men and women."

Marc was both relieved and chilled by his uncle's words. "How did Eckart imagine that *I* could help him?"

"He hoped that you knew some of my secrets. Especially where I keep *The Book*. I suppose you don't know about *The Book*?" When Marc shook his head from side to side, Charlie Wilson continued, "*The Templar Book of Life and Death*. Styled after the *Egyptian Book of the Dead*. It's a uniquely confusing conglomeration of history, mythology and spells. It combines Christianity, Islam, the Egyptian cults of Isis, Osiris and Horus, and early Satanism, which of course contains elements of the other religions anyway."

"Does it relate to the medieval Knights Templar?" asked Marc, drawing on his research.

"*The Book* was written by Jacques de Molay, the last Grand Master of the Templars, while awaiting his death by fire in 1314. One of the jailors smuggled the pages out of the prison days before Molay's death. In the final pages of *The Book*, Molay wrote that his death would accomplish the first half of a spell to bring Satan to earth. He said, 'I have unlocked the gates of Hell. It now remains but for some brave soul to open those gates and free Satan's terrible hordes.'"

"You don't have the original book from 1314, do you?" Marc asked in disbelief.

"Oh, no. This is one of the only two copies of the German translation, created by Karl Haushofer in 1932, just before the Nazis came to power. It's Haushofer's personal copy, *not* the copy supposedly stolen from Adolf Hitler in 1944."

"Jesus! How did *you* get hold of that?"

"I got it from my father, your grandfather."

You mean that smiling fat man who dispensed candy so freely? Oh yeah, I've been told he worshipped Satan. Still, what could he have to do with this?

"You must know that he was with the occupying forces in Berlin. He never told me exactly how he got *The Book*. I always imagined that he had to kill *someone*. Anyway, Father told me he'd give me *The Book* if I studied German in school and received high marks. Your father wouldn't have been interested, but I certainly was."

Donna walked in to announce that two bowls of soup were laid out on the table in the adjoining dining room. Marc and his uncle moved their conversation into the next room, waiting until Donna left to continue their conversation.

Marc asked, "So, does Eckart want *The Book* because of his Nazi background?"

"I'm sure that is a factor," said Charlie Wilson between spoonfuls of hearty vegetable soup. Marc couldn't bring himself to eat, with thoughts of poison still fresh in his mind. "But mainly Eckart wants *The Book* because it is powerful, and the Committee knows of its power. For all of his bragging, Eckart doesn't have the power to challenge *The Book*."

"How do you know how much power Eckart has?"

"His act's gotten smoother, but he's still the same incompetent he was twenty-five years ago. I'll never forget the day he came to that meeting and announced that Satan had come to him in a dream, commanding him to lead us all."

"Really? He's been saying that to his followers now."

"See? Same crap. When we didn't believe him, Bill was livid. At the next meeting, he burst in late, yelling that he would show us all. He chanted a few dramatic lines in German, then broke a vial of fluid against the ground. The smell was unbearable. For years people called him Stinky Bill."

"Then what happened?"

"He was quiet at subsequent meetings. If he had any more dreams or spells to try out, he kept them to himself. He never even put himself up for deacon or celebrant, as the positions became available over the years. He never seemed to get over the shame of that incident."

Marc found it hard to picture Eckart having been so powerless and pathetic. "Who else on the Committee was there twenty-five years ago?"

"Not many of us left now," Wilson said. "My God! There's none of us left. Norm Maxwell died two years ago. Then Thornton, Knight, O'Neill, Baylor and Spender. I'm the only one left."

"So, Eckart had more than one reason for going after each of them."

"But how did he do it?" Wilson wondered. "Has he developed some abilities after all?"

"Do you really believe in magic?" Marc asked.

"Yes, but it's an overused term. True magic is exceedingly rare."

"*The Book* is true magic?" Marc tried to hide his skepticism for the sake of informative conversation.

"Yes. I proved my right to leadership of the Committee by performing a spell from *The Book*."

"The spell worked?"

"We were all convinced that it had. Convinced enough never to use *The Book* again."

"What was the spell?"

Judge Wilson was silent. He squeezed his eyes tightly closed, and Marc could see the tension in his jaw as his teeth clenched. Then Charlie Wilson spoke simply: "It was a mistake to use *The Book*." He opened his eyes and continued emotionlessly, "But I had proven that I had the Power."

Charlie Wilson was a convincing spokesperson, but Marc still found it hard to believe in magic. Nonetheless, Marc continued the discussion on and with his uncle's terms. "And Eckart *wants* the Power."

"I doubt that Bill Eckart could ever have that Power. But he'll try anything to get it. Bill Eckart would dare to complete Jacques Molay's curse, to chant the second half of his death-spell and bring Satan himself among us. Not even Adolf Hitler would have attempted such folly."

Enough of this mumbo jumbo. Time to get real. "But what can we do to stop Eckart?"

"Well, I'll keep *The Book* hidden. He's already sent men

to break in and ransack every inch of my home, but they didn't find it."

"Will he make a move against you without *The Book*?"

"He might, if there was no other way. Support for Eckart has become pretty strong. And now he's been claiming responsibility for the Committee murders, boasting of his strong magical powers." Wilson's disdain was obvious. "If only I could find out how he's *really* killing these people, I could use it to discredit him. That, combined with some blackmail ..." Judge Wilson trailed off, as his mind ran through countless appealing possibilities.

Marc once again considered telling Charlie Wilson all about the German poison. *Hell, why not? He's my only hope. Maybe I should stop holding back on him.*

"What if I found out how Eckart was doing it?" Marc asked. "If I helped you prove that Eckart was a fraud? Could you stop him?"

Charlie Wilson thought for a long moment. "If I had that information, *and* I knew where they were having their anti-Christmas, I could undermine Eckart's support, bring his followers back to the Committee. Drive him out."

"Would Eckart have to be killed?" Marc asked.

"We might not be able to save him. If we wanted to."

The doorbell sounded, loudly enough for them to hear it on the second floor. They could not, however, hear the voice of the visitor from where they sat. Marc and Charlie looked at one another quizzically, neither saying a word.

Donna appeared to announce the caller. "William Eckart, Judge. He says you may not have been expecting him."

Charlie Wilson looked amused. Turning to Marc, he quipped, "Speak of the Devil." Then Judge Wilson laughed good-naturedly at his own joke.

Marc wasn't laughing. The blood must have run out of his face, because his uncle said, "Relax, son. He's not a ghost. And, of course, I *have* been expecting him."

I've got to get out of here.

Wilson told Donna, "Send him up to the living room in one minute." Then he instructed Marc, "Don't worry. Finish your soup. Listen in if you like. He'll never know you're here." As he stood up to walk to the adjoining room, Charlie Wilson added, "Anyway, he wouldn't dare do anything to you while you're *here.*" Marc's momentary confidence was immediately reduced as his uncle clutched his side in visible pain.

Seconds later, Wilson shrugged off the discomfort and disappeared around the corner into the living room. A minute later, Marc heard Donna enter the living room with the "guest." Marc literally felt a stab of sheer terror in his gut as he pictured the amiable grin that accompanied the oily charm in Bill Eckart's voice.

"Charlie, old pal! It's been so long! Where have you been hiding?"

"I'm not hiding," Marc heard Wilson respond coolly. "See, you knew where to find me all along."

"Are you going to ask me to sit down?"

"I wouldn't presume to ask you to do anything. You'll do as you like."

Marc could hear the faint sounds of two chair cushions depressing, as Eckart said, "This meeting is long overdue."

"True. I expected you hours ago."

"Traffic was murder," responded Eckart, then they both chuckled.

Marc felt nauseous. "Am I too late for the Early Bird Special dinner?" Eckart asked. "What delights has Antoine been serving up in that lovely dining room next door?"

Marc could almost feel Eckart's eyes staring at him from around the corner. Without even thinking, Marc squeezed up tightly against the wall to the left of the passage between the two rooms. He held his breath while waiting for his uncle's response.

"Too bad you didn't make it a few minutes sooner. You could have joined me for my lonely gruel."

"But now you couldn't eat another bite, right?" said Eckart. "Even if your life depended on it?"

"I'm content," said Wilson.

"Yet you have a gnawing feeling that something is amiss. Something's eating you, tearing you apart. In short, you've got a tummy ache that no chicken soup can fix."

"Cut the crap!" Judge Wilson abruptly thundered. "What have you done, poisoned me?" *Wow! Good guess! Was it possible that he knew?*

"Nothing so mundane." *Good lie, Eckart!* "I am a powerful magician. You have not given me the respect I am due." Eckart had now switched to a slow, deep deadly serious tone. "As a result, your days are numbered."

"I'm shaking." Two beats later: "Stinky."

Eckart wasn't amused. "Fool!" he hissed before he could regain his composure. Then, more evenly: "Believe this. Unless I reverse my spell, you will surely die."

Despite the threat, Wilson's tongue remained in his cheek. "For the sake of conversation, what would it take to get you to remove your spell?"

Marc could barely hear Eckart's next words. "I think you know."

"No, what do you mean?" Wilson was obviously playing dumb to annoy Eckart.

"*The Book.*" Again Eckart spoke softly. Marc pictured the awe and reverence on Eckart's face as he discussed it. "The wisdom of the ages, the basis of your power, the stuff of your nightmares. You're an old crybaby, suppressing the will of our Dark Lord." Now Eckart let loose his fury: "Give me what is rightfully mine!"

"You have no rights!" Judge Wilson screamed back. "You have no ..."

There was a moment of silence, then Eckart's determined voice. "I have the right *and* the power to take your life. You're dying, slowly, according to my plan."

Shit! Uncle Charlie is dying. And he's my only hope.

Charlie Wilson spoke again, full control restored. "Don't forget, this is my house. And the Committee is *my* Committee. Respect me, or *you'll* die fast, according to *my* plan."

"That's okay, Antoine," said Eckart to the new arrival in the living room. "Charlie and I are just having a friendly airing of differing viewpoints. No need to get excited."

"Wait outside," said Wilson. "Right outside." *Good. At least he's still in charge. For now.*

"Where's Tony?" asked Eckart. "Isn't he still first in line for your dirty work? Or has he deserted the sinking ship?"

Tony? My mom's new bodyguard?

"Don't worry yourself about my men," Wilson answered. "They'll be around long after your fanatics have killed each other."

"Touching. You're so trusting."

"Except when it comes to you, Eckart. How could I ever make a deal with you?"

"*You* don't trust *me*?" Eckart forced a chuckle. "You may be the high-and-mighty judge, but don't pretend that you're honorable. Not to *me*. How can I trust a man who ordered his own brother killed?"

No! It can't be! Marc massaged his aching stomach. *I couldn't bring myself to think it.*

"What the hell are you talking about?" Judge Wilson demanded self-righteously. "I loved my brother!"

Fucking bastard! How could you kill your own brother? Marc clenched his hands in rage, then blinked a tear out of his eye. He remembered his father's strong hands on his shoulder. *You piece of shit! If Eckart hadn't already poisoned you ...*

"Right," Eckart said sarcastically. "But when he threatened to expose the Committee, you didn't hesitate."

"That's a lie!"

Marc knew that Charlie Wilson knew that he was listening from the next room. *Now that you know that I know, will you kill me? Or were you already planning to?*

"I think your nephew figured it out." *Why is Eckart talking about me?* "That must be why he hates you so much."

"You don't know what you're talking about," said Wilson dismissively.

"Did Marc ask you about it, Charlie?" Eckart's voice sounded like it was getting closer. Marc cringed. *Trapped,* he eyed the windows. "What type of lie did you tell Marc? And what else have you lied to him about? He's smarter than you give him credit for. You can't just use him against me, then throw him away." *Could Eckart know that I'm here? Is he lying about my father? Well, if he gets any closer he'll definitely see me.*

"I won't even discuss this with you," said Charlie Wilson. "You're making up crazy things."

Marc had to leave. He had to escape from both Eckart *and* his uncle. *Can't trust anyone.* He walked over to a dining room window and unlocked it. He had to save himself.

"Who did the actual dirty work for you that time, Charlie? I know you *said* it was magic, but was good old Tony driving the rental car that totaled Mitch Wilson?"

Tony? "And how many others has he murdered for you since?"

Now Marc had a new purpose and a destination: he had to get his mother away from the killer they had sent after her. *Can't let them use her against me.*

"Just get out," Marc heard Charlie Wilson order. "This meeting has become totally pointless."

Damn! Marc had to leave before Eckart did. Marc couldn't face his uncle's return to the dining room. He couldn't summon up the strength to tell Uncle Charlie that he believed him. What would his uncle do when he realized that Marc hated and feared him? Maybe he would kill Marc sooner than originally planned.

Slowly, quietly, Marc eased open a window. From the next room he heard Eckart saying, "As always, Chuck, you're afraid of the truth." *Have to leave now. Don't want to run into Eckart on his way out.*

Marc stuck his head out the window and looked down. There was no fire escape or anything to climb on. There was nothing between him and the street one floor below except a sheer stone wall and a few gargoyles.

"Get the fuck out," said Wilson simply.

Ten feet between Marc and the hard street below. And temporary freedom. He looked desperately around the dining room for anything that could serve as a rope.

What the fuck, Marc thought as he climbed out the window. *Maybe I can reach that gargoyle a few feet down.*

"Very well then, Chuck." Eckart's voice had regained its full measure of false charm as it receded toward the front door. "If I don't see you again, rest in peace."

Hanging from the ledge, Marc swung his body to the right and reached out for the snarling gargoyle below. He grabbed it with one hand, then two, but the stone head came loose from the wall. Marc and the gargoyle hit the sidewalk at the same time.

Marc ignored the pain in his hands and knees as he scrambled to his feet. But he stopped and stared in dumb amazement at the smashed head in front of him. He reached into the pile of stone and picked up the old black book.

"Marc!" Eckart yelled as he stepped out onto the street.

Marc darted past the waiting black limousine, across Fifth Avenue, and into Central Park before Eckart could pursue.

Twenty-Seven

First Marc reached for his cell phone ... *Shit!* The phone had been in his overcoat pocket.

A few blocks from Charlie Wilson's brownstone, Marc used a pay phone to call his mother. "Darling!" she said. "Nice to hear from you. How was Germany?"

"A lot like New York," Marc replied, trying to keep his teeth from chattering in the chill December air. Again he regretted leaving his overcoat at Uncle Charlie's.

"Are you feeling a little better about work?" she asked.

"Listen, Ma, are you busy right now?"

"Not really. I'm just watching a little television ..."

"I'm coming over, okay?"

"Great. Are you hungry?"

"No, I'm not hungry, Mom. How fast can you pack?"

"What are you talking about?"

"Tell me, how fast can you pack?"

"I don't know. An hour, I guess. What's this all about?"

"I'm sending you to Florida. Tonight. Happy Chanukah."

Might as well kill two birds. I didn't have time to buy that gold necklace.

"Tonight? Are you crazy? And Chanukah isn't till Saturday night ..."

"So? This year in Miami Beach. I got a great deal on the plane tickets." *There must be some seats still available. Whatever it costs, it'll be a bargain.* "You'll go for ten days." At least. Hopefully things will be resolved by then. "Do you think you can stay with Cousin Gertie down there?"

"I suppose."

"Give her a call."

"What about my job?"

"I already talked to Judge Green," Marc lied. "He said it was fine."

"Well, I guess it would be nice ..."

"You bet it will. Start packing."

"What time is the flight?"

"Uh, soon. I'll be right there. Keep all the doors locked. With the chain. And don't open up for anyone but me." It was less than a half hour later when Marc jumped off the R train at Continental Avenue in Forest Hills, Queens, and broke into a jog, but the streetlights were all on. *Please, God, let her be okay.*

Despite his fears, Marc knew that his mother was probably safe. Even with a killer standing outside her door. *No one has any logical reason to kill her. But they might want to hold her hostage. To get me. And* The Book. Marc would feel a lot better when his mother was safely out of the state.

As Marc approached his mother's little house from the opposite side of the street, he got scared. He didn't see any sign of Tony. Marc had hoped and expected to see Tony standing right outside the house. It would be difficult for the big man to hide. But there was no sign of Tony on either side of the street.

As he approached his mother's house on 70th Road, Marc listened for sounds from within. He thought he heard voices in two different registers, but it was hard to be sure. He eased his key into the top lock and turned it. He undid the bottom lock and swung the door open slowly. He was horrified to see that the chain was hanging from the door, its original end having been torn from the adjoining wall.

Marc resisted the urge to run in for another moment, while he quietly closed the front door and stood in the entranceway to the dark living room. Now he could hear Tony's voice from upstairs. "Get going already," said Tony. He heard slow footsteps.

Marc stood to the side of the stairs. He placed *The Book* down softly beside him and drew his gun. He didn't know what he was going to do. The stakes had never been so high in his whole life.

Marc returned the gun to his pocket. He would try to avoid gunfire in his mother's presence. He looked around the living room in desperation.

He spotted and picked up his mother's tall glass vase, sitting empty on a shelf since the death of his Thanksgiving bouquet. The vase felt good in his hands—long and solid, like a stickball bat. *I had good luck with the vase in Judge Kelly's chambers*, he remembered.

Marc stood perfectly still, holding the vase by its open end in a two-handed batter's grip. He saw his mother's feet first, as she stepped down cautiously. Marc hoped she wouldn't see him in the dim light and tip off Tony.

Marc waited until his mother's hand was on the front door. "Run, Mom," he yelled.

Marc waited a moment, while Tony turned from Sylvia Wilson toward him. "Run!" Marc screamed again, as he swung his glass bat into Tony's outstretched right hand. The gun went flying before Tony could fire.

Marc tried to swing back lefty into Tony's head, but the man reacted too quickly. Tony caught and stopped the vase, wresting it from Marc's grasp with ease.

Marc withdrew several steps, pulling his gun. "Drop it," he barked at the big man. Tony stood still, but he didn't relinquish the vase.

"Where'd you get that pea-shooter?" Tony asked skeptically.

"It belonged to a judge I iced. Now drop it!"

Tony took one step forward.

"You heard what my son said!"

Tony stopped, surprised.

Marc looked quickly to his left. His mother had disobeyed his orders to run, circling around the two men to retrieve Tony's weapon. Her two-handed grip on the gun was steadier than Marc's.

"But don't drop it," she said. "Put the vase down carefully."

Tony gently placed the glass *objet d'art* on the floor. "Look, it's not what you think ..." he began.

"Now come around the stairway and take three steps to your right," Mrs. Wilson ordered.

Tony did as he was told. "Listen, I was just ..."

"Take off your coat, slowly, and drop it," said Marc. "No sudden movements."

Tony took off his coat, while saying, "I was just taking you someplace safe."

"Then why did you break in and point a gun at me?" Mrs. Wilson demanded.

"Would you have come with me if I didn't?"

"I never thought I'd say these words to you, Mom," said Marc, "but could you keep him covered while I search him? I don't want to give him a chance to get my gun."

"Go ahead, Marc. I've got him in my sights."

Marc put his gun down on the coffee table and approached Tony. The chauffeur stood still and stiff while Marc patted him down. "He's clean," Marc announced.

Without warning, Tony took a step forward and trapped Marc in a painful bear hug, pinning his arms against his sides.

"Marc!" his mother yelled. "What should I do?"

Marc smashed the top of his head against Tony's chin, then charged forward, banging Tony into the wall. Marc's knee snapped up into the big man's groin, forcing him to release Marc and sink to the floor, holding himself.

Marc retrieved his gun and aimed it at Tony. "Stay there," he ordered the injured man. "Call a cab company," he advised his mother. "Ask for two cabs, five minutes apart."

"Two cabs? Where are we going?" she asked.

"I'll tell them when they get here," Marc answered. "Just do it. Please, Mom."

Sylvia Wilson reluctantly left to use the phone in the kitchen.

Marc turned on a light and looked down at Tony. The man still appeared dazed.

"Tell me," said Marc. "Do you remember my father, Tony?"

"I don't know."

"What do you mean, you don't know? You don't remember my father, your boss' brother?"

"I don't know. Maybe." He was trying to hide it, but Marc could tell that Tony was getting nervous.

Marc's mother reappeared from the kitchen, still holding Tony's gun. "The first cab will be here any minute."

"Great. Now get up, junior. Slowly. Mom, you'll wait here, okay? I'll be right back."

Marc stood two feet behind Tony as he opened the front door. "Don't try anything and you'll be fine," said Marc. "We're going to let you go. On our terms. Just walk out slowly toward the curb."

As he followed Tony out, Marc said, "The gun's in my suit pocket, but it's still pointing at you."

Fortunately for Marc, no one was around. *I've got to do this,* Marc thought. *Can't have you doubling back and following us.*

Just before they reached the curb, Marc drew his gun out by the barrel and slammed the steel grip against the back of the chauffeur's head. *That didn't feel too bad,* Marc thought as Tony went down face first into the sidewalk.

Marc couldn't tell which had done more damage, the gun or the pavement, but the man wasn't moving and a pool of blood was forming. His momentary euphoria past, Marc worried that he had hit the man too hard.

Marc pocketed the gun and bent down to examine Tony before looking around again for witnesses. *Thank God. He's still alive. And no one saw.*

Marc bent down and tried to drag Tony to his feet, but he couldn't do it.

A man and woman turned the corner and walked several feet before noticing Marc and Tony. They stopped in their tracks, stunned.

Marc looked down at the chauffeur's bleeding head, then at the approaching couple. Then at his mother, running over from the house, Tony's overcoat in her arms.

"Help me!" Marc called to the strangers. "I told him he'd had too much to drink, but he wouldn't listen."

"Jesus, buddy," said the man. "What happened? Did he fall?"

"Oh my God!" said the woman when she saw the trickle of blood up close.

"Yeah, he fell," Marc answered. "Thank goodness, I stopped him from driving! We called him a cab. Help me lift him up, will you?"

The man bent down with Marc and each of them grabbed an arm and hoisted the dead weight until it rested on both of their shoulders. *I was nuts to think I could lift him myself, even just a few feet.*

"Hey!" said the man. "How come this guy's bleeding on both sides of his head?"

Sylvia Wilson answered before Marc had a chance. "He fell twice. Can you believe he got up after the first time?"

"Jesus!"

"We'd better call an ambulance," said the woman.

"Nah. Just help me get him into a cab and we'll be fine."

"Are you sure?" asked the man.

"Yeah. Here's the cab now."

The driver balked when Marc and the other man started

to load the bleeding chauffeur into his back seat.

"Hey! What's wrong with him? I don't want no blood back there! Take him out of my car!"

"It's an emergency," Marc said. "I'll put his jacket under his head. And give you an extra twenty."

"Uh, I don't know," said the driver. "What happened to the guy?"

"He was falling-down drunk." Marc thought a moment, then added, "His mother died this morning."

"Oh. Well, get in already."

Marc climbed in next to Tony. "Thanks a lot," Marc called out to the waving couple. "I couldn't have done it without you."

"Where are you going?" asked Sylvia.

"I'll be right back," Marc told him. "Hold the other cab when it comes."

A couple of blocks away, Marc asked the driver to pull over. "I have to go back to the funeral. Here's one hundred bucks. Can you take him to 200 Flatbush Avenue, Brooklyn?"

"Will he get out when I get there?"

"Of course. He'll be fine. He just needs to sleep it off in his own bed." *Wherever that is. Just as long as he's far away from us.*

At that, Marc hopped out and walked briskly back to his mother's house.

Marc flung his arms around his mother and held her tight. "So, are you packed?"

"It's inside. Where's your overcoat?" she asked.

They went inside for her luggage, *The Book*, and his father's overcoat. When they came back outside the cab was waiting.

"What's going on?" asked Mrs. Wilson, as the cab headed for La Guardia.

"I can't tell you much," Marc answered. "I don't want you to be involved."

"Too late. I'm your mother. I'm already involved."

"You should have left when I told you to run."

"Didn't I help?"

"Well, yes. But I can't let you take chances like that. I should have sent you away sooner. If only I'd understood how serious things were earlier."

"Are you going to come to Miami with me?" Sylvia asked.

"I can't. I have to resolve things here."

"I can't run away while you're in danger."

"You could *put* me in danger. Do you understand that you were being taken hostage? So Uncle Charlie could make me do his bidding."

"Uncle Charlie?" she asked incredulously.

"And it's only a matter of time before Eckart goes after you, too. They want to control me, and they want this book here."

"What's so important about an old beat-up book?"

Marc looked down at *The Book* on his lap. Its pages were yellow and frayed. Its thick spine had been broken and repaired in several places. If it had been any other title, no book dealer would have paid more than a dollar.

"It really is a long story," said Marc. "Believe me, none of these people are up to any good. I have to stop them."

"What are you going to do? Is it dangerous?"

"You're going to have to trust me. You've always given me a lot of credit. More than I deserved."

"You've always been a good boy ..."

"No. But I want to be. For once, I know what has to be done, and undone, and I'm going to do it." *I just don't know exactly how yet.*

"What sort of mother would I be if I go to Florida while you're in trouble up here?"

"I hate to break it to you, but you don't have a choice. I won't let you stay, and I won't go with you."

Sylvia Wilson looked at him intently. "You're right. You're *not* a good boy. You shouldn't boss your mother around."

Marc hugged and kissed his mother in the back of the cab.

Marc managed to put his mother on the 9:55 p.m. flight to Miami. At 9:05, after waving goodbye to his mother, he took a deep breath and wondered what to do next. *Might as well head back to Manhattan. But not to my apartment.* Recalling years of television advertising, he checked into the Milford Plaza, the self-proclaimed "Lulla-buy of Broadway." The hotel was fully decked out in its Christmas finest. *This could be fun under other circumstances.*

Marc thought of calling Sam. He wanted to talk to her. He *really* wanted to see her. He imagined how wonderful it would be to have her here with him, high above the seasonal splendor of Times Square. But he was hesitant to call her, because of the potential risks to each of them. Then again, Marc was sure that she would want him to call.

At 11:55 p.m., Marc called Sam from a public phone. *Maybe some of the bad guys are asleep by now,* he hoped. Marc thought it best not to use his own name or voice, just in case anyone was monitoring. Marc wished that they had set up a code in advance for just such a contingency. *Maybe we did ...*

When Sam said "hi," he responded in a deep, theatrical tone.

"Who is this?" she asked.

"This is Vargas," he answered, maintaining his attempted Charlton Heston impression. "You must remember me from that little Mexican border town."

"Mexico?" she repeated in confusion. Then, "Oh, yes, Mr. Vargas. How's your lovely wife, Janet?"

"Fine, thanks." *Janet Leigh played Charlton Heston's wife in* Touch of Evil, *but that wasn't her character's name, silly.* Marc was relieved that Sam had broken his code and joined in the game. *Might as well make this quick.* "Can you meet me now?"

"Well, okay. Where do you want to get together, Mr. Vargas? The theater where we first met?"

"Good idea. Come alone. See you soon."

Marc was happier than he'd been in a long time. Since he had last seen Sam. She was the greatest. Not just because she was clever enough to guess who "Vargas" was and to suggest a meeting place that no eavesdropper could decipher. Marc had confidence that she would lose her pursuers, if any, on her way to the Film Forum.

Sam lived only a ten-minute walk from the theater, but she took twenty minutes, going in and out of stores and subway stations. When first setting out, she had noticed a young man a block behind her, seeing him again a few turns later. By the time she arrived at the Film Forum, she hadn't seen him for at least fifteen minutes.

Marc hopped on the downtown 1 train at the Times Square station, which took him quickly to within two hundred feet of the theater. Sam was waiting just inside, having only arrived a minute before.

They held each other for some time. She felt wonderful in his arms. Eventually she whispered, "We're too late for the movie."

He laughed. "What's playing?"

"There's a Bergman festival in Theater One. *The Seventh Seal* and *The Magician.*"

"Damn!" he exclaimed in mock despair. The theater personnel, lounging around while waiting for the last shows to end, looked at them with mild curiosity. "Then let's get out of here."

As she opened the door to leave, Marc asked Sam, "Are you sure you weren't followed?"

"Pretty sure."

"Why don't you get a cab and drive to Eighth Avenue. I'll join you there."

Upon entering the taxi on Eighth Avenue, Marc told the driver to go to Broadway and Forty-Fifth Street.

"What's going on?" Sam asked.

"I'll tell you when we get where we're going," he whispered in her ear, before kissing it.

"Very well," said Sam, wrapping her arms around him and commencing to kiss him for the rest of the trip.

Explanations had to be delayed a little longer than planned. When Marc took Sam up to his comfortable room, neither could resist the invitingly turned down bed. They melted together, each rediscovering the wonders of the other's flesh with a sense of undeniable urgency. Marc watched Sam for signs of withdrawal or traumatic flashback, but she didn't hold back in any way. For an hour, the world was simple and contained in one room.

Afterward, they lay intertwined while Marc told Samantha every single thing that had happened to him since they had parted. He described every conceivably relevant event he could remember, holding nothing back. Sam listened intently, sometimes nodding, sometimes gasping.

"So you don't think you're poisoned, right?"

"I don't see how I could have been. I guess I'm getting an ulcer."

"You're going to have to lay off some of that weird food you like," she said, jabbing him lightly in the stomach.

"So, do you know what I should do now?" he asked hopefully.

"When did Paul say was the next meeting of the neo-orthodox Satanists? The day before Christmas?"

"Right. Next Saturday morning. And the next full Committee meeting and party are in the early afternoon. So the Committee members can be out of their orgies in time for Christmas services that evening. Appearances must be maintained, as long as there are a few important non-Satanists left."

"I guess we have to plan something for that Saturday."

Marc didn't question her use of the word "we." "That's what I've been thinking," he said. "And keep out of trouble until then."

"But what do we do on Saturday?"

"Ah, that's a good question. We don't even know where the splinter group is meeting. They know security was breached on their old meeting place." He rested his head on her flat stomach and closed his eyes for a moment. *What a fucking day.*

"I'm beat, too," she said. Looking at the clock radio on a nightstand, she announced that it was 3:40 a.m. "And I have a test at 10:00."

"Oh shit! I'm sorry. I completely forgot that you were in the middle of finals."

"That's okay. I know you've been busy, but I've been studying. Can you spare me tomorrow morning?"

"Of course. Actually, I don't think you should spend the night."

"What? You're kicking me out of bed?"

"I hate to do it, but I think it would be better for both of us if no one knows that you spent a whole night out. They may not be sure if you lost them on purpose earlier tonight, and they might think you just went out to meet a friend or something. But if you don't come back tonight, they'll probably figure out that you stayed with me. Unless there's another guy I don't know about ..."

"Oh, shut up," she said, hitting him gently with mild irritation. She climbed out of bed and into her jeans. "Just don't start offering me cab fare."

She looked so wonderful as she wriggled into her clothes. He sat up and stared admiringly. "Wait a minute. What's new with *you*? I haven't let you talk."

"You know. Same old. Only thing new is that Dad keeps calling, asking me to dinner. He keeps getting the machine."

"You should call him back, you know."

"I know. I've been getting up my nerve. I don't know what to say to him."

"Of course." Marc could only imagine what Sam was going through, trying to come to terms with who her father was. "Are you still having nightmares?"

"I don't think so," she said. "Not while I'm asleep anyway ..."

He kissed her gently. "Did you remember anything new?"

"Yes. That first time, before they put me in the cage, they introduced me to three men. They all smiled, but they threatened me."

"What happened?"

"One man was dressed as a policeman. One man was a

doctor. And the other one wore a judge's robe. 'We all know who you are,' they said. 'And we'll know if you tell anyone about this party.' They said, 'If you tell, we'll make you very sorry.'"

Marc could only put his arms around her.

She continued calmly as he held her. "Sometimes I want to kill them all. But then I remember that I'm one of them."

"You were a little girl. You had no choices. That wasn't you. You're a unique, kind, clever, loving woman. I love you."

Sam was sobbing quietly. "I love you," she whispered. "I didn't think this could ever happen to me."

A few minutes later, Marc found the strength to take Sam to the door of the room. "Call me as often as you like. I'll pretty much stay in for the next few days. Never know who you'll run into."

"Okay. We'll come up with a plan before Christmas."

As soon as Sam left, Marc felt sad and lonely. With his mother safely out of town, Sam was all he had. She was everything to him: friend, lover, confidant, advisor. Would they ever be free of her father and his uncle and all the other dangerously evil lawyers in this town?

He missed her so much already.

There was a knock at the door. Marc jumped, then ran to the dresser for his gun. *It can't be anyone I want to see.*

But it was. "It's me," she whispered from outside the door. "Sam."

It *was* her voice. What could she be doing back here so soon? An image of Sam being held at gunpoint and forced to return to his room leaped into his mind.

"One minute," he whispered back. He threw on pants and picked up his gun.

She was alone, except for a copy of the New York Post in her hands. She looked scared.

"It's the early morning edition," she said. "Just hitting the stands. You're not the cover story, but you are referenced on the front page. 'Berserk Lawyer Attacks Judge, details on page 5.'"

Twenty-Eight

Marc grabbed the paper from her hands as she came in and sat on the bed. Sure enough, the whole fake story was there. Marc had inexplicably gone crazy and pulled a gun on Judge Kelly. "Wilson hadn't worked at all for a full year before talking his way into a position at the high-powered firm of Ballen, Warren & Dow," said the *Post* article. "'Evidently Mr. Wilson snapped under the pressure and long hours which go with the life of a big-time Manhattan lawyer,' commented Acting District Attorney Jill Montana." Elsewhere, the author of the article quoted Court of Appeals Judge Charles Wilson as regretting his inadvertent role in aiding his dangerous nephew to escape: "I only knew that Marc had been depressed lately. If I had any idea how serious his condition was, I would have made him seek medical treatment."

Worst of all, there were pictures. One okay recent photo from the Ballen Warren website, plus an older, vaguely familiar and remarkably unflattering picture ... It was his law school yearbook picture. *How strange and embarrassing.*

How had the newspaper obtained that picture? They must have looked up where he went to law school on the Ballen Warren website, after which the easiest thing would have been to contact someone in the administration at Rutgers Law School, say that an alumnus named Wilson had attacked a federal judge, and ask for a picture of the fugitive.

Marc wondered which dean had handed him over. Was it his old nemesis, Dean Orlando? Maybe she muttered something like "I'm not surprised. I always suspected that he cheated on exams."

How incredibly mortifying.

Thank God they didn't call my mother before I sent her away. Hopefully, they don't find her cell number.

"I've got to get out of the city," Marc thought aloud as he paced. *Then again, maybe I'd be safer in the hands of the police. Maybe, but I can't take a chance on trusting the law.* "Somewhere quiet and deserted. Where I can hide out until the meeting on Saturday? And how can I get a few changes of clothes without going back to my place?"

"I've got it!" Sam declared. "Think about it before you say no, okay?"

"Yeah, what is it?"

"Fire Island. Dad's place." She ignored Marc's skeptical expression. "It's perfect. Practically no one lives in Saltaire this time of year. No one will find you there. Who would go all the way out there just to check?"

"Interesting. I know Uncle Charlie would never look for me there. Also, maybe I could learn something while I'm there, maybe find something useful." *Maybe something to discredit Eckart with his followers, like I discussed with Uncle Charlie.* "Paul said that the splinter group had at least one ceremony and orgy there, a few months ago." Marc couldn't help remembering Paul's story about Jill Montana servicing four Satanists at once.

"Dad seldom goes there after October, and he never goes during the week. I have a set of keys in my apartment. You could catch a morning ferry and be communing with nature before noon." Although Marc was becoming convinced, Sam continued. "You're almost the same size. Dad has a full wardrobe out there. And lodging would be free, of course. This place must be costing you a fortune."

"Right. And I should get out before the desk clerk sees this picture and recognizes me."

After Sam checked Marc out of the hotel, they headed back toward her apartment. Then they staged the paranoid ballet which they had choreographed in the taxi downtown.

The cab dropped them off two long blocks west of Sam's apartment. While Sam walked two blocks east to her place, Marc walked two blocks further west to a diner and sat in a far corner. Fifteen minutes later, Sam showed up at the diner and sat near the window. She ordered blueberry pancakes and decaf coffee, then headed back toward the women's room.

Marc popped out of a stall in the deserted women's room and embraced her. "These two are the front door keys. On this paper is the address and the phone number there in case you have to give it out to anyone."

"I doubt I'll do that. So the Bayshore ferry will take me right to Saltaire, and the house is walking distance from there?"

"You've got it," she said. "So, I guess you can call me as Mr. Vargas, if you have to. Otherwise, I'll call you there. I'll probably be the only person calling, but turn up the volume on the answering machine and screen, just in case. Afterward you'll erase my voice, of course."

"Of course. What type of spy do you think I am?"

Sam laughed quietly. He kissed her smiling lips, then parted them with his tongue. A little later, he said, "I guess you ought to get home and sleep a couple of hours. Thanks so much for everything."

Neither of them wanted to leave the restroom. It was scary out there.

⚖⚖

After getting another few hundred dollars from a cash machine Marc took a train from Penn Station to Bay Shore, Long Island, then hired a taxi to take him to the ferry dock. He boarded the 10:10 a.m. ferry to Saltaire, making stops at Kismet and Fair Harbor.

He started to relax on the ferry. The water looked almost Caribbean blue and calm except for the ship's wake, and the passengers were few. He sat indoors near a window but was still a little cold. Yesterday's suit was starting to feel like a clammy second skin under his father's overcoat.

The couple sitting nearest him were reading the *New York Times*, fortunately. Marc had purchased a *Times* at the train station and ascertained that his story was buried on page A24. And there wasn't any picture.

Marc bought several days' worth of groceries in a small general store near the Saltaire dock, then followed Sam's directions to find the Eckart house. He admired the snow-covered splendor of the area as he traversed the tree-lined, wood-planked walkways.

During his ten-minute walk with the groceries, he began to wish that Fire Island allowed cars. He passed a church called Our Lady By the Sea and a frozen pond on which one young man was skating. The kid whizzed around effortlessly, while Marc trudged along with his groceries, almost slipping on several patches of ice.

Shortly after passing a snow-covered softball field, Marc turned onto Eckart's "street." Fortunately for him, there wasn't anyone around as he unlocked the fortress of his enemy.

It felt strange and scary to be entering Eckart's vacation home. Marc tried to convince himself that he couldn't feel Eckart's presence.

After locking and latching the front door, and putting away the groceries—the refrigerator had been almost empty but was on—Marc started to explore the place. Hesitantly at first, then with great interest. Although Marc realized that there was probably a limit to how much damning material he could uncover in a vacation home to which Sam had the keys, it was still fascinating to have the opportunity for this behind-the-scenes look.

The furnishings were simple and attractive, tending toward the primitive and natural. Many decorations and pieces of furniture appeared to be of Native American origin. Nothing on display had an obvious Satanic connection.

Luckily, the furnace fired right up, making the modest two-floor house warm in a short time. Marc lay down on a couch in the ground floor living room to rest for a minute and fell asleep for two hours. He awoke feeling jumpy. He had to survey his surroundings and make sure they were as safe as they could be.

At first, Marc tried not to handle things, not to move anything. Then he realized the futility of such an endeavor. First of all, it would probably be impossible for him to stay here without leaving any traces that he had done so. Secondly, by the time that Eckart could conceivably know that Marc had been here, the situation between Marc and Eckart would probably have been sorted out once and for all, one way or another. Realizing this, Marc began searching every drawer and closet.

Marc was disappointed. He didn't find anything juicy. No secret notes, no bloody clothing, no dead animals or people. Nothing that didn't belong in the summer home of an upstanding citizen and devout Christian.

While searching the drawers, Marc changed into jeans and an Oxford shirt that must have belonged to Eckart. He looked forward to showering later. Then Marc found a suitcase and packed it full of clothing that might fit him. He placed *The Book of the Templars* in between all the shirts and underwear. He left the sealed suitcase, along with his father's overcoat, prepared by the front door.

In a room adjoining the living room that looked like a study, one deep drawer in a desk was locked. Marc jimmied the lock open with a letter opener to reveal a weapon collection: five small guns, three ornate daggers, some type of rifle and bullets. Marc checked the barrel of each gun and saw that they were all loaded. Thinking ahead to the possibility of danger, Marc placed at least one weapon in almost every room of the house.

Those preliminaries taken care of, Marc sat down in the kitchen with a microwaved dinner and a glass of milk. He had bought a gallon of milk. He was going to coat his stomach and minimize the pains he'd been feeling.

While he ate, Marc thought about the night ahead. And the days and nights after that. He was frightened to sleep in Eckart's house. What if Eckart or one of his cronies arrived, to find Marc sleeping there like a modern-day Goldilocks? It was unlikely, but Marc should be prepared.

For starters, Marc placed the suitcase so that the front door would hit and drag it. Then he propped a chair against the back door so it couldn't be budged. He made sure that every door and window was locked, every shade closed.

He took a quick shower, trying not to imagine Bill Eckart in an old woman's dress stabbing him through the shower curtain. Then he lay down again on the living room couch to read magazines and books from Eckart's shelves: *Time* and *Money* magazines from last month, as well as the complete Sherlock Holmes stories.

At 6 p.m. he called Cousin Gertie in Miami Beach. After they had exchanged brief pleasantries, Gertie put Sylvia Wilson on the phone. "It's beautiful here," said Sylvia. "I went to the pool today, and I've already met lots of people in the building."

"That's great," said Marc. His mother had always been a go-to-the-pool-even-when-you're-right-on-the-beach sort of person.

"How are *you* doing, honey?"

"I'm fine," Marc answered.

"Really? Is everything going to be okay?"

"You bet," he said. "I miss you already."

"I'll miss you when we light the Chanukah candles tomorrow night."

Marc felt lonely and nostalgic when he hung up the phone. He had only missed lighting Chanukah candles with his mother one year, when college finals had kept him too busy to come home.

It didn't help that this place was every bit as quiet and secluded as he had hoped. Between the lack of people and the blanket of snow absorbing all sounds, the silence was complete and unnerving.

Marc was startled when the phone he had just hung up began to ring. It rang just once, then stopped. For a moment, Marc thought that he had imagined it. Then the ringing resumed. He waited for the machine in the study to pick up, while he listened nervously. When he heard Sam's voice, he grabbed the phone like a life preserver. "Darling, I'm glad you called."

"Is everything okay?" she asked with concern in her voice.

"Oh, yes. Comfortable even. I just miss you. Terribly."

"I miss you too. Just heard some Peter Gabriel on my iPod."

"Nice. I shouldn't put on music here, though, so I can hear if anyone's coming."

"Well, you know, the ferries from the mainland only run in the morning. But I suppose people with money to burn can hire water taxis."

"Right. Or take a helicopter," he said, only half-joking. "In any case, I'll be ready. So, what's there to do around here?"

"In December, at night? Get under a blanket with a good book. Or think of me ..."

"I've been thinking of you a lot. Including under the blankets."

"Likewise," Sam cooed over the sounds of colliding traffic.

Marc forced his brain back to business. "Have you noticed anyone following you?"

"You bet. A couple different guys, both about your age."

"Is one of them missing a finger?"

"Like in Hitchcock's *Thirty-Nine Steps?*"

"Yeah."

"I can't tell from here."

"Well, keep acting normal. Did you call your father back yet?"

"No," she confessed. "I'll do it right now. It's early enough. Maybe I'll get his machine."

"That's the spirit. Stay tough. Maybe when you call me tomorrow we'll talk about a plan."

"Good. Keep thinking," she said. "I love you."

That was sorely needed medicine. "Then everything will be okay."

After hanging up, Marc remembered to erase the message.

⚖

After talking with Marc, Sam started walking north as she pressed a pre-programmed key on her cell phone. She didn't want to wait until she got home to call her father, because he might be in by then. Now he was probably still in the office.

After the third ring she felt home free. One more ring, then the machine answered. *Thank goodness*, she thought, mentally reviewing the message she had composed in advance. At the beep, Sam spoke in a light, friendly tone, "Hi Dad. Sorry we haven't been able to hook up, but I've been ..."

"Hi," said Bill Eckart as he picked up the phone. "Wait a second. Let me turn down this volume ..."

"Dad! You're home! Glad I caught you."

"Sorry, baby. I was on the other line. So, what's new with you?" He sounded so innocent, so nice, so like the father she used to love. Could she *still* love him?

"I've just been so busy. I'm in the middle of finals, working on papers ..." All of that was true. She *would* be considered busy even if she hadn't been helping her lover to escape and plot the downfall of the Committee.

"Sorry to hear it. But at least you like what you're doing. You do still like it, don't you?"

"You know it."

"Great. That's so important. Are we at least going to spend Christmas together?"

The thought of all of the happy Christmases she had spent with her father and mother made her feel sad. And sick to her stomach. "Believe it or not, I'm still going to be finishing a couple of papers for Monday. Pretty pathetic, huh?"

"My heart bleeds for you. So, when can you spare a little time for your father?"

"I don't know, Dad. Maybe next week. A quick lunch."

"That would be fine. Shall we say Tuesday?"

"Let's say Tuesday, but I'll call you in the office Tuesday morning to confirm. Okay?" She was ready to hang up, congratulating herself on her performance.

"Sure. So how's Marc doing?" he asked without skipping a beat.

"Oh, I don't really know." She injected irritation into her voice. "He hasn't been returning my calls." An inspiration: "Tell him if he doesn't call me back by tomorrow, he shouldn't bother at all."

Eckart didn't respond immediately. *What do you say, Daddy? Will you admit that Marc hasn't shown up to work for a few days?*

"Okay, honey. I'll make him contact you."

After he hung up with his daughter, Bill Eckart placed a call. "Hi. It's me," he said. "She's still playing hard to get. So go and get her."

⚖

Marc slept on the couch, so he could hear if anyone tried to get in, as unlikely as that might be. *They'll never look here.* He put down a sheet and a pillow, and it was pretty comfortable. Nonetheless, he tossed and turned for an hour. If he had known being in Eckart's vacation home would make him so irrationally tense, he would never have come out here. *I've got to get some sleep*, he thought to himself, over and over until he finally started to drift off.

By the time he heard the back door, he was surrounded. Dan and Larry each took hold of an arm and dragged him off the couch onto the floor. Then they held him down while Eckart bent over him. "Look who's been sleeping on my couch," Marc's boss announced with a grin.

Eckart had one of the ornate daggers in his right hand, poised above Marc's crotch. *How did Eckart find the daggers where I moved them?* Marc struggled but he couldn't budge Dan or Larry. *Was this how it would all end?*

"What have you been doing with Samantha?" Eckart demanded, using the dagger to lightly trace a circle around the offending area.

"Nothing that we haven't all been doing," said Joe and Scott from the next room. *How long have they been here?* The two men walked out of the study and into the living room, each naked, erect and bloody. The blood wasn't their own.

What the hell is going on here?

Marc wrenched his head to the side, trying to see into the study. "You've had your turn," said Joe. "Now she belongs to us. Oh, and Satan, of course."

"Of course," said Eckart, unzipping his fly to let loose his enormous golden phallus.

No!

Marc awoke when he fell off the couch. He checked all the doors and windows, but everything was still locked against the unbroken darkness of the night. Afterward, he stayed awake for a very long time.

Twenty-Nine

The next day, everything looked better. The snow-covered trees were still and lovely. The air was fresh and crisp. No one had come after Marc, and he was starting to think that no one would. *This was a good plan. They'd never expect me to hide here. Even if they did, they'd never come all the way out here just on a hunch.* He felt great, having slept from 4:30 a.m. until 11:15.

Eleven-fifteen! The 10:30 ferry must have pulled in a few minutes ago. Involuntarily tense again, Marc stared out a window for signs of approach. An hour later, he was relaxed once more. And bored.

By two in the afternoon he was feeling a little stir crazy. He peered out the windows, seeing if any of his neighbors were in town. It was difficult, since he couldn't check driveways for cars. There weren't really any signs of life, but he kept checking every fifteen minutes. At 3:45 p.m., he saw a man leave his house two doors down and head in the general direction of the dock.

A few minutes later, Marc decided to take a walk for a few minutes behind the house. As far as he could figure, he would only be visible from two other houses, neither of which seemed to be occupied. Donning his father's winter coat, Marc stepped out into the cool fresh air. It was a wonderful liberation, even if he only planned on pacing back and forth in the back yard for a few minutes. Everything was completely quiet.

Back inside, Marc stared out the window for several minutes, but didn't see anything or anyone. He missed Sam. He couldn't wait to talk to her tonight. He settled down to read another Sherlock Holmes story: "The Redheaded League." Twenty minutes later he put the book down on his chest and closed his eyes.

He awoke and reached for the gun under the couch cushions. Thank God, it was still there. But something was wrong. He must have heard something, but he didn't know what. He held very still, the gun gripped tight in his right hand, listening. *Am I going crazy?* Then he heard it: another creaking stair. Then absolute silence. *Could a human be that skillful? He must have climbed up the side of the house, broken in a window, then started tip-toeing down the old stairs, remaining entirely still between steps.* Did the intruder know that Marc was awake now? Had he known that Marc was asleep in the first place?

Marc resolved to move the next instant that he heard a sound from above. His muscles bunched in anticipation as he broke into an unseasonable sweat. The stress of waiting in such a tense state of readiness was becoming unbearable.

Creak. Marc rolled off the couch toward the study. As he heard the other bound down the remaining steps, Marc climbed to his feet and ran into the next room. He stood beside the door to the study, his gun pointed at the entrance. He tried to steady his right hand by the addition of his left, but both hands were shaking. Could he really shoot? He didn't even know who was out there. Until now, he had held a couple of people at gunpoint, unbelievable as that seemed to him, but he had never fired a gun. He had never tried to shoot someone.

Who was out there? Everything was quiet again. Minutes went by. Could the guy have left? Marc wiped the sweat off his forehead with his left hand, then resumed his two-handed vigil.

I can't stand here forever, Marc thought. *Maybe I should take the offensive. Run out shooting.* No, that was crazy. Marc had no idea where the other guy was.

The phone rang. Marc literally jumped. *Could that be Sam already?* Marc re-aimed his gun.

It rang again. It was the only sound in the house, except for Marc's breathing. *I guess he's not going to answer it.*

The answering machine picked up on the fourth ring. "Honey? Pick up. Come on. You must be there ..."

Shit! Whoever was in the house was hearing Sam's message. *I have to warn her. If I make it out of here alive.*

"Okay then," said Sam. "I'm about to go down into the subway, so you won't be able to reach me for a while. I should be home in forty, fifty minutes. I guess I'll call you later." *Click.*

Still no other sounds from the living room. *What patience! This guy must be a big game hunter. Well, man's the most dangerous game ...*

Marc realized that there was one bright side to this latest attempt on his life. It offered further evidence that he hadn't already been poisoned. Hopefully, that wouldn't be a moot point.

Marc cracked his neck and massaged his back. He wished that he could lie down.

What if I just peeked out for a second? Just to see where he is? Would that be so risky? He must be tired, too. Marc fought the temptation for the next ten minutes. Then he gave in.

Silently, slowly, he took one step forward. Then he stretched his whole body gradually in the direction of the door, while keeping his feet firmly planted. Still no sounds from the living room. Could the other man still be there at all?

Marc stretched his neck slowly forward toward the door. Another two inches and he'd be able to see. *Careful. Be ready to pull back. One more inch ...*

There! It was impossible. The man had been standing there, right in front of the doorway, for God knew how long, without making a single sound. *I'm dead* was all Marc had time to think.

A fist sent Marc flailing backward toward the desk. "Let

go the gun!" the man yelled, training his pistol at Marc's heart. Marc sprawled up against the desk, letting the gun fall from his hand.

"Throw it out the window," the man ordered. Marc complied, causing a loud crash of glass followed by a cold breeze. Then Marc stared at the person who held his life in his hands. *"Dumkopf! Schwein!"* the man called out, then laughed. Marc and the skinhead recognized each other, although the German was wearing a different toupee.

"You hit me twice," the Nazi informed him in fluent English, with a minor German accent. "Once in Munich, once in New York."

"I'm sorry," Marc muttered, staring at the man's gun. *Why is he toying with me?*

The youth smiled, but Marc took no comfort there. "I am Otto."

"I thought you went back to Germany."

"It seems my work was here."

"Were you going to Germany just to kill me?"

Instead of answering, Otto said, "We have a common friend."

"Bill Eckart?" *Keep him talking and think of something.*

"Paul Johnston." A broader smile.

Marc wasn't surprised. Just sickened. He remembered how Paul's body had been battered, almost beyond recognition. This was a man who loved his work.

How did Eckart know I'd be here? How could he have been sure? Can he really read my mind, as I always feared?

"Away from the desk," Otto ordered. "I know that's where Eckart keeps guns. Go stand in the corner, on the left."

With slow, steady steps, Marc walked back and stood in the far right corner of the room, next to a bookcase.

"The *left* corner, I said!" He waved the pistol furiously. "Are you deaf?"

Calmly and politely, Marc said, "I thought you meant *my* left. Sorry. Do you want me to ..."

"Just put your hands up. *Schnell!* And don't move!"

Otto calmed down after Marc had obeyed. Otto stepped toward the phone on the desk and spoke to it. "Do you hear me, Eckart? I have the bastard. He's sweating like a stuck pig."

Some sort of bug in the phone. The single ring before must have triggered it. I'm just not a natural at this spy stuff. Still, how could Eckart have guessed?

Otto looked up at Marc and explained simply, "Mr. Eckart is much smarter than you. You never had a chance against him. And me."

You may be right. But I've got to try ...

"Enough chit chat," said Otto, speaking slowly and taking pains to pronounce properly. "Tell the boss how sorry you are that you hit him."

"I'm sorry."

"That's not enough." Otto looked down at the phone. "Is it, boss?"

Now! Marc only had seconds. He brought his right hand down to the bookcase, snatching out the dagger he had placed behind the first books. He threw it and hit the floor in rapid succession, yet the gunshot rang out between the two events. Knowing that the odds had been against his mad dagger toss, Marc didn't waste a moment checking its results. Hopefully, Otto was still surprised, recovering his balance from ducking or sidestepping. Leaping to his feet, Marc ran toward the broken window and sailed out into the snow.

The gun! Where was the gun he had tossed out? There, embedded in the snow! He crawled quickly toward it, cutting his knee on a piece of broken glass. Marc scarcely noticed that or the gash on his left arm where it had hit the remaining window-pane.

Another shot sounded as Marc dived on the gun and rolled onto his back, facing the house. Miraculously, a miss. *No time to think.* As Marc saw Otto lean out the window to get a better shot, Marc squeezed off his first bullet. Instantly, Otto disappeared back into the house, but his blood was on the snow.

Shit! I did it! I shot him! But how badly?

Marc didn't dare go check. He lay there in the snow, wait-ing. He stood up. He walked slowly toward the house. *What if he's dead? What if he's not? But I can't stand here all day and night.* The sun was going down fast.

I should just leave. Hire a water taxi. Get out of here. But how can I leave without knowing? Have I actually killed a man? Or will he come after me again?

Then Marc remembered that he had to make a phone call. He had to warn Samantha, before it was too late, that her fa-ther knew everything. Did he dare call from the bugged phone? No. It could be helpful if Eckart didn't know right away that Samantha knew that he was on to them. If Marc left now, he could make it to the pay phone at the dock around the time that Sam had expected to arrive home. Of course her phone could be bugged, but *that* was an unavoidable risk. Marc turned away from the house, toward the dock.

Marc had only taken two steps on the wooden walkway when he wheeled about and stepped to the side on an impulse. Otto's bullet passed where Marc had been. Marc's bullet passed through Otto's left leg.

The skinhead was down, more blood in the snow. No time for indecision. *Got to end this.* Marc ran toward the youth as fast as he could travel, gun hand down for added speed. As he got closer, Marc could see that Otto was lying in deep snow, and his gun had landed several feet away from him. Otto was moving slowly, blood pouring from his leg and trickling from his ear. The pistol was still out of Otto's reach when Marc stopped and stood two feet away.

Otto looked up at him as Marc pointed the gun down at the man's chest. "No," said Otto. "Please. Get me a doctor."

Marc spoke slowly and calmly. "Why should I?"

"You're a good man." Otto gasped with exertion. "An American."

"Not good enough." *My God, am I enjoying this? And can I really shoot him again? Even him?* "Maybe I won't shoot you."

"Thank you."

"Maybe I'll just leave you here to bleed to death." Would he die? *It's a lot of blood, but what do I know about these things?*

"Take me inside. To a phone. Please?" His pleading voice sounded pathetic.

I know I should kill him. It's the most practical thing. It's arguably even morally right. I'm just having trouble doing it in cold blood. Maybe if I leave it to him ...

"Okay," said Marc. "Here's the deal. You get yourself up and walk into the house on your own. Leave your pistol where it is."

Otto couldn't stand, so he started to crawl toward the house. His progress was slow. For the first time since he had run outside, Marc looked around them. Still, no one was around. In that sense, Fire Island had been an excellent choice of locale, as it turned out.

Marc followed, several paces behind. Just before he reached the front door, Otto stopped, grabbed his left leg, then turned to Marc. Without hesitation, Marc shot him. The bullet went through one side of Otto's torso and out the other. Otto collapsed. He didn't move again. *I did it! My God, I did it!*

Marc walked over carefully, keeping the dead man covered. He felt the man's leg and ankle, searching for the spare gun or knife for which he had been reaching. Nothing. *It can't be.* There was no hidden weapon. The skinhead must have merely grabbed the leg in pain.

Marc felt numb and empty. He continued searching the man, feverishly. Finally, exultantly, he removed a second pistol from the Nazi's inner jacket pocket. *There. Surely he would have used that on me, eventually.*

Marc also found a half-empty bottle of Evian, presumably the secret German poison. *This could be useful*, he thought, as he put the bottle into his pocket. It would fit right into the plan he'd been formulating.

Marc unlocked the front door, pushing over the heavy suitcase he had left there as he forced the door open. Then he dragged the young man into the living room and dropped him. Marc didn't look at his face.

Marc wiped clean the gun he had used, placing it in the skinhead's hand for the hell of it. He put three of Eckart's guns and one dagger in the pockets of his father's winter coat. Then Marc picked up his pre-packed suitcase, closed the door behind him, and ran to the Saltaire dock.

No more time to think about the life he'd taken.

Thirty

Come on, Sam. Be home. Pick up the phone. Damn! The answering machine kicked in. *Please be screening.* If only he could have reached her on her cell phone; Sam's phone seemed to never work when it mattered.

At the beep, Marc blurted, "This is Vargas. It's important. Pick up the phone if you're there." *Shit!* "Well, listen carefully. They know. They know everything. Get the hell out of there. Now! Don't bother to pack. Run!"

Marc slammed down the receiver. *She'll be home any moment,* he thought. *She'll be okay.*

He stepped out of the phone booth, picked up Eckart's suitcase, and walked to the pier to look for a water taxi.

⚖⚖

Samantha Eckart was on her way home. As she approached her door, she heard a voice from inside. At first she was frightened. Then she realized that it was her answering machine. She yanked out her keys and fumbled with the lock. *Hurry up! It sounded like Marc!*

She flung the door wide open, leaving her keys in the lock, and ran toward the phone. The door bounced back and slammed shut as Sam dove for the phone and Marc yelled, "Run!"

"Hello? Hello? Marc?" *Fuck!* She missed him by a split second. But she could already tell that the message wasn't going to be comforting.

As she listened to Marc's voice, she started to tremble and she couldn't stop. What could she do? Where could she run? She was alone, without family. Nothing made sense anymore.

There was a knock at the door. Instantly, she snapped back into the moment. She lowered the volume on the machine's playback just before Marc yelled "run!"

Could she pretend she wasn't home? They might have heard the machine. But that didn't mean she was ...

The keys! In her rush to answer the phone, she'd left the keys in the lock outside. She stood up and ran to the door. As she grabbed the chain to put it in place, the knob turned and the door was yanked open. Two men in suits stood outside, one foot away from her. The three of them stood frozen for a moment, surprised by each other's sudden proximity. "I was just coming to open the door," Sam said.

"You've got to be more careful in this big city," said the shorter man.

As the newcomer handed her the keys and brushed by her into the apartment, Sam's attention was caught by his right hand: one finger was missing. "Not nice to stare," the man warned.

As the two made themselves comfortable on Sam's couch, they introduced themselves as Dan and Larry. "Sit down," said Larry.

Sam had hesitated too long to do anything else. Slowly, she stepped away from the door and sat on the love seat. She left the door open. "That's okay," said Dan. "We're going to have to leave in a minute anyway."

Who's "we"? Sam wondered, afraid she knew the answer.

Larry spoke up. "I'm afraid we've got some bad news for you."

Oh God! Marc!

"Your father is ill."

"What?" She was caught entirely by surprise. "I just talked to him yesterday."

Larry continued gravely. "He's had a serious heart attack. He's been asking for you."

Could it be true? she wondered. *Could the skinhead have used Dad's own poison on him? Or could it be a real, age-related heart attack?* If false, it was an ingenious story. As skeptical as Samantha was, it was hard to be sure, hard to dismiss the story as a lie and take a chance on never seeing her father alive again. But she had to take that chance.

"My God," she said. "Is he going to make it? How bad is it?"

"The doctors aren't sure," said Larry.

"But they're not making any promises," added Dan.

"Oh my God! I've got to go to him! Just give me one minute, please." She added, with a little embarrassment, "I was in the bathroom when you knocked."

Both men looked annoyed, but neither stopped her as she darted back and locked the bathroom door behind her.

When looking for an apartment, Sam had noted that, in Manhattan, one had a choice of a window in the bathroom or the kitchen. Few reasonably priced apartments had both, even though ventilation was desirable in both locations. Now she was glad that she had opted for the bathroom window.

She knew she had very little time. The window was high and a little small, but it would work. She stood on the edge of the bathtub and eased the window open. As she looked down, she thought of Marc and how he had jumped out his uncle's window. That wasn't an option here, three stories above the street. The good news was that her old building had a fire escape. The bad news was that the fire escape landing was one window over and a little lower, outside her bedroom window. She would have to ease herself out onto this window ledge, then reach over and grab hold of the grating.

Sam took several slow, deep breaths. She wondered what these men would do to her if she let them take her. What would her father *let* them do?

Cut the bullshit and go. This was the type of thing they did in movies *all* the time. Actresses wouldn't even use stunt people for something this easy. It wasn't like scaling Everest or anything. Her position would be perilous for only about ten seconds. *Just do it!*

There was a knock on the bathroom door. "Are you okay? Visiting hours are almost over."

"I'm fine!" she yelled. "I just need a minute. Please!"

"Okay. But hurry."

Larry spoke softly to Dan, "Give the girl a break, will you? Her Daddy's dying and she's got diarrhea."

"One minute," Dan announced, between clenched teeth. "Then I'm busting in and wiping her fucking ass."

Sam had to begin face first, doing a pull-up, then getting her knees onto the sill. She felt like she was back in high school gymnastics. She squeezed out the window onto the ledge and turned her body around to face the building. Clinging tightly to the brick face, Sam got her feet under her and managed to stand almost erect. Then she looked over at the fire escape landing, barely three feet away. It might as well have been across the Snake River Canyon. She didn't know if she could do it. She started to lean over and reach out, slowly, steadily ...

She heard the bathroom door come crashing in and she leaped the chasm. She only dangled for seconds before scrambling up and over the fire escape railing.

"You fucking, lying cunt!" Dan's head popped out the window, followed by his right hand and gun.

Sam started running. She took two and three steps at a time, tripping only once. She didn't look back until she was almost to the street. Dan couldn't get a decent shot, so he didn't risk one. There was also no way he was going to fit out the little window. "Fucking bitch!" he screamed as he climbed back in.

He wasn't used to fucking up. "Move your ass!" he yelled at Larry as he ran past him and out the front door.

The two of them raced toward the street level. In the middle of the last flight of stairs, they encountered an elderly couple and pushed them aside roughly. A young man near the foot of the stairs saw the incident and cursed them out, but Dan's fist sent him flying down the remaining few steps.

Sam hit the street running. She headed east. As she veered north at a street corner, she looked back to see Dan only about a hundred yards behind. She turned into the fourth store she saw and prayed.

⚖

On the train from Long Island back to Manhattan, Marc pondered his next hideout. Where could he be safe until next Saturday? Safe from Eckart, Charlie Wilson and the police.

If only there was someone in the police or the D.A.'s office that he could trust. If only Rosetti was still around. Could Rosetti have stopped Eckart if Marc had helped him from the start? Could he have avoided a grisly death if he had known more about what he was up against?

Poor guy. Dying naked and anonymous in a cheap Bronx motel. Framed so that the whole world thought he frequented male prostitutes. Rosetti had probably never even been to that part of the Bronx before.

That's it! No one Marc knew ever went to that part of the Bronx. And the people who did go there could be anonymous, locked in little rooms off the highway with the curtains drawn tight.

Before heading out to the Bronx, Marc stopped into a Penn Station electronics store and bought a small pair of binoculars. He paid with cash, then picked up more cash at the Citibank on his way out to Seventh Avenue.

Marc considered renting a car, but he was afraid. He'd have

to show his driver's license and use his real name. So he took a cab to the Bronx. The driver grumbled, but Marc politely reminded him that he was required by law to take Marc anywhere in the five boroughs of Manhattan.

As the taxi traveled northeast, Marc observed the splendor and squalor of a New York City Christmas. Lights were strung up everywhere, store windows were loaded with appealing sale merchandise telling a loose holiday story, and people were everywhere. Every man, woman or child was looking or buying or selling. Or giving or begging.

Marc passed several brightly lit Christmas landmarks. First the miracle of Macy's at Sixth and Thirty-Fourth, then the huge snowflake hanging suspended over Fifth and Fifty-Seventh, then the king of them all, FAO Schwarz at Fifth and Fifty-Eighth. The line to get into the massive toy store was just as long as Marc remembered from his three childhood visits, always after the Christmas show at Radio City Music Hall.

Marc didn't know the Bronx well enough to know where the motels were, and he doubted that the taxi driver knew or cared to drive around searching. Consequently, he steered the cabbie to the one Bronx motel he could locate, having seen it hundreds of times from the FDR across the East River. Minutes later, he was checking into the Ball Park Motel, just off the Major Deegan Thruway and a couple minutes drive from Yankee Stadium.

The man at the desk seemed a little surprised when Marc said he would be staying for seven or eight days, but he didn't comment. He didn't ask how many people would be staying in the room, nor did he seem to notice that Marc was a wanted criminal.

It was almost midnight when Marc entered his room, bolted and chained the door shut, and got into bed. He was happy to note that the bed was actually comfortable and clean.

At that moment Marc remembered that it was the first night of Chanukah. He doubted that there were any candles burning in front of the drawn shades of the Ball Park Motel. Amusing himself with fantasies of children opening gifts and spinning dreidels between the queen size bed and the bolted-down TV with pay-per-view, Marc fell asleep in minutes.

The next morning, Sunday, Marc walked a few blocks west, looking for a pay phone. He didn't have the luxury of worrying about the neighborhood being tough, although having one of Eckart's guns in his overcoat gave him some comfort. Marc lucked upon a gas station with a working pay phone and called Samantha's cell phone. Getting her voice mail, he identified himself as Vargas, out of habit, and promised to call back soon. "I'll tell you where I am then. I can't wait to talk to you. I really hope you're well."

Next he called his mother at Cousin Gertie's. "She's not here," said Gertie. "She went to the mall with Herb."

"Herb?"

"Yes, Herb. He lives down the hall. Between you and me, he's really got his eye on your mother."

"What's going on down there?" he asked. "I just sent her for a few days of vacation."

"Herb's a nice man. I think your mother likes him too. She keeps saying what a good dancer he is."

"When did she see him dance? She's only been there two days."

"Last night, at the Sahara. Herb took us all out. You want I should have her call you?"

"No, I'll be hard to reach. I'll try to call back later today or tomorrow. When's a good time to catch her?"

"I don't know. It's hard to keep up with your mother."

"Really?" Marc smiled. *Well, good for her. I guess.*

Marc spent the afternoon watching bad TV in a dark motel room. Periodically, he went out to the gas station pay phone and tried to call Sam's cell phone. *Please let Sam be okay!*

Finally, at 4:55 p.m., Marc got through. *Thank God thank God thank God ...* "Sam?" He was practically yelling with joy.

Silence on the other end. "Hello?"

"Hi Marc," said the voice on the other end of the line. Marc dropped the receiver and stepped back in fear. He looked around wildly, as if he were being watched. How had Eckart gotten possession of Sam's phone?

Marc retrieved the receiver and listened, but there was silence. "Eckart?" he asked hesitantly, though he had no doubt.

"You were expecting someone else?" Eckart's voice was as smooth as usual. "Sam can't come to the phone right now. ..."

"Is Sam alright?" Marc demanded nervously.

"You turned her against me, Marc," Eckart accused. "A little girl should love her daddy, but you turned mine against me."

"She *does* love you," Marc insisted. "She told me many times."

"That's touching. But she's nothing to me now. You can have her. For a price."

"What do you want?" Marc asked, pretending he didn't know.

"You know. Bring *The Book* to me and we'll make a trade."

Thank God I didn't destroy The Book. "I'm not coming to you. I'll meet you in a public place."

"I didn't think you'd want to be seen in a public place. Now that you're such a celebrity."

Eckart had a point. *Still ...* "Don't worry about me," Marc said. "I'll pick the place of our meeting." *Someplace crowded.*

"Okay, big boy. Where?"

"FAO Schwarz."

"Oh, goody," Eckart said flatly. "Very well. Tomorrow at noon." *Click.*

Thirty-One

The next morning Marc took a taxi back into the city, carrying *The Templar Book of Life and Death* in a plastic shopping bag. First he went to Greenwich Village, and stopped at a shop on Christopher Street called the Spy Store. He purchased a few items, arranging to pick up all but one later.

He arrived at FAO Schwarz at 11:50 a.m. He circumvented the really long line out front in favor of the much shorter one halfway down Fifty-Eighth Street. He noted the two wide security guards stationed just inside the door. Marc didn't know exactly where he was supposed to meet Eckart or his people, but he wanted to try to spot them before they saw him. Sam's safety was the most important thing.

Marc thought again of the possibility that Eckart was bluffing. After making the arrangement with Eckart, Marc had realized that Eckart might *not* have Sam. *Maybe she had fled when she got his message, and left her cell phone behind. I hope that's what happened. But I can't count on it.*

Marc walked back past watches and video games, taking the escalator to the second floor from the garish department known as Barbie on Madison. He didn't see any sign of Committee members or Sam on the second floor as he headed back toward the Fifth Avenue side of the store. *The Book* made a substantial bulge in the lining of his father's overcoat, in comparison to which the outline of the gun in his right pocket was barely noticeable.

He passed children stamping out random tunes on the *Big* piano, kids throwing tantrums and pieces of Lego sculptures, and youngsters play-acting death and destruction in the Action Toy section. People of all ages and sizes bumped and jostled him and each other. He spun around constantly, ready to challenge each new inadvertent offender.

Dan tapped him in Adult Games, near the front escalator. Marc wheeled about instantly, recognizing the man and grabbing him in a clinch.

"The gun in my right pocket is pointing at your heart," Marc said in his ear.

Dan backed off a couple inches, but Marc wouldn't let him go.

Dan said, "Cool down, lover boy, or you'll be sorry."

"Where is she?" Marc growled.

Only one or two people were looking. Marc didn't care.

"Over there," said Dan. "In Children's Games and Puzzles. With Larry."

Marc looked east, the way he'd come. Larry was there, amid the games of Chutes and Ladders and Candyland. Larry waved. He was pushing a woman in a wheelchair. She had long light brown hair, and was dressed in a scoop-necked peasant blouse. But the floppy hat on her head covered her face completely, and she wasn't moving.

"What have you done to her?"

"She's just resting. But it'll be permanent if you don't do everything I say."

Marc didn't stop Dan as he pulled away.

"You know what the big man wants," said Dan. "Hand me *The Book*. Right here. Now. Then I'll signal Larry not to stab your girlfriend. And we'll leave you two to your tearful reunion."

Marc held his anger in check, looking over at Sam's motionless form. "I'm going over there," Marc announced.

"No, you're not," Dan informed him. "Larry won't let you get that close. You'll give me *The Book* right here."

"She'd better be okay," Marc warned.

Then, without further delay, Marc reached into his coat and produced *The Templar Book of Life and Death.* "Recognize it?" Marc asked, maintaining possession.

"It fits the description," said Dan. "Anyway, I trust you."

Dan raised his right hand and waved at Larry. *Was that the right signal?*

Larry started to walk away from the wheelchair, in the direction of Dan and Marc and the escalator. Then he stopped and looked to Dan for further direction.

Dan held out his left hand. "Now give me *The Book* and we'll all be happy."

Marc tossed *The Book* at Dan and started pushing his way over to Sam. Dan caught *The Book* and headed for the escalator. Larry passed parallel to Marc as he also darted for the escalator to the front entrance.

It seemed like an eternity before Marc reached Sam's unattended wheelchair. "Honey," he said. "Are you okay?"

When she didn't respond, he put his hand on her shoulder and shook it gently. "Sam, darling."

No response. Marc took hold of both sides of the big floppy hat and gently lifted it off.

For a moment, Marc was confused. He noticed that the long brown hair came off with the hat. It was attached. Then he looked down to see Sam's face.

His mind reeled. A rubber balloon with a painted face smiled up at him. When he touched the "face," it became dislodged and floated up slowly toward the high ceiling.

A little girl nearby spotted the ascent and tugged her mother's sleeve. "Look!" she said. "A balloon."

For the first time in his life, Marc screamed. The pitch was low, but his anguished cry was clearly a scream. He was joined a moment later by two adult women.

Marc dropped to his knees in front of the headless corpse. He stared at it, running his hands over the body. The body looked and felt like it could be Sam's. And he was positive that the blouse was Sam's. But he couldn't be sure. And he had to be sure.

A man yelled out, "It's that guy! From the paper. The lawyer!"

"Hey, yeah!" said his wife. "He's the berserk lawyer!"

Half the people were fighting to get away, and the other half were pushing in to get a better look. Marc looked up from the body in front of him to see security approaching. It was only a matter of time before the police came.

Marc ignored the crowd.

Is this Sam? How can I tell for sure? If only she had a mole or something …

Marc reached out and tore the blouse off the body. Dozens gasped.

I should be able to tell. I loved her. I love her.

But he wasn't sure.

Suddenly, he leaned forward. As he grasped and lifted her left breast, he sobbed with relief. It was a horrible tragedy, who-ever had been killed. *But it's not Sam!*

Two security guards grabbed Marc and jerked him to his feet.

"It's not her!" Marc yelled, numb with relief. "She doesn't have the birthmark! That beautiful star-shaped birthmark…"

"Come on, buddy," said one guard. "The police will be here any minute."

"She's alive!" Marc wriggled then violently wrenched away from the guards and leaped into the terrified crowd. People tried to run out of his way as he pushed toward the front escala-tor, but the crowd was too dense.

At last Marc reached the escalators. The "down" escalator

was on the right, separated from the "up" escalator by a white sloping surface broken by white pillars and a gorilla in a big car. Marc ran onto the "down" escalator, but there was a policeman waiting at the bottom.

Acting instinctively, Marc vaulted the railing and grabbed hold of a white pillar. Next he climbed over onto the "up" escalator. Before reaching the top, he scaled the final railing and lowered himself onto a high ledge adjoining the escalator.

The ledge had been occupied by two king-sized stuffed animals, but Marc had inadvertently knocked over the donkey. That gave him an idea, as he looked at the ten-foot drop to the first floor. Marc intentionally tossed the huge cow overboard, then followed it down, his fall well cushioned by his predecessor.

Mixed in the dense crowd between him and the front door, Marc saw two security guards and a policeman. But it was too far to the back door. He had to attempt the straight line.

"Come on, brother." Marc scooped up the large stuffed donkey, holding it in front of him so it blocked most of his body and incidentally obscured his vision. "Coming through!"

Using his donkey as a soft shield and battering ram, Marc barreled his way forward, setting a Christmastime speed record. As he passed it, Marc knocked over a six-foot bear in royal robes into the path of a security guard. When he reached the door, he hurled the donkey back at his pursuers.

Once outside, he crossed the street, cut through the Plaza Hotel, then hailed a cab. "Seventy-fourth Street, between Madison and Fifth," Marc announced.

Marc stormed past Donna, the maid, and found his uncle in his study. Tony appeared in the doorway a moment later.

"Tell him to get lost," Marc ordered, pointing a gun at Charlie Wilson.

"Okay," said Wilson. "But you don't need that gun."

"I've gotten used to it," said Marc. "Now I feel naked without it."

"Tony, wait outside."

After Tony left, Marc began calmly, "I'm tired of getting pushed around. Lied to. Used. Let's not pretend to be friends. Let's just work together long enough to shut down Eckart's plans. I'm prepared to resume the discussions we began last week."

Charlie Wilson nodded slowly. "You have my attention."

"I also have something which will discredit Eckart with his followers. And, on Saturday morning, 7:00 a.m., I will have the location of Eckart's meeting."

"What about *The Book*? Do you have that?"

"That's a good news and bad news situation. Eckart has *The Book*." Wilson looked scared. "But I have the receiver which will locate the transmitter hidden in the spine of *The Book*."

Thirty-Two

Saturday, Christmas Eve day, Marc rolled out of his motel bed at 5:30 a.m. He had managed to squeeze a lot of nightmares into a few fitful hours of sleep. He stared at himself in the bathroom mirror. *This is it*, he thought. *No more inactivity. No more hiding out. No more running.*

It was exhilarating, but Marc was scared shitless. Was he up to the job ahead of him?

Of course he was worried about Sam. He had been trying hard not to think of her, or when he did he tried to think of her safe and happy.

Today, he *believed.* Things would be okay. He would do anything and everything it took. Sam *would* be okay.

Marc had moved out of the Ball Park Motel and into a different Bronx motel last Monday, just in case Eckart had traced Marc's call from the gas station pay phone. The Sunshine Inn wasn't as nice as the Ball Park, but it had sufficed. Marc shoved two guns and one knife into the pockets of his father's overcoat, and grabbed the receiver he had purchased for $2,200 at the Spy Store, leaving the rest of his stuff. If all went well, he'd check out later today.

When Marc asked the motel clerk how to get a cab, the man volunteered to call a gypsy cab he knew. Marc thanked him, not begrudging the man the kickback he would probably receive. Since the cab didn't have a meter, he and Marc agreed on a fare of forty dollars before starting (they were silent on the issue of whether there would be a tip above that amount).

Marc reentered Christmas season Manhattan, moving quickly despite the holiday because it was so early. He instructed the driver to cross town to the far west side and head down towards the 20s, the neighborhood of Eckart's last ritual site. Marc turned on the receiver and pointed it in all directions, listening for the signal that would tell him in which direction to go. The receiver sounded faintly in the direction of southeast.

Marc told the driver that he might have to circle around for a few minutes downtown, offering him an additional fifteen dollars for his time and trouble. The man agreed, not curious enough to inquire as to Marc's goals.

The signal grew louder and louder, then started to fade as they headed into the 40s. *A whole new neighborhood*, Marc thought.

Marc instructed the driver to head east a couple blocks to 8th Avenue, then start slowly back uptown.

The receiver response again peaked around 50th Street, so they traveled east on 50th Street until the signal peaked near 6th Avenue.

The trip having taken less time than anticipated, Marc gave the driver an even 60 dollars and stepped out onto 50th Street. He looked around the neighborhood, while sheltering the receiver as surreptitiously as possible in his arms.

He was basically on the Northwestern edge of the Rockefeller Center area. Less than a block away from the popular Del Frisco's Steakhouse, as well as the world-famous Radio City Music Hall, home of the high-stepping Rockettes and the world's most extravagant annual Christmas spectacular. Later today this neighborhood would be bustling more than any other this time of year, but it was still very early and the streets were mostly deserted.

Expensive real estate, Marc mused. *Not much residential or small business property around here. Well, that should make it easier to find.*

The receiver and its three-element antenna were too big to carry around the street inconspicuously. For that reason, Marc impulsively hid the device in a relatively clean trashcan and replaced the lid. He was close, but Marc would have to do the rest of the work himself.

He headed another block in the direction the receiver had indicated. He looked at his watch. It was 6:30 a.m. According to Paul, the meeting had been scheduled for 7:00 a.m.

Marc decided that he would duck into a doorway with a good view of the block. He would wait and watch. If he didn't see anything or anyone by 7:00, he'd go back and get the transmitter and take his chances with it.

Before Marc could choose a doorway, Dan Lessing popped out of an entrance two feet ahead of him, holding a gun in his left hand. "Step in," Dan invited. "We're having bagels and lox."

There was no time or place to run. Marc stepped into the deserted entranceway with Dan.

"Why were you following me?" asked Dan.

Marc was genuinely surprised. "I *wasn't* following you. But I'm going to the same place you are."

Now Dan was surprised. "Where might that be?" he asked. "And who invited you?"

"Don't you know? Eckart told me to be there. He said that this time I'd *really* see Sam."

Dan lowered his left hand a little. *This could work,* Marc congratulated himself. *Dan knows I'm not Eckart's friend, but he's reluctant to deprive his boss of a chance to torment me. Or to crush my hopes in advance and spoil Eckart's fun.*

"Sorry. I didn't know you were invited," Dan said with a sudden smile.

"That's okay. Let's just go."

Dan didn't move. "You know, you were rough on me, back in the toy store."

"Sorry," Marc muttered.

"That's okay," said Dan. "Any friend of Bill Eckart's is a friend of mine." Dan dropped the gun to his left side.

You know Eckart doesn't like me. Do you think you can convince me that I'm safe, increasing Eckart's fun later?

"No hard feelings," said Dan, taking a step forward and holding out his four-fingered right hand.

Might as well let him think he's fooling me.

Marc tried not to show his revulsion for the Satanist, smiling as he reached for the open hand.

At the last moment, Dan pulled his right hand back and reached out with his left. With a whisper-quiet report, Dan shot sideways through Marc's outstretched palm. Marc yanked back the bleeding hand and stared at it in amazement.

Dan stepped back and aimed the gun at Marc's heart. "You think I'm fucking stupid?" he demanded, raising his voice. "Bill Eckart would have told me if he invited you. But he would never do anything that stupid. Not like your uncle."

"No, you're wrong ..."

"You're a fucking atheist! But I'll prove to you that there's a Devil ..."

He's too close for me to avoid, but too far for me to jump. It's all over. Marc stared down at his hand and the pool of blood forming on the floor between them.

A man with a grocery bag pulled open the front door and looked stunned. As Dan dropped the man with a shot, Marc charged toward Dan. Slipping on his own blood, Marc sprawled up against Dan's legs, under the stream of bullets aimed where Marc's chest would have been.

Dan managed to keep his balance despite the impact. He looked down at Marc and aimed at his back.

Dan fell backward screaming after Marc used his left hand

to fire point blank into Dan's crotch. Marc had plenty of time to grope his way to his feet while Dan lay writhing and cursing. Dan had dropped his gun and grasped the wounded area tightly with both hands as if attempting to keep his fluids from escaping, but it was hopeless.

Marc looked around nervously. Surely someone would hear Dan's cries. Should Marc leave, call an ambulance, or shoot Dan again? And what about the guy with the groceries? He was bleeding from his side and unconscious. Marc couldn't guess at his prognosis.

Marc stood over Dan, gun in his left hand, asking, "Where's the meeting?"

At first Marc thought Dan incapable of focusing on the question. Then Dan gritted his teeth and grunted, "You didn't come up here for the Rockettes?" Dan didn't bother trying to reach for the gun a couple of feet away.

"Tell me or I'll kill you."

Dan pointed his right middle finger at Marc, the meaning momentarily unclear due to the lack of full five-fingered context. Dan coughed and laughed weakly at the same time. "You're too chicken shit."

Marc squeezed the trigger, sending Dan into bloody convulsions. Then he wiped Eckart's gun and dropped it on the twitching body. *I've got to get out of here. I've got work to do.* Marc pressed all of the intercom buttons, then walked briskly from the building. *Someone will call 911.* He couldn't hear anything from the street.

It was 6:45 a.m. *I hope they're not all there yet.* Marc walked only a few feet before he spotted a familiar shape ahead. Despite her overcoat, Marc recognized Jill Montana's figure and hair. He slowed his progress further, ready to duck into a doorway if she turned.

Jill Montana turned into a doorway herself. Marc was surprised, and wary. Had she reached her destination or was she next in line to ambush him? He crossed the street and pro-

ceeded to a building from which he could see the entrance that
Montana had used. Marc looked through his new binoculars,
but there was no sign of Montana.

Could it really possibly be there? Marc wondered.

Five minutes later, an older man and a younger one approached the same entrance from the other direction. Despite
their trench coats and hats, Marc recognized Judge Kelly and his
clerk. They too disappeared into the side entrance to the landmark building.

Marc could barely believe it. The Satanic rituals were going to take place in Radio City Music Hall.

They were in a rehearsal room four and a half flights up (the
internal layout of Radio City was complex, including many
half-levels), the one that was famously the same size as the main
stage so that even the largest numbers could be blocked and
practiced there. A movable rack of mostly red and white costumes had been pushed to the back, but most of the hundreds of
other Christmas Show costumes were in separate rooms nearby
on the same half-level.

The giant room was dark except for the flickering candlelight. Bill Eckart stood on a platform, next to a tall squirming
woman who was naked, gagged and tied to some sort of ornate
red and white chair: evidently some type of fancy sled, a prop
for the current (or a past) Christmas show. The young woman's
light brown hair spilled out the back of the tight leather mask
which muffled her anguished cries.

Eckart ignored the woman's struggles and addressed the
more than two-dozen, black-robed followers who were standing and facing him with anxious anticipation. "So much for the
traditional mass convocation. Today is a turning point. Today
we will rally the support of all the hosts of Hell. We will arm
ourselves with the awesome might of their blessing. Thus gird-

ed, we will take ourselves straight to that other group, to see those false servants who place comfort, convenience and the American dollar over the sacred commandments of our Lord himself. I think you know who I'm talking about. Do you know who I'm talking about?"

"Yes," the crowd sang out.

"We will *take* that group, take them back for the sake of our Lord. And then we will all work together, as he intended. Together we will work to bring Hell to Earth."

Several followers cried out spontaneously, "Praise Satan!"

"I, William Eckart, will bring all this to pass. Behold, I have *The Book!*" Eckart held high the aged volume. "*The Templar Book of Life and Death* is mine. No longer will it languish neglected, hidden from the wanting world by a weak and foolish old pretender. *The Book* is mine, and I am yours!"

"Praised be His Name!"

"Hail, Satan!"

⚖⚖

Radio City was still quiet this early in the morning. There was actually a show at 9 a.m., so most of the performers and stagehands, etc., would probably be arriving soon. For now, however, there was just one person apparent, an almost 6-foot tall blonde woman who could be a Rockette, who was opening a side door for Eckert's Satanists as they arrived in ones and twos.

Waiting was hard, but Marc bided his time until 7:42 a.m., when he hadn't seen anyone arrive for five minutes.

He knocked on the side door. As he'd mostly hoped, there was no answer. No time to play with the lock. After a quick glance around, he shot Dan's silenced gun into the area where he imagined that the lock resided. He was having to play the odds that no straggler would come behind him and realize that there must be an intruder.

He was relieved not to see or hear anyone as he came out

into the main lobby and jogged up the plushly carpeted stairs past the much larger-than-life wall-painting of a man in simple Asian garb making some sort of religious pilgrimage.

It was too quiet. Where can they all be?

He opened a door and started up a narrow, winding internal staircase with photos of mostly formerly famous musicians (Liberace, Barbara Mandrell, Liza Minelli, Bon Jovi, Elton John) hung on both sides. Just when he started to fear that he would never find Eckart and his bunch, he began to hear voices in the distance. As he got closer, he could tell that the voices were speaking in unison. Chanting.

⚖⚖

Eckart held up his hands to silence the crowd. "But I can only succeed in the wonders I would work on your behalf if all in this room believe in me and my power, and truly love our Dark Lord. Do you believe in me, and the power I wield?"

"Yes, we believe," they cried.

"Do you truly love our Lord, with all your heart, with all your soul, and with all your might?"

"Yes, we love Him."

"This thing we attempt today is dangerous, glorious, and mad. If we succeed in bringing His Infernal Majesty even one step closer to our world, surely we will be blessed and honored above all beings. Surely there will be nothing we desire but that we shall take it by the force of our wills and no human can stand against us." During this last sentence, Eckart reached out with both hands and grasped the breasts of the woman tied to the sled beside him. The woman wriggled and tried to scream, but the mask absorbed her protests.

"Take her! Take her!" yelled one of the women in the crowd. The chant was taken up by most of the men and women in the room.

Eckart reached into a deep pocket in his black robe and

produced his golden phallus. The crowd went wild, with many individuals running hands over themselves and others. A few started to pull up their robes, and were sternly rebuked by Eckart. "Enough!" he cried. "Contain yourselves! Pray to our Lord while I begin the spell and take the first fruit."

Eckart closed his eyes. He held *The Book* out from his body, between his two hands. The room was deadly silent, except for the sounds of the naked sacrifice struggling against her bonds. Bill Eckart began to chant in deep tones, speaking in old German, hitting each low guttural sound like a buzz saw. Many in the crowd closed their eyes as well. They began to feel a chill, like something was coming, something was changing, maybe forever.

Eckart continued to chant as he ran the golden phallus down the captive's exposed body. The woman tried to scream as her legs were pulled apart.

All plans thrown to the side, Marc flung open the double doors in the back and ran toward the stage. He dodged and shoved several stunned worshippers aside and was almost to the stage when two particularly strong and motivated men in black robes seized him tightly.

Marc squirmed just enough to free the hand with the gun. Unfortunately, the weapon was torn from his grasp before he could aim and fire at Eckart.

Now the two men secured their grip on Marc, pointing a gun at his head while verifying that he had no remaining weapons. As they each held one of his arms and dragged him toward Eckart and his near-naked sacrifice, Marc recognized Joe and Scott through their hoods.

"Hello there, Marc," Eckart stage-whispered. "Come to visit my lovely daughter?"

Now that he was closer, Marc concentrated his attention on the poor helpless woman, writhing helplessly against the Christmas show prop. Exhaling with sudden relief, Marc almost laughed.

"Yes, you've defiled my daughter often enough to know that this isn't your main squeeze." As he spoke, Eckart reached over and grabbed the prisoner between her legs, laughing.

"Yes," Marc spat at Eckart, raising the stakes in this sick variation on the classic father/son-in-law conflict. "I know every inch of your daughter's body ..."

"Shut up!" yelled Eckart. Then, calmly: "So it isn't her. But now that we've got you, we're sure to get her. Strip and help me with the sacrifice." Joe and Scott tore the coat off Marc's back. "Maybe I'll even let you use Big Bill here," joked Eckart, poking Marc with the golden dildo while Joe and Scott ripped off his shirt.

"Wait!" Marc screamed, turning back to the crowd. "You've all got to know something," he yelled to the faceless group.

What's keeping you, Uncle? Marc wondered desperately.

"Eckart's a liar!" Marc proclaimed. "He doesn't really have mystical powers. He doesn't really believe."

Eckart's punch sent Marc sailing backward, out of Scott and Joe's hands. Marc went with the momentum and fell off the platform and into the assembly. "He killed Baylor, Spender and the others with poison, not magic. He's a fake." Marc pulled the Evian bottle full of poison out of his pocket and tried to hold it up, but the faceless mass surrounded and held Marc anew. "I have the poison right here!"

Damn you, Uncle! I thought you had your reinforcements waiting when you got my call.

"He's crazy," said Eckart to the crowd. "*I* killed our enemies, and I alone. All the old, weak ones, those assimilated country clubbers. I willed them dead!"

"Then will *me* dead!" yelled Marc. "Or drink from the bottle in my hand."

All eyes were on Eckart, who sputtered with anger. "I won't waste my mystical energies on an insignificant pebble of shit like you. I am about to perform the most difficult and important spell ever attempted by man!"

"Yes," several members cried out. "Continue the ceremony!"

"Bring the infidel back to me," ordered Eckart, "that I can add his unbelieving blood to the spell I will work."

As Joe and Scott yanked him back up towards the stage, the back doors of the giant room opened again.

Two people stepped in. One was a black-robed guard and the other was an intruder, dressed in street clothes.

Larry beamed from within his hood, looking full of canary. "Look who I found; she just *happened* to be wandering around on the street outside!"

As everyone stared in surprise at the approaching newcomers, Marc mustered all his emotional strength to resist the urge to try to run to her, while using all his physical strength to twist around, trying unsuccessfully to break free and charge towards Eckart.

Fear paralyzed Marc a moment later at the sound of the gunshot. Relief followed instantly as he saw Sam running towards Eckart with the gun she had taken from Larry. He couldn't help feeling a moment of pride.

"You're going to let us go," Sam said to her father. "We won't tell anyone what we've seen or heard."

"Then why *did* you come here?" Eckart demanded of her. Then he turned to Marc. "Did *you* think you could turn my loyal followers against me? Who the hell are you?"

Marc was silent. He knew they shouldn't have charged in without his uncle, but he couldn't just stand by while Eckart had been doing things to that woman. Even if she wasn't Sam.

"Damn it, Dad!" Sam exploded. "Talk to *me*! Deal with *me*!"

"Don't let him upset you with petty mind games," said

Marc. "Let's get out of here."

Can't wait any longer for Uncle Charlie. Marc tried to communicate telepathically with Sam. *Let's get out of here with my audio recorder while it's still a secret.*

"Don't go, baby." Eckart addressed Sam directly, with devastating effect.

"What do you want from me?" she asked.

"How could you side with him against me?"

"Why have you done these things?" she asked.

"I'm sorry I kept things from you," Eckart said humbly. "I couldn't bear to lose you. I need your love. Don't tell me I've lost my little girl forever."

"Come on, Sam," said Marc. "Keep the gun pointed and make him lead us out."

"The things you did to me, when I was little ..."

"I've always loved you. You're Daddy's beautiful little girl. Remember those summers on Fire Island, just the three of us?"

Tears ran into Sam's mouth.

Eckart continued. "I've tried to make you happy, to show how much I love you."

"Do what Marc said."

"What?"

"Do what Marc said," she ordered. "Turn and walk ahead of us, toward the door. And tell them to let Marc go."

Eckart ignored her words. "I'm sorry for everything," he said. "You wouldn't shoot your Daddy. I know you wouldn't ..." He started walking slowly toward Sam.

Marc dragged his captors one step forward. "Sam!" he yelled. "Don't let him get too close."

"Stay back," Sam warned through her tears. "I promise I'll shoot."

"No you won't," said Eckart. "Give me the gun and I'll make everything up to you. Every day will be Christmas. We'll be a family again, just like old times."

"Look to your right!" Marc called out. Sam turned in time

to see a black-robed man heading toward her. She fired once, then stared at her bleeding handiwork.

"In front of you!" Marc yelled. "Your father!"

He was close. As Sam turned to aim, Eckart grabbed his nearest follower, the blond named Cindy. Holding her in front of him, he pushed her into Sam. Sam's gun went off as both women fell to the floor.

In the resulting confusion, Marc finally managed to break free, mount the stage and tackle Eckart with a flying leap. The two men rolled toward Sam and Cindy, each trying to reach the gun that now lay beside the two women.

Sam managed to push Cindy's dead weight off of her and turned to retrieve her gun. At that moment Jill Montana ran onto the stage and kicked the gun away. Sam yanked Montana's legs out from under her, sending her crashing to the platform.

Marc forgot himself and punched Eckart with his wounded hand. During the ensuing pain, Eckart pulled Marc down, then got behind him and thrust both hands under Marc's arms and over Marc's neck, creating a full-nelson hold. "I'll break your fucking neck," he told Marc.

"Freeze!" Larry pointed the gun first at Samantha, then at Marc.

"I've got this pussy taken care of," said Eckart. Indeed, Marc was forced to go limp to avoid breaking his own neck. "Search my daughter for any other hidden weapons. Like a serpent's tooth."

Larry relished the search, patting Sam down thoroughly. He found a dagger in a holder tied around her leg. And a small video camera attached to her belt. "She's been filming us," he announced, snatching away the device. Many in the crowd gasped.

At least they haven't found my audio recorder.

Eckart smiled grimly. "So, you wouldn't *tell* anyone, eh? Is this what I've paid my hard-earned tuition dollars for?"

Sam mustered the strength to reply, "Yes. This camera's state of the art. Small, but wide-angled. Omnidirectional sound recording. And best of all, capable of sending its signals live to a remote location."

Wow, we had similar ideas, but yours was much better…

"What?"

"This recording has already been sent to an external receiver at NYU. It's too late for you to do anything about it."

"You're bluffing," said Eckart.

Shit! Is she? How can he be so sure?

"What should we do with these unbelievers?" Eckart asked the crowd.

Many suggestions were called out.

"I'm not sure we can do *all* of those things …" Eckart smiled at his joke as he took a step toward his daughter.

Yet again, the back door opened. Larry whirled and aimed his gun, but fell to the ground a moment later with a bullet in his neck.

"Everything Marc told you is true," Charlie Wilson announced.

⚖⚖

The first couple dozen tourists had been seated in the theater at Radio City and were drinking in the giant art deco masterpiece while they waited. They had arrived over an hour early in order to properly absorb and prepare for the spectacle.

They had come from Kansas, Minnesota, Oregon and Japan, for starters. They were parents, grandparents, children, maiden aunts. They stretched their necks looking at the ornate ceilings and giant balconies so high above. They stared at the massive multi-ton deep red curtain and tried to picture what lay behind it. Children had to be held in their seats in order to prevent them from charging towards the stage. Programs full of colorful pictures were scoured for clues of what was to come.

⚖⚖

How long have you been out there? Marc wondered.

"Eckart's a fraud. He has no more magic than a light bulb." Charlie Wilson walked as fast as he could manage, breathing heavily and with some difficulty. None of the astonished on-lookers stopped him.

Judge Wilson halted in front of the platform, gun trained on Eckart's head. "You should all turn on him," he told the crowd, "but you're too stupid, aren't you?"

I thought you were going to win these people over. Couldn't you be more diplomatic? And where are the reinforcements you promised?

"Let Marc go," Judge Wilson ordered, gesturing toward Eckart's head with the gun. "You *know* I'll do it."

Released, Marc stood up, cracked his neck, and walked over to Sam, who was staring at the two dead bodies near her feet. Marc took the gun, the dagger and the camera from Larry.

"Samantha Eckart!" said Wilson. "Thank goodness we got here in time."

Marc aimed his gun at the gathered Satanists. "Stay away from the stage," Marc ordered those assembled. "And listen to Judge Wilson. Tell them about the poison," said Marc to Wilson, holding out the Evian bottle. "Maybe they'll believe you."

Charlie Wilson addressed the confused crowd again. "Bill Eckart doesn't really love Satan! He loves only himself."

Samantha took the dagger from Marc and walked over to the bound woman. The woman cringed away from her touch as Sam struggled to sever the ropes.

Marc forced the bottle into his uncle's hands. "Tell them. Like we planned," Marc insisted. Addressing the crowd, Marc said, "If we're lying about the poison in this bottle, maybe Eckart wouldn't mind taking a sip of clear fresh water."

The woman stared unfocused at her after Sam removed the captive's mask. Sam picked up the robe that had half-fallen off Larry and placed it over the woman's shoulders, while she just stood there.

"I doubt Eckart's even been following the spell directions," said Judge Wilson. "Did he tell you that this spell calls for a *fire* sacrifice?"

What are you talking about?

Members of the group murmured to each other.

Judge Wilson turned and said, "Marc, go check outside the door for the others." A moment later, he added, "Samantha, you help him."

"Both of us?" Marc asked.

"Yes. Now. I'll be fine."

"What about the *poison*?" Marc asked.

"*Go!*" Uncle Charlie shouted. "This is vital!"

Marc pointed the gun into the crowd and cleared a path for him and Sam. As if waking from a dream, the released sacrifice followed them out. They opened the two connecting doors but didn't see anyone outside.

"You see those handcuffs hanging from one doorknob?" Wilson called after them. "Step outside and lock the cuffs on both doorknobs!" he instructed.

"What?"

Charlie Wilson turned toward the door and yelled, "Do it! Lock the handcuffs!" Then he put his left hand under his coat, a pained expression on his face.

"Look out!" Sam screamed.

Eckart was almost upon Wilson when the judge's left hand reappeared, holding a flat bottle of Schnapps. Eckart was the one caught by surprise when the Judge broke the bottle against Eckart's head.

Eckart recovered a moment later and knocked the gun from Wilson's hand. As Eckart bent to scoop up the weapon, Judge Wilson pulled out his lighter and flicked it on. Eckart sprung up without the gun, his robe in flames.

"You fucking prick!" he roared, clumsily trying to pat out the growing fire.

Judge Wilson picked up his gun and ran through the

stunned crowd, shooting Joe as he rushed up to block him, and several sprinkler heads in the ceiling.

The fire alarm sounded loudly and the few working sprinkler-heads sputtered into action.

Uncle Charlie pushed Marc through the doors ahead of him. Sam ran out after them, followed by Jim the clerk. The Judge shot Jim in the heart, before slamming the doors closed.

Roughly half of the hooded crowd seethed toward the doors, while the others crowded around Eckart. Some of them made efforts to put out Eckart's fire only to be lit like fuses themselves, while others merely stood and stared in wonder as the flames approached them.

The doors opened a few inches, but no more, because Judge Wilson had succeeded in locking the handcuffs around both doorknobs.

Now the judge was hurriedly reloading his pistol.

"What the hell are you doing?" Marc demanded of his uncle.

"This is the only way. Don't try to stop me." Charlie Wilson pointed his newly loaded gun at Sam and Marc, who had let his weapon drop to his side.

"Drop it," Judge Wilson ordered.

Reluctantly, Marc complied. At that moment, the woman they had saved from sacrifice started running down the stairs.

"This is insane!" Marc cried out. "We can't kill all those people!"

Now most of those people were trampling each other, fighting for the chance to make the hopeless attempt to squeeze through the small space between the doors. Scott was in the forefront, pushing others out of the way as he yanked at the metal of the handcuffs. To no avail.

"Let them out!" Marc shouted. "I'll help you keep them covered."

"My father's in there," said Sam, more like a statement of fact than a request for mercy. She made no effort to wipe away the tears running down her face.

A blazing woman had managed to position herself under the best-performing sprinkler-head. Amidst smoke and steam and the peeling of raw blackened flesh, the flame subsided and the woman half-walked half-crawled towards the doors. Marc realized that the woman was Jill Montana.

"Why doesn't Eckart try to put out his own flame?" Marc asked aloud.

Far below, the fire alarm shattered the Christmas idyll. "What's that noise?" many of the children asked their parents.

Brightly dressed ushers rushed through the theater, attempting to gather up these early few while preserving holiday cheer. "I'm sure it's just a false alarm," announced an unflappably cheery old woman to her granddaughter, Amy, as she rose ever so slowly and bent to retrieve an American Girl shopping bag from the floor near her swollen feet.

Above the noises of the crowd and the smoke alarm, Marc could hear Eckart's voice swell in volume. He was chanting. Each harsh, violent syllable of old German grew louder than the last, as if a microphone were being slowly turned up to full volume.

Then they saw Eckart through a break in the crowd. He was a fireball. Flames were shooting out from his body, igniting people and objects in the room. But, like Moses' burning bush, it seemed that he himself was not being consumed. He held *The Book* high above his head.

"He understands more than I gave him credit for," Charlie Wilson announced nervously. "He has turned *himself* into the sacrifice. Now he truly has a chance of completing Jacques de Molay's spell."

Judge Wilson fired two shots back into the room, but it was impossible to tell if he had hit Eckart. It was impossible to tell if Eckart had even noticed the bullets.

It was easy for Marc to take the gun from his weak and distracted uncle.

"No!" yelled Charlie Wilson, reaching ineffectively for the gun. "They must be stopped. Satan doesn't belong on Earth!" Then he whispered, "May he forgive me..."

"Eckart's finished. And many of the others. Let the survivors run..."

Sam said, "No", but her voice was quiet and without force. She stood as if transfixed.

"Unlock the handcuffs," Marc ordered.

"I don't have the key."

Rather than argue, Marc shot the handcuffs off.

Marc stepped aside as the surviving Satanists burst through the doors. Marc braced himself for defense, but even Scott just ran past him, crazed and half-blind with fear and relief at deliverance. A cold stream of accumulated sprinkler water poured forth after them.

Inside the rehearsal space, Eckart seemed unstoppable. He was chanting faster and louder, swaying rhythmically from side to side, even as his flesh finally began to sear black. Sprinklers spit water five feet on either side of him, but Eckart paid no attention. *The Book* in his hands appeared almost entirely intact.

"Go!" Uncle Charlie ordered. "I need to make sure that Eckart's failed."

Before Marc could stop him, Charlie Wilson ran straight towards the blazing Eckart. Upon impact, Uncle Charlie literally bounced off and landed on his back nearby. Eckart seemed unaffected. Slowly Charlie rose to his hands and knees and started to crawl back towards Eckart.

It seemed almost coincidental that Eckart, without acknowledging Charlie Wilson's existence, started to flow toward the doors of the rehearsal space.

Then suddenly Eckart was moving swiftly out the back of the room and up the nearby stairs, leaving a singed and smoking line on the carpet as he passed. Marc ran after, with Charlie Wilson shuffling determinedly behind. Sam trailed them all.

Just a flight or two below they could now hear the sounds of fire personnel running up the stairs towards the rehearsal room.

A flight up, the door to the balcony had been left open. Eckart was most of the way down the aisle, one row above the ledge. Eckart faced them, rising to his full height, a flaming totem pole.

⚖⚖

"Look!" Amy pointed to the balcony, trying to get her grandmother's attention. "The fire's up there!"

Her grandmother stopped her slow progress down the aisle to bend her neck upwards. "My word!"

"It looks like a burning man!"

"Don't be silly…"

The nearest usher pushed a little as she tried to hurry them along.

⚖⚖

Charlie Wilson looked pale and desperate as he caught up with Marc. "He's almost done," Charlie exclaimed.

Eckart's skull-face was grinning like a jack-o'-lantern, still chanting, now without looking at *The Book*.

"Our Father, who art in heaven," Judge Wilson whispered urgently, "hallowed be thy name." Marc turned to him in shock, then turned back to Eckart.

"Thy kingdom come …" said Uncle Charlie.

Tiny tongues of fire played on Eckart's fingertips, an almost peaceful extension of the larger flames still engulfing but still not devouring him.

What's keeping Eckart going? He looks stronger than ever. Uncle Charlie, on the other hand ...

Marc fired at the smiling demon.

"Let him finish the spell!" Scott yelled. "Or I'll kill Samantha."

Marc and Judge Wilson both turned to see that a singed Scott had returned and was holding Samantha from behind, a gun to her head. Samantha wasn't moving.

"Thy will be done ..." Charlie Wilson returned to his chanting, even more anxiously.

"So, you came back, after running away, you chicken shit!" Marc goaded, trying to act tougher than he felt. *Have to stop Eckart! Have to save Sam! HOW?!*

"I was just laying low!" Scott asserted. "I would never desert Bill."

"Well, why not stop hiding behind his daughter? Let her go and shoot me if you want!" Marc offered.

"On Earth as it is in Heaven," said Uncle Charlie.

"Father," said Sam.

Eckart had stopped chanting. He looked triumphant. He looked expectant. He raised his arms high above his head. Despite the fire, the room seemed colder.

"It is finished!" Charlie Wilson observed, or perhaps announced.

Judge Wilson ran straight for Eckart. Eckart didn't seem to pay any attention as Wilson smacked into him, grabbing him around the waist and pushing. This time Wilson wasn't repulsed but his momentum carried them both forward, then over the ledge.

There was no sound associated with this event. Until the dull impact far below.

"NO!" Scott screamed.

Samantha jabbed an elbow back hard and ran from Scott's grasp.

Marc shot Scott, twice. Then a third time.

Marc and Sam both ran to the ledge and looked down.

All they could see was Judge Wilson's bloody, twisted body, lying on three broken seats.

There might have been ashes scattered nearby…

Marc and Sam couldn't fight through the firemen and policemen to get into the theater. He tried telling one fireman that his uncle was in there, but the man just said, "We'll get him out. But you've got to go now!"

Then Marc and Sam found themselves flowing with the crowd of Radio City employees, Radio City patrons and their grandchildren, unable to detour until they reached the street. A crowd had gathered in front, surrounding the five fire trucks.

Marc looked but didn't see any sign of the Committee survivors.

He regretted not seeing Eckart's body.

He continued to have a generally unsettled feeling, but he focused his energy on comforting Sam.

As Sam shivered in his arms, Marc remembered that it was Christmas in New York. He hoped that, once indoors, Samantha would eventually stop shivering.

And then, in time, maybe he, too, could stop shivering.

Assuming that Satan did not come to Earth that sunny Christmas day.

EPILOGUE

A month later, life was just beginning to settle down for Marc and Sam.

Sam had switched psychiatrists, to get a fresh perspective from someone who didn't know her father. She was making slow progress, with Marc's invaluable support.

Sam, in turn, was supportive of Marc, both emotionally and financially. Although Marc was never actually fired from Ballen, Warren & Dow, he couldn't face going back to work as a lawyer. Bill Eckart left Sam so much money that she would be able to support them both while she finished school and Marc figured out what he wanted to do. He was deciding between writing a novel and composing a rock opera.

So Marc parted with the law. With one exception.

Two weeks after the fire, Marc explained to David Gutierrez that the judge on his case had died suddenly. "But we'll get assigned a new judge. A better judge. And we're going to win this case."

"I thought you weren't going to be a lawyer anymore."

"I only left my firm. But now I finally can be a lawyer. When it matters. Now I finally have both the time and the resources. The desire and, I hope, the ability. We'll take it to the highest court that'll take us. Sooner or later, we'll find a good, honest judge."

"No offense, but I'll believe that when I see it."

"You and me both, Dave."

A week earlier, Marc had interrupted a young attorney ransacking his apartment. Marc had pointed Eckart's gun at the young intruder. "I guess you heard about the tape, somehow. But it's not here," Marc told him. "However, if anything happens to me or mine, several people will receive it. Make sure everyone on the Committee knows that." Marc didn't know who was in charge these days. "Now, leave me alone."

And, as of a month later, they had. In fact, somehow the warrants for his arrest seemed to go away on their own. No one ever followed up on them. Marc shivered when he considered the full extent of the Committee's power and influence.

Marc's mother had come back to New York as planned, but two weeks later she had already returned to Miami Beach. Marc was anxious to meet Herb, the great dancer with the "full head of hair" and the "wild gleam in his eye."

"You have to come down," his mother told him every time he called.

"Aren't you ever coming back?"

"I thought you *wanted* me to move down here."

"Okay. We'll come down during Sam's break in March."

Strange as it seemed, Marc was looking forward to his first double date with Mom.

Things were starting to look up.

Too bad I have to risk everything.

He'd talked it over with Sam and they'd agreed. They couldn't be part of the conspiracy of silence any longer. To paraphrase Marc's words to David Gutierrez, sooner or later they'd find a good, honest law enforcement official.

The odds seemed better outside the immediate area. Marc and Sam each crossed their fingers as they dropped a copy of the video into the federal mail system. They had researched the backgrounds of several Department of Justice officials and picked one.

Please, God. Let us get lucky this time.

ACKNOWLEDGMENTS

There are lots of people whose help and support I want to acknowledge. Thanks to my parents, Donald and Laura, who bought me a typewriter and believed that I could write. Mom, I still think of you often, especially as I am blessed with years beyond what you were allowed. Pop, you exposed us to classic movies and sometimes let us wake up in the middle of the night to watch them (before VCRs and DVRs), plus you coined classic movie titles like "Dead Men Fight for Their Lives" (a movie I still want to make or at least see). Thanks also to Elizabeth who has always been loving and supportive and who keeps saving the second half of Pop's life. Thanks to my brother Alan (a talented writer, actor, comedian, musician, computer geek and eventually director; basically he can do anything) for being the first to teach me that it's fun to make things up and write them down, and to my little sister, Shari (an engineer and lawyer who became the world's greatest teacher), for always encouraging me while pretending not to be creative herself. Thank you to my kids, Alicia and Jocelyn, who have so enriched my life, and who are both also excellent writers and theatrical triple threats; some day soon I may let you read this "inappropriate" book. And thanks so much to Jim Kelley, Jocelyn Kelley, Megan Kelley Hall and Gloria Kelley from Grey Swan Press and Kelley & Hall Book Publicity for their invaluable contributions to bringing this book into beautiful print and working tirelessly to help it find an audience.

Colophon:

This book was typeset using Minion, designed by Robert Slimbach in 1990 for Adobe Systems. This font family is inspired by late Renaissance-era type and is considered to be among the most legible and readable serif typefaces because of its fluidity and consistency.